FINAL OPTION

Praise for John R Hanny's Previous Books

Asleep at the Wheel:

"The political intrigue is incredible. This is Hanny's first novel and I can't wait for the second one. I know of no writer alive that can produce such a tale so close to reality. It's frightening but you must read *Asleep at the Wheel.*"

—EDWARD GEORGE PERES, LONDON, ENGLAND

"John Hanny has a great gift for telling a story. His novel is fast, accurate and timely." —IDAHO REVIEW

"This is a spellbinding story – real to the last word of the last page."

—DAVID ORRIN

"John Hanny delivers the action and *Asleep at the Wheel* has all the earmarks of a novel headed for Hollywood." —WRITER'S GUILD OF WASHINGTON

"One of John Hanny's finest skills as an up-and-coming master of the political thriller is his ability to combine reality and fiction."

—THE RECORD NEWS LETTER

"*Asleep at the Wheel* is five stars out of a possible four, unlike anything I've ever read." —PAUL JACOBS, LONDON STAR REVIEW

"Washington D.C. politics from an insider's perspective. It's ingenious and out paces anything I've read in years." —WILLIAM PENN BULLETIN

Secrets from the White House Kitchens:

"*Secrets from the White House Kitchens* is part White House cookbook and part culinary history lesson. This is a book to read and savor as well as use."

—ANA KINKAID, YOUR CULINARY WORLD

"Here is an overlooked reason to aspire to the Presidency and the White House—the food!" —JACQUES NOIR

"A delicious history lesson" —JOHN KELLY

"I love this book. History comes alive with each recipe."

—THE SOCIAL FOODIE

FINAL OPTION

JOHN R HANNY

COGENT
PUBLISHING NY
IMPRINT OF
THE WHITSON GROUP, INC.

Published by Cogent Publishing NY
Imprint of The Whitson Group, Inc.
3 Miller Road, Putnam Valley, NY 10579
(845) 528-7617 • www.cogentpub.com
cogentpub@aol.com

This book is a work of fiction. Names, characters, businesses, organizations, places, events, and incidents either are the product of the author's imagination or are used fictitiously. Any resemblance to actual persons, living or dead, or actual events is entirely coincidental.

Front cover designed by Frank J. Russom

Jack Hanny photograph on back cover by Meredith McKown, www.McKownPhotography.com

ISBN: 978-0-925776-46-4
1 2 3 4 5—21 20 19 18

Dedication

James Michael Hanny
1942 – 2004
"This one's for you, boy"

Acknowledgments

It takes several people to bring a book to the seller's shelves and I would like to share the credit that's so richly deserved by those who helped me reach that goal.

First is Debbie Willson-Hanny who consistently encouraged me for the sound advice and artistic style that she added to this manuscript. I am very appreciative.

To my children, Michelle, Lisa, Jane, Jennifer, Kristen and Jason, you're the best ever.

To my brother Bud and my niece, Tricia Browne, who together shepherd the success of our Eagle House Restaurant in Williamsville, NY. This has enabled me to do what I love the most.

Very special thanks to Dr. Paul Marrone for availing himself, not only with his knowledge of all things nuclear, but helping me translate that special language to something we can all understand, and to Dawn Proctor for her valued advice in shaping this manuscript into something readable. Also to Dr. Carlo Kopp for his invaluable information on the E-Bomb.

To Bill Derrick, Cheryl Stone, Tammy McClary, Peter Updike, Kevin McCarthy, Ian McPherson and Judith Pigg Carter for their special input; it's much appreciated. A special thanks to my dear friend Jim Chiswell, who has advised and managed our campaigns of life so beautifully.

To my agent and friend Ivor Whitson and his wife Ronnie for their advice for this book and books past.

A writer knows he is only as good as his editor and mine was the best. Thank you, Ann LaFarge for your excellent work and guidance. Rest in peace my friend.

"We knew the world would not be the same. A few people laughed, a few people cried. Most people were silent. I remembered the line from the Hindu scripture, the Bhagavad-Gita. Vishnu is trying to persuade the Prince that he should do his duty, and, to impress him, takes on his multi-armed form and says, 'Now I am become Death, the destroyer of worlds.' I suppose we all thought that, one way or another."

J. ROBERT OPPENHEIMER, FATHER OF THE ATOMIC BOMB, ON THE OCCASION OF THE FIRST SUCCESSFUL NUCLEAR TEST THE TRINITY TEST IN NEW MEXICO IN 1945.

Chapter 1

THE BLUE PARROT CAFE
GEORGETOWN

*T*ime was running out for NNC investigative reporter Lerrick McKenna. Sitting alone at the bar with a glass of wine, the twenty-eight-year old Midwestern beauty concluded that anyone who would leave a promising career at a major law firm for the thrill of reporting mundane news must be certifiable.

At the time the choice had seemed to be a no-brainer. After a bitter divorce she'd wanted a change of scenery, so when the position at NNC was offered, she leaped at the chance to leave her home town and head to the nation's capital. Things had always come easily for Lerrick, so when the offer included a probationary period she really didn't give it much thought, considering it more formality than obstacle.

Now however, she was facing the brutal truth: no story, no job. And to make matters worse, D.C. action in August was as stagnant as the weather. Everyone who was anyone had left town to escape the heat and humidity that prevailed during the dog days of summer. Lerrick was learning all too quickly that success in this town required high visibility and lots of discretionary income. Leaning back against the corner of the bar she faced the grim reality: she needed a story and she needed it fast.

She was considering another glass of wine when she saw her friend Jill walking towards her. "Hey, I think that good-looking guy at the far end of the bar is checking you out," Jill said as she sat down.

"Jill, you of all people, know I'm not interested." However, curiosity had gotten the better of Lerrick and she glanced towards the end of the bar, unexpectedly making eye contact with the handsome stranger. Blushing, she turned away and looked at her friend who was trying to stifle a laugh. The two women began to giggle, unaware that the young man was making his way over to their end of the bar.

"Hi, I'm Dr. Jeff Roberts," he said holding out his hand as he approached, "and you're Lerrick McKenna. I've seen you on NNC."

"Hi Dr. Jeff Roberts," Lerrick said as she shook his hand. "This is my friend Jill Lohr." Lerrick couldn't help but notice how handsome he was.

"Nice to meet you, Jill, may I buy you both a drink?"

"Thanks" said Jill before Lerrick had the chance to decline. "Come join us." Jill shot her friend a quick eye-smile to make sure she was on board.

"What would you both like?"

"Chardonnay," the two replied in unison as Jeff pulled up a chair.

As the three of them sat sipping their drinks and discussing life in D.C. Lerrick found herself enjoying the evening. When Jeff started to order another round, Jill discreetly declined, giving her friend a hug and bidding them both good night.

Once the second round had been served, Jeff looked down into his glass and said softly, "What if I could put you on to a story that could catapult your career all the way to a Pulitzer Prize?"

Lerrick laughed and responded with skepticism. "Why me and what would I have to do to get such a story?"

"To answer question one, you want a story, and I believe I have one, and as for number two; just listen. Let's go into the dining room, it's quieter and we can talk over dinner. When I'm finished and you decide you don't want any part of what I'm about to tell you, we'll go our separate ways. At the very least we'll both have had a good meal."

"Sounds like a plan," said Lerrick. As she followed Jeff into the dining room she thought to herself, no risk, no foul, and maybe, just maybe this is the break that I've been waiting for.

Their waiter approached as soon as they were seated. "May I bring you something to drink?" he asked.

They decided on Pellegrino water and when the waiter returned they were ready to order. They both chose the New Orleans chopped salad with garlic shrimp. Lerrick chose for her main course sautéed sea scallops with roasted red skin potatoes and veggies, while Jeff selected the beef tournedos grilled over mesquite with a Pinot Noir sauce, the same potato as Lerrick, and sautéed escarole.

Once they were settled Lerrick asked "Why didn't you call me at NNC?"

"I wasn't sure you would take my call, and if you did, I thought you'd probably hang up on me. This way I'm pretty sure you'll hear me out, that is if I talk fast and you eat slowly."

"Well you've certainly sparked my interest. How did you come upon this bizarre tale?"

"As I told you, I'm a doctor. I graduated from the University of Virginia Medical School and remained there to do my residency in psychiatry. This fall I'll begin a fellowship in forensic psychiatry at Georgetown. The lease on my apartment in Charlottesville was up, so I moved to D.C. at the beginning of the summer and decided to take a temporary position as a hospitalist at St. Elizabeth's. You remember St. E's, the sanitarium in Anacostia where John Hinckley went after he tried to kill President Reagan?"

"I'm familiar with it."

Just then their waiter appeared with the first course. After the food had been served, Jeff continued his story.

"Anyway, I work the night shift in the block reserved for the criminally insane. Some of my patients are so withdrawn that they rarely speak. Others exhibit violent behavior and require some form of restraint. I hadn't been there very long when I became concerned about one of the patients. He was always so heavily sedated that his speech was not much more than incoherent rambling. I'm not sure if you are aware of this, but the use of chemical restraints is very controversial in psychiatry today. Its use must be documented thoroughly, and it should always be given in moderation, even in an institution like St. Elizabeth's, yet every time I saw this man he was completely obtunded. Anyway, one night last week when I was making rounds I found him awake and more coherent than ever before. I checked his chart to see if his doctor had changed his medications, but everything was the same, so I figured it was an error on the part of the day shift nurses; they just forgot to give him his meds."

"Why was he sent to St. E's?" Lerrick asked.

"His records state that he was brought to the ward a few months ago with a diagnosis of borderline personality disorder and a history of committing multiple murders. Most of the patients have personality disorders and co-morbid diagnoses that blur the line between fantasy and reality. On this particular night he told me about a terrorist plot against the United States. I'm not sure why, but I believed him; maybe it was the way he kept eye contact, or the way he spoke, but whatever it was, I decided to consult with the attending physician in charge of his case. That's when things got really weird. Dr. Lyons is listed as a member of the staff but this guy Riley is his only patient and no one at St. E's has ever seen him. He has a private office in Georgetown but the phone number that's listed doesn't answer."

"I thought psychiatrists never interrupted a session to take a call," said Lerrick.

"They don't, but they always leave a voice message and an emergency contact number in case one of their other patients is in crisis."

"Go on," said Lerrick. "This is beginning to get interesting."

"Well, just wait till you hear all of it, "Jeff said, "I decided to begin titrating down his medications."

"Why not just stop them?"

"The physical ramifications, for one," replied Jeff, "and secondly, if I was wrong, I wouldn't want anyone to get hurt. Anyway, every time I made rounds he seemed to be improving. Then the other night when I went in to see him he was lucid."

Lerrick interrupted again. "Jeff, who is this guy?"

"According to his medical record, he is George Riley, but he claims he is Ian Tuttle."

"Not Ian Tuttle, the former Chief of Staff to President Walsh!"

"One and the same. Riley/Tuttle or whoever he is claims he's sane. He did admit that he suffered a nervous breakdown while serving time at the Lewisburg Penitentiary, but says he received treatment and recovered. He told me that the man who conspired to have him transferred to St. Elizabeth's so he could disappear forever was the same person who had paid him to manipulate the policies of President Walsh's administration while he was Chief of Staff.

"I remember when that story broke," Lerrick said, "Warren Dunn was an oil baron who hired Tuttle to be his White House mole so he and a few select members of an organization called the Bohemian Society could gain control of the world's oil supply. The plan went south and

Dunn was convicted on tax evasion and served time in Lewisburg. I'm sure he and Tuttle were there at the same time.

The story was tragic even by Washington standards. Tuttle was not only one of the smartest politicians in Washington; he had been David Walsh's closest friend since their college days. The President respected his opinions and trusted him implicitly. He threw everything away, he betrayed his friend, his country; I can certainly understand why he suffered a breakdown. I believe there was some talk of charging him with treason but nothing came of that and he was convicted on conspiracy charges."

"What made him do it?" Jeff asked.

"Greed. Dunn paid him vast sums of money in cold hard cash. What I don't understand is why Dunn would want him to disappear. I'm not sure they were friends but I guess you could call them cronies."

"Tuttle claims Senator Archibald Blake and a beautiful Arab woman, apparently working for al-Qaeda, visited Warren Dunn at Lewisburg Penitentiary every week," Jeff said.

"How did Tuttle find out about this?"

"Dunn invited Tuttle to attend these meetings. He probably thought Tuttle would want to exact his own pound of flesh from the administration. Tuttle claims he told them he wasn't interested, and the next thing he knew he was at St. Elizabeth's under an assumed name. He has steadfastly claimed he is not George Riley and for some reason, Lerrick, I believed him so I started to do some investigating on my own. I secretly searched for Riley's file in the archives' section of the hospital. If Tuttle was telling the truth, I didn't think that whoever arranged the transfer would want any evidence lying around, so I wasn't surprised when I didn't find anything on Tuttle. I almost got caught a couple of times, but I continued to explore his story. I found out that George Riley was a patient at St. Elizabeth's some years ago, long before my time. He died and no one claimed his body so he was buried in Potter's field with a number. I'm sure Ian Tuttle, is the patient incarcerated in my ward. He's terrified and doesn't trust anyone but me."

"He has good reason to be scared," said Lerrick. "It would take someone with a tremendous amount of power to pull this off. Now, tell me about the plot."

"It revolves around Warren Dunn, an Arab woman, and Senator Archibald Blake. Tuttle says he overheard some pretty wild statements from Dunn about an attack that would cost many lives and that was when he told them he wanted out. The next thing he knew, he became George Riley."

Lerrick sat silently for a few moments, then asked, "Jeff, have you talked to anyone else before you approached me, another reporter or the authorities?"

"No one."

"If what you say is true, would you be willing to let me use your name and will you give me and NNC an exclusive?"

"No to the first part, and yes to the second," he replied.

"Why not the first part?"

"I'm not a hero. I'm a doctor. And besides, I could stay on the inside and funnel information to you."

Lerrick paused to collect her thoughts. "Jeff, give me your contact information," she finally said. "Also, get yourself a beeper so we can keep in touch. I will beep you first and you can call back on your cell. Don't use any of the phones or pay phones at St. E's. I'm going to take this to my boss and get his OK to run with it. I'll call you within two days; here is my beeper number as well as my cell. Feel free to call me anytime in the next two days if you have any more to add. Just please be careful—whoever these people are I don't think they're going to lose any sleep over a little collateral damage."

Dinner was coming to an end with a shared dessert and another glass of wine. Lerrick feeling a little bit heady called it an evening thanking Jeff for the treat and company. They shook hands and Jeff walked Lerrick to her cab.

Chapter 2

NNC HEADQUARTERS

*T*he next morning, Lerrick met with her boss, Brian Landry. At first he wanted her to share the by-line with one of NNC's top White House correspondents but she convinced him to let her run with the story. Reluctantly, Landry agreed, and Lerrick got right to work.

Using the NNC network library, she gathered as much information on Tuttle, Dunn and Blake as she could. By the end of the day she had also verified Jeff's degrees from UVA. She did not contact St. Elizabeth's about his current status; that might raise a red flag that could jeopardize his job and hinder their investigation. She was relieved that Jeff was legit. That problem solved, she was ready to call him for a meeting.

She pulled her cell phone from her carryall and dialed. "Hi!" she said. "Is this Jeff?"

"Yes it is."

"It's Lerrick McKenna from NNC, I have some news to share with you."

"Good news, I hope."

"I don't want to talk over the phone. Can we meet sometime today or tonight?"

"I just got off. Do you want to come over?" he asked.

Feeling a little uncomfortable with that, Lerrick suggested they meet in Georgetown at Dean & DeLuca's for a sandwich and coffee.

"It's a deal," he said, "how about in 15 minutes?"

"I'm on my way."

Lerrick caught a cab and arrived just as Jeff was sitting down in one of the booths that line the walls. As she sat across from him, he immediately asked "What's up?"

"A lot," she replied, "I talked to my boss—no, pleaded with my boss—and he gave me the go-ahead. Now I have a plan and I'm going to need your help."

"You've got it," Jeff responded, "I told you that at the beginning."

"I know, Jeff, but this could get tricky, and I don't want to cost you your job."

"Understood, but that will be my call, okay?"

"Okay. I need you to get me a copy of George Riley's file. I'll get Tuttle's file from Lewisburg. There must be some collusion going on at the highest level for an inmate at Lewisburg to be transferred to St. E's and become a dead man walking."

"I hadn't thought of that," Jeff said.

"Well, my boss knows somebody who knows somebody at the prison. You know, the old boy's network; he's going to work on it from that end. However, I'll need you to get the records from St. E's."

"I can do that, but you're right, this is going to be tricky."

"I would never forgive myself if you threw away your career to help me." Lerrick suddenly realized she was beginning to sound more like a girlfriend than a reporter. She silently vowed not to let that happen. Now was not the time for personal attraction to cloud professional judgment.

"Okay, okay" said Jeff throwing up his hands in mock defeat, "but first, let me remind you that I'm doing this to help someone I believe has been terribly wronged."

"Then you'll help me get into St. E's so I can talk to Tuttle," said Lerrick. "Actually, I'll probably need to interview him more than once. Is this possible?"

"I think so, but I have to give some thought as to how I'm going to get you in there without both of us ending up in jail. And you have to promise me that if you get in and things go south you'll get the hell out, with or without the story."

"Okay, Jeff, but I already know that I would be arrested for breaking and entering, Brian gave me that lecture. But I get the feeling that there's something else. What is it?"

"There is an aide who works in Tuttle's unit. I'm beginning to think he has something to do with Dunn. He rarely does much with the other patients, but pays close attention to Tuttle's every move. They call him Manson and if he catches you, I can't guarantee your safety."

"Okay, I'll get out if I feel the heat, but, you know I work for some very important people."

"I'm afraid he does, too. Anyway, let's hope we never have to show our hand. First, I need to titrate down Tuttle's meds. That should take about twenty-four hours. I will meet you outside the rear entrance on Saturday night. That's a good night because we are short-staffed. Meet me at the rear entrance of John Howard's Pavilion at 11:15 p.m. That entrance is only used for deliveries and staff at shift change. The shift change is at eleven o'clock, and that's when the guard makes his rounds before returning to the front hall to watch TV. Park your car on a side street and walk to the Pavilion. Page me and hide near the rear entrance until I get there to open the door."

"Do you have a key?" asked Lerrick.

"No, but I do have the key that opens the emergency drawer where all the keys are kept. All the hospitalists are issued one. I think it is best to interview Tuttle in his room so you won't be noticed. I'll make sure I'm working on that floor that night. If there's a problem, page me using 911 and I'll be there in 30 seconds."

The two planned to talk the next day and as Lerrick left Dean & DeLuca she smiled to herself. This could develop into something big. And not just for NNC.

Chapter 3

ST. ELIZABETH'S HOSPITAL
WASHINGTON, D.C. – SOUTHEAST

*D*uring the Civil War, southeast Washington was a fine place to live. However, time was not kind to the beautiful old neighborhoods. Southeast was no longer pretty and no one cared. People lost their jobs, and their pride. Neighborhoods opened their doors to drugs, pimps and whores while the politicians turned their backs.

Lerrick decided to park on a dingy narrow side street where cars were parked on both sides amidst the broken glass and garbage of the rundown row houses. No taxi driver in his right mind would take a fare down there.

She parked her car, looked around carefully, and got out. Armed with a can of pepper spray, she walked the thousand feet or so to the hospital. The first thing she had to do was figure out how to get past the guard.

As she approached the guardhouse, Lerrick caught a lucky break. An ambulance, sirens wailing and lights flashing, pulled right up to the front gate. While the guard on duty was busily checking it in, Lerrick slipped behind the vehicle, and quickly walked past the blind side of the guardhouse to the safety of the tall evergreens that obscured the entrance to the lot. Once in the immense parking lot, she began to look for the John Howard Pavilion. She knew from her research that it was in the rear of the campus, away from the other buildings. To remain undetected, she walked around the outer perimeter of the parking lot until she reached her destination. Glancing at her watch, she realized she had plenty of time. She took cover in a small area to the far right of the rear entrance, with ten precious minutes before the guard would open the doors. She prayed no one would hear the sound of her heart pounding or walk her way to light a cigarette. A couple of minutes later the rear door opened for the shift change. All went smoothly; no one even stopped for a smoke or a pee. Breathing a sigh of relief, she waited for the guard to close and lock the steel door. At last it was time to contact Jeff. She punched 911 into her cell phone and waited.

He appeared and motioned to Lerrick to follow him up a darkened staircase to the main hallway. This was the quickest route to the patients' rooms.

"Hurry," said Jeff. "We need to get you to Tuttle's room without being seen. Fortunately, we're short staffed tonight. Manson requested the night off, thank God."

"I'm a bit scared, Jeff," said Lerrick, "are you going to stay?"

"I can't, I don't want to arouse any suspicions. But trust me, Mr. Tuttle is completely harmless and he knows you're coming."

"Does he know I'm from NNC?"

"Yes, he knows, now listen to me, you have exactly forty minutes to spend with him. Rounds are in fifty minutes, so when I come to get you I don't care if you're in mid-sentence, you're leaving."

Jeff inserted a key into the lock that kept Tuttle in his room and opened the door. The walls were pea soup green and the stench of urine and feces was sickening. Housekeeping left a lot to be desired.

Turning to Jeff, Lerrick said, "What the hell is the smell?"

Jeff whispered, "He gets such high doses of medication he can't control himself." He turned to Tuttle and introduced him to Lerrick before returning to his duties. Tuttle seemed fully cognizant of his surroundings and apologized for them. He spoke quietly, "I'm very sorry, Ms. McKenna, but this is the way I'm forced to live. I hope you're not too offended to help me?"

"Good evening, Mr. Tuttle," Lerrick said. "I'm not offended; I am horrified by your circumstances. Jeff has briefed me, and I sympathize with you. That's why I'm here. Now, let's get down to business; we don't have much time. As a matter of fact, I will probably have to make another visit or two before I get all the information that I'll need. May I call you Ian?" He nodded and she said, "Good, and please call me Lerrick. I have a feeling we're going to know each other really well before broadcast time."

With Tuttle sitting on the edge of his bed and Lerrick on the room's only chair, the interview began. Tuttle spoke first, saying, "I did my President and my country a terrible disservice, for which I lost my job, my home and very nearly my sanity..."

Lerrick interrupted, "Ian, may I record your statements?"

"Yes, I prefer it that way." Lerrick pulled a battery powered recorder from her purse and asked, "Would you start by stating your formal name and former position with the President?"

"My name is Ian Tuttle, and I am the former Chief of Staff to the current President of the United States, David Walsh." He went on to say that during his tenure he was convicted of tax evasion and accepting bribes and sentenced to the Lewisburg Federal Penitentiary for three to five years. While in prison he suffered a nervous breakdown.

"After going through therapy, I was able to participate in prison life," Tuttle continued. "I spent a lot of time with a man named Warren Dunn. He's the former CEO of Oil-Co who was convicted of bribery and tax invasion. Dunn and I have quite a long history. We first become acquainted through our work on Walsh's presidential campaign and the relationship continued once President Walsh was elected. I was considered a close confidante of Dunn's, so while we were in Lewisburg I was privy to several conversations he had with Senator Archibald Blake, and a woman affiliated with al-Qaeda."

"Why would a US Senator take the chance of being seen at Lewisburg Penitentiary?" Lerrick asked.

"Because Warren Dunn is still one of the most powerful and dangerous men in the world, and if he wants to see a senator, it's going to happen."

"OK, what about the woman?"

"I didn't know who she was, but I assume she represents the interests of al-Qaeda. I once overheard her say that we must honor the wishes of Bin Laden's legacy and dedication to the present War Council and his Jihad. His plan called for the complete destruction of the financial and governing system of the United States and that's just the beginning. He wanted every bridge, building and business in America destroyed, along with its people. The ultimate goal of al-Qaeda is to create a worldwide fundamentalist state for Islam headquartered on top of our graves."

Lerrick interrupted. "But what's that got to do with Dunn and Blake?"

"Before his conviction, Dunn was promised control of most of the world's oil supply in return for colluding with top government officials to secretly support al-Qaeda's interests in the United States. As I had been Dunn's White House mole, the three of them automatically assumed I would be part of their conspiracy. I told them in no uncertain terms that I didn't want anything to do with their plot. I had betrayed my country and my friends once and never again. The next thing I knew, I woke up at St. Elizabeth's as George Riley. I thought I would die here and I probably would have if Dr. Roberts hadn't gotten involved in my care."

Lerrick nodded and said, "It isn't every day a patient in this place gets a doctor who believes them. That is as fascinating as the rest of your story. Tell me what happened next."

Tuttle went on, "A guy named Manson was giving me my meds. When Dr. Roberts asked him for his license to administer medication, he became belligerent and wouldn't give the doc a straight answer. Doc decided to check Manson's credentials and found he wasn't licensed in D.C. or anywhere else. Dr. Roberts ordered the nursing staff to administer all my medicine, then took down the dose I had been receiving. Soon I became coherent enough to tell my story. We both believe Manson was planted here by Dunn to ensure my silence. We arrived on the same day."

"And both with false credentials," Lerrick added. "What happened to Manson? Did he get fired?"

"If Dunn has the power to get him here, he has the power to keep him here. I assure you he is still here, monitoring my every move." Tuttle smiled faintly, then continued. "What if I told you that I know these bastards are planning to blow up the Chesapeake Bay Bridge?"

"Do you know details?" Lerrick asked hastily. Her time with Tuttle was running out.

"Yes, but first I need your assurance that I will leave St. E's and have protection on the outside."

"You have my word," Lerrick said. "I'll arrange it with my boss."

The minutes rolled by quickly until Jeff interrupted them and quietly said, "Lerrick, it's time to leave."

Reluctantly she packed up her things, then turned to Tuttle and said, "Ian, I'm going to call my boss as soon as I leave. I know he'll want to speak with the National Security Adviser about your story and then I'll be back to see you. Jeff will let you know when."

Once in the hallway Lerrick began to talk but Jeff motioned her to keep quiet. Together they made their way back to the rear entrance. Jeff told her to call his cell when she was in the clear. After hurrying back across the dimly lit parking lot, she climbed in her car and locked the doors. Still reeling from the events of the night, she took a deep breath, paged Jeff, and then called her boss.

"Brian? This is Lerrick; I need to see you right away."

"Can't it wait until morning?"

"No."

"Oh, what the hell, come on over."

Lerrick arrived at her boss's condo in record time and was met at the door by a somewhat skeptical Landry. "Now tell me what can't wait till morning," he said as he handed her a mug of black coffee.

Lerrick started to tell him the story but then said, "Hell, Brian, let me play the tape so you won't hear this secondhand." The two sat motionless as the tape rolled, revealing Tuttle's story. When it ended Landry broke the silence. "Jesus, Lerrick, I have to call the White House and speak with Jim Sercu, the National Security Advisor. Go home, get some sleep and I'll call you after I talk with him."

Lerrick drove home quickly and headed straight for bed. She had just turned out the light when her phone rang.

"Lerrick, get ready," barked NNC's, chief editor. "We're meeting Sercu at the White House. My driver will pick you up in fifteen minutes. I'll see you there."

At 1600 Pennsylvania Avenue, Lerrick was immediately escorted to the office of the National Security Advisor. Her boss was already there and introduced her to Jim Sercu. After the introduction, Sercu told Lerrick that Brian had briefed him on the situation with Tuttle. The three of them sat down to listen to the tape. When it ended, Sercu broke the silence that shrouded the room. "I need to wake the President. Wait for me in the White House Mess. Get something to eat and I'll call you after I've talked to him."

Alone in his office, Jim Sercu picked up the secure phone and was immediately put through to the private quarters. "I need to see the

President right away."

"Yes, sir" came the reply and Sercu walked hastily down the hall toward the Marines who stood guard at the entrance to the President's private elevator. As he arrived on the second floor, President Walsh came out of his room. "Jim, what brings you here at this hour? It can't be good news."

"No, sir, it's not," said Sercu. "I have information that another terrorist attack on our soil is imminent, and it involves not only al-Qaeda but a wealthy American and a US Senator."

"A United States *Senator*?"

"Yes, sir," Sercu continued. "You need to listen to a tape that has come into my possession." Sercu briefed the President on the events leading to Lerrick's visit to St E's, her interview with Ian Tuttle, and the delivery of the tape by Brian Landry.

"Where are these two now, Jim?"

"Downstairs, getting something to eat, sir."

"Have them come up immediately and I'll start listening to the tape."

It saddened David Walsh to hear Ian's voice again. He had been a good friend at one time, but the greater concern right now was that someone or some group was plotting once again to attack Americans on their own soil, and that these same people had conspired to imprison Ian at St. Elizabeth's under a false identity. It would take tremendous resources and an extensive network to pull this off.

Sercu met Brian and Lerrick at the entrance to the residence and ushered them into the President's study. Lerrick felt intimidated in the presence of the most powerful man in the world and, sensing this, David Walsh made every effort to make her feel at ease. "You've quite a story here, Miss McKenna. Do you intend to air this on NNC?"

"Yes, Mr. President, as soon as possible."

"Miss McKenna," the President said slowly, allowing the weight of his office to amplify his message, "I need you to hold your story in the interest of national security." Landry began to protest but the President held up his hand and said, "Brian, you know I can't allow you to broadcast this information. It would create total panic, and you also know I have the constitutional authority to suspend habeas corpus if I see fit; however, I am not going to do that. I just want you to hold off releasing this story. Continue your investigation of Ian Tuttle. Find out everything you can about how he got to St. Elizabeth's and who authorized it. Do it quickly, because I question his safety."

"Yes, Mr. President," Brian said.

Brian and Lerrick took their leave and were escorted to the North Portico gate, where Landry's driver was waiting to take them back to the Washington Bureau of NNC.

Once the two reporters had left, the President said, "Before we go any further with this, Jim, we need to make sure Tuttle is legit."

"Mr. President, how in the hell are we going to tell if Ian Tuttle is sane or not?"

"We need to check this out ourselves and then talk to Ian, but first, we need to make sure the Chesapeake Bay Bridge is secure. Call FEMA and get them on site ASAP. If this is real we're in a race against the clock. I'm going to put in a call to Colonel Ziegelhofer."

"Thank you, Mr. President," said Sercu, taking his leave.

Sunday 0600
SOE Command Center
The office of Colonel David Ziegelhofer

When the secure phone on his desk began to buzz, it took no more than a glance from Colonel David Ziegelhofer to dismiss the two officers seated across from him. Once the room was clear, Ziggy reached for the phone. "Yes, Mr. President?"

"Colonel, we have an issue and I need you at the White House."

"Yes sir, I'm on my way."

The President had just finished appraising Ziegelhofer of the situation when Jim Sercu walked through the side entrance of the Oval Office. "What do you have on this Roberts fellow?" Walsh asked as Sercu walked to his chair.

"He's legit, sir," replied Sercu, "He completed his residency in Psychiatry at the University of Virginia and will start a fellowship at Georgetown in January. He was hired as a hospitalist at St. Elizabeth's and they think very highly of him."

"Verifying Tuttle's story and his sanity is our first step," said the

President. "Ziggy, you and Jim are to make a visit to St. Elizabeth's tonight. Enlist the help of Dr. Roberts, but I want you two to see Tuttle alone. You both know him so well that you'll be able to get a read on his condition instantly."

"Do you want us to get him out?" Ziegelhofer asked.

"That might not be a good idea, sir," Sercu said. "If Tuttle is telling the truth, his removal by any of us could cause the terrorists to expedite their plans."

"You're right," said the President. "Let's see what you come back with first, and then we'll decide what to do. I'm sure I don't have to tell you gentlemen that this has top priority."

Sercu and Ziegelhofer left the President. They had a lot to do in the next few hours.

Jeff was awakened by the sound of his phone and answered it to hear an unfamiliar voice. "Jeff Roberts, this is National Security Advisor James Sercu. Lerrick McKenna, whom I met last night, gave me your name. It is imperative that I meet with you within the hour. Would you please come to my office at the White House? The south gate entrance will be fine and someone will escort you."

Office of the National Security Advisor

"Mr. Sercu, Dr. Roberts is here," announced the director's secretary.

"Show him in, Annie, please." As Jeff entered, Sercu held out his hand, "Doctor Roberts?"

"Yes, sir," said Jeff. "It's an honor to meet you, sir."

"Thank you, Doctor." They shook hands. "May I call you Jeff?"

"Of course, sir."

"Good, let's get right to the point. Last night I was involved in a meeting with Lerrick McKenna, her boss Brian Landry, and the President regarding Miss McKenna's interview with your patient Ian Tuttle. I've been directed by the President to talk to Mr. Tuttle myself, and I need to do it quietly and covertly. Can you help me do that?"

"Yes, sir," said Jeff. "I will be working this evening if you want to visit Tuttle that soon. The only problem is that a man named Manson will also be on duty tonight. I'm sure he's connected to this somehow. He can cause everyone a lot of trouble."

"That's all right," replied Sercu. "I am bringing someone along who is more than capable of dealing with any situations that might arise. We'll be okay."

"All right then," said Jeff and proceeded to give the same instructions to Sercu that he had given to Lerrick.

Chapter 4

ST. ELIZABETH'S

$\mathcal{L}$ate that night Colonel Ziggy and Jim Sercu met Jeff at the rear of the Pavilion and went straight to Tuttle's suite, following the same instructions he had given Lerrick. As they entered, Ian stood up to welcome the two visitors. He was shocked to see the President's top men.

"Jim, it's been a long time," Ian said softly.

"Ian, you remember David Ziegelhofer," said Sercu.

"Of course." Ian held out his hand.

"Ian, we need to talk."

Ian nodded, "I'm glad you got here so quickly. There's a lot to be said." The men studied Tuttle closely as he relayed the same story he had told Lerrick. He was almost finished when the door suddenly opened.

"What the fuck is going on here! Can't you read? No visitors allowed!" Manson bellowed. He started to reach for the call button on the wall when the 6' 6" colonel's fist whacked the back of his head, sending him sprawling to the floor. Ziggy was throwing the limp body over his shoulder when Jeff rushed into the room.

"What happened?" Jeff asked.

"Get us out now," ordered Sercu, grabbing a surprised Tuttle by the arm. "Don't say anything to anyone. If someone asks, just say Manson told you he was tired of this shit and was out of this goddamn hellhole. The next thing you knew, George Riley was gone. Let them think Manson was involved in Riley's disappearance."

"Is he dead?" Roberts whispered, looking at Manson's limp body dangling over Ziggy's shoulder.

"No, but he'll wish he was," snapped Ziggy.

"Jim," Tuttle began.

"Quiet, Ian," Sercu assured his former associate. "Just stay close."

Jeff pointed the men to the back entrance where they escaped undetected and hurried across the dimly lit parking lot.

"Dump him over the fence," Sercu told Ziggy.

"What if a cop notices the body?"

"In Southeast? Hell, he's just part of the landscape."

"Ok," said Ziggy. He threw Manson over the fence with ease.

"Walk with us around the corner and stay close. We can't be seen by the guard" said Sercu.

Out on the street, the men retrieved their package and drove toward the White House.

"What now?" Sercu asked.

"Well, I need to interrogate sleeping beauty here and find a safe place for Ian," said Ziggy. "I'll probably store them both at the safe house in Gordonsville VA. Meanwhile, you can ask the President what he wants me to do with Tuttle."

"How's the President?" Tuttle asked, quietly.

"Good, but different than you remember him. Stronger, more confident," said the colonel.

"He's made his bones," Sercu interjected. "Hell, his approval ratings are through the roof and he has almost everyone in the Free World behind him."

Glancing in the rear view mirror, Ziggy noticed a tear in Ian's eye as he remembered the President and friend he had betrayed.

Sercu broke the silence. "Drop me off at the Capitol Grill, I'll walk from there. If we try to go through security with Ian and our friend in the trunk we'll be the lead story in tomorrow's *Post*."

"I sure don't want to have to explain that," cracked Ziggy.

"Here we are," Sercu announced as he opened the door and hopped out of the car. "See ya, Ziggy," he called back over his shoulder as he walked swiftly toward the White House.

Colonel Ziegelhofer, with cargo intact, drove to the safe house located in Gordonsville, Virginia.

The Residence

The clock in the private study read 4 a.m. when the President entered the room. He looked tired, and Jim Sercu apologized for waking him.

"Nonsense," said the President. "Bring me up to date."

"We had to get him out tonight, sir"

"Tuttle?" said Walsh, straightening in his chair.

"Yes sir. A man named Manson, whom we believe was sent to St. Elizabeth's to keep an eye on Tuttle, made us. Ziggy took care of him but we had to move quickly to ensure Ian's safety. When whoever was employing Manson finds out he's gone, shit's going to hit the fan."

"Where are they?"

"Ziggy is taking both of them to a safe house in Virginia. He's going to 'talk' to Manson, and Tuttle will be safe there until you decide what you want to do with him."

"What's your gut, Jim? Do you think Ian's all right?"

"I think he's sane, Mr. President. He gave us the same Intel that he gave to the NNC reporter. The terrorists have chosen three locations in the continental United States and one in London. Apparently, they're in their destroy mode."

"Did Ian give locations?"

"Only one, sir, the Bay Bridge. He backed out of the conspiracy before learning of the other sites."

"Damn," said Walsh.

Sercu looked at the President, trying to get a read on his boss and friend, but for the moment Walsh was playing his cards very close to the vest. Then, so swiftly that it startled the NSA director, the President reached for the phone.

"Jeannie, I want FBI Director Michaels and Jim Chiswell in my office at 8 a.m. Tell them not to say anything to anyone. And Jeannie, when you're done, get me Colonel Ziegelhofer." Turning back to Sercu, the President said, "Jim, go home and get some sleep. I'll see you later today."

"Thank you, Mr. President."

———————

Alone with his thoughts, the President pondered what could drive anyone to betray their country, especially a member of the most exclusive club in the world—the United States Senate. He wasn't surprised, however, that Warren Dunn had a part in this. Walsh had never liked the wealthy financier and had learned from past experience that his mantra was power. Dunn would never let a little thing like conscience keep him from his destiny. But who was the woman and what role did she have in al-Qaeda? Suddenly the solitude was shattered by the sound of Jeannie's voice.

"Mr. President, I have Colonel Ziegelhofer on the phone for you."

"Thanks, Jeannie," he said. "Colonel, I hear you're having guests."

"Yes sir."

"I don't need to remind you, Colonel, that time is of the essence. This Manson person is our best lead as to who and what we're facing."

"I understand, sir."

"Where's Tuttle?"

"He's with me. When we get to the house, we'll clean him up and get him some medical attention. I understand that he's been on some heavy-duty drugs. If he were to stop them cold turkey, I'm not sure how much he would be able to help us. We will also be able to reassess his mental status."

"What's your gut, Colonel?"

"I'd say he's sane, but he's definitely had a rough time, sir."

"Of course I want you to talk to Tuttle as soon as possible, Ziggy," urged the President, "but I respect your judgment."

"Thank you, sir, I'll do my best. Do you want me to pick up Warren Dunn and Senator Blake?"

"No, Colonel, I don't want to tip our hand. I'm going to call the FBI director and have the Senator placed under observation 24/7. I have something else planned for Mr. Dunn. Report back to me as soon as you get anything from Manson."

"Yes, Mr. President." The line went dead. Pausing for a moment, Ziggy decided Sercu was right. Manson and Tuttle's sudden departure from St. Elizabeth's will surely cause the terrorists to accelerate their timeline. He decided to start work on Manson immediately. Time was definitely not on his side.

Chapter 5

HOOPERS ISLAND
MARYLAND

On the Chesapeake Bay, surrounded by the Black Water Wildlife Refuge, was a small, secluded weekend cabin. The residents, Ali Atwa and Abdul Yasin, thought themselves very fortunate to have such a private place available to them. But then, they felt blessed in many ways. They had escaped a worldwide search by the United States government, gained entrance into the country by crossing the Rio Grande at Nuevo Laredo, Texas, enjoyed an uneventful trip across the country, and had been preparing for their destiny in the seclusion of Maryland's Eastern shore. Their only contact was a 36-year-old white supremacist named Leroy Michie.

Michie was a family man from Montana with two children. The leader of the 110th Regiment Militia, an ultra-right-wing group that believed the present government of the United States must be eliminated, he was considered extremely dangerous. Because he had broken no laws, he was able to operate under the radar of an ever-watchful FBI. This resume made him a perfect candidate for employment by Warren Dunn and al-Qaeda. His job was to babysit two fanatics who could not be seen around town. He provided everything they needed, even going to the mainland to a little grocery store in Cambridge called the Center Market to buy their food. Leroy didn't mind the menial tasks; the pay was good, it was cash, and it was short term. Very soon, Ali and Yasin would die as part of the holy war against the Great Satan.

The plan itself was simple; Ali and Yasin would drive across the bridge, stop at the anchor and detonate the bomb, blowing themselves and everything in their path to oblivion. They believed that when their journey was over, Allah would fulfill his promise of heaven, honey and dozens of virgins. Leroy was sure that a very grateful Warren Dunn, being of a more practical nature, would generously bestow rewards upon him as well.

The White House

President David Walsh had been down this road before. He knew that he needed to warn his friend, the Prime Minister of Great Britain, about the rumored attacks on the Chesapeake Bay Bridge and unspecified sites in London. He must advise the Prime Minister of Israel that there was a possibility, that they, too, could suffer an attack on their own soil. He hoped that Prime Minister Mordachi would be able to lend some additional insight into the political climate in the Mid-East. However, Walsh knew that before he made those calls he needed more information; information that only Tuttle could provide and Manson could confirm. The President needed more time, but time was running out. Ziegelhofer had to do his job, and do it fast.

Government Safehouse
Gordonsville, Virginia

Colonel David Ziegelhofer had replaced General Louis Blaine as the head of the President's Special Operations Detail. This organization is actually called SOE, an acronym for Special Operations Executive, but it's known as "the Detail" by its members, thirty-five men and women, all officers with the exception of a select few Master Sergeants, and all graduates of the Army War College with masters degrees in counter-terrorism. Their sole purpose is to carry out the covert orders of the President of the United States in times of crisis, and to this end they are bound only by conscience.

The stately manor house deep in Virginia horse country provided a perfect place to entertain a "guest" of the United States government. Towering pines and high stone walls completely hid the mile-long driveway. Cameras concealed in birdhouses high up in the trees recorded the arrival and departure of all who entered the premises. If the occasion dictated, speed bumps became titanium spikes that could render a vehicle useless by shredding its undercarriage. The inside of the manor house looked like most of the homes of the antebellum period, except that some of the walls were noticeably thicker. This alteration allowed an operative to walk between the studs and observe his "guest" through strategically placed two-way mirrors. The rear of the manor boasted a secure room where the members of the SOE interviewed the detainees; admission was by invitation only and gate crashers never left.

Colonel Ziegelhofer turned onto the long drive leading to the manor. While showing his credentials to the guard posted halfway up the driveway, so as not to be seen, Ziggy ordered him to summon Master Sergeant Kevin McCarthy and Colonel Steve Meyers to his office. By the time the two men knocked on the door Ziegelhofer was dressed in his black jumpsuit. His 18-inch arms, bulging in the tight clothing, made him look like a behemoth. Ziggy liked the power of intimidation. However, unlike his predecessor, he relished intellectual sparring with his prisoners more than direct physical contact, leaving the "bad guy" routine to other members of the detail.

Master Sergeant McCarthy was 5'6" of solid muscle, with a baby face that belied the intensity of the man. Enlisting right out of high school, he now embodied the spirit of the corps. The Army was his life, and he zealously defended the United States of America and the principals of freedom by whatever means he deemed necessary. Ziggy thought that as long as the armed forces had men like Kevin McCarthy, America would be safe.

Colonel Steve Meyers grew up in Baghdad, the son of an attaché to the US Embassy. During the summer his family vacationed in a Kurdish mountain town near the Turkish border. Imbedded with the local children, Meyers learned to understand and speak their language like a native. As the war on terror accelerated, so did Meyers' career in the armed services. His ability to speak a very rare dialect of Kurdish, as well as Farsi and other languages of the region, made him especially valuable. Loaned to Great Britain, he served an apprenticeship with the SAS, watching Saddam Hussein's son Uday. During this time his hatred of the Arab terrorists and the ruling family of Iraq became his passion. Watching the daily torture of innocent people, Meyers absorbed the techniques like a sponge, resolving to someday exact his own pound of flesh on those who committed these atrocities. He became a specialist in the art, earning the respect of the Mossad and Shin Bet as well as his own country.

Now, after assisting MI-6 for the benefit of the English government, Colonel Meyers had come home. Ziggy couldn't help but think that if Meyers were civilian, he would probably have ended up at

St. Elizabeth's; instead he found a home in the Corps, and the Corps protected him.

Following a knock on the door, the two men were ordered into the office by their commanding officer. Ziegelhofer briefed his team on the prisoner's rather sketchy background. Manson was a high school dropout who had spent most of his life on the wrong side of the law. A loner, he had no affiliation to any specific group or organization and was strictly a gun-for-hire. This was good news to the three men, who concluded that Manson was a man without conviction. A man without conviction is a man without loyalty, and a man without loyalty is a man who can be easily broken. They decided on a good cop/bad cop routine with their boss taking the lead and McCarthy playing his antithesis. Meyers was standing by in case this strategy failed. The only thing that would keep their "guest" quiet was if Meyers killed him.

When the two men entered the room, McCarthy ordered Manson to take all his clothes off.

"Why?" asked Manson. "So you can see what a real man looks like, you little asshole? "

Manson didn't have time to finish his insult before McCarthy slapped him across the face with a whiffle bat wrapped in duct tape. The unexpected pain was so intense that it brought tears to Manson's eyes, tears that flowed down his cheeks in a steady stream. The second blow came from an uppercut to the groin, bringing with it more unbearable pain. Moments later an angry, humiliated, naked Manson was handcuffed to the chair.

"Mr. Manson, my apologies," Colonel Ziegelhofer began. "Sometimes our Master Sergeant gets a little carried away. He's so used to dealing with barbarians that he forgets how civilized people can communicate. If you would be so kind as to answer a few questions, I'm sure I will be able to curtail his zeal. However, if you choose not to cooperate, he will make your life more miserable than you could ever imagine, and I doubt you would make it out of here alive." Manson was defiantly silent, so Ziggy paused, then said, "Master Sergeant, call Colonel Meyers. We don't have time for this. His 15 minutes of fame are up."

When Meyers entered the room, Manson immediately began to

protest, demanding his rights.

"Mr. Manson," Meyers snapped. "These are your rights, and these are your only rights. The President of the United States suspended the rest. You have the right to talk now. If you choose not to execute this right, it is my duty to inform you that you will probably die here, and no one will know what happened to you. Are we clear?"

Manson sat motionless, ignoring Meyers' threats.

"Good, I'm glad we understand each other," Meyers continued. "Now then, it will help this government to know who placed you at St. Elizabeth's."

The refusal blurted out of Manson's mouth before Meyers was able to offer him more time to think about his answer. Infuriated by Manson's arrogance, and while Manson was invoking his 5th amendment rights, Meyers removed two black rubber hoses from his bag and began wiping them down with Vaseline. When he finished, he attached them to the two water spigots in the room and called for McCarthy to give him a hand.

"Grab him from behind by the hair, yank back as hard as you can, and hold him there," Meyers instructed.

"Yes, sir," stated McCarthy, executing the move to perfection.

Manson was still "mother-fucking" everyone, including the President, when Meyers jammed a small crowbar in his mouth, effectively removing most of his teeth in one hit. Manson screamed in agony, spitting and choking on teeth and blood, as Meyers began to slowly push the black hose down his esophagus and into his stomach. He saw the fear of God in his prisoner's eyes as he wrapped duct tape around Manson's head to secure the hose. Next Manson's feet were shackled to a block and tackle, and McCarthy raised him off the floor, dangling upside down. Meyers inserted the second hose into his rectum, forcing it as far into the colon as possible, then Meyers slowly turned on both hoses so that the stomach and intestine would fill just before bursting. After a few moments, Meyers switched from cold water to scalding hot. Almost immediately, Manson began frantically to signal his antagonists. The men knew it was over, so McCarthy lowered him to the floor and quickly removed the hoses. Immediately Manson started to vomit and lost control of his bowels. Angry and humiliated, he began to sob.

"Mr. Manson," Meyers started. "I'm only going to ask you this once. Who hired you? What were your duties? Who else was involved?"

"I'm just a handyman. I guarded his house, cut the grass. I did anything he wanted me to do."

"*Who?*" Meyers shouted.

"Mr. Dunn, Mr. Warren Dunn," Manson cried.

Ziegelhofer did not wait to hear the rest. He left immediately to call the President.

Chapter 6

HOOPERS ISLAND
MARYLAND

*F*riday afternoon traffic on the Bay Bridge was at its peak. Toll booths were backed up for at least half a mile as families anxious to escape the heat of the city tried to get a head start on the weekend, and those whose occupations carried them out of town during the week headed home. Everyone was glad that the weekend was here. Especially Leroy Michie.

It was shortly after 4:00 p.m. when Leroy drove up to the little cabin on the backwaters of the Chesapeake Bay where Ali and Yasin had been patiently waiting to play their part in the Jihad.

"Soldiers of Islam," Leroy said. "It is time. Follow the plan and do not deviate. Soon you will be in paradise."

Ali and Yasin were ready. They had been trained in the best terrorist camp in the Islam world. Ali had actually met Osama Bin Laden when the leader spoke to his class, describing a greater life on the other side which he should be enjoying now. Ali and Yasin were highly skilled and deeply dedicated men, which enhanced their desirability with terrorist organizations worldwide. The two smiled gently, envisioning the havoc they were about to wreak on the dog from the west. Allah would surely welcome them.

To begin their journey, both men bathed and dressed in fresh clean white linen robes, as was the custom of those who were about to die, then changed back to jeans and t-shirts to avoid detection. The road to eternity has many paths. After bowing to the East for their last prayers, the two men took their positions in the truck and trailer loaded with Cem-Tex, a highly volatile compound so powerful that an amount the size of a can of paint could easily destroy a 3,400-square-foot building. The trip to the bridge would take approximately an hour and forty minutes, depending on traffic. They must be very careful to obey the rules of the road so they would not arouse the suspicion of any of the many troopers who patrolled the highways on the weekend. The town of Cambridge, Maryland, was the worst, and Ali made a mental note to be extremely careful there. Everything must go according to plan. After an hour and twenty minutes on the crowded road, Ali entered the wide apron to the bridge.

The Chesapeake Bay Bridge had been placed under federal guard. Humvees carrying National Guard troops with automatic rifles were in full sight, just waiting for something to happen. FBI profilers had replaced the men and women who normally worked the tollbooths. Ali laughed as he thought how arrogant the American dogs were for believing that these pimply-faced young guardsmen with unloaded weapons and those redneck cops carrying peashooters could stop the Jihad. He picked up his walkie-talkie and called back to the trailer.

"Yasin," he said, "We are at the entrance to the bridge." Yasin hurried to get ready. Everything in his life came down to this day. It was a perfect mission; it was a perfect day to die.

The traffic on the bridge was so heavy that the drive took a little longer than Ali had thought, but finally they were on the other side and looking for the anchor, a 4,000-ton block of cement that held the bridge cables taut from both ends. If these cables were cut loose from the anchor, the entire structure would buckle and the road would weave up and down, gaining momentum before finally collapsing into the bay. And that was exactly what was going to happen.

Ali located the anchor and turned on the truck's blinkers, feigning mechanical trouble. He slowed to a stop with the trailer still in the passing lane. Traffic was blocked, and police and soldiers were rendered helpless at each end of the bridge.

Ali radioed to Yasin that the moment of greatness had come, and Yasin did not hesitate. Screaming praises to Allah, he pressed the detonator switch and set off an explosion heard all the way to Baltimore. Cables snapped from their eyelets and started whipping about like strands of overcooked spaghetti. Girders and struts, no longer secure, rolled with the violence of a tidal wave before plunging into the water. Cars and trucks caught in the explosion shredded like pieces of paper. Shrapnel flew from the bridge with such force that the jagged pieces cut through three liquid propane gas tanks atop the *LNG Edinburgh* as she slid through the waters between the two spans of the bridge on her way to the harbor and the Baltimore Port Authority. Three million cubic feet of liquid propane spewed from its protective containers and reached the flaming cars above. The second explosion completely incinerated the ship and tugboats accompanying her to port. The mushroom cloud from the blast was so thick and black it could be seen 125 miles away in Richmond, Virginia.

Damage to the second bridge, known as the Twin Span, was so great that it, too, started to collapse. Hundreds of cars and thousands of people slid to their death in the flaming inferno of molten steel that was once the *Edinburgh*.

Leroy Michie was parked at Sandy Point State Park just below the western span, reporting back to Warren Dunn, when the heat from the blast overcame him. Both the noise of the blast and the ensuing silence pleased Dunn. Mission accomplished: no witnesses.

Camp David
US Army Communications Shack

It was a beautiful evening in the Catoctin Mountains, and the annual retreat that the President hosted for his Cabinet members and their families at Camp David was getting underway with the popular pig roast. Meanwhile the Chief Warrant Officer on duty was busy decoding a message that was coming off the wires. Once finished, he quickly placed the communiqué into an envelope marked "The President" and hurried to find COS Chiswell, who was attending the festivities in the picnic area, and handed him the envelope.

"Good evening, sir," he said.

"Good evening, Chief," said Chiswell, taking the envelope. "Thank you, that will be all for now."

"Yes, sir." The Warrant Officer promptly disappeared up the path, back to the Communications Shack.

Envelope in hand, Chiswell excused himself from the others, quipping that this must be a note from the VP Harry Dent's bridge club, excusing him for being late. He walked to the very edge of the picnic area and removed the message from its envelope. Stunned, he stared at the words for what felt like an eternity, then swiftly stuffed the message back into the envelope and hurried to find the President.

"Mr. President," said Chiswell, touching David Walsh lightly on the arm. "A moment, please?"

"Of course," said the President, noting the urgency in his Chief's voice. He excused himself and the two men walked to the edge of the picnic area closest to Aspen Lodge where the President's quarters were located.

"This just came in, Mr. President," Chiswell said, passing the message to his friend of many years.

"Oh my God, they blew the bridge. Those bastards blew the Chesapeake Bay Bridge!" Walsh crushed the note and threw it in the direction of his COS. "They think that because we cherish life we will be imprisoned by our fears, but they don't know us. They don't know us at all. As God is my witness I will destroy those bastards." The President moved toward the lodge so quickly that the secret service detail was momentarily caught off guard. As the men entered the lodge, the agent in charge immediately approached them.

"Mr. President, this message has just come in."

Walsh took the envelope from the agent standing before him. A wave of thanks came over him. The explosion, had just missed Marine Two. The Vice President is in the White House shelter, no wonder he's late.

Walsh then entered the communication shack to contact his dear friend.

"Mr. President, please follow me to the bunker," directed the secret service agent in charge of the President's detail. "Your chief of staff and the NSA director will accompany you."

"First I need to speak with the members of my cabinet."

"Mr. President, you need to come with us now."

"Let's go then," the President said. "But I want the Secretary of Defense there, too."

"Yes, Mr. President," replied the agent, leading the two men toward the presidential bunker buried beneath Camp David.

Reports detailing the carnage were coming in faster than the staff could decode them. The scene was an inferno. Thousands were presumed dead and many more would die before rescue workers and medics could penetrate even the outermost perimeters, due to the extreme heat and smoke from the blast. No one, especially a first responder from the emergency services, would hazard a guess as to when the site would be stable enough to send in help.

"Mr. President," Chiswell said as soon as they were secured several stories below ground. "I know that some measures to ensure Continuity of Government go into effect automatically, but I believe you need to order FEMA to implement the entire plan. I don't think you can wait on that. The people need to know that their government is secure and able to lead."

"You're right, Jim," replied the President. "Put me through to the director of FEMA. I also want to speak to the people as soon as possible. We have to avoid mass panic, and you know as well as I do that, the networks will saturate the airways with enough carnage to drive anyone to the brink."

The President turned to Jim Sercu, who had just arrived with Defense Secretary Bill Cassidy. "Has Ziegelhofer been able to give us any more news other than what he told me already?"

"Nothing yet," said Sercu. "I'll tell him to turn up the heat."

"Do that. We need to know people and places before the whole country goes up in smoke. I know it's Walter Dunn who is behind this, but I want more information."

"Right away, sir," said Sercu, as he reached for one of the secure phones that lined the bunker.

"Bill, what's your first move?" asked Walsh, looking to the Defense Secretary.

"Close the borders and clear the air," Cassidy said. "I also recommend that we move all military facilities to DEF-CON 2. They may have plans for other locations as well."

"Agreed," said the President, and he began issuing the orders that would not only seal the borders but place all major ports, airports and train terminals under the protection of the armed forces. The North American Aerospace Defense Command, often called NORAD, was ordered to implement the Security Control of Air Traffic and Navigation Aids plan. Known as SCATANA, it was developed in the 1960s to clear the skies following confirmed warnings of an attack from the Soviet Union. Today, it is a valuable tool in the war on terror.

The plan to ensure COG (continuity of government) was ordered in its entirety. Jim Chiswell informed the President that FEMA had already activated its contingency plans to move the Speaker of the House, the President Pro-Tem of the Senate, and other congressional leaders who remained in the area to the High Point Special Facility at Mt. Weather in Berryville, Virginia. Those who had already left for summer recess would be contacted by the White House Communication Corp and escorted to one of the 75 safe bunkers located throughout the country. The rest of the cabinet would be taken to the Communications Center at Raven Rock Mountain until the all clear could be sounded.

"Thank God our Ike had the foresight to build bunkers and devise plans that ensured continuation of government in a time of crisis," said the President. "For the last few terms, no matter who held the majority, it seems that we spend so much time fighting each other that we often lose sight of who the real enemies are. How can we be so damn stupid?" It was not a question, just frustration verbalized under intense pressure. The words hung in the air as if to chastise all those within earshot.

"Mr. President," Chiswell said, breaking the silence, "What's the status of the military?"

"We are going to DEF-CON 2. This will alert 'Looking Glass,' the military's fleet of airborne command posts, and put the National Airborne Operations Center on the ready. I have to get back to Washington, Jim. The people will feel better if their President is in the White House. You and I have the tools to lead from any one of many locations, including Air Force One, but the average person doesn't. People need reassurance right now. Besides, Harry must be going out of his mind and don't forget how weak his heart is. Just the other day Harry talked to me about retiring. I'd sure hate to have anything happen to him now."

"As soon as it's safe enough to move you, Mr. President," Sercu replied.

"I also think it's necessary for you to address the nation, sir," said Chiswell. "The people do need to hear from their President."

"I agree. Do we have any numbers yet?"

"Not yet, sir, the site is still too unstable. Rescue crews can't even cross the perimeter," said one of the support staff manning the phones.

"But the early reports say the bridge was packed with people, so I'd estimate the death toll is well into the thousands."

"Has anyone claimed responsibility?"

"No sir, Mr. President," Sercu told him. "Not yet."

NNC
Breaking News

"At approximately 6:25 this evening, a massive explosion beneath the Chesapeake Bay Bridge sent a portion of the huge structure plunging into the Bay. As yet, rescue crews have not been allowed into the area due to gases emitted during the blast and the intense heat from fires that continue to burn.

"There is suspicion of terrorism and that is being investigated, but so far no one has taken responsibility.

"We have confirmed, however, that Vice president Harry Dent was flying close by the bridge when it exploded but was not hurt. He is now at the White house waiting for President Walsh.

"Stay tuned to NNC as we report the details of this terrible tragedy. This is Lerrick McKenna at the site of what was the Chesapeake Bay Bridge."

Lerrick put her mike down on the hood of her news wagon, and the cameras went silent. She thought of Jeff and what went on the last couple of days and cold chill overcame her mind and body. She became teary wondering why she was the chosen one to have discovered this mess in the first place. She was scared and with reason. She knew it was a terrorist act but could not divulge that information until the President said so.

Raven Rock
Camp David

NSA Director Sercu retrieved the envelope from the officer standing at the entrance to the President's bunker, and quickly removed the message inside.

"Dismissed," he called over his shoulder as he entered the inner office. "Mr. President, this just came from Colonel Ziegelhofer."

"What's he got?"

"Well, as we suspected, Manson—the guy Ziggy snatched out of St.E's—worked for Dunn. Officially, he was the gardener, but he got his hands really dirty as Dunn's personal henchman. Manson worked directly under Dunn and didn't have much contact with others in the organization, a sort of a loner if you will. Anyway, he did make one acquaintance, a man named Lewis Michie, a caretaker at a cabin that Dunn owns on the Bay. It seems Michie has ties to a white supremacy group out of Wyoming that is openly anti-administration. We've been informed that other members of that group are also suspected of aiding terrorist cells in the west and are presently being watched by the FBI. Whenever these two would see each other, Michie would brag about how important he was and how much he knew, and sometimes he would back it up with facts. One time he told Manson he was taking care of two Muslims staying in Mr. Dunn's fishing cabin. Michie couldn't tell him what they were going to blow, but when it happened, Manson and the whole damn world would know."

"Did he say who else was involved?" asked the President. "I want to know who that Arab woman is."

"Manson said Warren Dunn and Archie Blake were also involved." Sercu added.

A knock at the door left the statement unfinished. When Chiswell opened it, Lieutenant Moses handed him a sealed message. The COS thanked him, and then handed the message to the President.

"Read this." The President handed the envelope back to Chiswell when he had finished reviewing it.

"Gentlemen," Walsh said somberly, walking to the sofa and motioning both men to sit. "Al-Qaeda has just claimed responsibility for the bombing of the Bay Bridge."

"Along with an American businessman and a United States senator," Sercu murmured with disgust.

"Bastards!" shouted the President. "Those sons-of-bitches should lose their heads."

"Mr. President," said Chiswell with palms up, "That might not be to our advantage right now. If we plug them into Echelon, we can not only give them enough rope to hang themselves, but we can listen to them doing it."

"Brilliant," exclaimed Sercu. "I just love the idea of those two SOB's conversing with Islamic terrorists while the leader of the free world listens."

"They're so damn arrogant," Walsh added. "They probably think we're too stupid to catch them, especially Blake. As a ranking member of the Armed Services Committee, he's very familiar with the capabilities of Echelon. He simply thinks he can fly under the radar because he believes I will never do anything to compromise the integrity of the U.S. Senate by spying on one of its members. But he's wrong. He's *dead wrong*."

"Get me back to Washington Jim," the President ordered, "and soon."

NNC
Breaking News

"This just in from the Maryland State Police. At approximately 8:14 p.m., a communique was received and was handed over to the Secret Service. Al-Qaeda has taken responsibility for the bridge destruction because we did not heed their warning about dropping all financial and diplomatic ties with Israel. The President has been advised and we were told from sources that he will talk to American citizens shortly.

"Rescue crews are on the apron of the bridge and facilities have been set up on either side to treat those injured by debris

from the blast. All area hospitals are on
emergency status and all employees are asked
to report to their units, as the number of
casualties is expected to rise. We will
remain on live to bring you more details as
they come to us.

"For NNC, this is Lerrick McKenna."

Once again Lerrick put down her mike and wondered how this was
going to work out. She knew so much more and believed at the right
time the President would not forget her.

Chapter 7

THE PRESIDENTIAL PALACE OF PRESIDENT IMAM AL FAREED TRIPOLI, LIBYA

Fareed addressed his friends: "It is a fine day, my brothers, when I am allowed by the Great Allah to entertain two such great leaders of our cause. Allah has truly blessed this day. Now, we must carry this quest forward in his name. Allah sent the Arab world a great gift when he blessed us with Saif al Adel as the new leader of al-Qaeda, and his representatives Halem and Farhad who continue the work of the late President Saddam Hussein. You and your countries have suffered the wrath of these dogs long enough. I feel my heart leaving my body for your people. You have lost hundreds of thousands to America's bombs and although they have been embraced by Allah and are now in heaven forever, Allah demands retribution. He will have it, and we must give it to Him."

Farhad Atwa responded, "Remember, these infidels are cunning. They have virtually cut the flow of money and have made it next to impossible to operate in a world market. They have destroyed my country and killed Saddam's sons. I will participate in any way that will bring total destruction to these dogs of the western world."

Halem Saran: "It's true, we have all suffered Imam. The American bombs killed your family and forced you to roam the countryside, taking shelter in a tent to avoid your own death. We rejoice that you are no longer content to sit by and watch the Jihad; you will now join with us in the annihilation of the Western world, starting with America. The will of Allah demands retribution. When the Americans dropped bombs on Iraq and Afghanistan, Allah spared me so I could one day seek revenge against the West in His name."

"We have now officially declared war on the Great Satan by destroying their bridge. I am sure this attack has killed more than those towers in New York."

NSA Headquarters
Washington, D.C.

The three men conferred, unaware that 100 miles above the earth their conversation was being recorded by a U.S. spy satellite from the National Reconnaissance Agency. Pictures were being taken, as well as recordings, all forwarded directly to NSA for analysis. The system, called ECHELON, is one of the NRA's most sensitive and ultra-secretive methods of surveillance. It links satellites to a series of high-speed parallel computers, enabling NRA and NSA to intercept and decode virtually every electronic communication in the world in real time. By recognizing key words, ECHELON can identify and segregate messages of national interest in any language, including dead languages such as Latin. The system is capable of listening to millions of conversations at once, and can determine with pinpoint accuracy exactly where any conversation is taking place. All of this information is funneled to waiting NSA agents in order of importance.

"Pay dirt!" exclaimed the NSA technician reading the Intel from the ECHELON satellite. His job was to search for Iman Al Fareed, the new leader of Libya, who had exited the world stage after the death of his family. His only sighting had been his assistance to Gaddafi during the bombing of Pan Am flight 103 over Lockerby, Scotland. This was presumably to avoid scrutiny from the Americans while amassing billions from Libyan oil. Recent chatter had suggested that Iman had returned to add his support and enormous wealth to the Islamic Jihad.

Seconds after finishing his transcriptions, the tech called his superior. "Sir, I believe I have received something of major importance from my satellite." After reviewing the message, the supervisor knew he was right. The recorded conversations and photos were of paramount importance to national security, and needed to be reviewed by the Director immediately. Within minutes, Director Sercu had the full report and was knocking on the door of the President's quarters in the bunker.

Further Translation of the conversation between Imam al Fareed, Farhad Atwa (representative of Saif al Adel of al-Qaeda) and Halem Salan (representative of the Republic of Iraq).

The Presidential Palace, Tripoli, Libya

Via ECHELON:

Al Fareed: "Farhad, allow me to praise you. Once again the Great Satan has suffered the wrath of Allah with the bombing of the great American bridge. We are all brothers joined in a common cause by our former great leader Osama bin Laden."

ATWA: "I accept your praise humbly and I in turn praise you for opening your heart, as well as your doors."

Imam: "You are too kind, Farhad. You have been my guest in my home these past two years, and the West is ignorant of that fact. They are still searching for you and your leader in Tora Bora. Little do they know of the plans we have in store for these infidels. Allah has been good to us all in spite of America's bombs. He has united us in friendship and brotherhood to further avenge his glory."

HALEM: "In the years since the Americans invaded our land, I have not been able to lead my nation. I have lost hundreds of thousands of my people. They have taken my oil and left me powerless. My family is dead, and now Saddam and his sons are dead as well. Saddam was a great leader. Their court and so-called justice stripped him of his dignity. He was treated not as an international prisoner of war but as a common criminal. By the will of Allah, I was able to escape. Only with your kindness, Iman, was I able to exist with some pride and dignity. I never had time for Allah. I thought he never answered my prayers, but I was wrong. It is now clear that he has plans for me, and I will follow him."

Al Fareed: "You are very angry, Halem, and you will remain angry for a long time. We are all very angry, but we must be careful that our anger does not cause us to make a mistake. We must funnel it to Allah's advantage. Allah demands that our mission be a success. I pray he regards Saddam and his sons as martyrs. Perhaps he too regards my beautiful family from my second wife Safi as martyrs. They were just babies, an innocent family, when the Hollywood President Reagan dropped his bombs on my home and killed them. He killed Muammar's little girl as well. We both suffered greatly. Osama was thrown out of Saudi because his beliefs were considered a threat to the Royal Family. The American dogs engineered that decision with the Saudi royals because of their thirst for the black gold. The Saudis abandoned their people to line the walls of their counting houses with US dollars and gold."

FARHAD: "Allah has his reasons for everything. I can see why He has brought us together. He has chosen the three of us as his leaders of Islam. We will avenge Allah. When our enemies in the West are destroyed, we will then deal with our Arab enemies. Our mission is to destroy all our adversaries."

Al Fareed: "Allow me to tell the two of you what I have done so far. I have remained very quiet these past years. I have let the Americans think they defeated me when they killed my family and bombed my country, but they did not. The Americans and English thought they contained me, so they did not worry about me. They should have, for I am their worst nightmare. My absence from the world stage allowed me to amass billions of dollars to use in financing our cause. Silence is golden. Besides, they were more interested in Muammar than in me."

"Members of the Russian underworld have been in touch with me. Their leader, Nikola Romanatuv, paid me a visit. He told me that he could make available the 22 bombs missing from the old Soviet arsenal. These are what they call suitcase bombs; they are 1 to 15 kiloton nuclear bombs. One kiloton is the equivalent of one thousand tons of TNT. They were smuggled into the United States and Great Britain during and after the Cold War. They have been placed in London and several other cities in England, as well as throughout the United States, in cities such as Washington D.C., Las Vegas, New York, the Hoover Dam and Niagara Falls."

"The Hoover Dam supplies the power to most of the west coast and the power project at Niagara Falls lights the northeast. The location of these bombs is known to only a few. I have now purchased these bombs, their locations, and the codes to detonate them."

HALEM: "How is it that these bombs were never detected?"

Al Fareed: "The bombs were originally sent to the United States and England during the early 1960's. I am told that when they arrived in the Baltimore harbor, a truck with diplomatic plates was waiting to deliver them to the Soviet Embassy. They were stored there until the KGB distributed them. The fact that they are small—about the size of a sea trunk—and encased in lead shields, made them very difficult to detect. Even if the FBI knew of the bombs, I'm sure they realized that locating them would require a search of every house and building in each of the suspected cities. That would create severe panic. After the Cold War, everyone became complacent and forgot about the bombs. Americans are such trusting fools. Some say there still is a bomb stored in the attic of the old Soviet Embassy, now the Russian embassy. That's how stupid these Americans are."

FARHAD: "Allah has truly blessed us. He has brought you back from the desert to join with us and allowed you to reap the riches of His earth so that you may finance our destiny. Praise is to Allah. Please, Iman, go on with your plan, and tell us more."

Al Fareed: "My plan is this. First we send the American President David Walsh a second letter detailing our demands as we did in the first one. We warn him that we are in control of those 22 bombs which we will detonate them at will if our demands are not met. If he does not believe us, we provide a demonstration. Finally, we will send a communiqué to NNC and all the other networks. If the news does not reach the American people, we will broadcast it ourselves through Al Jazeera."

HALEM: "The plan is brilliant and simple. I agree that we should concentrate on the United States first. We can eliminate the British at a later time. Through the American press, panic will permeate their country, and the western world. That alone will kill tens of thousands of people. It will also cause their economy to implode. It is Allah's wish to see all Americans die a terrible death."

Al Fareed: "There are certain Americans who believe in our cause. They had befriended Osama before me. One of them was jailed and is now free. I'm sure he had a light sentence because the President did not want to be embarrassed. This man contributed heavily to the President's campaigns. The other man I befriended was a United States Senator. These two men are ready to betray their country for money and power. They are the worst of the worst of American dogs. We will use them, and then destroy them with the rest of the curs on that continent. They will never see a drop of oil. We will make them all vanish."

End Translation

These three leaders—men who once hated one another—plotted to show the world that for the common cause they were united and were, indeed, brothers. They talked on, unaware that in minutes their conversation would be reviewed by the most powerful man in the world.

Reflections & Tough Decisions

The President read the new report and wished for the umpteenth time that he was just a citizen, operating his ranch with his wife Sarah by his side. He regretted going into politics. The decisions that he had made during his presidency were far too weighty for one man to bear. And now, even before he had a chance to address the American people after a terrorist attack that caused the death of thousands of American citizens, there was more disastrous news with even greater consequences.

"Get Seifert, Chiswell and Cassidy in here," ordered the President to the military attaché standing at attention outside the office door.

"Yes, sir."

David Walsh turned and closed the door behind him. Can't lose your cool now, he thought to himself, there are too many people who need you, just too many people…

His thoughts were interrupted by the arrival of the Chairman of the Joint Chiefs, his own Chief of Staff, and the Secretary of Defense. They settled in as secure conference lines to the Cabinet members were activated. "Approximately half an hour ago we received information linking three terrorist organizations to the Russian mob," the President said.

"The Russian *mob!*" Chiswell blurted. "How did they get involved in this?"

"During the Cold War era," NSA Director Sercu began as he took the floor, "the Russians planted nuclear suitcase bombs in this country and around the world. This all came to light during the Reykjavik, Iceland, summit meetings when President Ronald Reagan and Russian Premier Mikhail Gorbachev agreed to a treaty which called for the depletion of the nuclear inventories of both countries. Much to Gorbachev's embarrassment, he was forced to notify President Reagan that 22 suitcase bombs were missing from the Russian inventory. We don't know where these bombs are, but there are rumors that there's one in the old Soviet Embassy on 14th Street in D.C. Anyway, following the fall of Communism, the Russian government was in turmoil. Many officials turned to corruption as a means of survival. We've heard that during this time the Russian mob came into possession of these bombs, paying hundreds of millions of dollars, if not billions, for their locations and activation codes. That information was never verified, and the Russians became our allies, more or less. Tonight, we've learned that not only did the Russian mob get those bombs, but they've sold their locations and codes to Hamas, Hezbollah and al-Qaeda so they can pursue their Jihad against the west."

"What's our first move?" asked Chiswell.

"Mr. President," Secretary Cassidy interjected. "I must advise you to board Air Force One; it is the one place you'll be safe."

"No, Bill," said the President. "I'm not going up top. I need to return to Washington and address the people from the Oval Office. I don't want them to think I've left them, and if they see me hunkered down in a bunker or cruising above the turmoil, that's exactly what they'll think. After the speech, we can move to the Emergency Operations Center below the East Wing of the White House."

After the last attack on U.S. territory, the President created a line of succession within key agencies of his Cabinet. The automatic transfer of power would be done without fanfare and ensured the continuation of government in the case of the death or incapacitation of a ranking Cabinet member. President Walsh remembered how difficult it had been to get the legislation through. It was peace time, and most congressmen thought there were more important pieces of legislation to deal with. In the end, though, the President had persevered. He now wished he had included the Vice Presidency in the bill. He would have to appoint a successor if Harry were to resign. Just more to think about.

"Mr. President." The sound of Chiswell's voice startled him. "It has been over four hours since the bridge blew, and the early numbers are staggering. Casualties are in the thousands. News networks are sensationalizing and creating panic. Roads everywhere are full of frustrated drivers escaping from the East Coast cities."

"Well, then, gentlemen," said David Walsh quietly, "it's time for me to go home. Jim, I need a moment with you."

"Of course sir," Chiswell said.

"I want you to make the necessary arrangements to ensure the safety of the families of staff members, Congressmen and the Cabinet. The Greenbrier in West Virginia can accommodate a large number. Who knows, we may all end up there."

Powell hesitated before responding, "Mr. President, I'm not sure that we can do this without the public finding out. I was under the assumption that, to avoid panic, we were going to maintain as much normalcy as possible. Then, if necessary, we would try to move them out later."

"No," said Walsh. "I've changed my mind, and I want the Greenbrier to be an option. You and I know it's too far away for our use, but it's perfect for our families." Noticing that his Chief of Staff was somewhat perplexed, Walsh continued, "The men and women who serve this country will be asked to make decisions that could impact all mankind for decades to come. They will be separated from the comfort of their loved ones, confined to spaces either underground or in a mountainside for an indeterminate amount of time, and forced to take actions that could cause the deaths of Americans and Islamic people alike. Remember that Americans are, for the most part, people of inclusion. Put simply, we believe that all men are created equal. Unfortunately, not all nations or religions agree with that creed, so when those influences combine with the shrinking resources of our planet, conditions exist which allow for the perfect storm. I'm afraid we are sailing directly into it, full throttle. So, if I can lighten the load of the members of my Cabinet and the congressional leaders by ensuring the safety of their families, I'll do it. It's going to be difficult to do without the general public finding out, and I am aware of the consequences of public panic. The damn press is doing a good job on that. The chaos will be as deadly as any explosion, but I will not waver on this. It's an order."

"Yes, sir," said Chiswell as he turned toward the door. "And, sir, thank you, from all of us." His words were silenced by the President's raised hand.

––––––––––

The President, his Chief of Staff, the Secretary of Defense, and the NSA Director walked swiftly to the waiting presidential limousine. The Secret Service insisted on returning to Washington by motorcade because the bomb-proof limo made the journey safer. It was an impressive sight that sped down Park Central Road to Route 77. Overhead, there were six Sikorsky UH-6 Blackhawk Gunships, fully manned with Delta Force Special Ops Personnel on board. They were flying as low as fifty feet above the front and rear of the entourage. The three identical limousines were all displaying presidential and U.S. flags on their fenders. Between each limo there was an armored Chevrolet Suburban, each carrying Secret Service agents fully armed with nine-millimeter Uzis. Following them were two fully equipped ambulances with two doctors and two nurses who specialized in trauma. Tucked in the tail of the motorcade was a specially built Ford van called the HAMMER—Hazardous Agent Mitigation Medical Emergency Response—which was the President's personal anti-biological warfare attack vehicle. A warning system was connected to a small biological sniffing device that constantly analyzes the outside air. If there was an attack on the motorcade and the President or his staffs were in danger of contamination with biological agents, an alarm would sound and the President would be immediately brought to this vehicle. Secret Service agents assigned to HAMMER were always prepared, wearing specialized breathing masks and suits that were ecologically safe from 95% of the known bio-weapons available to the world via the black market.

When the motorcade arrived, 1600 Pennsylvania Avenue was at Def-Con 2. The White House was completely surrounded by regular army personnel, each one carrying a M-16 automatic rifle. The silos on the White House roof and lawn were wide open and at the ready. Each silo contained one SAM-D Patriot Missile, a long range, high altitude surface-to-air missile guided by a multifunction radar system. Each was capable of separating moving targets from background clutter, identifying incoming collateral at low altitudes, and providing a swift response to any attack on the President's House.

The President and his staff got out of their cars and made their way into the White House with the Secret Service in a tight circle surrounding David Walsh.

The President was very anxious to talk with his Vice President, and to relieve him. He was worried what this kind of stress could do to his weakened heart.

Below the West Wing of the White House there's a 10,000 square foot room reserved solely for the use of the President and his closest advisers. Unlike the Situation Room or the other two bunkers hidden in the gut of the White House, the Command Center is a state-of-the-art facility featuring the most advanced technology. Built by systems engineers and naval architects who specialize in the design of nuclear submarines, not one square inch of space is wasted. The walls are crammed with the latest technological equipment, allowing the President to receive information within seconds from all corners of the earth.

The walls are of reinforced steel, three feet thick, that virtually seal the inhabitants off from radiation and chemical or biological weapons of mass destruction. The living quarters are comfortable but Spartan, with enough food and water to last six months. The air is recycled, waste is emptied directly into a sealed septic system and heating and air conditioning systems are entirely self-contained. The Center is even equipped with a fully-staffed four-bed hospital capable of performing surgical procedures. It also houses a crematorium. Ancillary staffs of thirty people, ranging from cooks to generals, accompany the President to the Center so he can run the government from within its walls.

The war room contains a large oval oak table and comfortable leather chairs, as well as the most sophisticated communications system in the world. All data that filters through Fort Dietrich, Fort Meade, and the FBI, the CIA and the Defense Department, plus many other American security agencies including the Department of Homeland Security, is routed to this command post. Five movie screens show every view of the globe from a hundred miles above. The imagery from the MH-11 satellites is so precise that even on a cloudy day you can see a license plate on a car in Haiti, or watch a black widow spider eat her mate in the desert sands of the Sierra. The President has the technology to talk with a soldier in the field or the Commander of a nuclear sub any time he chooses. Translations of foreign languages are instant, and just hooking up to ECHELON allows him to monitor conversations in any part of the world.

———————

The elevator dropped gently to what was the equivalent of five stories below ground. When the massive door opened, two armed Marine guards snapped to attention and saluted their Commander in Chief. Walsh returned the salute before stepping up to the camera at the Center's entrance; a specially designed system that identifies people by reading their eyes, then permanently recording the identity of all who enter.

Soon after arriving, the President received a memo from the Surgeon General detailing the protocols that would be implemented by all health departments and clinics in any location that could be considered a terrorist target. All institutions would be open 24/7 to distribute potassium iodide to anyone who walks through the door. PI can prevent radiation poisoning within a ten-mile radius of ground zero if taken 24 hours before a strike. There was enough PI in stock for the general population to receive the medication for 30 days; after that, the supply would have to be reserved for the military. The President almost laughed out loud, saying to himself "thousands of lives can be saved, but only if our enemies comply and detonate their bombs within thirty days."

Jim Chiswell knocked on the door to the President's quarters and announced that it was time to go upstairs to the Oval Office. Within minutes of the President's arrival, his longtime friend and reigning Press Secretary Asa Ransom entered the room.

"Mr. President, we'll be ready in about 20 minutes. I've notified all the networks that there should be no interruptions and no questions. Your secretary is waiting outside, and we're good to go. And, sir, we're all behind you, wherever this leads."

"I know," said the President, feeling the weight of his friend's words. "I know."

Live from the Oval Office

"My fellow Americans, I come to you in this late hour with a heavy heart. At approximately 6:15 this evening, the Chesapeake Bay Bridge was destroyed by an act of terrorism. Although we are still assessing the damage we know that thousands have perished. I mourn those whose lives were lost, pray for those who grieve, and vow that those responsible for this massacre will be held accountable for their deeds. History has taught us that conflict with an unconventional enemy is complicated and challenging. History has taught the world that

we are equal to the task.

"Because the perpetrator is not a nation but a band of cowards who hide in the shadows of the desert sun, their crimes must not be misinterpreted. They have committed acts of war against the United States of America, and for that they must suffer her wrath. To that end, I will be asking Congress for a formal declaration of war against the terrorist groups Hamas, Hezbollah, and al-Qaeda and any others who test our freedom, our liberty and our resolve.

"In times of crisis, Americans have been called upon to make sacrifices, and during the days and weeks that lie ahead, you will be asked to do so once again. I know that some of you will question the necessity of these sacrifices, but let me assure you that they were dictated by the nature of the enemy and the enormity of the crimes.

"Certain measures have already been put into place. All airports are closed to commercial and private flights, leaving the skies open to military aircraft only. All borders are sealed. U.S. Embassy personnel posted in all nations have been put on alert and, if necessary, will be evacuated. All ships, with the exception of military vessels, will remain in port or be turned back out to sea.

"Tonight I am asking for the help of each and every American. Never before in the history of this country has personal responsibility been so crucial to the preservation of our freedoms. If we are to protect our shores, our families, and our futures, we must come together, without prejudice or malice, as one nation under God. Thank you, and God bless this blessed country and her people. Good evening."

Lerrick McKenna was among the many journalists assembled in the Oval. The President wanted to make sure she was rewarded by a special invitation and made it possible. He personally invited her and Jeff to witness history in the making.

NNC Breaking News

"This is Lerrick McKenna reporting from the south apron of the Chesapeake Bay Bridge. It has been several hours since the massive explosion destroyed the bridge's main structure and sent the LNG *Edinburgh* into its fiery waters along with four escort tug boats and crews. At the time of the explosion they had been nosing through the waters under the bridge and were impacted by the blast, and sinking before they could reach Baltimore Harbor. The Twin Span sustained unrepairable damage, and many of those who were crossing at the time of the blast were thrown into the inferno below.

"Makeshift medical facilities have been set up on either side of the bridge to treat the walking wounded and evacuate those with more serious injuries to area hospitals. Authorities thus far will not speculate as to when first responders will be allowed on the scene due to the instability of the area. So, we wait and we pray.

"The surreal atmosphere that pervades the scene is amplified by the darkness that has descended over the bridge and the fires that continue to burn on the water. Somewhere in the corners of our minds and our hearts, we believe that the dawn will see travelers crossing the bridge and the *Edinburgh* docked in the harbor unloading its cargo. But we will awaken to reality. Dawn will only bring us more images of devastation and more victims of the war on terror.

"This is Lerrick McKenna for NNC."

The Oval Office

Immediately after the President's speech, the White House was a flurry of activity. Cameras and crews rushed to make their deadlines; the press secretary reviewed the talking points with members of the press. David Walsh had just fixed himself a drink and was about to sit down when Jim Sercu came into the room and approached him. "Mr. President, with all due respect, sir, I was caught off guard by your decision to ask Congress for a declaration of war against the terrorist organizations. It was my understanding that a Congressional declaration of war can be issued only against a nation or state that harbors terrorists, not against organizations that may have several different locations. Have you conferred with Secretary of State Howe and Secretary of Defense Cassidy, or was this a personal decision?"

"I did what needed to be done," the President replied sharply. "We are in a situation where every minute, no, every second counts. We can't afford politics as usual. Sit down, Jim." The President motioned for the NSA Director to join him in the sitting area of the Oval Office. "It's something that I've been contemplating, and I feel it is the right thing to do. This is warfare unlike any that we have ever known. This enemy is stealth. It is not distinguished by a uniform or language; instead, it moves about freely, many of its soldiers calling America home and enjoying the privileges of our citizenship. One is even a member of our Senate, if you recall. Our radar cannot warn us of an impending attack so that we may shelter our families and ourselves. The tools of our destruction are already in place, just waiting to be detonated. Just because this enemy does not have a geographical boundary does not make it any less a nation, for by definition a nation is "an aggregation of persons of the same ethnic family, often speaking the same or cognate language." The President continued, "This enemy is the most dangerous we have ever encountered. It is evil, elusive, and it could look just like you or me. If we are going to prevail, every weapon that we have in our arsenal, both strategic and military, must be available at a moment's notice. That is only possible with an official declaration of war."

"Mr. President," said Sercu, "I apologize. We're damn lucky to have a Commander-in-chief like you."

"Balls!" said the President, and both men laughed for the first time in what seemed like eternity. "Get some rest, Jim. I'll see you in the morning."

"Thank you, Mr. President; I'll be here bright and early."

Chapter 8

THE WEST GATE
THE WHITE HOUSE

"Good evening, ma'am, or should I say good morning," said the soldier stationed at the West Gate Guard shack as the young woman approached. "You shouldn't be out in the city this late at night; it's not safe."

"I will be fine, but thank you for your concern," said the lovely young woman with long black hair and large brown eyes. She was dressed in nursing scrubs. "I've only come to deliver this tape to the President. It's from a doctor who vacationed with the first family last summer. I work nights and offered to deliver it on my way home. Please see that the President receives it."

"Certainly ma'am, but I urge you to go directly home," said the uniformed SS guard. "I wouldn't want to see anything happen to you. My sister's a nurse; you do great work."

"Thank you, I assure you I love my work," she said as she turned and disappeared into the black morning.

———

The manila envelope containing the tape was delivered to the Secret Service office for clearance at 3:30 AM on Saturday morning. The identity of the woman was still unknown, but with the pictures taken by the security cameras, Interpol was soon able to identify her as an Islamic radical with ties to al-Qaeda. After the envelope was ascertained to have no explosive capabilities, it was sent directly to Tom Holloway for translation. As soon as the translation was complete, Holloway was on the phone to his Director, James Sercu.

"What is it?" Sercu demanded, reaching for his glasses on the nightstand.

"A package was delivered to the West Gate at approximately 0330 this morning. It contains a letter and tape addressed to the President from the leaders of Hamas, Hezbollah, and al-Qaeda. Sir, you need to see this ASAP."

"I'm on my way. Have the full translation delivered to my office. I'll take it personally to the President."

"Yes, sir,'" said Holloway as he prepared the most infamous document in the history of this nation.

Translation
File # 89389 4979-2-626-9235
6th Jumad AI Awal, 1425 Year of the Hegira

To the President of the American Republic: Greetings. May this message convince you that the Jihad against your country and others is going to go forth. I hope this message reaches you in time, for only you can prevent the total destruction of your country. Either you submit to our demands, or you will be destroyed. There will be no negotiating.

The brothers of my faith, with the full will of Allah, demand for the third time the complete divorce of all diplomatic, economic, and military ties with Israel. You as well as the Jews are our sworn enemy. We will destroy you as sure as you have tried to destroy us, but we will succeed. There will be no more demands, just total annihilation.

We write you as men of compassion. It is now time that all of the Western world pay for exploiting the Islamic world. Our people have suffered, and our eternal desire is justice. The imperialistic western powers have seen to it that the oil-rich Arab lands have been taken over by degenerate infidels, only to quench the great thirst of their nations. Soon this will stop. The day of contaminating our brothers with wine and whores and igniting them with your greed has ended. Soon Israel will no longer exist, and our lands will return to us.

Your country and Great Britain, Mr. President, started this. Your President Roosevelt divided the Middle East and took its oil. Your President Truman soothed his guilt by becoming the first head of state to recognize Israel. From that day forward, Mr. President, we have suffered. Allah holds your country and England responsible for these terrible crimes. You and administrations before you have forced us to accept Western policy. No more. What is good for America is not good for us. Allah demands that we live according to His will and that His blessed children carry His word throughout the world. Because of this, we must remain pure and uncontaminated by your motives.

You say that you wish peace in the Middle East, and I beg Allah's favor upon you for that, but that is not enough. My brothers and I are also men of peace, but we all know that without justice, there can be no peace, and there can be no justice as long as America and Israel exist.

I pray Allah will deliver this communiqué to you in good sense so that you may not make the mistake of retaliating against any of our Arab brethren. I pray that Allah sees fit to return to us our sacred lands from the hands of the Jews. May Allah grant you much wisdom and compassion at this most difficult time in history.

IMAN AL FAREED
PRESIDENT, THE LIBYAN ARAB JAMAHIRIYA

HALEM SALAN
THE REPUBLIC OF IRAQ, THE IRAQI ARAB JAMAHIRIYA

FARHAD ATWA
REPRESENTING SAIF AL ADEL, LEADER, AL-QAEDA

End Translation

For the second time in a week, Jim Sercu dialed the inside line to the President's private quarters. "Jeannie," he said as the familiar voice came on the line, "it's Director Sercu. I need to speak with the President. It's urgent."

"Yes, sir; I'm going to place you on hold for a moment while I see if he's available."

"Of course," Sercu responded, trying to avoid irritation at the patented reply.

"Director Sercu," Jeannie said, returning promptly. "I'll put you right through."

"Jim, what is it?" the President asked as he picked up the phone.

"It's here," said Sercu simply.

"What's here?"

"The letter with the terrorist's demands was delivered to the West Gate at approximately 0330 this morning by a woman matching the description of the one Tuttle said he had met with Dunn and Blake at Lewisburg. I'm on my way in, and the letter is being delivered to my office as we speak."

"Okay, Jim, meet me in the Oval."

"Jeannie," the President said, picking up his private line again. "Get me General Seiffert, and Secretary Cassidy. Have them meet me here in the Oval Office immediately."

"Yes sir, right away."

Saturday
0600 Hours

"What kind of mumbo–jumbo crap is that egotistical son-of-a-bitch talking about? Everything's negotiable!" Chief of Staff Chiswell exclaimed.

"Apparently not," said Defense Secretary Cassidy.

"He's talking about taking us down," said General Seiffert, "and I believe he can do it."

"I do too, General," the President said. "Jim," he continued, turning to Chiswell, "I need to address a joint session of Congress tomorrow evening to formally ask for a declaration of war. Draw up the request and send it to the Speaker of the House ASAP. We need this to be a show of solidarity. Be sure all branches of government are represented under Presidential order. I want to show those bastards what we're made of; I want to show them we will not be intimidated. After the address, we will move everyone back to safety."

He quickly gave instructions to those in the room. First, turning to his NSA Director: "See what Colonel Ziegelhofer can find out from Tuttle about the woman who dropped off that tape." Then to the Commander of the Joint Chief: "General, get me any intelligence pertaining to the sale of those suitcase bombs. We need to know how much time we have. If any." He then proceeded to dismiss all except Jim Chiswell: "We'll meet back here in the Emergency Command Center at 1600, except you, Jim, I need you to come right back with a speech writer so we can get to work. It needs to be understood that absolutely no advance copies will leave this office."

"Yes, sir, I'll get right on it" answered Jim as he hurried out the door. The others began to follow him when the President said, "Bill, stay behind a moment. I need to ask you something."

When the room cleared, the President turned to his longtime friend and trusted colleague. "Bill, Harry Dent is facing some very serious surgery. He needs a heart transplant and will not be able to complete his tenure. I want you to be my Vice President. This country is facing the perfect storm, and if anything should happen to me, the next President must possess not only political savvy and military experience, but a strong will and a level head if he's going to steer her through it. What do you think?"

"I'm honored, Mr. President. Of course I will serve you and my country in any way I can."

"Good," said the President. "I'll have Chiswell start the confirmation proceedings as soon as Harry serves me with his letter of resignation. He will also make arrangements to get you to Mount Weather. As you know, the Vice Presidential designee and the President must be separated as outlined in the COG."

"Yes sir, I'm aware of that. Until the arrangements are made, I will be in my bunker office."

"Good."

———————

Alone in the massive office, David Walsh pondered what had gone wrong. Only weeks into his Presidency he had guided his country through a major threat to her survival. He thought he had cut off the head of the serpent by destroying everything but the oil fields in Iraq; however, he had underestimated his enemies' ability to survive and strike back. Now they were back and deadlier than ever. *No more* he vowed to himself. *No more.*

As President he has at his discretion the entire might of the United States military. Tomorrow night he would go before Congress and ask for what no President has ever asked: declarations of war against an enemy who lives everywhere and can look like anyone. And, the President thought to himself "I will get it."

The sound of Chiswell's voice broke the silence. "Mr. President, everything that you asked has either been done or will be completed in the next few hours. The Greenbrier has been alerted, and the evacuation has already begun. Transportation arrangements have been made for the members of Congress, the Supreme Court Justices, and the Joint Chiefs. The Central Locator System found all involved. I enlisted the use of special aircraft that will be waiting on the Capital grounds to move everyone safely out of town as soon as your speech is finished."

"Thank you, Jim, but here are a couple more things," said Walsh. "I want to meet with all of the congressional leaders as soon as the session ends. I need to explain the pending threat in more detail than I feel is prudent to divulge to the American people at this time."

"And Jim," he added, "I want Sarah to be in the Gallery. She is so full of great wisdom and as you know has been my anchor. I would like the British and Israeli ambassadors to sit on either side of her as well as two other special guests."

"Who might they be Mr. President?"

"The two young people who brought this to my attention, Lerrick McKenna and Jeff Roberts. They deserve to be honored."

"They do indeed sir."

Jim Chiswell prepared to leave to make the arrangements as the President concluded, "Now, before we get the speech writer in here, I need to speak with both the British and Israeli Prime Ministers. When I finish talking with them, get me the Russian President."

The White House Communication Corps initiated the protocols that allowed heads of state to confer with each other on short notice. The

Hot Line, as it became known, was installed by Ike's administration during the Cold War. Today, it is an invaluable tool in diplomatic relations worldwide.

The principle was basic: Heads of state could talk on secure links, together with translators who were familiar with the dialect of the region where the participant lived. This was to ensure that both parties had a clear understanding of what was being said. Today, with all of our modern technology incorporated into the system, heads of state can sit at their desks and look their peers straight in the eye.

"Mr. President." A marine's voice shattered the silence. "We are ready, sir. The lines are open to London and Tel Aviv."

"Thank you, Major," replied the President. "Where do you want me?"

"Right at your desk, sir," said the young major. "Your Yiddish translator will be positioned just to your left, in case Prime Minister Mordachi chooses not to speak in English."

"Okay," said the President as the final preparations were made. "Let's do it."

Within moments, the images of England's Prime Minister John Lawton and the Israeli Prime Minister Eli Mordachi were flashing on the monitors set up in the Communications Office.

The President spoke first. "John, Eli, good day to you both. I hope that all has been well."

"Thank you, David," replied John Lawton, the President's close friend and staunch political ally. "We had a lovely holiday in the country. It was certainly refreshing to escape the London heat in August, if only for a fortnight."

The pleasantries ended abruptly as the abrasive Mordechai interrupted. "David, did you call me to discuss the weather or is there something that you wish to tell us?"

"Eli, I haven't paid any attention to the weather since I took office," Walsh retorted. "I am calling to tell you about a letter that was delivered to the White House from Iman al Fareed, Halem Salan, and Farhad Atwa. Once again they are demanding that we sever all diplomatic, economic and military ties with Israel or the Jihad against our countries will go forth. They say they will not negotiate nor warn us again, and the attack on the Chesapeake Bay Bridge was just a small sample of what they are capable of."

"Nonsense, everything's negotiable. Besides, this is old news" interrupted the ornery old man. "I know that your CIA cannot compare with my Mossad, but really, David..."

"Eli," said the President sharply, beginning to lose his patience, "we have also learned from a satellite recording of a conversation between al Fareed and his merry band that they have come into possession of a number of nuclear suitcase bombs, 22 in fact, that were hidden throughout this country and Great Britain during the Cold War and we have to believe that there are a few planted in your country as well. When the Cold War ended and Russia and the U.S. began holding hands, Gorbachev reported them missing but nothing was ever done about it."

"How did the terrorists get the bombs?" asked Prime Minister Lawton.

"The Russian Mob," said the President.

"Of course," growled Mordachi, "those bastards are so crooked they would sell the souls of their Mother for pound sterling or American gold."

"Well, gentlemen, that's the story. I will keep you both in the loop on a daily basis and share all Intel; and you can stay abreast of what is happening first hand. I will contact you both after I address Congress and the nation tomorrow evening. I am asking for an official declaration of war on all terrorist organizations."

Both men agreed and offered condolences on the victims of the Bay Bridge. They offered a pledge of support, and then the conversation changed to how Vice President Harry Dent was holding up. "Not well" said the President, "He is hanging in there but just barely. As you know, he is a candidate for a heart transplant and will officially resign after my speech to the Congress tomorrow. For your information I will be appointing Secretary of defense Bill Cassidy to that post. I'm sure he will do nicely all the way around." At that point they each pledged support to one another and the conversation terminated.

"What was your take on all that?" the President asked the young soldier who had been analyzing the voice and body language of both prime ministers during the conversation.

"Mr. President, I need to take it back to the Communication Shack for further inspection, but if you're asking me for a first read I'd say that this was not a surprise to Prime Minister Mordachi."

"I agree."

"Sir," the major continued, "we are moments away from a connect with the new Prime Minister of Russia, Vassily Gorginakov. Your translator will once again be to your left."

"Thank you Major."

Within seconds, the image of the Russian Prime Minister was on the screen.

"President Walsh, let me say how sorry I was to hear of the tragedy that has befallen your country. What is it I can do for you?"

"I am calling to ask for your cooperation concerning a matter that involves the Russian underworld. We have learned from our intelligence that your Mafia has sold the location and codes of over 20 nuclear devices found to be missing during the Gorbachev era to Muammar Al Qaddafi and his henchman Iman al Fareed. Al Fareed's intent is to use them against the United States and Great Britain to further the Islamic Jihad. I need to find out the name of the person or persons responsible for the sale and when the transfer took place."

"David, I cannot help you. My government is a fledging one and my position is tentative at best. I'm sorry for your dilemma, but I cannot help you."

"You can, and you will, for not only is your government weak, it is a house of cards," said President Walsh. "Your position is tentative because your military is undermanned and inexperienced, with no leaders who know what they're doing. If you do not do everything in your power to rectify a problem that was born from the ignorance of your predecessors, I will go to the United Nations and ask for sanctions that you do not want and your country cannot bear. Mr. Prime Minister, I want those names within 48 hours."

"I'll do my best," said the prime minister abruptly, "but what good will it do? It sure wouldn't cure your dilemma, would it?" And the screen went blank.

Later that day, the President was advised that he had asked the

Russian leader for a promise he could not fulfill, even if he wanted to, without forfeiting his life. The mob runs mother Russia, and they would never allow that information to become public. It was only a shot in the dark. Vengeance was not his this day.

Chapter 9

EMERGENCY COMMAND CENTER
SATURDAY 1600 GMT

"Gentlemen," said the President, addressing his chief advisers. "I'll make this brief as we all have work to do. Today I asked Secretary of Defense William Cassidy to be my Vice President. I believe that his military expertise and political savvy will allow for a smooth transition if anything should happen to me. I hope, if that should happen, that you will give him the same support that you have given me."

"Jim," as he turned to Chiswell, "I need you to expedite the confirmation hearings. This is no time for our country to be without a Vice President."

"Yes, sir." Chiswell realized that for the first time in history, a presidential appointment would have to be confirmed via teleconference. "I'll get right to it."

"Good choice, Mr. President. You have my full support, and I can also speak for the entire Chiefs of Staff," General Seiffert said.

"For what it's worth, Mr. President," Director Sercu added, "I'm in complete compliance. If I can be of any assistance just let me know what I can do."

"Thanks to all of you," said the President. "Now let's get down to the business at hand. General, what have your sources been able to find out about the sale of those suitcase bombs? I think it necessary to know everything we can about what we're facing and what we can do about it."

"We're working on it, Mr. President, but they haven't come up with anything concrete yet," the Chief replied.

"What is strange to me is the attempt to hit us twice. First the bridge, now this threat," Seiffert said. "Chief, if there are other bombs placed around the country, as they say, then this is just the beginning."

"General," said the President sternly, "today I had a teleconference with Prime Ministers Lawton and Mordachi. Afterwards, the consensus was that the Israeli Prime Minister was aware of our predicament.

Perhaps it's time to enlist the help of the Mossad. The Israelis certainly have a stake in this, and I'm not sure how effective our CIA can be when the clock is running. There seems to be too much turmoil within their ranks."

"What did Ziegelhofer find out from Tuttle?" He asked Jim Sercu.

"Nothing that we didn't already know. Tuttle only saw the woman on one occasion, and she was introduced to him as a representative of Saif al Adel. Shortly after that meeting, Tuttle decided he wanted out and ended up at St. Elizabeth's."

"Very well," said Walsh. "Keep working on it. If anything breaks, report back here ASAP. Otherwise I'll see all of you tomorrow night."

Chapter 10

The United States Secret Service had ordered a complete shutdown of all commercial businesses within a two-mile perimeter of the Capitol to ensure the President's safety. All streets were blocked off; even the manhole covers along the parade route were sealed. Only the hospitals and news bureaus were allowed to operate normally. It was the tightest security in history, with signs warning "Authorized to Use Deadly Weapons" posted around the Capitol Building and down Pennsylvania Avenue.

With D.C.'s finest leading the way, the President's limousine streaked past the soldiers lining the streets and pulled up to the Capitol steps. As the President emerged, he was immediately surrounded by Secret Service agents who quickly escorted him through a side entrance to the right of the steps.

From there, an elevator took him directly up to the first floor VIP Suite. Several of the nation's leaders already lined the hallway, anxious to greet the President, but David Walsh strode right past them. The niceties would have to wait for later.

Just outside the waiting room, the President noticed Senator Archibald Blake approaching with his hand outstretched. "Not now, Senator," said Chiswell forcefully as he blocked the man's path.

"You better get the hell out of my way boy," snarled Blake. "You're talking to a United States Senator."

The President overheard their exchange and directed his Chief of Staff to escort the senator into the waiting room. Blake, fully expecting an apology, glared at Chiswell with contempt. Knowing that he was about to get the last laugh, Chiswell smiled to himself as he led the way to the private anteroom at the end of the hall.

"Jim, it is important that you witness this," said the President as soon as the door had closed behind them. Turning to the senator, a man he had come to detest, Walsh began, "Archibald Blake you are a traitor. I know what you've done, and it's unforgivable. I plan to announce your treasonous acts to the Country and Congress in about twenty minutes unless you resign right now."

Blake stared at the President in disbelief. "How dare you accuse me of that? I'm not some off the wall fool, you know. I'm a United States Senator!"

"Wrong on both counts, Archie," shouted the President as he shoved the resignation letter towards the defiant Blake. "You are a fool for thinking that you could deceive your country and get away with it; and no, you are not a Senator, not any more. It's all in this letter, in case you need to have your memory refreshed." Blake tried to speak, but the President was on a roll. "In about 20 minutes, I plan to advise the Joint Session of Congress of your part in this conspiracy unless you sign this letter of resignation immediately."

Blake reached for the pen and signed the letter in silence. As he handed it back to the President, there was a knock at the door. Colonel Ziegelhofer entered at the President's command.

"Colonel," ordered the President, "place this son of a bitch under arrest and get him out of my sight."

"Yes, sir," responded the Colonel, grabbing Blake's arm.

"On what charges?" protested Blake as he tried to pull away from the Colonel's grasp, "I don't see an indictment??"

"I must have forgotten to mention that," said the President. "You are under arrest as an enemy combatant. Simply stated, it means that you have committed an act of treason against the United States of America. Now leave quietly so you won't become more of an embarrassment to your family and your country than you already are. Colonel, get him out of here."

The colonel decided to escort the former Senator out the side entrance of the Capitol Building to avoid drawing the attention of the media. As they were approaching the car, a desperate Blake suddenly bolted away from the colonel and sprinted out of the parking lot. Stunned, Ziegelhofer screamed for the man to halt, but Blake kept running. A soldier standing guard at the perimeter of the lot ordered him to halt. The order was ignored, and once again the soldier ordered him to stop. When Blake again ignored the command, the soldier raised his rifle, took aim, and fired a single shot that entered the back of Blake's head and exited the front in an explosion of skull and brain matter. The two men arrived at the crumpled body of Archibald Blake and immediately Ziegelhofer ordered the body taken to Walter Reed Army Hospital with strict instructions not to release any information unless it had been cleared through his office. The next call he made was to the President. He dialed the number to Chiswell's cell to inform him of the most recent events.

"Chiswell," answered the voice on the other end of the line.

"There's been an incident," reported the Colonel. "Blake's dead. He was shot by a soldier guarding the perimeter as he tried to make a run for it. I had him bagged and sent to Walter Reed."

"Suicide by soldier," Chiswell said in disgust. "Well, at least the chicken shit son-of-a-bitch saved the taxpayers a lot of time and money. I suppose that's something. Thank you, Colonel. I'll let the President know."

The House Chamber

The massive doors opened, and the familiar words "Madam Speaker, the President of the United States" resounded through the chamber as David Walsh started down the aisle. It was a walk that he had made many times before, but tonight was different. Friends and supporters did not fill the gallery. Instead, military personnel who would all too soon be put in harm's way filled the seats. He saw his beloved Sarah, who had come to town to be with him tonight, and on either side were the British and Israeli Ambassadors showing their countries' support. Two very special honored guests. Lerrick McKenna and Dr. Jeff Roberts took their seats directly in front of the First Lady.

The Vice President and Speaker of the House Judith Pigg Carter were in position behind the podium. As the President reached it, he completed the tradition of handing copies of his speech to his VP and the Speaker. He was introduced and all who were present shouted their support for a full two minutes.

"Ladies and gentlemen," the President began, "would you please bow your heads in a moment of silence for all those who lost their lives during the attack on the Chesapeake Bay Bridge."

He then cleared his throat and continued: "Mr. Vice President and Madam Speaker, members of the House and Senate, the Justices of the Supreme Court, and members of the Joint Chiefs of Staff, as well as the United States Diplomatic Corps. Thank you for forsaking your personal safety so that our enemies may know that the American spirit is alive and undaunted. I also want to thank the members of my Cabinet, and the Ambassadors who defied both personal and political peril to be here tonight. My heart goes out to the American citizens who lost their lives, and their families who have to endure this terrible loss. Let me assure you we share that loss with you. *You are not alone.* Because of this misplaced hatred of our enemies, I promise you, they have not died in vain! Freedom has been attacked, but freedom will be defended."

When the President paused for breath, the room again erupted in a roar of approval, then hushed as he resumed.

"We have been attacked by an unconventional enemy. They have no borders, they do not come from one country or region, and they are stealth. They do not dress or look alike; nor do they wear uniforms, except a scarf to hide their faces in shame. They may live in the desert, in the cities, or in your neighborhoods. They are alike only in their determination to destroy our way of life, and they will not rest until we no longer exist.

"We thought the monsters were dead. We thought we could go forward with plans for peace. We were wrong; the monsters are alive and walk among us. Saif al Adel, the new spokesmen of al-Qaeda and his predecessor, is the shadow of Hitler and like Hitler is one of the most reviled screeds in modern history. He hides in the mountains of Tora Bora and I have recently become aware that his subordinate, Farhad Atwa, has formed an alliance with Iman al Fareed of Libya and Halem Salan, who replaced Sadam Hussein as the illegal president of Iraq. Al Fareed is financing the efforts to eliminate the Western world and anyone else who does not embrace Islam. Well, I say to them: Not on my watch. So starting right now, the United States will hold every country responsible for its own citizens, and we will hold accountable all those who harbor, train or finance terrorists. There will be no exceptions.

"President Fareed, our people believe in their desires. They want respect and peace. They want their families to be safe, happy and free. They want prosperity for all, and above all they want liberty and are prepared to fight anywhere to protect our natural born rights as Americans and human beings. I pray that we find the path to a peaceful coexistence, but if this is not your wish I pray not to be sheltered from the danger, but to be fearless in facing it. If you refuse to recant your threat, I will do what I must to defend my people and my God. You, sir, have now been warned. Unless I receive a communiqué from you by midnight tomorrow, Greenwich Mean Time, I will ask for a formal declaration of war against you and the factions that have aligned themselves with you into perpetuity.

"Iman al Fareed, for the good of your people, you do not need to do anything but surrender unconditionally. To that end, you must lead your people away from conflict and harm to a place where peace and harmony will abound for all."

The applause was tumultuous, and the President paused before his summation. "That, sir, is attainable."

"Ladies and gentlemen, the goal of this nation is peace. It always has been, and it always will be. Tonight I am inviting all countries, friends and foes alike, to partake in this process. All nations will come to the table as equals. All must speak, and all must listen. Together, we can stop the slaughter of innocent lives and move forward, away from the violence that has become the legacy of many. Together, we can build a world where children are safe, a world where tolerance replaces prejudice and where words are mightier than weapons. I pray to your Allah and my God that this becomes the commitment and responsibility of all mankind."

"Thank you, ladies and gentlemen, and God bless America."

The Chamber resounded with unanimous approval as the President made his way back down the aisle.

The large oak double doors separating the House Chamber from the reception room closed and David Walsh slumped into an easy chair and closed his eyes. He said, "Give me a minute, Jim."

"Sorry," said Chiswell as he approached the President. "I have some news: Archibald Blake is dead. Apparently he broke away from Ziggy and was shot by a soldier standing post in the parking area."

"Cowardly bastard," the President said in disgust. "Does anyone know about this yet?"

"No, sir. Ziggy sent the body to Walter Reed and ordered the soldier to keep his mouth shut and sent him back to his headquarters."

"Good," said the President. "You know, Jim, this may be a blessing in disguise. The press is going to have a field day with this. Hell, they'll be so busy extrapolating about the treasonous bastard's death that we may actually be able to get something accomplished. Tell Asa to get a statement out telling what happened and I mean fully transparent. I'm not in the mood to sugarcoat his deeds. The country must know that there may be more of those traitorous bastards out there."

"You know what to do, Jim. Just keep me in the loop. By the way, give this story to that young journalist from NNC, Lerrick McKenna. She deserves it for not releasing her story about the Bridge at my request. See to it please."

"Yes, sir," said Chiswell. He made a mental note to make sure the President got some much needed rest after his meeting.

When the President walked into the adjacent meeting room, the members of his Cabinet and key leaders from both houses of Congress had already assembled. He came right to the point. "Ladies and gentlemen, I'm going to make a brief statement, after which I will open the floor for discussion. As you know, approximately 48 hours ago. al-Qaeda claimed responsibility for the bombing of the Chesapeake Bay Bridge. What you don't know is that we received intelligence that President Iman al Fareed of Libya has gained possession of 22 nuclear suitcase bombs, implanted by the Soviet Union around the western hemisphere and Israel during the Cold War. We believe several of the bombs are already in the United States, and one or two are known to be in London. Recently, Fareed purchased the locations and detonation codes from the Russian mob. He, along with the leaders of al-Qaeda, plan to use the bombs to further their Jihad against the West. I received a communiqué from President Fareed demanding that we sever all ties with Israel or he will use the bombs. I'm sure you see why we could not divulge this information earlier; if it got out that bombs were already in the U.S. and this fool was threatening to detonate them, it would cause mass panic. We must avoid that at all costs. Now I'll entertain comments or questions, if anyone has any?"

"Are we going to pursue diplomatic channels with our allies in the Arab Peninsula?" asked Secretary of State Howe.

"Yes, of course, Barbara" replied the President. "However, we must negotiate from a position of strength. Therefore, I believe our first move should be to reposition the Sixth Fleet just off the Libyan coast. Not 200 miles out; just 3 miles will do. Let the son of a bitch see our boats."

"Mr. President, I presume that you've spoken with Prime Minister Mordachi. Does he think Fareed will pull the trigger?" asked Senator Mike Hardy, Chairman of the Armed Services Committee.

"Yes, but I think the Prime Minister is wrong in his opinion of Fareed being crazy, because he's crazy like a fox."

"Well, crazy or not, I can't believe Fareed went through all this to enact revenge against the West and doesn't care to be alive to see it. He's way too narcissistic for that," Cassidy said. "I think we must convince him that his plan will accomplish nothing but total destruction for both sides. He needs to know that we're serious. I fully concur with repositioning the Sixth Fleet."

"I second that," said Senator Hardy.

"Okay, Bill. Notify the Joint Chiefs to contact the NATO Allied Supreme Commander. It is imperative that we use the appropriate chain of command as a fail-safe measure when we pass the order to the Admiral of the Sixth Fleet. Agreed?"

"Agreed."

"There is one more thing I want to discuss with you tonight," the President said. "I have asked Secretary Cassidy to assume the role of Vice President. As you know, Harry is very ill and will not finish out his term. I hope you will ensure the Secretary's rapid confirmation. I need not remind you of the peril that surrounds us all."

"I can't think of a worse-case scenario than a top-level conversation between Iman al Fareed and a female representative of the Western World," added Secretary Barbara Howe.

"Madam Secretary," said the Senate Majority Leader, "You are respected worldwide."

"Sam, thanks for the vote of confidence, but you know as well as I do that as a woman, I could never effectively negotiate with any Arab nation. It's not about respect, it's about religion and customs, and it's never going to change. They respect their camels more than their women."

"You're absolutely right, Barbara," the President said. "At best Fareed is going to be difficult to deal with. If we do anything he views as disrespectful or that causes him to lose face, he will walk away from the table. But be that as it may, you are my Secretary of State and that's final."

Everyone in the room nodded in agreement, and the President adjourned the meeting. It was late, and they all needed to get to higher ground.

Once they were back in the motorcade, Chiswell turned to his boss. "Mr. President," he began, "Earlier today, before the shit hit the fan, so to speak, Ziegelhofer gave me his letter of resignation. He said that the time had come to decide whether to remain in the military or go into the private sector. He chose the latter. I believe that his wife's illness has had a lot to do with his decision."

"I wish I could join him," the President said. "Sorry, Jim, bad joke. Resignation accepted, but make sure he gets his star before he leaves. He's worked hard for this country; he deserves to retire as a flag officer. What have you heard about this Colonel Steve Meyers?"

"He's one tough son-of-a-bitch," replied Chiswell.

"He sounds to me like the old Lou Blaine. He just might be the right man to replace Ziggy. Have him meet with me tomorrow at 0700 in the bunker."

"Yes, sir, Mr. President." The motorcade pulled up to the North Gate. "And, sir, I'm sure it's been a while since you've had a solid six hours, so if you take a rest, I'll stay in my office with orders not to disturb you without going through me first."

"Yes, Mother," chided the President. "See you bright and early, my friend."

As soon as the President opened the door of his private study, he saw the smile that always melted his heart. "You were brilliant tonight, darling, but then, you always are," Sarah said as she put her arms around him.

"I just pray to God that I can pull this off."

"You will, I'm sure of it," Sarah said, but the shudder that rippled through her body belied her optimism. Sarah was scared, but then, so was he. Finally she broke away and took him by the hand, leading him into the bedroom.

As they readied themselves for a good night's sleep Sarah reached for her husband and held him tight. "I will do anything you ask of me, David. You know I have a great amount of diplomatic service with State. Perhaps I could be of service as a goodwill ambassador in the Arab Peninsula. Barbara could do her thing as Sec. State while I go to separate venues, working with the schools and children while establishing good will with the ruling families. This could be the beginning of what should have been done many years ago. When you're as powerful as we are we must show real transparent compassion to those who are not."

"What a great idea. You could leave immediately and the goodwill you would project could very well be one of the keys to our success. I'm going to mention this to Chiswell and have him make it happen."

She kissed her husband long and hard. Then they fell asleep in each other's arms.

At promptly 0645, Jim Chiswell strode to the North Gate of the White House to greet Colonel Steve Meyers. Powell knew Meyers only through his reputation as someone who got the job done. He was impressed by the number of decorations that adorned the Colonel's dress uniform, which he wore for his meeting with his Commander in Chief.

"Good morning, Colonel," Chiswell said. "Follow me, please, and I'll take you right to the President."

"Good morning, sir, and thank you." Meyers followed Chiswell down the hall. Moments later they were ushered into the President's private office in the Bunker. Meyers returned the salute of the young marine standing guard outside the bunker door and stepped in to greet his Commander-in-Chief.

"Jim, please give us a moment," said the President. "We need to talk privately."

"Of course, Mr. President, I believe I can find a few hundred things I need to do. Good to meet you, Colonel."

"Good to meet you too, Chief," said Meyers as the door to the inner sanctum closed.

"Colonel Meyers… may I call you Steve?" asked the President.

"Yes sir, of course."

"Good. Now then, I have asked you here because this country has a serious problem, and you may be the person to help solve it. The issue is highly sensitive and outside of your normal duties as an officer. If you decline, you will return to your regular duties with absolutely no repercussions."

Meyers answered without hesitation. "Mr. President, I will serve in any way deemed necessary. I'm honored, Sir."

"Good," said the President, thinking that Meyers didn't get all those ribbons by being a pussy. No wonder Lou Blaine and Ziegelhofer were so impressed with this guy. "I want you to eliminate an enemy of the state. Warren Dunn is a wealthy businessman who made headlines a couple of years ago by donating large sums of money to my campaign. I was naive and thought he believed in my politics; however, that was not the case. Unbeknown to anyone, Dunn had aligned himself with al-Qaeda, who, of course, relished an alliance with someone who could influence U.S. foreign policy, especially as it pertained to Israel. Their plan was simple. Dunn would use his influence with me to initiate a foreign policy that called for the U.S. to sever all ties with Israel. In turn, Dunn would control the oil regions in Iraq, a sizeable reward."

"However, the plan failed when Dunn couldn't control me. Israel is still our ally and many of the oil fields in the region have been nationalized. As you know, Dunn was convicted of tax evasion and ended up doing a couple of years in our federal lock-up in Lewisburg. We believe that during his time there, he rekindled his relationship with al-Qaeda, only this time the stakes were higher, possibly even a new world order. Senator Archibald Blake became involved, as well as other members of the Bohemian Society and their sister organization in Holland, the Bilderberg Group. These organizations are comprised of top-level American and European leaders as well as the captains of world industry and the intelligentsia of our universities. In their secret meetings, they explore ways to change the world, usually to suit the needs of the top 1% of the world's wealth. We are unsure how extensive this new alliance is, but we do know that besides Senator Blake, a Muslim woman made several visits to Dunn while he was in the penitentiary. We presume she is linked to al-Qaeda, and is the conduit between them and Dunn. As you know the men who blew up the Chesapeake Bay Bridge stayed in a cabin that belonged to Dunn and were looked after by a member of Dunn's staff. Of course you also know that al-Qaeda has taken responsibility for the bombing."

"Yes sir."

The President continued. "Warren Dunn has not only committed treason against the United States of America, he participated in the senseless murder of her citizens. I want him dealt with like the pond scum he is."

"Do you want this to be a solitary mission?" Meyers asked, "Or can I call up my team? I work with three men and one woman, each at the top in their respective fields."

"Use anyone or anything you need."

"And, sir, if I may speak freely?" said Meyers, "Why not eliminate the Arab leaders as well? It seems to me that if you have a problem with rats and you exterminate only one, you still have a problem with rats."

"Well said. That's exactly what I have in mind, but first things first. I don't know how far I can take this on my own."

"Mr. President," said Meyers, now on a roll, "I'm not at all sure that you need to shoulder this responsibility. That's the thing about war. Collateral damage replaces political assassination."

"I see your point," said the President. After a brief pause, he asked, "Has this special squad you mentioned been in existence during other administrations?"

"Yes, sir, many." Meyers answered, so succinctly that the weight of the message was underscored by the simplicity of the reply. The two men stared at each other in silence until suddenly the President rose and came around from behind the desk. "You're right, Steve," he said. "We'll consider this collateral damage. Here is my private number. Call me when it's over."

"Yes, sir, Mr. President."

Alone in his office, David Walsh sank into the chair behind his desk. He thought of Lincoln and Roosevelt and wondered what they would have done given the same circumstances. At least their enemies had countries, their battlefields had lines, and uniforms differentiated friend from foe. The art of war was simpler then, he thought. Today, our enemies can be our friends or our lovers: they can be found in the communities where we live and the places where we work; and much like the soldiers who fight for this nation, they are willing to sacrifice their lives for what they believe in.

We are the wealthiest, the most wasteful, and the most imitated and yet the most hated nation on earth. We have the strongest military anywhere, equipped with the technology to safeguard everything from our farmlands to our borders, yet we are defenseless against just one man with a bomb and a conviction. What's happened? Was it our quest to build weapons capable of destroying the world that perpetrated this change in strategies? Were we so naïve that we believed these weapons would act as a deterrent to conflict?

Guilty on all counts, thought the President sadly. Hubris in the name of progress has taken the nobility out of war and left us with suicide bombers and assassination squads. Well, if those are the rules of the game, then, by God, those are the rules I'll play by.

Lincoln and Roosevelt didn't know how lucky they were.

Chapter 11

336 40TH ST. NW
GEORGETOWN

errick and Jeff were feeling a bit heady as they left the Blue Parrot after a wonderful dinner and great wine. The events of the last few days had served to remind them both of how fragile life really was, so when the driver stopped in front of Lerrick's home, she leaned over and asked Jeff if he would like to come in for a nightcap. The invitation was readily accepted, and the two walked hand-in-hand up the steps of the brownstone as the cabby drove off into the night.

Once inside, Lerrick poured two glasses of the same Chardonnay they had enjoyed at the Parrot and brought them over to the sofa where Jeff was sitting.

"Here's to all we have been through together," Lerrick said, raising her glass.

"Here's to the future," countered Jeff. "I have this feeling that we will be going through a lot more together, for better or worse."

Putting down his glass, he pulled her close and kissed her. They held one another closely as the joining of their souls merged from the crossing of their paths.

"For better or worse," whispered Lerrick.

Presidential command center

Shortly after 0800, Chiswell returned to the bunker to go over the day's agenda and wait for the Attorney General. Within minutes, the secretary in the outer office of the bunker buzzed the President to let him know that Mark Ferrell had arrived, along with the President's good friend Ian McPherson.

The flamboyant Attorney General made his usual grand entrance but the confines of the inner office made him appear more comedic than commanding. Chuckling to himself, the President welcomed his trusted friends. This was a close-knit group of the most valued political allies, the men he turned to in times of crisis.

As usual, Attorney General Ferrell was first to speak. "I have good news," he exclaimed. "In my hand is an indictment of none other than that fucking traitor Warren Francis Dunn."

"How in the hell did you get it so fast?" Walsh asked.

"Well, when you ordered me to get things done, I just thought, what the hell, let's do it sooner rather than later. I convened an emergency session of the Federal Grand Jury. I chose a different venue so the press wouldn't pick up the scent."

"Where did you take them?" Chiswell asked.

Mark smiled sheepishly. "Dunn's office building in the District. I signed a search warrant for his private office, and I tried to save the government some money by killing two birds with one stone. We convened in his board room." The four men broke out laughing and shaking their heads.

"Well done." The President patted Ferrell on the back. "I wish I could be a fly on the wall when he finds out we used his board room to get an indictment for him."

"I hope nobody tells him," Chiswell said. "He'd probably send us a bill."

"Or sue us for trespassing," McPherson added.

"I don't give a damn!" said the President, thoroughly enjoying the moment. "I'd love to see the bastard's face."

After a few more laughs, the President said "As you all know, I have asked Bill Cassidy to be my Vice President. Jim, are we up to speed on his confirmation?"

"Sir it should be done in twenty-four hours."

"His appointment leaves me without a Secretary of Defense, so I'm asking you, Ian: Will you do me the honor of serving as my Secretary of Defense?"

McPherson was overwhelmed. He and David Walsh had always been like brothers. Since his friend had become President, Ian had put in many hours working with and advising not only Walsh but also others in the administration. He was, after all, an extremely knowledgeable and well-connected man. A highly decorated soldier during the Viet Nam War, Ian became an extremely successful businessman in private life. And now he had graduated from the kitchen cabinet to the official Cabinet.

"Mr. President, I'm honored."

"Jim," began the President; but his Chief of Staff was already on top of it.

"I know, Mr. President, ASAP," said Chiswell as he stood up. "Mr. President, if you don't need me right now, it sounds like I have something that needs to be attended to. Ian, let me be the first to congratulate you, and welcome aboard. Mr. President, if you don't need me further?"

"Go, Jim, work your magic. And by the way, the First Lady had a brilliant idea. She has offered to do a goodwill tour of the Arab Peninsula. Please set this up with the Travel Office. We might as well let her do her magic as well."

"Thank you, sir," Chiswell said as he took his leave. The President then said to his two friends, "Honest to God, Chiswell is like Radar in the TV series Mash. Everything's done before I tell him." They all laughed, then got down to business.

Alone in the room, Attorney General Farrell turned to David Walsh and said, "Mr. President, are you still going to go up top?"

"No, Mark, it would be like a captain abandoning his ship. I can't leave the people of this country in harm's way while I'm safe and sound aboard Air Force One. I'll be in the bunker with my immediate staff, connected to the outside world via electronics. I've actually been outside the bunker too much already. The Secret service is ready to kill me."

The President's weak attempt at humor fell on deaf ears. "Mr. President, I think you're making a grave error, not to mention a dangerous one," said Ferrell. "In light of this threat, we can't say how safe these bunkers are. We don't know enough about the capabilities of those suitcase bombs. For the sake of this country, it's important for you to be elsewhere, just in case."

"For the sake of the American people, I'm staying here. I've made up my mind. Besides I'm more comfortable in the White House."

Signaling that the meeting was over, the President stood and made his way toward the door. "Let me know if there are any problems with Ian's confirmation. I don't anticipate any, but you never know."

"Will do, and thank you, Mr. President." The two men then took their leave.

The President was feeling stiff and uncomfortable in the confines of the bunker office. Maybe it was the idea of being underground that had him so on edge. More likely it was the upcoming separation from Sarah. She always provided the calm amidst the chaos, and heaven knows he was going to miss her.

Perhaps, he thought, he would have his favorite chair moved down here. He could catch a power nap once in a while and maybe he'd stop feeling so tired.

Chapter 12

The President's motorcade pulled up to the National Cathedral by 10 AM. The morning was beautiful. Not too hot, cherry blossoms everywhere. A perfect day, except he had arrived for a memorial service for those who lost their lives at the bridge.

The Secret Service opened the door and the President asked them to shut it; he wanted a moment to reflect. There was so much to do but this memorial, albeit dangerous, had to go through. He would speak briefly, then make his way back to his bunker.

President Walsh then knocked on the door and it was readily opened to a thunderous applause. Average citizens hollering "three cheers" and "we're with you Mr. President," made him feel especially kindhearted toward his people. Citizens were giving him high grades and he was most humbled by the gesture.

There was the usual crowd of political well-wishers waiting at the entrance. The President wanted to work both crowds, but the Secret Service said no, so he did not shake one hand; he just waved.

Inside the Cathedral the Washington Opera choir began singing with the music to the "President's Own," the United States Marine Band. As soon as he stepped inside, the band started to play "Hail to the Chief," and David Walsh, with a somber face, made it up to the reserved pew. With tears in his eyes he waited to be introduced to the world.

Chapter 13

The President's secretary buzzed, announcing that Secretary of State Barbara Howe had arrived for their meeting. The President wanted to send her to Amman, Jordan, to meet with the leaders of the Arab nations and get an idea of how the political winds were blowing.

"Mr. President," said Howe, "are you sure it's a good idea to send a woman? Maybe those nations with whom we have already established relationships would turn a polite cheek, but the more radical leaders could use it to sway public opinion. If that happens, there might not be enough time to even begin a dialogue."

"You're my Secretary of State" said the President, "and this time it's on my terms."

"Yes, Sir," she said, "I just hope they won't leave me sitting on the tarmac at the Jordanian Airport."

"Anyone who does will be considered an ally to the other side and sanctions will be placed on their country immediately."

"You mean if anyone is left to implement those sanctions," Secretary Howe said, refusing to yield.

"What do you think, Jim?" the President asked his Chief, who had been sitting in on the meeting.

"The Secretary has a point, sir. If they won't talk to her, it won't matter how capable she is."

"Maybe you're right," Walsh said after a long pause. "I'll ask Bill Derrick to go along. I can't think of anyone who has a better understanding of the Arab mind than he. You win, Barbara."

"Thank you, Mr. President. We all win," she said, realizing that she had come very close to crossing the line.

"I know," Walsh chided his friend, "you could talk the paper off a wall. Jim, get ahold of Derrick for me right away. We need to get this show on the road."

"Will do, Mr. President," Chiswell said as he left the inner office. "Safe trip, Madam Secretary."

"Barbara," said the President when the door had closed, "make sure to keep Prime Minister Mordachi in the loop and I'll keep John Lawton up to speed. Good luck."

"Thank you, sir."

The President sat back, feeling confident. Those two will make a good team he thought. A damn good team.

Chapter 14

CLAM LAKE, WISCONSIN

*H*idden in the northernmost part of Minnesota is a small military base with no name. It is known to the men and women who serve there simply as 'The Reservation'. Officially it's called the Sanguine Project and is the main communications center for the US NAVY to all its submarines around the world. The base is surrounded by thick woods that are home to an abundance of wildlife and beautiful rolling pastures dotted with cattle. The Reservation operates under the guise of an experimental farm. There is no housing, no PX store, and none of the other amenities that one would expect to find on a military installation.

There are no high antenna towers, and the Navy Seals who patrol the perimeter give the occasional passerby the impression of a farmer and his dog tending to his cattle or checking his crops.

The highly secret installation was designed solely for the purpose of communicating with American Submarines. Deception and technology were integral to its success. The 'Reservation' was fenced and cross-fenced with miles and miles of razor wire that served as the main transmitter to our nuclear missile-bearing subs at sea. The wire remains in a constant state of transmission. It employs extremely low frequency radio bands that have a unique capability. A frequency that is below 10 hertz produces very long waves that are able to pierce ocean waters at the depths where nuclear submarines lurk. Each of the subs lying on the ocean floor trails its own aerial, a thin strip of wire that is identical to the razor fence back in Minnesota from which it receives its messages. With this technology, the President is able to communicate directly with the Commander of any submarine in the U.S. Fleet.

It took less than sixty seconds after President Walsh issued the order for nuclear submarines *The Cato* and *The Daniel Webster* to join the Sixth Fleet in the Bay of Sidra off the Libyan coast. Modifications to the patterns emitted by the razor wire were picked up by the radio operators of each submarine and immediately sent to the duty officer for decoding. That officer in turn sent the message to the Captain. Upon receipt of the decoded message, the Captain and First Officer opened the ship's safe by simultaneously inserting the keys that they wear 24/7 on lanyards around their necks. After the safe is open, pre-programmed orders on punch cards are inserted into the computer. Then the 20 Poseidon Nuclear Missiles, with all the data necessary to complete their mission with astounding accuracy, are ready at a moment's notice.

The Webster and *The Cato*, now the deadliest war machines in the world, were ready.

Chapter 15

"Mr. President," said Chiswell as he entered the inner office, "I've just spoken with Bill Derrick. He's in Buffalo, but said he would be here as soon as he could gas up the jet and pack a bag."

"Good," said President Walsh. "Jim, I've been thinking. I want to talk with Imam al Fareed. I owe it to the American people to pursue a peaceful solution to the problems while we quietly position our military."

"Mr. President, of course we should make every attempt to circumvent a military confrontation with Fareed and company; however, we must be very careful how we deal with him. He's dangerous, unstable, and right now he's holding a detonator. If you think Derrick is the foremost authority on the Islamic culture, I suggest that you get a profile from him before proceeding with any plans for a one-on-one with that madman."

"You're right, and be sure he knows that our time is limited; quick is not good enough. If we have to delay Secretary Howe's departure for Jordan it's going to send the wrong message."

"Will do, Sir," said Chiswell as he reached for the phone.

"Good," said Walsh. "I think I'll go stretch my legs for a while."

———————

Upon arrival Bill Derrick, the President's personal advisor on all Middle East affairs was immediately escorted to the War Room.

"Bill," welcomed the President, "thank God you're here. I know how busy you are, but thanks so much for getting here this quickly."

"Not a problem, Mr. President," replied Derrick. "I'm always glad to be of service."

"Good, then let's get to it. Has Jim had a chance to brief you yet?"

"Yes, sir, on the way in from Reagan. He said that you are planning to speak directly with Imam al Fareed."

"That's correct. I feel that it's necessary to initiate a dialogue. Even if the talks break down, we may be able to buy some time to mobilize our forces before we have a nuclear showdown with this madman. But before I begin I need to know what makes him tick. I need background information—how he thinks, what he feels, and what, if anything, could make him stand down. I'm not interested in hearing from the CIA; I already know what's in their files. What I want are your personal feelings."

"Sir I have known the Libyan leader for some time, and I can tell you that he is a very complex man. He is highly intelligent yet very insecure. As a young boy, his father sent him to school in rags while the other children had nice clothing and shoes. Now he believes that because he was raised in poverty, the elite of his country does not accept him. I believe this is the reason that he craves the respect and attention of the world's leaders, even if he detests what they stand for. He is a deeply religious man who regards himself as a visionary who will lead the world to total Islam. He is not a fanatic, but he's rigid in his beliefs, and he holds his followers to the same standards that he holds for himself. He once publicly shaved the head of his Prime Minister because he violated the principles of the revolution by consorting with several escorts while traveling in Italy. Even though Fareed believes he is a great man, he requires constant affirmation from those around him. He and Quadafi authored the now famous 'Green Book' in which he chronicled the ideals of his revolution and made it required reading for all of his followers. The idea came from Chairman Mao who wrote The Red Book and who he greatly admired. Quadafi also was Fareed's mentor. The two have been together since the overthrow of King Idris. He retreats to the solitude of the desert several times a week to meditate and sleep. During these pilgrimages, only his most trusted people know where he stays. He is paranoid about his safety and often obsesses about his own murder."

Derrick took a deep breath before continuing, "Fareed is a cunning and aggressive strategist, but what makes him so dangerous is his patience. Failure is unacceptable, and he has been known to wait months or even years to ensure victory. In 1969 he and Muammar overthrew King Idris with a small band of revolutionaries. During the years after the new regime was established, Fareed and his partner systematically eliminated anyone who posed a threat to them. Only the Prime Minister has remained in place."

"What the hell kind of a madman are we dealing with?" exclaimed the President.

"Egomaniacal, paranoid, volatile, ruthless," Derrick enumerated. "Fareed wears many faces. Once handsome and charming, he is an introvert devoted only to his wife and children. He never got over the loss of his fifteen-month old daughter when President Reagan bombed his home. It is also reported that since that time, he has suffered from migraine headaches, but this has never been confirmed. I do know that he is subject to unpredictable mood swings, and has been known to throw temper tantrums so violent that he will smash furniture and roll on the floor of his office in an uncontrollable rage. Some say he's fearless; most say he's crazy. I think he's both. Do you remember when President Reagan sent the Sixth Fleet into the bay of Sidra? Well, Muammar and Iman met them aboard a 60-foot cabin cruiser waving golden swords, ready to do battle. That's how eccentric they were."

"I do remember that, now that you mention it, and I must say that it doesn't make me feel better," said the President, shaking his head. "So, which Fareed should I play to? Which one's going to show up, Imam 1 or Imam 2?"

Derrick sat back in his chair and closed his eyes. He knew what he needed to say; he did not know how his President would take it. "Mr. President, study his eyes and his facial expressions, and you will get a pretty good idea of who he is. However, you must remember that this is a man who has been ridiculed all his life. You must make him believe that you think he is a great man, even if the very idea is repugnant to you. Listen while he extols his principles and beliefs. Flatter him. Remember, no one in the western world takes him seriously and that's what causes him the most pain. If he thinks you do not respect him, you will lose him; if you lose him, you will never get another chance."

"To do anything," said President Walsh, letting the ominous words hang in the air like a thick morning fog. "Bill, I want you here when I talk with him. I need your analysis of the conversation."

"However I can help, sir."

"I spoke with Chiswell and Sercu earlier today, and they told me we're on for 2200 tonight; I believe that's 0700 in Libya. I will speak to Barbara, and the two of you can get going as soon as we're finished here."

"Sounds good, Mr. President," said Derrick, thinking that he could use a good meal and a few hours' sleep. The next twenty-four hours were going to be very long, very long indeed. "Mr. President, if you don't need me for anything else, I think I'll get a room at the Hay Adams and relax before things get started. I'll be back here by 2130."

"Good," said Walsh, as he came around his desk to shake his friend's hand. "See you tonight."

Chapter 16

NNC BREAKING NEWS

"This is Lerrick McKenna reporting to you live from NNC headquarters. Last night, President David Walsh, in a history-making address to a Joint Session of Congress, served notice to the terrorists' organizations of Hamas, Hezbollah, and al-Qaeda that he intended to ask Congress for an official declaration of war unless a peaceful coexistence can be negotiated within forty-eight hours. He asked all Americans to unite without prejudice or malice so that we can defend America, her people, and the ideals for which she stands.

"The session started with a tribute to those who lost their lives in the recent attack on the Chesapeake Bay Bridge.

"Attending the memorial service this morning at the National Cathedral, President Walsh underscored the nature of a faceless enemy determined to destroy us all and assured Americans everywhere we are at the ready.

"Just before the President's speech U.S. Senator Archibald Blake was arrested for treason. In trying to escape Blake was shot by one of the soldiers guarding the Capitol Building. Mr. Blake was involved in a plan with al-Qaeda to take over our government using the world's oil supply as a weapon against it. More on the subject as the news develops.

"For NNC, this is Lerrick McKenna, live from Washington."

2130 Hours

Bill Derrick entered the Presidential Command Center for the second time that day after a brief rest and a good meal. The delay had added to his apprehension about the President's impending conversation with Imam al Fareed. The events of the last few days had left the President on edge, and Derrick knew that Walsh must keep his emotions intact and stay on course during their conversation or the consequences could be devastating.

As the door to the President's office opened, he saw the NSA Director, Chief of Staff Chiswell and Joint Chiefs Chairman General Ned Seiffert in a heated discussion, with the General leading the charge.

"Why in hell are we going through with this exercise in futility?" bellowed Seiffert. "Normally, I would agree that every diplomatic possibility should be explored before entering into a military solution, but not in this case. Any attempt at diplomacy will be interpreted as weakness, and you know how far that will go. He'll disconnect, laugh, and blow us off the map. Besides all that, what happened to our policy to never negotiate with terrorists? Our only chance is to strike first. Drop a little teaser, and then promise the big one on his capitol doorstep if he doesn't give up the locations and codes. What do we have to lose? It can't be anything more then we're going to lose anyway. If you ask me, we're wasting time we haven't got."

"Nobody's asking, general," Sercu snapped.

"Mr. President," Derrick offered in an attempt to deescalate the tension filling the crowded office, "if I may."

"Of course," said the President, getting up to shake his hand. "Please, we're relying on your input."

"Thank you, sir." Derrick took a seat in one of the few empty chairs. "Fareed is an Arab first and a leader second. His goal is to complete the Jihad against America and her allies in the West. If his country is destroyed in the process, so be it; the end justifies the means. The only thing you can hope to gain from any dialogue with Fareed is time."

"What about Israel?" Chiswell asked. "Maybe they can accommodate us for a change. After all, we keep them alive. Tell them if they don't move out of Palestine, the goose that laid the golden egg is going to be dinner. Frankly, Israel should want America healthy almost as much as we do. If Mordachi is worried about losing face, he can tell the world that we forced them to acquiesce."

"Good point, Jim," said Sercu.

The President was becoming frustrated by delays and the indecision of his senior staff.

Turning to Sercu, he snapped, "Jim, the clock is ticking. Whatever we're going to do, let's get started."

"Yes, sir." Sercu was concerned over the President's escalating anxiety. Of all the qualities that defined David Walsh as his nation's leader, it was his mental toughness in times of crisis that Sercu most admired. Sercu couldn't put his finger on it, but his sixth sense was now telling him that his President was beginning to unravel. "Mr. President," he said, "You will be using the H. L. satellite system for the first time. The photo transmissions will come from a plane staffed with a team of experts working with those here at Command Central. They can determine if the subject is lying by analyzing his eyes and expressions and relay that data to you in seconds. Another advantage this technology affords is that it can filter your expressions so that he will not be able to interpret your true feelings. You will have the advantage."

"You must remember," interrupted Bill Derrick, "Fareed is a carbon copy of his mentor and is as irrational as Muammar was. This is the first time in twenty years that he has had a dialogue with a leader of the Western world, and he didn't resurface to make an empty threat. It is obvious he has the bombs. It's very possible that he will escalate during your conversation, so you must set the tone in the first few moments. Treat him as a visionary and not as a terrorist. He dreams of acceptance by the world's leaders, so if he senses your disrespect, he may become aggravated and make an irrational decision. If at any time you feel that the talks are deteriorating, change the subject; philosophize with him but do not acquiesce to his ranting for he will see right through you. He does not admire compassion; he detests weakness."

"Mr. President," said Chiswell. "Don't forget, we're not after peace right now. We're after time."

"Okay, okay, let's get this son-of-a-bitch on the line," the President said, then changed his mind. "No, wait, I want to talk to Prime Minister Mordachi first. I think you're right, Jim, we've supported them long enough. It's about time they return the favor."

"Yes, sir," snapped Chiswell. "I'll set it up."

Chapter 17

TEL AVIV

*I*n an anteroom adjacent to the Prime Minister's spacious living quarters a small office housed the communications center serving Israeli Prime Minister Eli Mordachi. The officer in charge read the message as it came across the lines. It was clear and to the point: the President of the United States needed to speak with the Prime Minister. The officer awakened the sleeping Mordachi with the news of the President's urgent call.

Eli Mordachi, a longtime friend of David Walsh's, had been made aware of the developments from the Mossad, probably regarded as the most effective intelligence agency in the world. Wearing slippers and a bathrobe, Mordachi shuffled to the office and picked up the phone still known as the hotline.

"Mr. President, to what do I owe this honor?"

"Eli, I apologize for waking you at this hour, but I have only a few minutes before I speak with Fareed and I want to run this by you first."

"Yes, David, how can I help?"

"I want to tell Fareed that we have convinced you that Palestine should become an independent state and you are willing to restore the borders that were in place before the U.N. awarded you the additional land in 1948."

The silence after the President had finished seemed endless. Prime Minister Mordachi finally replied "No. Mr. President, the answer is no. First, I must remind you that those lands were ours 4000 years ago. Secondly, we do not negotiate with terrorists. Whatever we give them, they will demand more. If we negotiate now, the war will not end; this will just be the beginning. I'm sorry, Mr. President, the answer is no."

"Eli, for God's sake, they already have the bombs in place. If I can't give them something, we're dead in the water and you may be as well."

"If you want me to assassinate them, absolutely. Negotiate, forget it."

"I thought our relationship was better than this." Without

another word, the President replaced the receiver. "Son of a bitch, that ungrateful little bastard. He won't lift a finger to help us. Has he forgotten that Israel is the reason we're in this mess in the first place? I'm not sure why Harry Truman pushed so hard for those borders, but now Israel is so vital to the region and the security of our assets that we do nothing but kiss their ass and keep them alive."

Presidential Command Center

The President was flushed with emotion when he turned to Chiswell and Derrick. "Here we are, facing possible annihilation, and this bastard says no. Does he think this does not mean his destruction as well? He thinks they have us by the balls because they know how vital they are to the security of our assets. Well, he might want to stop and think what's going to happen to them if we're blown to bits and no longer need those assets."

The President's tirade had silenced the room. Derrick knew they needed to get back on track. "Mr. President, what if we put the weight of global salvation on his shoulders? This will give us a stay of execution and time for our experts to find those bombs. Tell him you are aware that previous administrations have turned their backs on Palestine. While you believe that Israel deserves to exist as a country, you also believe that Palestine does as well. Cite the Fourth Geneva Convention, Article #14, which states that citizens of one country cannot become Colonists in the territories that their country occupies. Proclaim that Israel should not be above the law. Assure him that you will seek an end to the thirty-five year occupation of Gaza and the West Bank and that your administration will support dividing the aid between Israel and the newly formed state of Palestine. Let him know that you are aware the Palestinian economy has suffered greatly and that you feel strongly that no one should be expected to raise a family on an average of three dollars a day. Repudiate the laws that grant lenience to Jews while Arabs are given penalties that are far more severe. Assure him that we are interested in rebuilding the Palestinian state, but only if it remains a peaceful region. Tell him that America has made mistakes but not on your watch."

"Jim," the President said "I like what you've said, and I may use it at some juncture, but in this initial talk, we need to set some ground rules and get to know each other."

"Mr. President, this may be our only chance."

Derrick's appeal was silenced by the appearance of the communications officer. He said, "Mr. President, the AWAC plane is just seventy-five miles off the coast of Libya and the satellite is in perfect position."

"Thank you, Captain," responded the President. "Hook me up."

Tel Aviv
Home of Israeli Prime Minister Eli Mordachi

The Prime Minister of Israel was having second thoughts. He walked from the private office in his home to the kitchen where he poured himself a glass of orange juice. He saw Sadie, his beloved wife of forty-five years, standing in the doorway.

Although they had not shared the same bedroom since he had become Prime Minister, because of the constant awakening of her husband, she could always sense if something was troubling her life's partner. Her intuition was a never-ending source of amazement to him.

Without a word she slipped past him and poured herself a glass of juice. "You couldn't sleep, my darling? Is there something wrong?"

Mordachi looked at her. Through the years she had become a trusted adviser and he valued her opinion, but he could not share what he had just learned. How could he tell her they would not survive another week? He could not, so he simply said, "Nothing's the matter. I just couldn't sleep, that's all."

Chapter 18

PRESIDENTIAL COMMAND CENTER

The President was ready to go. He blessed himself, realizing that he only prayed when he needed something. He made a mental note to pray more often and place more trust in the Lord.

When he looked up, unaware that the connection had gone through, he was stunned to see Imam al Fareed staring at him. He quickly composed himself and addressed his adversary: "Mr. President, I bring peaceful greetings from the people of the United States of America. I'm sure you understand how important it is for the two of us to talk before we embark on a path of mutual destruction."

The Libyan stared at Walsh for what seemed to be an eternity. "Mr. President, I just had the pleasure of watching you pray. I did not know that you were a religious man and respected your God."

Walsh was startled to hear Fareed speak perfect English, and the surprise registered on his face. Fareed reacted quickly, eager to spar with his opponent. "Mr. President, you look surprised that I speak your language. As a matter of fact, I am fluent in five languages, so, you see, I am not the mindless fool that your Generals portray me to be."

"Mr. President," said Walsh calmly, "I'm not aware that my Generals have referred to you in that manner, but if that is the case, please accept my apology. However, we both know that we have more pressing things to discuss."

"Of course," Fareed replied. "However, for our two nations, respect is always an issue. So tell me, President Walsh, what is it you want to talk about?"

"I believe that the two of us, by working together, can solve many of the problems that are facing our nations and perhaps the world. I am hopeful that, given time, I will be able to institute the changes my administration has already been working on which will facilitate this process. I believe that if you hear me out you will find them acceptable."

"Mr. President, as far as we are concerned, whatever your changes, they are too late."

"Please call me David and may I call you Imam?"

"That will do" replied the Libyan. "Need I remind you of the destruction my country can cause if provoked?"

At this point Chiswell slipped his boss a note, cautioning him not to anger Fareed, but the President brushed the note aside. "I am trying to prevent this, Imam."

"David, your contempt for me and my people resonates in the sound of your voice and the choice of your words. Or do you threaten all whom you hope to negotiate with?"

"Imam," continued the President, again ignoring Chiswell's advice. "Our commitment is total, and I'm NOT speaking with contempt. I have asked Congress for a declaration of war against your country and any that align with you. As we speak, we have nuclear submarines and the entire Sixth Fleet speeding toward your shores. Ask the terrorist leaders, whom we know you are harboring, what Afghanistan and Iraq look like. I'm saying, Imam, that technology has made this world smaller than it was twenty years ago when you could hide in the desert. Today, we are able to hunt you down, and your friends along with you. However, if you choose to accept a peaceful resolution to our differences, I promise you that your place at the table of history as one of the men who prevented this destruction of our countries will be secure. Your legacy as a world leader will be assured."

"Mr. President, I know full well what you and your Air Force can do. I have seen it on my shores and on the shores of my neighbors. However, the question may very well be: Do you know what *we* can do to *you*? We have bombs in place in several of your cities and with the touch of a button, I can cause your destruction. Do not threaten me with your submarines and your declarations for you will only make me laugh. All Arabs will stand together; if you kill one, another will take his place. You may have invented stealth, but we perfected it; we are not only invisible, we are unstoppable. I bid you good-bye, David Walsh. I do not want to talk anymore today."

The line went dead and the picture disappeared from the screen. The President leaned back in his chair and put his hands on his head. Concerned that Walsh could not tolerate a barrage of questions, Chiswell quietly cleared the room.

Breathing deeply and exhaling through pursed lips, Walsh regained his composure and looked at his Chief of Staff. Chiswell assured him, "It's not irreparable, sir. Fareed did not say he would not talk again, just not anymore *today*. You were speaking from strength."

"Bullshit! I wasn't speaking from a position of strength; I was speaking from desperation, and he knew it. It's ironic, isn't it? He's the one that craves respect, and I'm the one who ended up the laughingstock. Dammit Jim, what have I done to us?" The President slumped back in his chair and closed his eyes. He felt overwhelmed and inadequate. The job was too much for him, he thought; this job was too much for anyone.

He yearned to see Sarah. He realized that sending her to the Arab Peninsula was the most prudent course of action, but she was his soul mate and he never felt completely whole without her. Deciding that something was better than nothing, he asked one of his aides to connect him to Sarah. He then turned to his Chief of Staff and asked how Bill Cassidy's confirmation was progressing.

This was the first time that confirmation hearings had been held away from the Capitol Building but that did not deter Congress from acting swiftly. Chiswell informed him that both Secretary Cassidy and Ian McPherson would be confirmed by the end of the day. Walsh then directed Chiswell to assemble his top military advisers to discuss the consequences of a nuclear explosion in a major city.

As Chiswell was leaving the office, the Communications Officer arrived to let the President know that the First Lady was on the line. Walsh grabbed the phone, anxious to hear her voice.

"Hello, Darling," said Sarah. "Are you all right?"

His beautiful Sarah, thought the President. How he yearned to be with her, to be away from all this. "As well as can be expected, I suppose. I only wish I was alone with you, away from all this madness: no Secret Service, no Imam al Fareed and no bombs, just the two of us."

"I will treasure that," replied Sarah softly. "I miss you, and I love you, but I know that until your term is over, I must share you with the world."

The President paused for what seemed like an eternity before delivering his own bomb. "Sarah, I have made a decision, and I want to talk to you about it before I discuss it with anyone else. I am planning to resign the Presidency immediately after this crisis is resolved. I am being devoured by this job. By the time it's finished, there's not going to be anything left of David Walsh. Again, I am faced with the possibility of ordering a nuclear attack on a population guilty of nothing more than living on soil controlled by a madman. Couples on their wedding night, mothers nursing their newborns all will die at my hand. I disdain my enemies, yet I wonder if I am any different. I must not be, for the world has grown to hate us. The French do not allow us to fly over their territory, nor do the Italians. Look what we have done for Israel: we give them money and protection, and what do they do for us? Nothing. Hell, sometimes it feels like we support the whole damn globe and with the exception of Great Britain, we have no real allies. I'm tired Sarah, very, very, tired and I do not wish the legacy of being the destroyer of the world as the Vishnu. Bill Cassidy is a good man, and he will make a very fine President."

Sarah had heard enough. "David!" she exclaimed, "I'm shocked. I can't even imagine what you're going through, but I do know that now is not the time to talk about quitting. Now is the time for you, and you alone, to stand up for the values that have made our country great and will make the world a better place for those newlywed couples and mothers you spoke of. When we are all through this, then, and only then, will we discuss your resignation. My heart goes out to you, my love. Your road has not been smooth, but neither was it for many of your predecessors. They didn't quit and neither should you. I promise you that when this is all over we will take that vacation and many more. You know I love you more than life itself. Good-bye, my love, call me soon."

The line went dead, and David Walsh leaned back and closed his eyes. He knew she was right; she always was.

0800 hours
Presidential Command Center

The President's top military and environmental advisers were gathered in the Command Center along with Dr. Paul Marrone, a world-renowned nuclear physicist. The President entered the room and motioned for everyone to keep their seats.

"Good morning, gentlemen," he said. "Thank you for assembling on such short notice. I'll get right down to business. General Seiffert, what would be the expected outcome of a nuclear explosion in a city the size of Washington or New York?"

"Mr. President," said Seiffert, "the man who can best brief you on this is with us today. Let me introduce you to Dr. Paul Marrone."

The President acknowledged the man seated at the end of the table. "I am familiar with Dr. Marrone's reputation. Thank you, Doctor, for getting here on such short notice."

"Certainly, Mr. President," replied the soft-spoken Marrone, who was widely accepted as the leading authority on nuclear warfare in the US.

"Dr. Marrone," the President began, "I need to fully understand the devastation, or should I say, the progression of the devastation, from a nuclear device starting at ground zero and extending out through the various perimeters to an area that could be considered safe. I also need an approximate time line that could direct initial cleanup efforts."

"I'll do my best, sir" said Marrone, "but I must start by saying that in no other type of conflict does the advantage lie so heavily with the aggressor. That's why during the cold war we embraced the high wire act known as Mutually Assured Destruction. MAD, as it was nicknamed, was developed to convince the other side that even in the face of a nuclear attack, a retaliatory force would destroy them as well. Most members of the scientific community, however, realized that the only thing this concept could assure was the destruction of two nations instead of one. President Eisenhower had no illusions about the magnitude of this threat and ordered a report called the 'Doomsday Scenario.' Officially named the "Original War Plans Document," it was classified as top secret for obvious reasons. During the Reagan administration, the Secretary of the Air Force, Russ Rourke, mistakenly declassified it. Although the error was quickly remedied and the document re-classified in a matter of hours, two copies were released. One copy was used as a basis for the book titled *The Doomsday Scenario*. The scientific community used the other for further study and to document the effects of a nuclear attack."

After a quick pause to gather his thoughts, Marrone continued. "Today, advanced technology and history itself have created variables that no longer allow us to deal in absolutes. Even in the light of advanced warning systems and with greater medical technology, the consensus of the scientific community remains steadfast in its belief that there is no way to mitigate the effects of a nuclear attack. Should terrorists detonate a small nuclear device in a major city such as New York, everything within a one-and-a-half mile radius from ground zero will cease to exist. Should the attack occur in Washington D.C., the initial perimeter would extend further because the buildings in D.C. are relatively small in comparison to the skyscrapers of New York or Chicago. Radioactive material or 'Black Rain' *will drop on everything*. All living matter will be obliterated. Beyond the initial perimeter, variables such as buildings and weather will dictate how far the landscape will be blurred with smoke and haze and littered with debris and contamination. Survivors will suffer wounds and burns that will cause their skin to peel away from their bodies. Others will develop acute symptoms over the next few months—fever, blindness, Leukemia, and other forms of cancer. If the explosion occurs during working hours, two to three hundred thousand people will die. If the wind is blowing in the right direction, it could affect everyone within a seventy-five-mile radius. As many as four million people could be poisoned and die. Those may be the lucky ones. For the rest, government control will be seriously jeopardized and central federal direction will be virtually non-existent. The social fabric will cease to exist, confusion will run rampant, and there will be no customary control such as police or army. There will be no surviving labor force. There may be emergency rations available at distribution centers, but highways will no longer be viable, nor will the railroad. You can initiate an airlift several miles out from ground zero, but the question remains as to how the population will receive it, or how a government will distribute it. Bartering and looting will replace the monetary system, and the small amount of the population that is alive must dispose of the dead before more disease erupts."

Marrone directed his next statements directly to President Walsh. "The problems, sir, are endless. The White House will no longer exist. You will be dug out by special equipment housed in a special underground garage specifically for that purpose. Theoretically, you should be safe, but will anyone be alive to dig you out? And where will you go when you have reached ground level? You will be safer staying where you are. There will be enough food and supplies to last for several months and by that time the radiation should have dissipated. But once again, we cannot be 100% sure."

"Doctor, what about potassium iodide?" the President asked.

"There are some who think that potassium iodide is a cure for radiation sickness, but in reality, it is only effective for those who suffer a light dose. Perhaps a resident of Leesburg will survive if the winds were going the other way, but I can assure you that it will not save those within a three-mile radius of ground zero."

Jim Chiswell asked, "Doctor, do you believe our bunkers are safe?"

"I cannot answer that with absolute certainty, sir, but my guess is not 100%."

"With all due respect, Doctor," bellowed Director Bowen of the CIA, "we are not in a position to rely on guesswork. We need to leave the betting and percentages at the racetrack."

"As I said before, Director," Marrone replied, "there are many variables that do not allow us to deal in absolutes. Human nature is one of them. You see, to maintain a perfect shelter, a strict schedule of checking and rechecking is required. I believe that the maintenance on these shelters has not been kept up to date. As you know, most of our bunkers and shelters were built decades ago, during the cold war when the entire nation was in a state of hyper-vigilance. When the Reykjavik Treaty was signed and the Wall came tumbling down, the American people replaced their omnipresent fear with a sense of security. I'm not insinuating that we became complacent, but if those bunkers were not strictly maintained, they could very well leak. Even the smallest of leaks could have the gravest of consequences. "Unfortunately, now when we need them, it may be too late to right the wrong. However, what applies to the goose, applies to the gander. The type of device that the terrorists claim to have access to is the Russian-made suitcase bomb. These nuclear devices were encased in lead and hidden where they would not be detected. If they were to be of any value today, they must have been strictly maintained. All of this is possible, but not probable, and all it takes is one of them to be in good condition for Armageddon."

Marrone paused and again addressed the President directly. "Mr. President, I know that you want a time frame and a distance reference. I can't, with any amount of accuracy, give you that information. I know that we will have trauma centers available in Richmond, Charlottesville and Baltimore, but I cannot tell you how soon we will be able to transport survivors or what methods we will need to employ. The same can be said for delivering emergency supplies to those nearest the perimeter. There is one more variable, one that gives us the best chance to emerge from this and rebuild a stronger, smarter nation: the dauntless spirit of the American people. History has numerous examples of our indomitable spirit in the face of overwhelming adversity, and these have taught us that it is a nation's leader, either political or religious, that binds the fabric of society. The people will need to see you, and they will need to hear you. That is why I believe that it's imperative that you remain safe: 100% safe. I'm sorry, Mr. President, but with everything I have learned about nuclear warfare, I believe the safest place for you is in the air."

"I agree, Dr. Marrone," replied the President. "Thank you for your expertise and your honesty."

Turning to the Cabinet members and military advisers attending via satellite, the President closed the meeting, saying, "Dr. Marrone has given us a lot to consider; however, my aide was just informed that Prime Minister Mordachi is on the line, so we will have to reconvene later in the day. Bill, stay with me. I want you to hear this."

"Of course, sir," Derrick replied.

"Thank you, Mr. President," those in attendance chorused, either in person or via the many screens that lined the walls of the Command Center.

"Thank you, everyone," said the President as he exited the room. "We'll talk soon."

As soon as the President, accompanied by Chiswell and Derrick, secured the door to the private office, an aide announced that Prime

Minister Mordachi was on the screen back in the war room.

"David," the Prime Minister began, "there must be some way to destroy those bastards. I pray to God Almighty that we will always stand with our friends, but you must know that we cannot negotiate with those curs. They are the dogs of the earth, and they should be destroyed."

"Believe me, Eli, I want that as badly as you do," David Walsh responded. "But we must first deal with the problem at hand, and I have to come up with a plan to get us out of this mess. Fareed knows that we contribute heavily to your economy, and he wants us to leverage our position and force you to return the Gaza Strip to Palestine. If I go to the United Nations and issue an ultimatum to Israel, it might just buy us some time. However, it is of the utmost importance that no one in your Cabinet knows about our charade or Imam al Fareed will blow us out of the water quicker than a blink of an eye."

"Send in the Mossad?" Mordachi asked. "I believe that is the best way to deal with the bastards; however, that discussion is for another time. You will have my full cooperation, David. You have my word."

"Thank you, Eli," said the President. "We'll talk soon."

When the Prime Minister disappeared from the screen, Walsh turned to Bill Derrick and asked for his thoughts.

"It's tricky, Mr. President," Derrick said. "If Iman even suspects that we're playing him in front of the United Nations, he'll pull the trigger. He must believe that what he wants is possible and that the United States is strong enough to force Israel to comply. We do have a couple things working in our favor. We hold Israel's purse strings and the world knows that. And that certainly lends credence to our ability to pressure Israel. Show a lack of compassion for the Israeli people and that will come as a surprise and should benefit us in any negotiations with Fareed. Compassion is synonymous with weakness in the eyes of an Arab. I cannot emphasize strongly enough that you must appear in control. It's imperative that you wait for him to call."

"Okay," snapped the impatient President. "We'll do it your way, but if you're wrong, we're running out of time and I'm running out of options, I don't want to be the first President in history to strike three times. But if that's all that's left on the table, so be it."

"Be careful, Mr. President" Derrick cautioned. "He'll pull the trigger rather than take a chance that you'll get the drop on him."

The conversation was interrupted by a call from the Communications Center; a transmission from Libya was being received. "Good, very good," said Walsh with a sigh of relief. "Well, gentlemen, score one for the good guys. He called back."

"It's something," added Derrick, "but be careful. Don't read too much into it. It's just a start."

"Okay," said the President. "Jim," he said as he turned to Chiswell, "Have the Communication Center wait one minute, then put the call through to me."

"Are you sure he won't get pissed off and hang up?"

"I'm not sure of *anything*, but I believe we must portray ourselves as the powerbrokers that we profess to be or he will smell a rat. He's no fool, that I'm sure of,"

"Yes sir, Mr. President," said Chiswell, as he directed Communications to forward the call.

"Imam," the President began, "since we last spoke my advisers and I have continued to review the message that you delivered to the White House three days ago. The process has been arduous, to say the least, for even though I can appreciate your passion, I abhor your methods. It is wrong to threaten any nation. I am aware of the issues that divide us; however, my government is not responsible for choices that were made on someone else's watch, and we are certainly not responsible for what the Crusaders did 800 years ago. Further, sir, you know nothing about me. We have never had the opportunity to sit together and talk about our differing philosophies, the hopes we have for our children, the plans we have for our countries. We have never had the chance to listen to each other, to look into each other's eyes. I'm sure if I get the opportunity I will be looking at someone I can trust. I don't think we're that far apart."

"You have spoken well, Mr. President, and may Allah preserve you for that. We will talk again." Then as quickly as he had appeared, Imam al Fareed vanished.

David Walsh sat back in his chair, allowing the tension to ebb from his body. Chiswell was smiling and giving the thumbs up, but it was Bill Derrick's analysis that the President was interested in. "Bill, how do you think it went?" He asked.

''You kept the door open and bought us some time, Mr. President. But don't let him bait you. Even though it seems he wants to engage in a dialogue, do not take this as an overture of an alliance. I'm not insinuating that this was not a giant step forward; I'm just telling you to be careful."

"I'll heed your warning," Walsh said, feeling too ebullient to let his enthusiasm be quelled. Paging his military aide, he ordered a connection to the Prime Ministers of Great Britain and Israel. "I need to bring John and Eli up to speed on these latest developments. I'm sure they're walking on eggshells about now."

Twenty minutes later, the Communications Officer, had Prime Minister's Lawton and Mordachi on the line. The President looked up at the huge screen, now filled with the images of both men, and said, "gentlemen, I may have some good news." He then related the details of his earlier dialogue with Fareed

"Careful, my friend," said Mordachi. "Remember, Fareed learned from Muammar and is a wily old bastard. I think he has something up his sleeve."

"I must agree with Eli," said John Lawton. "I'm having trouble envisioning you and that Libyan discussing your philosophical differences over brandy and goat meat. Need I remind you that we represent the only countries in the world that you can trust? Everyone else is either too scared of these radicals or they're doing business with Libya and don't want to upset the "oil" cart. There are nations, David, whose support we have counted on in the past that may now distance themselves from us. If there's a showdown in the United Nations, just remember, bullies are feared, not liked."

"David," Eli interrupted, "I believe that an assassination squad is our safest and most efficient way to resolve our problems. I know that it's against the law in your country, but it is not in mine."

"Nor in mine," said John Lawton. "I would love the chance to send my boys in there."

"I'm glad you agree with me, Prime Minister," continued Mordachi, "but the Mossad has been in and out of the palace for years, developing their covers and gleaning intelligence in preparation for just this type of mission. My country has a protocol already in place in the event that something like this should become necessary: I must sign a document of reason ordering their deaths. By doing so, I take full responsibility. However, in this case, I don't believe anyone would oppose me, even without knowing what we were up against."

"I like the idea, David," said Prime Minister Lawton, "especially with all three of the bastards in one place."

"So do I," the President agreed. "This will allow me to focus on protecting our shores, and I can use the Seals and Delta Force to better advantage on this side of the pond. I think we should allow Eli to formalize his plan."

"Gentlemen," said the Israeli Prime Minister, "I told you, we've had a plan in place for years. Agree with me by word only, and I will take care of business."

"Agreed," said, both the President of the United States and the Prime Minister of Great Britain.

"Good. 1 will advise my people and keep you both in the loop." With that, the transmission ended.

"Well, gentlemen, it looks like we have a plan," the President said, sitting back in his chair and allowing himself the luxury of a little guarded optimism. "Bill, I have kept you long enough. You need to catch up with Barbara and see which way the Arab sands are blowing. Should, God forbid, someone leak this, we don't want Eli running into any trouble in his own country."

"Very well, Mr. President," said Derrick, "As soon as I hear anything from my people over there, I'll let you know."

"Bill," said Jim Chiswell, "I'll notify Howe's office that you are on your way to Andrews."

"Thanks, Chief, and thank you, Mr. President." With that one of the President's top advisers took his leave.

"Jim, I want you and the Vice President to go to London to keep your finger on the pulse. If there are any problems, John can send in MI-6 and Cassidy will be there to speak for me if need be. The trip can be heralded as Bill Cassidy's first official visit abroad as the new Vice President. Who better to receive him than our good friends on the other side of the pond? I'll call Prime Minister Lawton and let him know you're coming. He can get his office to put together an itinerary; you know how good the Brits are at ceremony."

"How soon do you want us to leave?"

"ASAP, Jim. I want to know what's going on and I need to know their perspective."

"Yes, sir, I'll coordinate with the Vice President's office and be at the ready. Is there anything I can do for you before I leave?"

"Yes, be safe." Then he quickly asked his Chief to bring him up to speed on Ian Tuttle. "Ian's been on my mind quite a bit lately. I'd like to do something for him, maybe a pardon, when we're through with this mess."

"That's a fine idea, Mr. President. I'll see that you get that information right away."

NSA Communications Center

ECHELON received a transmission that was picked up over the Presidential Palace in Libya shortly after the President and Imam al Fareed finished their conversation. As ordered, the officer on duty had the message transcribed and immediately contacted National Security Director Sercu.

After receiving the document, Sercu buzzed his aide and had him place a call to the President. "Mr. President, we may have already caused an explosion in Libya," he reported. "ECHELON picked up some chatter from the Palace in Tripoli, and it seems that after you and Fareed played nice yesterday, those three crazy Arabs started fighting like snakes with their tails cut off. Saif al Adel is furious because he thinks Fareed is more worried about his own legacy than the Jihad. Al Adel is concerned that a continuing dialogue with you could soften his position on the West. They prefer that Fareed discuss only the efforts of the Jihad, because to him nothing else matters. It seems that as much as he hates America, Fareed sees these conversations as an opportunity to establish himself as the world leader he envisions himself to be."

"So, what do you think, Jim?" the President asked.

"Sir, I think you're going to get another telephone call."

Chairman of the Joint Chiefs General Ned Seiffert and Secretary of Defense Ian McPherson arrived at the bunker for the meeting they had requested with the President. Both men were eager to discuss a new weapon that could very well trump al Fareed before his house of cards came down.

Once both men were seated, McPherson began to brief the President. "Sir, General Seiffert and I have been apprised of a new weapon that might be of immense value. It's called the E-Bomb. It stands for EMP or electro-magnetic pulse. We didn't mention it to you previously because it is still in the developmental stages; however, when we contacted the developer, he said that he had three prototypes ready to go."

"What the hell's an E-Bomb?" asked the President.

"Let me explain," General Seiffert began, taking over the conversation. "As reported by Dr. Carlo Kapp in an article on www.auspower.net, the E-Bomb is designed to destroy all electronics and electrical systems and grids in the country that are under attack. Upon detonation, all telephones will be silent, computers will shut down, and power grids will be rendered useless. If they have GPS systems, they will burn out. Most of the country will be left virtually in the dark—and defenseless I may add. Fareed himself will be prevented from making a simple phone call. Transportation will be the same as it was 2000 years ago—camel or horse. Automobiles will stop in their tracks; planes, if near the detonation, will drop from the sky if lower than 2000 feet or approaching an airport, but only in the country under attack. Not only will a complete meltdown occur, but it will happen without causing the death of thousands of people. Their only salvation is to escape to a different country or live like Nomads. It is something that came from the effects of nuclear explosions. Many countries have been trying to perfect the EMP since the 40's. The basic principal is to create a magnetic field and an electric current simultaneously to produce a field that could be aimed at a target. This pulse within its range would produce a surge in any electrical system large enough to put it away forever."

"Mr. President, this could buy us the time we need to find

those hidden nukes," McPherson interjected. "Libya could be down for years to come. Their oil wells are operated by two to four diesel engines each. The motor blowers, hoisting systems, and everything else associated with those engines would be destroyed. Their economy will be destroyed, and who knows, it might even ignite another revolution. At the very least, it will cause Fareed some very serious problems at home and abroad. Our intelligence says that Libya has the codes to detonate the bombs that are implanted here and if that is correct—and I believe it is—then the Electro-Magnetic Bomb has the potential to save hundreds of thousands of lives on both sides."

The President listened with serious intent, for his mind was spinning rapidly. "Sir," said McPherson, "in his article Dr. Kapp further describes the E-bomb; saying it is, to quote, 'a well-designed weapon that will flood the target with a GigaWatt class 'chirped' pulse, or a short train of pulses, capable of coupling through cables, ventilation grills, or gaps, producing gate punch-through or avalanche breakdown effects in semiconductor electronics.' In other words, nothing electrical will survive. It will produce a crippling effect which, I would think, is exactly what we want."

The President's aide suddenly interrupted the conversation to report that a transmission was coming in from Libya. The President motioned to his advisers to stay seated, then ordered the soldier to put the call through. He also asked the aide to get Bill Derrick on the line from the Secretary of State's plane. Within minutes Fareed's image was before him on the screen.

"Greetings, Mr. President, and May Allah and your God preserve you," Imam al Fareed said in perfect English.

"Good evening, Mr. President, and May our God and Allah preserve you as well," the President countered, feeling like he was playing nuclear chess and praying that he was not a pawn. "To what do I owe this communication?"

"I have been entertaining two of your friends in my private quarters and..."

"Let me assure you, Imam," President Walsh interrupted, "I am in no way a friend of your two guests. They have tried to eliminate my country, its people, and our culture. Al-Qaeda and its emissaries have no country. Osama himself was made persona non grata, as were all al-Qaeda Central members by the Saudis after they pursued the overthrow of their royal family, even though they had once welcomed his father, and made him a very wealthy man. It is a good thing for your world and mine that he now sleeps with the fishes. Why do you need people such as these? Has your influence in the region diminished, or are your friends afraid that your conviction to the Jihad could be softened by words of peace?"

Fareed stopped speaking English and reverted to Arabic. No one talked to him this way in his country and lived to tell about it.

Suddenly, Walsh changed his tone. "Mr. President, I believe that you and I can find common ground to bring lasting peace to your region and the world. Israel will be here long after you and I are gone, that's a given, but it will be back to its original borders. I have spoken with Prime Minister Mordachi, and he has agreed to this. That is a giant step in a journey that is both difficult and deliberate. Peace requires patience and nurturing."

Fareed was still muttering in his own language when Walsh turned to his interpreter and said "I am ordering you to translate every word of what I am about to say exactly the way I say it. No polite diplomatic terms. I want this verbatim." Then he leaned forward on his elbows and said "But let me assure you, Imam al Fareed, I will not be bullied. I have taken an oath to defend freedom at any cost, and I will use any means that I deem necessary to keep that promise. At my fingertips is the power to destroy every living thing in your country. Every man, woman and child, including your own, will perish. You may be able to take out some of our cities, but Americans have the resolve to rebuild. That is our heritage. You, though, will have no hope of recovery."

Suddenly, Atwa and Salan appeared next to Fareed and caught the President off guard. "Mr. President, ..." Atwa began in broken English.

Furious at this turn of events, the President interrupted him immediately. "President Fareed, I will talk to you and only you. I refuse to speak with people I'm inclined to despise. I will break all communication with you if they do not step back and leave the room."

Atwa continued. "You must listen to me. I have instructed my people who are at your door, residents in your country. I have ordered them to show how committed we are and how vulnerable you are. We do not care if we receive any communication from you. We are only concerned with the Jihad and the destruction of the Great Satan. Should we die, then we will be welcomed by Allah. We are not afraid; that is our belief."

As soon as Atwa stopped speaking, the line went dead.

The President looked at his Secretary of Defense for his reaction and was met with a shrug of his shoulders and a shake of his head. "I'm not going to let that son-of-a-bitch ruin this country."

"It certainly looks like he's going to try," said McPherson.

"What's your take on all this, Bill?" the President asked Bill Derrick, who was skyped in from Secretary Howe's plane.

"Well, Mr. President, judging from the way Atwa seemed to be speaking for the three of them, I am certain that al-Qaeda is running the show from who knows where. I think Fareed wanted to return to the world stage and financing the Jihad was his ticket. I believe he sees his destiny as different from the others; they see themselves as servants of Allah and he sees himself as a soldier of Allah. He'll call, Mr. President. Believe me, he'll call."

"Thank you for your input Bill, I'll be in touch." With that, the screen went blank and the President turned back to his advisers. The Secretary of Defense was the first to speak.

"I'm not sure it matters if al Fareed calls. Bill just said that Atwa was calling the shots, and he's not going to be happy until the West goes up in smoke."

"I concur with Ian." said General Seiffert. "In my opinion, I believe we should take the initiative, and at present, the E-Bomb is our best friend."

"You feel good about this even though it is still in the experimental stages?" the President asked Seiffert.

"Yes, sir, I spoke with the developer myself."

"Okay," said the President. "What's our next move?"

"Give the order and 'Operation Lights Out' will get under way," said General Seiffert. "I'll contact the developer and have him prepare his prototypes for pick-up by a US Army convoy. As soon as they're ready, the bombs will be loaded onto a flatbed truck and transported under military escort to the Naval Base in Norfolk. There, they will be loaded onto three separate C-2 cargo planes that will deliver them to the *USS Ronald Reagan*. We're going to use three planes to ensure the success of the mission. The loss of all three of these bombs, for whatever reason, would be devastating and could shift the balance of power right back to Fareed. When the delivery has been made, Secretary of Defense McPherson will instruct the Commander of the *Reagan* to commence. One bomber and four fighter escorts will deliver the first payload. As soon as the bomber is over Tripoli, it's lights out for Libya."

"General, in your opinion, can we knock out the nuclear codes with this device?" the President asked.

"If the codes are in Tripoli they will be rendered useless," said Seiffert, "but if they are in the hands of an operative 100 miles outside the city, they could only be incapacitated if a telephone was used as the detonator. You see, sir, there are three ways to detonate a nuclear bomb that is already in place. The first and easiest is to enlist a kamikaze to guard the device and set it off at a certain time. If that is the case, neither the E-Bomb nor anything else will save us. The second is to detonate the bomb by telephone. This process requires that a power pack be attached to the phone, but that is simply a matter of connecting a few wires. After the pulse of an incoming call is routed through a preprogrammed signature detector, it opens the circuit to a microprocessor in which the code has been stored. The microprocessor automatically compares the stored code with the incoming code and, if they match, a five-volt charge of electricity is released into the bomb. All anyone would have to do is call the number from anywhere on earth and feed in the codes. The catch here is we have no way of knowing whether or not the Soviets had this technology when these bombs were placed, and there's no time to find out. However, we don't believe Fareed and company, or any other terrorist, would use a phone. Too much could go wrong."

"Like the E-Bomb?" the President quipped.

"Yes, sir, exactly," replied Seiffert. "We believe they will use the third and most efficient method, low frequency radio waves that bounce off the ionosphere and come back to earth to detonate the bomb. Choosing a radio would give the terrorist more flexibility and greater security than other methods. It operates independently of any existing communication system and its origin is impossible to track."

"How does it work?" the President asked.

"For example, if the radio was on a ship in the Mediterranean Sea, it would take one megahertz or one million cycles to detonate a bomb."

"Is there a reason you used that particular example?" McPherson asked, breaking his silence.

"Putting myself in Fareed's place," Seiffert replied, I would want a failsafe system; a tramp steamer already at sea or a terrorist cell in place in another country, even somewhere in the US. That way his plan could be implemented with the greatest amount of certainty."

"Well," said the President "let's hope Fareed will hate us so much that he wants to control the activation. If we drop the E-Bomb and he's powerless as long as he's within one hundred miles of the drop, then we must make sure we can somehow contain him. Anything else, General?"

"I have only one more thing to add, sir," General Seiffert concluded. "There is no technology available that can block a transmission or code coming into the USA. The E-Bomb is our only option, other than a proactive nuclear strike."

"Then let's hope it works. Thank you, General." President Walsh stood to adjourn the meeting.

As the two men moved toward the door, McPherson suddenly turned and asked, "Sir, we are about to bomb another country. Terrorist haven or not, we need a formal declaration of war."

"We have it. The Speaker of the House sent it over this morning."

Congressional Declaration of War
on
The State of Libya
10 September 2015

JOINT RESOLUTION: Declaring that a state of war exists between the Government of Libya and the Government and the people of the United States of America, and making provisions to prosecute the same.

WHEREAS: The Government of Libya has committed

unprovoked acts of war and terror against the government and the people of the United States of America. Therefore it is resolved by the Senate and the House of Representatives in Congress assembled, that the state of war between the United States of America and the State of Libya, which has been thrust upon the United States of America is hereby formally declared: and the President of the United States is authorized and directed to employ the entire naval and military forces of the United States and the resources of its Government to carry on war against the Government of the State of Libya and any and all other countries who harbor, train or finance terrorists on their lands: and to bring the conflict to a successful termination. The Congress of the United States hereby pledges all the resources of the United States of America.

DAVID J. WALSH
PRESIDENT OF THE UNITED STATES

JUDITH PIGG CARTER
SPEAKER OF THE HOUSE OF REPRESENTATIVES

APPROVED: BY THE UNITED STATES CONGRESS IN JOINT
SESSION ON THIS DAY
TIME: 1400 HOURS, GMT,
10, SEPTEMBER 2015

Chapter 19

MOSSAD HEADQUARTERS
KING SAUL BOULEVARD
TEL AVIV

The Mossad, formally known as the Institute for Intelligence and Special Tasks or (ha-mossasle-modin ule-tafkidi m meyuhadim) is the most ruthless organization of its kind anywhere in the world. Since its inception in 1951, Israel had used the Mossad to perpetrate violence and terror against its enemies. Focusing mainly on Arab nations and those individuals that Israel considered a danger to its state of being, the Mossad is relentless in its pursuit of a target and will not hesitate to 'burn' an agent to save a mission or capture a spy. This highly efficient intelligence agency is comprised of eight separate divisions ranging from intelligence to covert operations and counter terrorism.

The Special Operations Division, AKA the Metsada, is responsible for highly sensitive assignments, such as sabotage, paramilitary operations, and psychological warfare projects. This team will receive the warrants of execution making Imam al Fareed, Farhad Atwa, and Halem Salan marked men.

Members of this division are trained to work as a team, but until they receive their orders, their identities are kept secret. The Case Officer, or Katsa, is the person to whom the other members report. A Kidon is an operative specializing in assassination. He or she usually lives in the country where the operation will take place. These operatives are inserted into the population of the host country with TUED—perfectly forged identity papers. They are even supplied rent receipts, credit cards, and employment in dummy corporations. Fluent in the area's language, they hold regular jobs, raise families, and pay taxes. Kidons are so well buried that their identities may be unknown even to their families.

Before any plan can be initiated, the operatives are briefed on every aspect of the target or targets. Daily routines, personal idiosyncrasies, and family relationships are reviewed, as well as the design of the target's home and the amount and type of security that surrounds them; no detail is too small. After the preplanning has been reviewed and approved by Director General Halvery, then and only then will the orders be given to initiate the termination of one or more persons who threaten the State of Israel or her friends.

The Mossad is known for running its organization with ruthless precision. Today, however, General Halvery was not ready to approve the plan that would culminate in the deaths of the three Arab leaders. He had voiced frustration at Prime Minister Mordachi's order, believing that Israel should not be doing America's dirty work. After a brief and one-sided discussion with the Prime Minster, the Director was made to understand that this was to be the most important assignment of his career. Realizing that a swift response was paramount to the success of the mission, Director General Halvery returned to King Saul Boulevard to implement the orders and contact the Katsa already living in Libya.

Al Birkah, Libya

Three hundred and fifty miles south-east of Tripoli, just over the border from Tin Alkoum, lived a family of nomads. Ali Bin Rachide and his family lived near this small border town mainly because it provided the Mossad Kidon with the opportunity to easily escape the country. Ali knew firsthand how difficult that could be.

Ali was his given name, and he was actually a native of Libya. He immigrated to Israel under the name of Rali Solomon with what was left of his family after his mother and father were killed when Colonel Quadafi overthrew the government and installed himself as the new ruler. The family had been strict Royalists; his father was House administrator for King Idris at the time of his death. Ali was lucky to escape and vowed that someday he would return to Libya and avenge his father's death. He became a citizen of Israel and, when he was old enough, he sought employment within its intelligence service. What better recruit for the Mossad?

Years had gone by since he had received his training and was ordered back to Libya to don the filthy robes of a desert dweller. It was a hard existence in a godforsaken part of the world. At night, he and his family survived temperatures close to freezing and during the day they worked in the parched desert sands. Ali, as he was once again called, lived the life of a Bedouin tribesman, roaming the great Sahara. As a camel trader and breeder, he could move freely about the country, but he preferred to adhere to the Bedouin way and only came into town periodically for supplies. He wore a sheep's wool hupla and a hat that identified him as a Sarami tribesman. The Sarami were the oldest sect of the Islamic Sufi and roamed the Sahara for centuries. They were fanatical in their beliefs and were greatly feared by the other tribes, even the Wahabi. The Mossad had created the perfect cover for a person who was trained to kill.

Ali was making one of his periodic trips to town when he saw a vaguely familiar person walking toward the coffee house. After corralling his herd, he cautiously followed the man inside to see if he could get a better look. As the man approached, memories came roaring back and Ali knew immediately that his waiting days were finally over.

The two men talked quietly for some time, and then Ali left the coffee house and finished his business in town before returning to Riana, his wife. He did not want to jeopardize this chance by drawing any attention to himself. Sitting together that night, he gently touched her hand and told her that the time had come. For the first time, Ali saw his wife's eyes well with tears as she whispered to him that she was sad, not only for her children and herself, but also for him. They held each other as they had on their wedding night, and slowly fell asleep.

Two days later, Riana took her children into town where she was met by a couple who told her she could stay with them until she could be reunited with her husband in Israel. Riana sadly began her journey, doubting that she would ever see her beloved Ali again.

With his family safe, Ali left for Tripoli. A journey of 350 miles across desert sands. He had plenty of supplies and the remainder of the herd that he had not sold in Al Birkah. His plan was to stop midway through the journey at an oasis where he could sell the rest of his herd, or scatter them to roam the desert and blame another tribe for stealing them while he slept. There, he would meet his Katsa and together they would travel the rest of the way. When they had completed their journey and Ali had been safely placed with 'friends'; then and only then would he learn of the enormity of his mission.

Chapter 20

PRESIDENTIAL COMMAND CENTER

*T*he President looked up when the Communications Officer was escorted into his private office. The distraction made him realize how much he depended upon Chiswell for everything, from the smallest detail to saving the world. But he knew that the new Vice President needed Jim, especially if things turned sour over here.

"Mr. President, you have a communiqué from Prime Minister Mordachi," the young soldier said as he handed the envelope to his Commander in Chief.

"Thank you, Lieutenant," said Walsh. "That's all."

"Thank you, Mr. President." He saluted smartly and took his leave.

David Walsh leaned back in his chair, opened the communiqué, and read the words:

Documents signed. Plan initiated.

The President look a deep breath and thought to himself, "Christians one, Lions zero." They could complain all they want about the Jewish psyche, but when the chips were down, they were one of a handful of friends left for America.

President Walsh's National Address

NNC carried live the first Presidential message broadcast from the East Wing bunker. The sparse surroundings were a sharp contrast to the President's previous speeches, which had been staged in the opulence of the Oval Office. The disparity was ominous to an already terrified nation, as the people saw their leader buried 150 feet below the symbol of the Presidency itself, sleeves rolled up, dead tired, leading the fight against the religious fanaticism that sought to destroy freedom.

Looking straight into the camera, speaking slowly and deliberately, the President began his transmission.

"Good evening, my fellow Americans and peace-loving people around the world. It is with a heavy heart that I come to you tonight. The triumvirate of Imam al Fareed, the new leader of

Libya, Halem Salan, and Farhad Atwa has threatened to initiate nuclear war against the people of the United States of America and the principles by which we live. We can no longer remain in the abyss of political diplomacy while the factions of evil seek to destroy us. For these reasons I have decided that the best way to deal with these terrorists is not to deal with them at all.

"To this end, I have today signed an official declaration of war against Libya and any other country that harbors terrorists. All diplomatic options remain open and America, as always, is committed to a peaceful resolution of our differences. However, as of now, I have been unable to convince our enemies that although our philosophies differ, our goals are the same: love, family, respect.

"Because of this national emergency I have ordered all Islamic students holding an educational visa, or those holding visitor or work-related visas, to leave the United States within 48 hours or be detained as enemy combatants.

"To our enemies I say to you: America is a generous nation that will always provide shelter to those seeking emancipation from tyranny. The American way is to welcome all who seek the freedom to worship as they please, love with their hearts, and pursue their dreams. Americans will defend those principles with the same conviction that permitted our forefathers to persevere during the long winters at Valley Forge. We are not afraid to fight or die for what we believe in; that is our heritage and that is our promise.

"Former Secretary of Defense William Cassidy has been confirmed as the new Vice President, with Ian McPherson replacing him as Secretary of Defense. As you see, we will go on. Thank you and good night."

With that, President David Walsh left the homes of the people he loved.

Chapter 21

NEST HEADQUARTERS
WASHINGTON, DC.

*S*ix years ago, Homeland Security created a high level department known as NEST to find any unaccounted-for nuclear devices and render them harmless if possible. The missions usually entailed searching for nukes that had fallen from airplanes; however, since its inception, the team has responded three times to direct threats of nuclear retaliation. Because of the urgency of these missions, NEST is allowed to search and retrieve without permission or warrants. The last three situations were just threats, mostly a sick mind's fantasy or al-Qaeda trying to cause panic. But Jake Perry knew this time was different. A graduate of MIT with a degree in structural engineering, Jake is the Chief Investigator for NEST, and the reason for its success.

It was a warm September morning when Jake received his orders from David O'Brian, the Director of Homeland Security: Search every building in the District and beyond for Russian made suitcase bombs installed during the cold war. After consulting with the other members of his team of engineers, Jake decided to focus the search on only those buildings constructed prior to 1983 and to pay particular attention to Federal historic sites. There were three teams of two men each, plus a woman nuclear physicist on loan from the Mossad who Jake had met at MIT undergraduate school. Laura Preston and Jake Perry were friends and worked very well together. Jake knew that having Laura on board would make life much easier because of her reputation and experience in the field. She also held a doctorate degree from Oxford in nuclear physics, and had a highly regarded reputation in her field for her cleverness in searching for these bombs.

While at Oxford she was recruited by the Mossad as a Honey Trap—a person who lures enemy targets to her lair for assassination purposes. She would then set them up for the kill with a Kidon, which is an operative specializing in assassinations. The recruiting officer was Anna Kleberg, who became her best friend and operating partner.

Now, with a doctorate in her back pocket, Laura led a very interesting life. Israel receives more nuclear threats than any country in the world, so she had become a very busy woman. The Mossad was pleased that they could kill two birds with one stone. Each NEST team had the use of a van specially built by GM and equipped with the latest nuclear detection devices. Aside from Geiger counters, the vans carried highly sensitive sniffers, custom tools, and robots to find and retrieve nuclear bombs.

Jake decided to search the area around the White House and Treasury himself. Beginning with the Executive Mansion, he and the other members in his unit worked their way down Pennsylvania Avenue. When Jake was approaching the FBI building on the corner of 14th Street, a thought suddenly hit him—it would be almost impossible for anyone of a foreign nationality to deliver and install a 350-pound suitcase bomb encased in a sheath of lead in highly guarded buildings. However, it could be accomplished if the bombs were placed in areas that were easily accessible, like parking garages or hotel basements, and there were plenty of those. Jake notified the members of his teams to concentrate on buildings with delivery services that had easy access, and little or no security. If he was right, it was an ingenious plot. He also instructed them not to touch anything until he and Laura investigated it first.

The unit continued their search down Pennsylvania Avenue to 6th Street. Jake was ready to go back to the office for a working dinner when he decided to look at one more building.

601 Pennsylvania Avenue was home to several offices and a famous restaurant called the Capital Grill, a favorite with Washington's elite. Just around the corner on 6th street is the entrance to the parking garage that services the entire building. Jake knew that he needed to investigate the storied old building now. Throughout his career, he had learned to trust his gut and he was not about to stop, not with the clock ticking.

The two entered through the service entrance, and separated to check out every inch of the basement before working their way to the other floors. Jake immediately noticed something about the heating and air conditioning equipment that just didn't look right. There was too much apparatus for a basic system. This small system had probably been added for someone's office back in the fifties and was never removed when it became obsolete. The newer system was stored on the roof. After reviewing the blueprints and mechanicals of the building one more time, Jake and his assistant headed back into the basement. At first, they didn't notice anything out of the ordinary. Suddenly, Laura shouted, "Jake, get your ass over here! Is this furnace sitting on a metal box or am I dreaming?"

"What have you got?" he asked as he ran to her side. She had already started testing for radiation leakage.

"Look at this; you know there is no way a company reputable enough to work on a building like this would do such a shoddy job. Have you ever seen anything like this gray steel box before?"

"It looks like painted cement, Laura, to make it look like a part of the installation," he said. "Get the HAZ-MAT suits and a hand drill out of the truck. If my hunch is right, we're going to need to report this to Homeland right away and see how they want to handle it."

Preston came back with the equipment, and the two donned their suits. Jake turned on the sniffer and Geiger counter while she tried drilling a one-inch hole in the side of the box. Neither one of them had any idea how thick the metal was, so she took her time. Drilling very slowly, she broke through the coffin-sized box without incident and sure enough, it was made of lead. Jake turned the sniffer and Geiger counter toward the box and the counter started clacking like an old lady. The alarm from the sniffer also sounded, causing some men who were working in the parking garage to come running.

"Christ Almighty!" exclaimed one of them. "What happened?"

"We got ourselves a live one," Preston exclaimed, and before Jake could put a lid on her, she announced, "Honest to God, a real live frigging nuke, and a Russian one at that."

Jake knew that he needed to report to the Agency immediately. He dialed the direct line and addressed his boss. "Mr. Secretary, we just found the bomb. It's probably forty – fifty years old but it looks good as new. It was encased in lead so it couldn't be detected. I have a bomb truck on site. We found the thing in the parking garage of the Capitol Grill. What's the next step?"

Jake's orders were to load the bomb onto the truck supplied by the bomb disposal unit and deliver it to a US Naval ship docked at Camden Yards in Baltimore.

Four men carefully extricated the bomb from the site where it had been placed decades before. Homeland Security decided to clear the area of pedestrians, and the restaurant was evacuated. Jake and Laura chuckled to themselves at this benign gesture, for if the bomb exploded everything in its path for a mile and a half radius would cease to exist.

Jake decided to drive the truck himself and asked his partner to ride shotgun. He knew he could depend on Laura; she knew exactly what to do in a situation like this. There was no one that he trusted more.

The two of them traveled to Baltimore under police escort via the beltway which was closed both ways to all traffic. They remained silent for most of the trip. These two had very different personalities. Jake was gruff and demanding, while Laura was a tall athletic girl who smiled a lot. Jake was sweating profusely and Laura wasn't stressed at all. "You know, it doesn't make any difference if we are on top of this thing or a mile away," she said. "We're cooked if something goes wrong."

"Thanks for the encouragement; that really makes me feel real warm and fuzzy. You really know how to say the right thing to a guy. How in the hell did you ever keep a relationship with someone?"

"None of your business, Jake, just keep your mind clear and out of the gutter for once and pay attention." The two laughed, knowing that venting was the best possible stress release.

Jake's cell phone began to ring; he saw that it was the Secretary of Homeland Security. Flipping up the cover, he heard Secretary O'Brian's voice booming out of the tiny earpiece.

"Jake, there's been a change of plans. We're going to deliver the bomb via helicopter to the *USS Paul C. Holmes*. She's a destroyer located about 100 miles off shore, just east of the mouth of the Chesapeake. Her Captain, Lou Irmisch, has already been notified and they'll be ready to accept the package. The navy is sending three nuclear engineers to the *Holmes*, but I want the two of you to go aboard and supervise the off-loading of the bomb. There will be no more changes. It was bad enough that we were going to load the thing on a naval ship that didn't have access to the ocean. Incredibly, or should I say sadly, no one factored the collapse of the bridge into the contingency plan, even though we have all been watching the carnage on NNC for days now."

"Where are we meeting the chopper, sir?" Jake asked, annoyed that not only did he and Laura have to baby sit the cargo but when they arrived they would have to supervise a team that probably had questionable experience to handle such a situation. The Secretary should have given that job to him and Preston in the first place. "Camden Yards," replied the Secretary. "Good luck, Jake," and with that, the line went dead.

"Slight change of plans, Laura." When he didn't hear her customary tirade, he glanced over at his friend. "Did you hear me?" Jake repeated.

"I'm just thinking," she said.

"Sorry," said Jake, wondering what he had done to antagonize the person he needed most right now. His shrink would have a field day with that; if he lived to tell him about it that is.

"Why the change?" she asked

"It's unbelievable. Our government is one big FUBAR. The problem is they don't confer with one another and when an emergency arises, the left hand thinks the right hand has taken care of the problem and the result is the problem doesn't get fixed."

"What the hell are you talking about?"

"I'm talking about contingency plans. Everyone with a brain knew the fucking bridge was blown and the channel was blocked, but here we are, driving to the harbor with a nuke in the back seat so we can load it onto a ship that has no access to the sea. That's what I'm talking about."

"Man that just can't be true!" Laura said.

"Oh, yes, it is. After all, they've known since the 80's that the bombs were hidden somewhere in the U.S. It was documented in a top-secret report that was put on the back shelf when we started playing footsy with the Ruskies. What bullshit! Wouldn't you, as President, search every frigging building in every major city?"

"I don't know, Jake, I don't know. Maybe he was afraid of public panic, who knows what those people do? I guess that's why I'm driving around with a nuke and not living at 1600 Pennsylvania Avenue. I think we should stop bitching and just get the job done. Then we can make ourselves heard. That is, if there's anyone left to listen."

The exchange at Camden Yards went off without a hitch, and the pair, with the bomb, was airlifted to the *Holmes*.

Chapter 22

ON BOARD THE USS PAUL C. HOLMES

The Captain of the *Holmes* had just issued a new set of orders: The use of all cell phones, personal computers, and E-mail were now prohibited due to the sensitivity of the incoming cargo. Captain Irmisch worried about his jittery crew, many of them newly enlisted and away from home for the first time. Emotions had been running high on deck ever since he had briefed them on the nature of the incoming cargo, and these new restrictions weren't going to help bolster morale. He couldn't blame them; he wasn't too happy about these new orders either.

As Captain Irmisch looked out over the sea he loved, he pondered the decision that could very well end his life. Disillusioned with the politics of medicine, he had walked away from his lucrative practice for another tour of duty and one last chance to see the world through a porthole. Older than most of his peers, he knew full well that he would be facing retirement or a dockside desk the next time around. At the time, he thought it was worth it; now he wasn't so sure. What the hell, he thought to himself, I would still rather have the challenge of bringing on a 40-year-old nuke for deactivation than remain a medical examiner or go into research trying to develop a cure for rectal itch. Excitement beats boredom every time.

He was at his desk when the intercom rang twice. Two pings signaled the necessity of a stat response, so he quickly picked up the receiver. "Yes, what is it?"

"Captain, a Coast Guard helicopter is approaching from the west. The pilot is asking for you, sir."

"I'll be right up. Notify him that he has permission to land, and I'll see him on deck."

Irmisch replaced the receiver and left immediately for the Hilo-Pad to greet his cargo. Minutes earlier, the chopper carrying the nuclear engineers enlisted by the Defense Department had landed.

Once on board the ship, Jake and Laura supervised the off-loading of the cargo and secured it so it would not move about in the heavy seas.

They had gone below to get some coffee and wait for their ride home when the chief engineer approached them, requesting their assistance and asking if they would remain on board overnight. Neither one was pleased, but they both knew that one phone call would change the request to an order, so they just shrugged their shoulders and followed the scientist to the Captain's Galley. The meeting with the three civilian engineers lasted more than an hour, and it was decided that Jake and Laura would stay while the others left the ship. They felt that due to the age of the bomb and the conditions that they would be working under, the mission was too dangerous to undertake. Besides, they were not military and they did not have to obey orders. Jake arranged for the three civilians to fly back to Baltimore, then called Secretary O'Brian with the news.

Perry and Preston left the galley and went straight to where the bomb was tethered. A tent had been set up over the weapon so they would be sheltered from the wind and spray. Their first step was to cut away the square-shaped lead shield and lift it out of the way so they could inspect the bomb. They both looked down and then at each other, nobody making the first move.

"What the hell," said Laura, "I guess it's ladies first?" She reached inside the lead container and inspected the wires. After concluding that they were in good condition she proceeded to the next step. Jake stepped up to the bomb to confirm what she had claimed.

"What do you think?" he asked.

"You know of course, the purpose of the lead shield is to prevent leaking radioactivity. The fact that it prevents detection by sniffers or Geiger counters and protects the device from the elements is secondary. In order for the device to work properly, everything must be kept away from the armed payload. If any other mechanisms, such as the code receiver or timer, were to deteriorate because of age and interfere with the payload, the danger would increase tenfold."

"I know that, Laura."

"I know you know," she replied, "I just need to talk out loud. This looks good. No visible signs of rot; the wiring looks fresh and dry. However, the neuron flux of the bomb's payload is strong enough to short out the internal circuitry and cause premature detonation if we're not cautious."

"So just how bad do you think it is? Are we going to see the light of day?"

"Just say a prayer, stop talking, and give me a hand. I'll check for trick timers and you check the fuses. Remember, they are also installed as a safeguard to prevent an accidental detonation. Our biggest nightmare is if they are too old. These things are usually set near the surface of the nose of the bomb so they can be easily installed, usually right before launch. But these were set decades ago, and that makes them even more dangerous."

Laura trailed off without finishing her thought, focusing instead on something she discovered. "What's wrong, Laura?" Jake asked.

"This thing looks like it was made by a rogue nation rather than the Soviet Union. The uranium though, is most likely U-235."

"Well, if this thing explodes, it won't make any difference what kind of uranium it is. I don't know why we just don't drop the fucking thing in the ocean and go home. All it will do is kill a few sharks."

"Not really, Jake. A sub-surface explosion is the worst of all possible worlds, you know that. The contamination will stay around for years before it dissipates, and that alone would prevent any cargo or military ship from approaching the Bay. It must be dismantled here and now."

"Okay, then let's scan her and see what we've got."

After inspecting the mechanics of the bomb with an x-ray, the two concluded that there were no tricks inside the casing. The lead shield had prevented air and pollutants from deteriorating the inner workings. The consensus, however, was that a radio altimeter would be the method used to detonate the bomb. This made sense, for a terrorist could be anywhere in the world and all he had to do was push a button when he was ready to detonate.

Jake went up to the bridge to check the weather report and returned with a scowl on his face. "Laura, the weather's closing in. Let's do this thing now and get the hell out of here. Okay?"

Laura suddenly stepped away from the bomb, "Something's not right."

"How so?"

"The timer should be below the casing that holds the uranium. It's that way on all nukes."

"Could this be a booby trap? Do you think we stumbled onto something before we were supposed to, or do you think there may be two timers?" Jake asked. "And if there are two timers, which one do we pull out first?"

"I'm not sure this thing's not a fake, my friend."

"What makes you think that? We ran the tests together on-site, and the sniffer detected uranium. What's so difficult about that?"

"I'm not sure what's going on. Perhaps they planted a fake to throw us off course and the real one is placed somewhere closer to the White House or the Capitol Building. After all, those are the locations that would exact the maximum amount of damage to your government."

"What in hell are you talking about?"

"Just listen to what I say. If death and contamination is the objective, then a surface bomb is the way to go."

"You're right," Jake said. "Besides, a surface bomb like this is designed to blow up bunkers. Super detonations are made to lift up radioactive material; bombs of this design are capable of going down 320 feet below the surface. If the President is in his bunker and the thing explodes, bye-bye Mr. President."

"I thought the shelter below the White House was impervious to everything."

"How do you know? Has anyone ever tested the strength of the steel that it's made of? Besides, you know as well as I do that when the cold war ended, everyone eased up. There's no telling when the last time that bunker was thoroughly examined. The government says it's safe, but I'm not so sure."

"Well," Laura said, "let's let the big guys worry about that. Our job is to dismantle this monster."

"Let's x-ray it again and maybe we can come up with some better answers," Jake proposed. "Say a prayer, and hope it goes from our lips to God's ears."

The two continued to dismantle the bomb, methodically taking it apart, one small piece at a time. It seemed to take an eternity, but when they finished, their suspicions were confirmed—the bomb was a fake. There was a possibility that it was Russian-made, but there was no signature on any of the parts. Jake left to call the Secretary of Homeland Security, and Laura started packing up the pieces, wondering who would go to all the trouble to plant a dead nuke. When Jake returned, he told her that the bomb was going to be stored in a secure warehouse for forensic study, and they were to go back to D.C.

And to square one.

Chapter 23

TRIPOLI
REPUBLIC OF LIBYA

*T*wenty minutes after the E-Bomb exploded, Tripoli was dark and chaotic. All electronic devices, as well as electrical grids and equipment within a hundred-mile radius, had been fused by the blast. Everything from hearing aids and car batteries and airplanes to the diesel engines that run the oil wells were wiped out permanently. Communication ceased and animals were the only mode of transportation. Anything with a battery or electrical was dead.

The United States had dropped only one of the strictly experimental bombs. Top strategists decided that crippling Tripoli could buy the U.S. enough time to find the hidden nukes, so they delivered only one of the E-Bombs and opted to save the others for a rainy day.

Al Fareed was reeling. Ever since he helped depose King Idris, he had dedicated his life to eradicating all other religions from his country. His hatred of Western degeneracy had become an obsession in recent years, so much so that he had devoted all of his waking moments—and many millions of dollars—to destroying the Great Satan. But Fareed was wise and knew he had made a mistake. He had let ego and ambition make an old man out of the dedicated soldier of Allah. The American President had tricked him; President Walsh did not want to discuss philosophy nor was he going to ensure him a seat at the table where the leaders of the world met. Imam al Fareed had been deceived, and he would seek revenge.

Fareed needed to detonate just one bomb to bring the Western dogs to their knees, and Washington was at the top of the list. If the symbol of liberty and freedom were destroyed, panic would permeate the nations of the West and chaos would rule. Fareed would also exact his revenge on the American pig that made a fool out of him. But to accomplish this, he must leave Tripoli. Now.

Mossad Safe House

Ali bin Rachide had been waiting for this moment. Ever since arriving at the safe house, he had spent hours memorizing the original plans of the Presidential Palace. He knew how many steps there were from the steel door that separated the sewer from the cellar of Fareed's private quarters, to the chambers of Farad Atwa and Halem Salan. The assassination itself had been rehearsed with the members of his team many times and all concurred: The time was now.

The Mossad Kidon left the safe house wearing a Kevlar bulletproof vest and armed with two weapons in addition to his usual fighting knives: an Uzi with six extra clips and a Glock 9MM with a silencer and additional clips carrying 15 rounds of ammunition each. He made his way through the streets of the powerless city to the place where the sewer intersected the river. The team had decided that this was the safest approach to the palace.

Ali had gotten into position by the entrance to the sewer when an explosion rocked the city and the capital began to burn. Fearful of what was happening, he quickly debated whether to return to the safe house and determine if this unexpected disaster would compromise his mission or continue on as planned. He checked his surroundings. Street lights had lost their power, automobiles had stopped dead in their tracks, and cell phones had become passé. Pandemonium was everywhere.

Ali decided that the confusion was a gift from God. It would now be easier for him to gain entrance to the palace and carry out his mission while the guards were distracted by the chaos. He would go now; he *must* go now. Long ago, Ali had made a vow to avenge his family and serve his adopted land. He was not going to let anything divert him from his destiny. He had waited so long, come so far, and was so close, so very close. He entered the sewer and edged along until he reached the entrance to the palace. He was in the process of rigging a small explosive device to the steel grill of the door that separates the cellar from the sewer when he was discovered by three of Fareed's soldiers on patrol. The men had been sent by the Commander of the Guard to inspect all exits and entrances in the palace after the E-Bomb hit and the security systems went down.

The first guard grabbed Ali by the thick of his hair while the other slammed the butt of his rifle into Ali's kidneys. The riveting pain was beginning to subside when Ali was forced to his feet by the two guards while the third started screaming at him. "Look at the sewer rat, crawling through the shit to sneak into the palace. Fucking rat, I'll show you what we do to fucking sewer rats around here." He aimed his nine-millimeter Berretta at Ali and shot him in the leg.

They then dragged him into a holding cell where he would remain without medical attention, food, or water until they received further orders from their Commander. Fareed, distracted by the blackout, ordered one of his deputies to interrogate Ali and, when he was finished, just kill him.

Forty-eight hours elapsed without word from Ali, and the Katsa feared him dead or worse. If Ali had revealed the details of their plan, it wouldn't take Fareed's advisers long to figure out the Mossad was responsible for the attempted assassination. From there, they could merely follow the dots to Israel, Great Britain and the United States. This information would not only damage the reputation of the Mossad, it would compromise Israel's ability to negotiate with other nations in the Arab world, one of which may have the bomb soon. The President, however, would never learn the truth, for the bullet that had pierced Ali's leg severed his femoral artery and Ali bled out in his cell without ever uttering a word.

Fareed was holding a rare meeting with his top advisers and the Director of Security. The group had failed to come up with any tangible plan and the impatient President was becoming enraged. Suddenly, he announced that he would travel to the town of Hun, a journey of approximately 200 miles across the desert.

Fareed remembered that before the embargo, one of the Dutch oil companies had installed a sophisticated communications system. During the insurrection, Gaddafi had taken it over and converted it for his own use; now it was his. A tribe of Bedouins now occupied the town and that made his plan all the more viable. He hoped that if he reached Hun, he could contact the agent waiting for his order to detonate the 15-kiloton bomb hidden in Washington D.C. The leader prayed to Allah that Hun was not also in darkness.

Fareed ordered his Director of Security to assemble a band of twenty accomplished horsemen to accompany him across the desert. He wasn't waiting for anyone, just as destiny was not going to wait for him.

This is where Allah's work would begin.

Chapter 24

BALTIMORE, MARYLAND

$\mathcal{L}$aura Preston had just finished supervising the off-loading of the disconnected bomb to a storage building in the harbor. Turning to her boss she mused, Listen to me for a minute. Back in the fifties, if someone was planting a fake bomb and a real bomb, wouldn't it be easier to plant both bombs in the same building? Then, if the fake was easier to find, it would make the chances of discovering the real nuke almost nil."

"Jesus, Laura," said Jake, "I never thought of that, but you're right. I'll get another team on it right away. If they find anything, I don't want them to proceed until you and I get there. You're the only one I can trust to handle the mechanical work on this deal."

"Thanks," she said.

———

Back in D.C. the first call Jake made was to his deputy in charge of the team during his absence, instructing him to return to the recovery site underneath the Capital Grill. The second call was to the Secretary of Homeland Security, advising him of what was about to transpire and requesting that all traffic be blocked for a square mile from the site.

Jake and Laura arrived and consulted with the teams that were already on sight. The preliminary search had not turned up anything even remotely suspicious, and Jake was about to call it quits when Laura pulled him aside.

"You've got to listen to me," she pleaded. "In those days, we perceived that Russian enemies worked only white-collar jobs. Everyone watched every move that any Russian made if he or she was wearing a suit. So my guess is that whoever planted the bombs probably worked construction or some other blue-collar job. Most of the construction work in the Capital is done at night so traffic flow during the day won't be interrupted. No one would give a second thought to the sight of a construction worker at night; not even the Metro Police."

"Okay, okay," said Jake, "You've convinced me. Let's go back in."

After a preliminary walk-through, the two focused their attention on the site where the fake bomb had been discovered. The investigation was going nowhere, and Jake was becoming irritated with Laura's insistence that the real nuke must be hidden there when both noticed something strange about the steel construction in one corner of the building. The brick facade that held the beams in place was unlike the rest of the construction and the shore posts in the area where the Capital Grill stored their meats seemed to be out of whack. They'd been made to look like the rest of the walls, but upon further inspection, Jake realized there were actually two corners instead of one, which created a room with no entrance. Jake quickly reviewed the original building plans once again before putting in a call to the D.C. building department. The two came up empty; it was not in the original plans and no application had been submitted to alter the building—ever.

Jake took one more look, then grabbed a sledgehammer. After he struck the wall several times, pieces of shattered brick fell to the floor and revealed a room that reminded him of a cistern in an old building, used to store water. He knew the building was old, but not old enough to necessitate storing water the way they did 100 years ago. He flashed his light inside and there it was—a coffin-shaped box similar to the bogus bomb that was discovered earlier, only this one was five times bigger. Jake couldn't risk premature detonation by using the two-way radio, so he left everything as it was.

Laura was at the bottom of the ramp that led out of the garage speaking with Secretary O'Brian when she saw Jake walking quickly toward them. "This is the worst of the worst," he said. "This thing is probably booby-trapped. There's no way we can move it out of the building." Secretary O'Brian sighed deeply. "You need to get the best and the brightest to look at this monster."

"The best already has," said Jake with an uncharacteristic smile.

"Jake I realize that, but I just got word that Laura must leave immediately and fly home now. She's been recalled for whatever reason."

With that said, the secretary and Laura Preston stepped into his limo for a quick ride to Dulles International where Laura boarded a private flight by El Al to Israel.

The Town of Hun
South West Libya

Imam al Fareed was mythical to many of the people who lived in the small town of Hun. For those who witnessed his arrival, astride a black Arabian stallion and dressed in a white flowing kaffyieh and multi-colored headdress, just like his predecessor, the vision would forever perpetrate the legend. Flanked by a band of riders, his unexpected arrival sent waves of fear through the streets of the small town.

Fareed was in no mood to allay the fears of Hun's citizens.

Reining his horse to an abrupt stop, he demanded to know where the secure phone was and if their systems were working. A stout man stepped from the doorway of a meeting room to tell the leader that the system was indeed working, and that he would take the President to its location. When they entered the room, Fareed ordered the man to leave immediately. Thankful to be alive, the man turned and vanished into the streets. The startled Director of Communications placed the earphones on his head and awaited his orders. Fareed gave him a code that only he knew to initiate the transmission. Once that was done, he gave the officer a series of numbers and letters to relay to the person on the other end. When the transmission had been completed, Fareed drew his pistol and shot the officer in the back of the head. He would still be the only person on earth who knew the codes.

1700 Hours GMT
Aboard the Steamer *Aubin Faisal*
The Indian Ocean

Mahatma Khalfan was glad the waters had finally calmed. The rough seas of the last two days had forced the entire crew to work around the clock, but now there was time to rest. As the ship glided smoothly through the tranquil ocean on its way to its destination, Mahatma was relaxing with some of his crewmates in the galley after the evening meal. Years of rigorous training as an al-Qaeda agent had prepared him for his duties as an Able Seaman on board a "friendly freighter" owned by a staunch supporter of Bin Laden long before his death.

Shortly after dinner, Mahatma was summoned to the bridge.

There was a call for him in the radio shack. Knowing that the time to serve Allah had come, he entered the shack and, with transmitter in hand, he received the codes. He did not know the significance of what he was about to do, but it didn't matter; he was a loyal soldier. He worked diligently, setting the radio to the right frequency and readying his phone transmission. Once the code was programmed, it would route through the atmosphere to a preprogrammed signature detector. The powerful pulse would then open a circuit that was connected to the stored code. If the code were properly identified, it would ignite and set off the bomb. It was an advanced system, considering the age of the bomb.

1100 HOURS
Office of the Secretary
Homeland Security

The Secretary of Homeland Security returned the phone to its cradle and put his hands to his head in frustration. He had just returned from Dulles Airport and was talking with the President who refused his request to evacuate, electing instead to sequester himself and his immediate staff in the bunker far below the White House. O'Brian had argued each and every excuse, but the President was either the most stubborn human being on earth or in complete denial. When the President said he must remain with the people of Washington, O'Brian had countered that there were citizens in other states who needed him as well. When the President insisted that the bunker was bombproof, he had countered that Homeland Security had learned these bombs were capable of going hundreds of feet below the earth's surface; but that was dismissed as nonsense. When the President decided the short trip to Andrews was too risky, he countered that the 'smart money' wouldn't agree. He shouldn't have said that, O'Brian thought to himself; not only did it antagonize David Walsh; it also insulted the office of the President. Wondering if he had said too much or not enough and chastising himself for his inefficiency, O'Brian cursed out loud and silently prayed that he would have time to try again. He then left for Camp David on his chopper.

Bomb Site
Corner of Pennsylvania and 6th St. NW

Everyone in the vicinity was questioning the blockade that encompassed a square mile around ground zero. Some were satisfied with the explanation that it was just a precaution taken by the district because they were working on such an old building; others were not.

NEST had moved a portable scientific lab closer to the location of the bomb. It looked like any other black van, with the exception of six gray metal disks about the size of coffee cups attached to the roof of the vehicle. The disks were connected to a unit that detects neurons and other nuclear material from something as small as a pinhead of plutonium or nuclear dust. The square pod located on top of the van connects to a gamma ray scanner that transmits images to a flat screen television via minicomputer and together act as an oscilloscope.

Jake replaced his HAZ-MAT suit with a fresh one and once again cautiously approached the bomb. Observing the monster from another generation, he said to himself, "I don't think this thing is a 10-kiloton bomb. I think it's larger. It may be a 15 or 20."

He turned to one of his engineers. "The casings are larger than those of a 10-kiloton bomb, not that it makes any difference; either of them can do a shitload of damage. So let's go see what we've got."

The two men started to dismantle the bomb. After only a few minutes, Jake discovered frayed wires in the back of the casing. "We got to pull up," he shouted. "This thing's too old and too unstable to dismantle here. We'll all get blown to bits."

"What the hell do you want me to do?" The new guy shouted back. "Let this thing roll around in the back of a truck for thirty or forty miles with those frayed wires? One thing's for sure, we wouldn't have to worry about loading it onto a chopper."

"Sorry," Jake said, "I was just thinking out loud. I know this thing's too damn old to fool with, and I know that if it blows here it will take out everything: the White House, the Capitol, you name it. I just can't seem to come up with another option. We're damned if we do and we're damned if we don't. Take a break, and I'll run this by the home office."

Jake never had a chance to make the call.

The sun was descending into the sea when Mahatma walked onto the deck and stood along the railing, proud to be a soldier of Allah. Holding the transmitter, he carefully entered the codes. Seconds later, the unimaginable exploded into reality.

Chapter 25

WASHINGTON, D.C.

*I*n less than a second most of our symbols disappeared. The White House, the Capitol Building, the Supreme Court, Union Station, the FBI Building, the Federal Mint and the Department of Justice all were in the zone of direct impact. Our friends and neighbors, our families, our churches and temples, our homes and our work places, were all gone.

At least 250,000 people were severely injured or dead. It happened so fast they didn't have a chance.

Damaged but not destroyed were Reagan National Airport and the Pentagon. The Washington, Lincoln, and Jefferson memorials were still standing, but ruined. The National Archives Building was severely damaged. No one yet knew for sure if the Declaration of Independence and the Constitution had been lowered to their emergency chamber far below ground level. Odds were against it.

Within minutes of detonation, fire was everywhere. Temperatures reached 2000^0 F and winds climbed to 175 miles per hour. The damage beyond ground zero was incalculable.

An atomic explosion comes in waves of four. The searing bright light can cauterize a human eye unless one wears a black lens shield. Next comes the heat, intense enough to incinerate everything in its path. After that comes the shock wave, which knocks down buildings, committing them to rubble. Finally, the long term effects of gamma radiation, which can last years and, sometimes, generations. These rays cause carcinomas and malformations of huge proportions because of the winds. Wind carries the rays far from ground zero and contaminates communities many miles away.

The effects of the blast reached for several miles beyond ground zero, affecting a six-kilometer radius. The fallout for most of the NW area and Embassy Row created a firebrand that caused razor-sharp projectiles to fly through the air at supersonic speed like unguided missiles.

Plate glass, furniture, and other building and home contents, plus their façades, joined street signs and automobiles that whipped around the atmosphere like pieces of paper. The asphalt streets peeled up and flowed like molten lava. When the bomb exploded, the loss of life was almost incalculable, instantly disintegrating thousands. Those who died immediately were the lucky ones; the ones left behind faced the horrors of burning skin and peeling flesh. Their death could take days.

After an atomic blast, winds are reversed because they're sucked in from the peripheral to the center of the explosion. Anything alive that hasn't been vaporized will perish due to asphyxia. The possibility of harm to residents of the Virginia Highlands and other outlying communities was a great possibility. They could expect serious fallout and radiation poisoning if they couldn't escape. For the living, suicide would take precedence over life. It would be weeks, perhaps months, before authorities could claim "Safe Haven" status for rescue personnel to enter the area and to offer medical help. Even then, proper first aid and provisions such as food, water, mail, and other services, including hospitals and transportation, would be far too inadequate to care for all the injured. What was left of Washington and the surrounding area would become a jungle where people became animals in the wild, stealing and hoarding food and water, not knowing they were prolonging their own agony. A scrap of non-contaminated food or a jug of clean water would be priceless, far more than a piece of gold.

These victims were truly dead men walking.

The White House

Ground Zero was less than three city blocks from the White House and the Capitol Building. The explosion was not kind to these buildings. The bunkers deep below the east wing of the White House, called the Presidential Emergency Operations Center, were destroyed within seconds of detonation. President David Walsh was in the bunker when the explosion occurred. The ground-level detonation lifted his stainless steel bunker totally out of the ground and the heat caused it to melt. The President and his staff were killed instantly.

Control of a situation of this magnitude was virtually non-existent.

The United States has a plan for COG (continuation of government), but FEMA needed time to implement it. The written versions of the plans were safely held in several bunkers around the country, but the people with the responsibility of implementing these plans were dead.

PART II

Chapter 26

THE AMERICAN EMBASSY LONDON
10:40 GMT

*V*ice President William J. Cassidy and President Walsh's Chief of Staff Jim Chiswell were having dinner with the American Ambassador in his residence when the Chief of Station delivered the terrible news.

The communiqué simply read; "Nuclear device detonated near White House; President and staff dead; Do not leave American Embassy; Inventory of live personnel being taken; Will advise of damage ASAP, signed: Admiral Lee Gunn, Chief of Staff, USN, Norfolk, VA."

Just two days before, President Walsh had sent his Vice President and Chief of Staff to London to talk secretly about the American and British terrorist situation with Prime Minister John Lawton. Chiswell joined Cassidy's team on the President's orders, because Chiswell and Lawton had been in school together when Jim's father was posted to the American Embassy. They had maintained their friendship ever since, and the President felt this friendship could help to solidify agreements between the two countries.

Everyone in the room fell silent when Ambassador Osborne spoke. "My God in heaven, what has caused these people to be so extreme? Where do they get off thinking they can do this to us and get away with it?"

Chiswell immediately jumped in, saying, "Mr. President, please tell us you're going to take Admiral Gunn's advice and stay put for a couple of days before returning home?"

Cassidy looked puzzled at the comment, and then admonished Chiswell. "First off, don't call me Mr. President: I haven't been sworn in yet. Give me a chance to think and make contact with people I can communicate with."

Sensing his hesitation, Chiswell quietly said, "Sir, when there is a loss of a President, the Vice President automatically becomes Commander and Chief. He is not required to be sworn in. However, it is important for the American people to witness the continuation of their government so it is in their best interest that they see you take the oath. We can do it right here in the embassy." Turning to Ambassador Osborne, Chiswell said, "Ambassador, will you swear in the Vice president?"

"Of course, we will use my study."

A visibly shaken Bill Cassidy was escorted to the ambassador's private study by his wife Kristan and Jim Chiswell along with the rest of the dinner guests. The historic ceremony was brief, sad, and over in minutes.

The ambassador addressed the new President. "Sir, are you ready to take the oath?"

Bill Cassidy replied, "Yes, I am, Ambassador."

"Then please raise your right hand and repeat after me. I, William J. Cassidy, do solemnly swear that I will execute the office of President of the United States, and will to the best of my ability preserve, protect, and defend the Constitution of the United States."

Cassidy repeated the words and added "So help me God." The new President was now ready to take the reins. He was grateful that he had asked his wife Kristan to accompany him on this trip. With her own demanding job, she had not traveled much with her husband on official business. He was also thankful because if she had stayed in Washington she'd be gone. He thanked God for their safety at the moment and promised to seek vengeance on those responsible. He was also thankful Chiswell was safe and with him. He wanted him to remain COS.

Under normal circumstances the President would wait until he was on his own shores to make such an important address, but Cassidy knew he must make a statement immediately. He must address those who were responsible for what had happened. He decided to do it from the study where he was sworn in. A short statement would suffice, he decided, just enough to let the American people know they had a President and a continuity of government was in force, and to let all the guilty parties know who was in charge.

President Bill Cassidy then sat down to compose the most important message he would deliver in his life.

Chiswell knocked and entered to tell the new President he had an hour before broadcast time. He also assured Cassidy that although his Secret Service detail was smaller than it would be in the future, Britain's famous MI-5 intelligence service would add to it. As his first order of business, Cassidy asked Chiswell to stay on as his Chief of Staff. The answer came back—an emphatic yes.

The hour went by quickly, and Bill Cassidy began his address to the free world.

The Ambassador's Private Study
Live Broadcast

"Good evening, my fellow Americans. A short time ago, the United States of America was attacked for the second time in just a few days. This time it wasn't an explosive of the type that was used to tear apart the Chesapeake Bay Bridge, but instead, a nuclear device that we believe had been housed in the Washington area since the cold war. It is believed to have been a fifteen-kiloton bomb which is equal to 15 thousand tons of TNT. That is about the same size as what we dropped on Hiroshima during the Second World War.

"This attack destroyed our capital city, but not the American resolve. In 1945, the United States employed the use of nuclear power not to make war, but to end war, and it did just that.

"In no other type of warfare does the advantage of terrorism lie so heavily with the aggressor. So I tell you here and now, this aggression will be stopped before the world, as we know it, ceases to exist. America will never acquiesce to the demands of her enemies. We will hunt them down and destroy them, one by one.

"We will never give up until the job is complete. The time has come when we cease to walk on diplomatic eggshells to appease private interest groups or countries that align themselves with us because we keep them alive. Diplomatic saber rattling and hubris are now unacceptable. We will not tolerate the order of terrorism or their threats any longer.

"We have many important matters to attend to. We must

ensure that our shores are safe and we must rebuild our national heritage. Our enemies believe they have not only destroyed our government and its symbols but the American way. Let me tell all of you in this world who seek to destroy us: America stands today as it did yesterday, a beacon of freedom for all to see.

"Thank you and good night."

Sweat rolled off the new President's face. Decisions had to be made with no way to consult the members of his administration. He was very much alone, in the loneliest job in the world. Hell, they could all be dead for all he knew.

The previous problems in the administration had resulted in a strict need-to-know policy for information and that fact, coupled with his newness as a Vice President, meant that Cassidy was not fully informed. He could operate the government adequately, but he wished Walsh and his staff had taken the time to fully brief him. Now, within less than a month, he was President. The last time that happened was when Harry Truman took over after the death of Franklin Roosevelt. He thought of what Truman would have done, and he sensed he was on the right track. Harry "gave them hell" and that's exactly what Bill Cassidy was going to do.

So far, the only person he could trust and get advice from was Jim Chiswell. He would have more information in just a half an hour. Thank God Walsh had the sense to send him on this trip, he thought, otherwise the situation would be much worse. He couldn't help but wonder if Walsh had had a premonition.

Cassidy, Ambassador Osborne, the Chief of Station at the embassy, and Chiswell met in the ambassador's residence to discuss plans. Embassy staff was running around in circles, not knowing what to do next and worrying about their families. They clogged the phone lines with calls home, which made the new President nervous. Cassidy was a very orderly man; commotion and chaos did not suit his personality. The order went out for all staffers to stay off the phones until the Communications Corps completed the special telephone hookups. Meanwhile, the President could use the secure phones of the embassy.

Emergency plans are always made before a President or Vice president sets foot out of Washington. When the Principals travel, an identical plane with all the same communications gear and amenities follows Air Force One or Air Force Two. If, for example, there are engine problems, the follow-up plane takes over. It is also standard operating procedure for the Presidential and Vice Presidential limousines to advance the principal wherever he travels. These are the safest cars in the world, and there's a special communication system outfitted in the automobile. This was first made evident when Nixon and Kissinger visited the Soviet Union and were told that the KGB was photographing them in their bedrooms. The Secret Service discovered the cameras and listening devices built right into the new American Embassy walls; by using local labor, the KGB had installed several dozen of these devices. The only safe alternative was for these two men to communicate in the limo.

President Cassidy received a full briefing from Chiswell. As Def Sec he was familiar with DEF-CON and was well aware of the military operations that had been ordered by President Walsh, including the placement of a nuclear submarine and the 6th fleet just off the shores off Tripoli. He also had previous knowledge of the "football."

For security purposes, a Warrant Officer travels with each of the principals, carrying what is called the 'Football,' a briefcase containing the codes which, when activated, will send the message to retaliate if the USA is attacked by a foreign power. This system is called "MAD" or Mutual Assured Destruction. Two keys are needed to activate the system. The officer on duty carries one, and the other is worn around the neck of the President and Vice president. The name "football" comes from the way the officers pass the case from one Warrant Officer to another at shift changes.

Cassidy contemplated the difficulties of dealing with the Arab nations. Since the E-bomb had been dropped on Tripoli, all communications from there had ceased. He decided that there would be no negotiation with any Islamic country until things were sorted out—even allies like Pakistan or Saudi would be kept in the dark.

Chiswell suggested going airborne. British hospitality was nice, but there was a limit to what a new President could do from foreign soil. "The first stop, Mr. President will be Ottawa, Canada; it will be a secret landing. Canada is part of NORAD. From there we can determine if the air space over the USA is safe. Then we'll move on to Tampa, Florida and to Central Command. There you will receive a complete briefing and a view of D.C. and the surrounding area in digital detail."

A decision had to be made as to where he would set up a temporary capital. The bunkers were fine for a while, but the people—the world for that matter—needed to see the President of the United States. Because of the attack on US soil, every country in the Western world now suffered from insecurity. Cassidy needed to reassure each of them with a personal phone call. He couldn't allow allies to slip away because of fear. They would then fall into the terrorists' hands. The President's mere presence would have a profound effect on the world's economy, so he must be seen making the right decisions. Perhaps Nebraska, at the old SAC headquarters where George W. Bush was taken on 9/11, would work, or Mount Weather, in Maryland, about 20 minutes outside of Washington, where all the equipment necessary to govern was available. His handlers would know where to go but Chiswell is correct that "Command Central" is the most logical choice. But how safe was it to travel, and should the President be at a destination so close to the fallout?

The President turned to Chiswell and said, "Let's get the hell out of here, Jim, but for safety reasons, I want my wife to stay here at the embassy. Now take me to the motorcade."

En route all streets and highways were blocked on both sides until the President's entourage had passed, and were not re-opened for a half hour. The SAS and his own SS detail did a superb job in assuring his safety. At the speed they were traveling, Heathrow was just a few minutes away. Air Force One—formerly Air Force Two—was fueled and ready on the tarmac. Normally when Air Force One is about to take off or land, no other plane is allowed to enter its air space for two hours. In this case the Brits suspended all flights in or out of Heathrow Airport for 12 hours.

Once on board, President Cassidy rolled up his sleeves and went to work.

Aboard Air Force One

The first order of business was to find out who, in Walsh's government, was alive. The Speaker of the House, now in direct line of succession, was dead. Cassidy wanted to keep all the Cabinet members as holdovers. Some did not share his philosophy, but they were all very loyal, and besides, it wasn't prudent at this time to make personnel changes.

Secretly, Cassidy knew the Declaration of War that was already in place would be very useful. It would give him the very broad powers that he would not have under normal circumstances, and he intended to use them to the fullest. He could never understand why the previous administrations, ever since FDR, had kissed the Arabs' asses. If it was just oil, we would be better off taking it and leaving them to camp at the oasis with their camels, or better yet use our own oil. We had created a monster, and the time had come to sever its head. This could be done, and it would be done. Soon.

Frankly, it's the only way of life those people understood. Not one of the countries in the Gulf Region understood the words freedom and liberty, let alone democracy. It would take several generations, if ever, before democratic governments in the region would be created and tolerated. Cassidy couldn't waste the time. His priorities were to protect the borders of the United States and re-establish the security and morale of the citizenry.

"Our enemy is silent, deadly and stealth," he said to the staff on board Air Force One. "Hell, I don't even know what country they're from. We could respond with wholesale elimination at first, which would show off our power, but I believe that our enemies should be made to suffer one by one, quietly, and with no bravado. Not everyone who is Muslim is guilty, but I believe this is our best option."

Cassidy would begin by changing the way the US did things. Business as usual would cease until further notice. Cassidy had busted his backside to get where he wanted, and he did it with very little political support. In every election, he ran as an independent. The only reason he was President was because he was appointed VP, and then the unthinkable happened. He truly owed his party nothing, and this placed him in a great strategic and political position. It kept the hacks away from his door, and he didn't have to waste precious time listening to the bullshit they all had to say. He could shelve that political bullshit by making it come to an end real quick, and he was thankful for that. Everyone on both sides of the congressional aisle, plus our allies, should understand this, but they probably wouldn't. He just hoped he had a Congress that would work through this mess with him.

The President picked up the phone and asked to be connected to the Prime Minister of Israel. The connection took all of 20 seconds before Eli Mordachi was on the other end. "My sorrow is with you, Mr. President," the Prime Minister began. "We as a nation open our hearts and facilities to you. You are welcome to headquarter here in Tel-Aviv until you see fit to leave."

"Thank you, Prime Minister, but that might endanger your country further. I called to tell you I will be landing in Ottawa in about two hours. Once there, I would like to have a teleconference with you and the British Prime Minister. We have never met, sir, but I can tell you President Walsh had great respect for you and the Zionist cause. I want you to know I share the same sentiments. Our nations are partners and always will be."

"That's good to know, Mr. President," said Mordachi. "I believe we will make a good team. I will await your call. God bless our common endeavors." The line went dead.

The President placed a similar call to John Lawton of Great Britain. They spoke for five or six minutes, and President Cassidy ended the call with his personal thanks for all the Prime Minister had done while he was on English soil. Lawton also agreed to the teleconference call coming up in a couple of hours.

The phone rang: the Secretary of Defense was on the line. "Ian, for God's sake, where are you?" the President asked. "Tell me who survived and who didn't, and tell me if COG went into effect."

"Sir, as far as I know the Cabinet has survived, or most of it anyway," the Secretary replied. "When you were out of the country the decision was made to move the cabinet and their families to Camp David for a working weekend. All but a few of us are still there. Probably the luckiest one of all is Chiswell. Being with you saved his life. Secretary of State Howe was the only one missing from Camp David. She was ordered by the President to leave for Amman, Jordan with Bill Derrick.

"Thank God, Ian, but I want her back," said Cassidy. "Now tell me about Washington."

"What about Washington, Mr. President? There is no more Washington. For the most part, Washington is leveled."

"There will always be a Washington, Ian" the President said. Just because it's leveled doesn't mean we won't re-build, and it's there in spirit as well. I think that's why we need to set up something that's very close, but safe, so we can operate."

"I agree, sir, and that's what FEMA is working on right now. They were sure you would want to be as close to D.C. as possible. If nothing else, it would be a symbol to our citizens and the world. A very important symbol, I may add."

Cassidy continued, "Please get me a list of survivors besides the secretaries so I know who I have to work with. I'll be landing in Ottawa shortly, and I would like some answers by then. Contact Chiswell and give him the Intel because I'll be having a conference call with Lawton and Prime Minister Mordachi. And Ian, one last thing, I'm contemplating the use of SOE, the Special Operations Executive. Contact the Commander and order him to meet me at Central Command in Tampa."

"Yes, sir."

Next on the President's list was to double-check how many Congressmen had survived. The few who did not go home when Congress recessed for the summer were probably dead, but if they were away from the blast they would be picked up by Marine helicopter if possible and flown to Mount Weather. However, he believed that most of them had been in their own districts and not in D.C. when the bomb went off. He hoped so anyway. He had also ordered one of his aides to contact the proper people at Fort Meade outside of Baltimore to find out what the chatter was and what they were hearing from the other side. He received a call from the NSA and was told that the sympathizers to the Jihad were dancing in the streets in most Islamic countries. NSA at Fort Meade had the best technology available, so he would stay in direct contact with them. Cassidy was tired and stressed, but he responded quickly and decisively. He was a champ at multi-tasking.

The President kept moving forward, making decision after decision and slowly getting the answers he needed.

Under any other emergency situation, there were plans in place so that the continuation of government could go forward. In this case, President Cassidy had no idea if there were any grunts alive to implement the COG. He didn't even know if a back-up plan to COG existed. Much had to be done, and he hoped he had the manpower to do it.

The flight commander announced Air Force One's entrance to Canadian air space and received permission to land in their capital in one hour. Cassidy thanked God for America's good neighbor and prayed for strength for his return home.

2:46 AM EDT
Ottawa, Canada

The approach to Ottawa International Airport was quick and smooth. Once on the tarmac, the huge plane taxied to a large hangar where armed security from the Royal Canadian Mounted Police and a contingent of Secret Service Agents from New York City surrounded the plane.

The President's limousine had arrived 20 minutes earlier and was waiting. As soon as everyone was offloaded, the motorcade headed for the American Embassy. Once there, the President would contact Canadian Prime Minister Jacob McKenzie to thank him for his hospitality. They agreed to meet that morning.

The first order of business, however, was setting up the teleconference and video call to Tel-Aviv and London. The time was 4:10 AM, EST.

Several members of the US Army Communications Corps travel with the President and Vice President. These five men had the responsibility of setting up the teleconference among the three leaders. When in the White House Situation Room, this is no big deal; the President can reach out to anyone anywhere in the world almost instantly. He could have made the conference call while he was in the air but he wanted to use the time to gather his thoughts.

As soon as the lines of communication were open, the President was notified. He proceeded to the secure room.

"Prime Ministers," he said, addressing the two allies, "As you know, we desperately need help. Although I have no figures as to the damage caused or lives lost in Washington, I can assure you your embassies have vanished, as did the White House and Capitol. Frankly, a lot more than that disappeared, but you can understand where I'm coming from. Our only way to communicate is the way we're doing it right now until I can establish a temporary capital.

Unless your Ambassadors were re-called, I must presume they perished with everyone else caught in the firestorm. I am making some decisions at the moment that you both must be included in. I am hoping I may have your complete cooperation because I will need the efforts of MI-5, the SAS and the Mossad. What I have in mind is a complete stealth operation that will be ongoing for years, if not generations to come. I want to clear them out forever.

"I am in the throes just now of working out the details and when I finish, I would like to present them to you. As you know, if we are to survive, the terrorists must be decapitated and, frankly, the CIA is too caught up in their own hubris to do the job and I'm sure their headquarters in Langley doesn't exist anymore. Homeland Security is still trying to organize, so I must lean on you and our friendship. Your countries are the most trusted allies we have, and we need you desperately."

Eli Mordachi responded first, saying, "As far as I'm concerned, Mr. President, you may have all the support Israel can give."

"And I echo Eli's comment," said John Lawton. "Whatever we can do to help, we'll offer it to you. We're as close to you as a phone call."

"One last thing, Mr. President," added Mordachi. "As far as I'm concerned, it's a great feeling to finally have an ally that's on the same road as we Jews. We've been going it alone since 1948 or before, and from my fighting days with the Haganah I can tell you, take no prisoners. Cut the head off the snake quickly. I might add to that and say, kill their families as well, women and children alike. I know this might offend the way Americans do business but if not, they'll come back to haunt you."

Cassidy winced but said nothing.

Lawton commented that his country did not have the problem that Israel did until of late. "London has a different type of Jihadist. He is a natural born Englishman, a second generation Muslim who has learned his skills from several mosques that dot London neighborhoods and from their AQ training camps. Then they become martyrs, all of them, giving their lives for an empty promise from a leader who fears death just like you and me."

"They hardly know how to read or write," Said Eli, "but they can recite the 6236 verses of the Koran verbatim."

Cassidy interjected, "Gentlemen, thank you for the faith you have in me. It certainly makes life easier to have friends like you in our corner. I will make contact with you the day after tomorrow, once I talk over my plans with some advisors. Again, thank you."

The lines went dead, and the President stretched out on the couch for a much needed nap.

Later that morning, Cassidy met with Prime Minister McKenzie at Government House. They agreed that all borders to and from their countries would be closed until further notice. McKenzie also agreed to triple the border guard on his side of the line. The Prime Minister also agreed to deport all Muslims who were in Canada on a visa. They would be ordered to leave within 24 hours. This would add to the safety at the border and prevent anyone from sneaking over.

The President then placed a personal call to the President of Mexico and told him the US border to his country would be closed. The Mexican President agreed to cancel visas and deport anyone from a Muslim nation. Cassidy also told him that the US Border Patrol has received orders to shoot on sight anyone trying to illegally cross the border into the US.

President Cassidy got no argument from Raul Linares. The Mexican President was upset, but he could understand the situation. He secretly wanted to get rid of the people who sneak over the border into the US; he had no use for them.

It was time to confer with Chiswell and McPherson. Cassidy had ordered his Defense Secretary to Central Command in Tampa, Florida ASAP; at the moment, that was the best place to do business. The Secret

Service wanted him to fly to SAC headquarters in Nebraska until the situation in D.C. had stabilized, but the idea repulsed Cassidy. He had no desire to emulate the jihadists by living in a hole. He overruled them and insisted on remaining in Tampa until more permanent arrangements could be made closer to Washington.

The flight from Ottawa was uneventful. Air Force One departed at exactly 7:30AM, EST and was escorted from Ottawa to Tampa, Florida by six F-16's assigned by NEADS (North East Advance Defense System) which were dispatched from Rome, New York.

Chapter 27

CENTRAL COMMAND
TAMPA, FLORIDA
1:40PM

*T*he flight was smooth, although they had to fly around the destroyed capital rather than over it to avoid contamination. This gave the President extra time, allowing him to make some serious decisions that would not endear him to certain wings of his party. But, he thought privately, the hell with them. He knew that most of America, and at least half of the world, would be on his side, and he had no illusions. What he was about to do had never been done, from the days of George Washington's administration to the present. He had no fear of his legacy and didn't give a damn. He just wanted to save the country.

The plane landed smoothly and pulled to the side of the tarmac. There to greet him were General Cyrus Taylor, Commander of Cent Com, Chairman of the Joint Chiefs Ned Seiffert, and Admiral Lee Gunn. At the head of the line was Def.Sec Ian McPherson. The President was shaking hands with all the brass when he turned to Chairman Seiffert who brought news from Washington. The emotion was getting the best of him and he thanked God that these men were safe.

Looking at them, he was overcome. "I never thought I would see you again Ned, your whereabouts information was temporarily lost in the fire at the Pentagon; thank God you're alive. The communications failed miserably but I'm so glad you're here. As you know, Ian was able to reach me, but so many others seemed to be lost or gone."

"Mr. President, when all else fails, you drop a quarter in a pay phone," said Seiffert. "I began calling on my way to Norfolk, but the lines at the Pentagon and everywhere else around the Capital were useless. Cynthia and I were going to be guests of Lee Gunn's for the weekend.

I'll never forget it as long as I live," said Seiffert. "My cell shit the bed and so the next best thing was a fistful of quarters."

"Son of a bitch," said the President. "Kind of reminds me of Grenada. You remember Grenada, General. That's when Reagan sent in a force to rescue some medical students. When the Colonel, who was the CO, radioed back to the ship, his batteries were dead. He used a fistful of quarters to call the Pentagon to get directions."

They all remembered and laughed, which helped to lighten the mood. "When all else fails, old Ma Bell saves the day," said Gunn. "Wouldn't you think there would be some communication in place for such emergencies?"

"There is, sir, but the nature of the attack rendered the whole system useless. We used our emergency backup system at the Naval Communications Department in Norfolk. I called Lee, and he made the necessary calls from his office to several base commanders on the outskirts of D.C. to get a damage assessment. Some answered the call, but most were dead."

Bill Cassidy liked the initiative that he saw in his team. He ordered everyone to meet with him in his quarters in a half hour.

The President had settled in and was making a mental agenda of what he wanted to say when the phone rang. Chiswell picked it up and handed it to the President. Jim took leave through a side door and went to the meeting room to announce that the President would be joining them in a few minutes.

On the other end of the line was Colonel Steve Meyers, calling as ordered from Houston, Texas. "Mr. President," said Meyers, "as requested, sir, I'm calling in."

"What was this mission you were assigned by President Walsh, colonel?" Cassidy asked.

"I'm not on a safe phone, Sir," replied Meyers. "Perhaps it can wait until we meet."

"Colonel, have you accomplished what you set out to do?"

"No, sir."

"Abort the operation, Colonel; I need you at Cent-Com immediately."

"Yes sir, Mr. President, I'm on my way."

As the President entered the meeting room, all the brass stood until he was seated. "Gentlemen, look at the screen on your right and you will see what is left of Washington, D.C.," Cassidy began. "Frankly, I don't know where to begin. I was never briefed as VP because I only held the office for a short time, but now I'm the President and I intend to make things happen."

"Mr. President," interrupted McPherson, "As you know there are two sets of plans. Both have been implemented. COG continuation of government is Plan A. Plan B, if used, is to attack the enemy from the sea using nuclear warheads. The FEMA Director also is informed of Eyes Only but was in Washington and is assumed dead. The Secretary of HLS, of course, is informed as well and is presumed to have just have landed at Camp David, just in time, from Washington. He is working with the rest of the cabinet at SITE-R. If you wish, he could be here in four hours. Better yet, we could hook him up via Skype."

"Good, do the latter. I'm not sure yet if I want to use Plan B, but keep it in place just in case. Now let's begin. This is going to be a long day."

General Seiffert started the ball rolling. "Sir, the rebuilding of Washington will have to wait until the city is clean and that will be a long while. The cleanup will take at least a year or maybe two. This is not my department except for the military installations, but looking at these videos, everything of importance, as we know it, was destroyed. When this happens, the plan for COG automatically goes into action.

"COG has been implemented twice; once in the great power failure of the Northeast during the LBJ administration. At that time we all thought we were being attacked by the Ruskies. It turned out to be a problem at the source in Niagara Falls which supplies the whole Northeast with electricity. It worked out very well then, and again on 9/11. I can only presume it will work out as well this time, and, of course, the plan has been updated and that's a good thing. You do have a government in place, Mr. President."

"Except Washington wasn't attacked back then. Frankly, God forgive me for saying this, but it's a lot easier if an attack like this would happen in a city other than DC." The President then turned to his aide and asked when the Secretary of Homeland Security would be ready.

The connection was made instantly and the Secretary was in focus. "Mr. President, I presume you need a briefing as to where we are in this crisis and what we plan to do."

"Hold on for just a second, Mr. Secretary." He turned quickly to General Seiffert.

"General, you said the re-building would take a long time but that can't be allowed to happen. We must re-establish ourselves quickly. The American people need to know they will have a capital again, and soon. The morale of our citizens, and the rest of the world for that matter, is paramount." He turned back to his HLS–Scc and said. "Go ahead Mr. Secretary."

"Yes, well, as you can imagine, chaos reigns in this area. Officially, everything is down. We have no way to even drop food and medicine to the living, if anyone is alive. We can't use helicopters for fear of contamination, so it's impossible to drop supplies from the air. I can only imagine how horrible it must be down there. It must be like the Stone Age.

"The FEMA Director is officially dead, as are his assistants. He was caught in his office, as were thousands of others in that department. Most of the Under Secretaries and Deputy Secretaries are also gone. The only saving grace is if a few of them were in their hometowns on holiday or on the road.

"We are still checking as to the condition of some of the bunkers that took a direct hit. I believe a few of them could not withstand the blast. They were too close to the explosion. But that still remains to be seen. Because of the fallout we can't enter the area. If anyone is alive, the only way to know is if they find a way to contact us, which is doubtful. We can look over the area via satellite, but even our military satellites can't produce good quality pictures because of the haze. I have taken the liberty of partnering with Ian to assume the control of COG until you say differently. Plan 'B' cannot be set in motion until we identify those responsible for the attack. That's a Presidential and military decision."

"Mr. Secretary I will make that decision, and soon."

The President then asked, "Has anyone from the National Reconnaissance Agency taken the trouble to look down from the sky?"

Admiral Gunn offered his opinion. "I believe NRA at Fort Meade is doing just that, sir. Their pictures are the highest quality but we don't know if they can get an accurate image through the fire, smoke and fallout still consuming the city and surrounding areas."

"Admiral, have them get their results to me by tonight, whatever the quality," said Cassidy. "I don't care what time."

"Understood, sir." Gunn stood to make the call.

"The next thing I want to talk about is how and when we answer these sons of bitches that did this to us."

"Lee is right, sir," said Seiffert. "With the technology we have now, we can take out any S.O.B. on earth, pluck them right out of the sky if we have to."

"With the exception of senior AQ operatives and al Zahwari himself," said Cassidy. "We've been trying to get those bastards for years; that's why we're the laughing stock of the civilized world. 'Wanted dead or alive.' What a crock of horseshit."

The room quieted with the uncharacteristic outburst and then the new President continued, "I'm here to tell you all, I will not accept anything less than complete capitulation from those responsible. However, as of now retaliation through Mutual Assured Destruction is not an option. I have no interest in bombing every Islamic nation around the world killing innocent people; that makes no sense. However, Libya leaders with ties to al-Qaeda and all the Jihadists must go and its leadership is what we must concentrate on first. I just don't know how."

"Well," said Seiffert, "we had a good start with the E-bomb, for sure."

"As a former Defense Secretary, Mr. President" said Gunn, "you know that we lead the world in covert technology. This may be the only kind of retaliation that would allow us to get those responsible with as little collateral damage as possible. We have something that has never been used to counter an attack of this magnitude; our enemies may be thrown completely off guard."

"I think that's an option that I can live with, Admiral, and we do have Drones as well. We can surgically strike when we want and we most likely will, but I want something on a grander scale to start. We should all give these options careful consideration. Now there are other things that we need to address.

"Our borders to and from Mexico and Canada will be closed indefinitely. I know this will have an impact on trade, but right now the order of the day is to survive. I have also given the order to shoot on sight anyone ignoring this edict. They cross, we shoot, and both leaders understand this. Mexico is already making noise about no oil and all the usual crap if we don't acquiesce to their demands, but we can't afford to and that's the bottom line. Hopefully, someday soon everything will be back to normal. Till then we run our own railroad with no foreign interference. The bottom line is our doors are sealed like the Papal Conclave. No more foreign nationals on our soil, at least for now."

"Second: every Islamic nation will receive serious economic sanctions from the US and its allies until they hand over the pond scum. If the acceptance of a jihad is their choice, or if we find out that training of terrorists on their land exists, then their government will not. As I said before, not everyone is guilty, but if the training camps are flourishing, the people know and must be punished. It's rather like Germany during the war. Ask anyone living in that era if they knew about the camps and cattle cars full of people, and they'll deny it. They're full of shit, they had to see something, and that's the way it is with those fucking nomads. Of course they know what's going on, and they're guilty as hell. Unfortunately, we must be able to prove it. Until then, we hold our temper."

McPherson asked, "What about the United Nations, Mr. President? Perhaps we should depend on them more and lessen our load. For instance, we could send in their people covertly."

"Ian, you know they're a joke. How the hell are you going to trust the UN? They're a dirty lot and therefore not acceptable. We'll do our own work as we have in the past, depending only on England and Israel, is that clear? From now on, I want NRA to pass over these countries randomly so they don't know we're coming, and I want pictures on my desk every day to prove it.

"Gentlemen, we must force these degenerates to their knees. We must encircle them and control their every move. Life must be made impossible for our enemy. If they think SHIRA is difficult, just wait and see what we can do. Hopefully, their grandchildren will see and learn to cooperate within the human circle. If not, they go as well. No humanitarian efforts will even be considered and that's a given. No food, no clothing, and no medical supplies or anything else. Our ships will block any foreign vessel from approaching their waters. When they surrender, we will consider lesser sanctions. But only then.

"Third: Admiral Gunn, as of this minute, my signature is on an Executive Order ordering you to enter any Islamic port of call you see fit. You will consider any ship caught smuggling oil or anything else as an act of war and you are to sink her, preferably in the port of origin so we can clog their harbors and it doesn't happen again. I don't care what flag they're hiding behind. Saddam had parameters after the war, governed by the UN. For humanitarian purposes only, he was allowed to trade his oil for food and medical supplies. What a farce that turned out to be! He lined his own pockets first, then several in the UN, then his cohorts; next to nothing went to his people. Any ship may invade or evade our blockade at their peril. The usual three warnings are all that's necessary. Understood?"

"Yes, sir," said Lee Gunn, privately wondering how long this blockade would continue. The President sensed his thoughts. "As long as it takes Admiral, do I make myself clear?"

"Crystal, sir," responded Gunn, shocked at the mind read.

The President continued. "Fourth: Ian, along with our satellite system we must use anything else available: drones, predators, and what have you must be fully operational by tomorrow morning. I want a special emphasis placed on Western Pakistan and Tora Bora Mountains with armed predators unless Intelligence tells us differently. Maybe we can get lucky this time around and score a big one for the good guys."

"As far as the home front is concerned, give some thought to rationing as we did in WWII. It's high time we limit the use of automobiles. It's crazy for momma, poppa and all the kids to drive separate cars. Let's use our own oil. Think what we can do about it. We're at war, gentlemen, and it's high time we win for a change."

Turning to Chiswell he ordered, "Contact Bill Derrick and see where we are on oil production in Iraq. I believe we own the wells.

After all, we earned them. And if not, take them, and find out what our own reserves are like. With rationing, we should be okay but I want to hear it from the horse's mouth. Tell Derrick to report to me as soon as he can."

Looking back at the military leaders, the President said, "I have a lot more to say but we will gather once again tomorrow morning at 7AM. General Seiffert, I know you and Ian want to talk further, but keep me in the loop."

Standing up for a stretch, the President turned again to Chiswell. "When is this Colonel Meyers arriving?"

"He's waiting for you now, sir. He arrived with Master Sergeant McCarthy an hour ago. They're just biding time at the mess hall until you summon them. When would you like to see them sir?"

"I want to see Meyers alone in about an hour."

"Very well, sir, no problem," said Chiswell. "It'll be done." He walked away, wondering what was going to happen next.

When Chiswell came back, Cassidy asked, "Do I have a press secretary, Jim?"

"I don't believe so, sir," replied Chiswell. "I've been trying to contact Asa, but I'm sure he was in the President's bunker with Jim Sercu and several others."

"If that's the case, try to contact that NNC reporter Lerrick. If she's alive, ask her to help out. President Walsh respected her, and that's as good a recommendation as you can get." What's her name— McKenna?

"Yes, sir" said Chiswell. "I'll get right on it."

"And Jim please get hold of Sarah Walsh for me. I'm sorry, General, please continue."

"Mr. President," said General Seiffert, "I think this is the best time to tell you about some new technology that's been developed over the past two years. It's still classified, but it might be useful for our purposes now. We've tried it over Afghanistan and Iraq, and it's been very successful at taking out difficult targets, not the big guys but several of the little guys hiding out in the mountains. It would be very efficient at depleting their army. We don't want to go after the AQ leaders just yet because we don't know exactly how accurate this weapon is. I can tell you, though; so far it's hit every mark we've aimed it at."

"We finally have in our hands a weapon that will prove itself truly invaluable in the fight against terrorism. It will strike fear in their souls. The guy who dreamed this one up deserves a medal. I guess he must be some kind of genius because it will rank supreme in the arsenal of world weapons. So far it has passed every test with an A-plus, and budget wise it's great because we have a load of C-130A's we can transform to accommodate this weapon and others. The services, especially the Army and Air Force, want this weapon. We call it "the Dragon." We've been very successful with it, and I'm going to recommend that it be put at your disposal within the month."

"Tell me how it works, Ned," said the President.

"It's very simple, sir," said the General. "We got hold of a Lockheed Martin Hercules AC-130, and converted it to a first-class gunship. We can circle at 20 to 30 thousand feet looking for targets above a cloud layer without being detected, just like a drone, only more efficient. The engines run almost totally silent, as if it were a glider. We can peek right through the cloud cover as good as Keyhole. Once we're airborne, we hunt for targets. As soon as they're identified, we take them out—with no misses I might add—thanks to the special mechanics we've installed. It's like a Sniper Plane. From Defense's point of view, this plane is as nasty as you'd ever need to get."

"The whole inside of this C-130-A was gutted and outfitted with an array of tech designed to search, locate, target and destroy the bad guy. It is a 50-million-dollar piece of technical wonder that can deliver the bad news quicker than the blink of an eye. Once airborne, the plane automatically assumes the locate mode. In that mode, it does not depend on conventional radar as we know it. It can take a picture in good weather or bad. Raytheon Corporation built synthetic aperture radar and an infrared thermal imager that can pick out anything that emits body heat. Even something as small as a mouse in the middle of a snowstorm can't go undetected. It can snap pictures deep in the jungle as if they were being taken in the middle of an empty field. The image is not a blur; rather they can show every detail of a subject, down to the pimples on someone's face. The only way to beat it is to cover yourself with at least 36 inches of dirt or just kill yourself before the Dragon does it for you. We can even kill a target hiding in a cave because the new equipment allows us to fire from the plane horizontally. Think of it like a smart bomb." He paused for a brief moment, and then went on.

"The destroy part of the package has three options. The heaviest is the 105mm M103 Howitzer, which is much too large to use on a single small target. The second choice would be the 40mm Bofors Cannon. This is a Belgian anti-aircraft weapon, and it is a very fast repeater with lots of muscle. It can rip through a building and tear it apart using depleted uranium rounds and penetrate a tank and wipe out its contents in seconds. Finally, Mr. President, if the target is a man or several men, for instance, riding horseback along a trail in the Tora Bora, then you might want to go with the third choice. It's the newest weapon we have in our arsenal and probably the most effective. This is a steroid of a machine, and it's called the Model 50 Dragon. This weapon is basically what you see at the top of Humvees on patrol in Iraq but with shortened barrels and four of them instead of one. With the help of the developers we've been able to include the 'Mighty Dragon' on board as part of our family of weapons by using a specially built mounting system. It's lighter than the current M2-50 machine gun by at least 33 percent, and after it's converted, it will be more accurate and handle easier than before. The best part is, it fires 1,100 forefinger size rounds per minute. Its predecessor can only fire 450 rounds per minute. Hell, we've been doing that since Hitler was a Corporal. Everything the Dragon hits converts to dust. The firepower is so intense because each round is three times the size of its predecessor and four times 1,100 equals 4,400 rounds. It will destroy an entire domed football stadium within minutes. Nothing will survive. All that's left is a bloom of dust vapor. However, in order to use this weapon effectively, it must be fired from 3000 feet or less. The two other choices are more effective at higher altitudes."

He took a deep breath... "Mr. President, once the Dragon is locked on a target and fired for 60 seconds, dispensing all 4400 rounds, the target would disappear as well as the poppy fields he's hiding in. Burial is unnecessary."

The President responded, "Thank you, General. While you were talking, I received a note saying they're ready with the Keyhole satellite pictures of Washington. Let's have a look."

The lights dimmed and a view of the D.C. sky came before their eyes. In real time, Keyhole focused on the White House. The entire building had disappeared, with the exception of a piece of a guard shack and a column at the front entrance. Pictures of the Capital and FBI buildings showed the same devastation. The Supreme Court building was farther away from ground zero, but it was badly damaged, as was the Pentagon. The Pentagon, because of its construction, survived better than the court building but it was unusable. Focusing back on the White House, the men could clearly see how deep the hole was under the East Wing. Zooming in for a close-up view of the bunker, the President could see nothing but shiny shards of stainless steel and titanium pieces strewn all over the ground. Scoping further into the Rose Garden, they found where the ten-ton bunker door was. It looked as if it had peeled off the wall and folded in a half circle from the intense heat. There was no chance the President and his staff could be alive. For that matter, there was no chance anyone with the federal government in downtown D.C. was alive to tell his or her story.

Cassidy continued to view the screen and said a silent prayer that God grant him the resolve to go forth and to rebuild the world's most powerful capital. Was he prepared to do it? With His help, he thought so. "I've seen enough for now," said the President. "Send me Colonel Meyers immediately."

Following a soft knock on the door, Colonel Steve Meyers entered the small makeshift office. A snappy salute and one returned by the President put both men at ease. "Colonel, come in and sit down," said Cassidy. "I need your help, so let me get right to the point, but only after you tell me exactly what you were ordered to do for President Walsh."

Meyers explained the operation in detail and what the President had ordered. Cassidy had been aware of Warren Dunn and what he was trying to do with a few members of the Senate and a woman the government had considered a 'person of interest' for two years. Even though it was widely believed that she was an agent for al-Qaeda, she hadn't been arrested because the FBI Director was convinced she might provide valuable links to others involved in the conspiracy.

"Colonel, I am rescinding your orders for the time being. Trust me, we'll take care of that son of a bitch, but right now I have a situation that takes precedence. I need you to put together a group for a covert operation in Afghanistan, notably the Tora Bora. I have information that there is a very large training camp there and I want it destroyed."

"Do you have a target in mind, Mr. President?"

"Ayman Al-Zawahiri would be nice, with all his merry men who run his organization along with about 500 trainees and soldiers. I promise you'll have everything you need: money, equipment, anything else it takes. I know that it will take time to plan but I want just a few highly skilled individuals going in, not the whole damn Delta Force, or Seal team six. I want someone to infiltrate and gain their trust and I want this to be done as covertly as possible." Meyers started to speak, but the President held up his hand, "I don't care how long it takes as long as there are results. Got it?"

"Got it, sir," replied Meyers. "Mr. President, there is one thing I'd like to ask for. When I put together this group, I would like to ask permission to include one man who was assigned to us when Clinton was President."

"He's not one of ours?"

"No sir, he's SAS, and if I may speak freely, he's the meanest SOB on the face of the earth. My feeling is that on the eighth day God made Nick Malone and the devil stood and saluted. In the past, when we've borrowed personnel from other agencies we have mostly used the Brits. Their SAS and MI-6 are as efficient as the Mossad and are considered among the toughest anti-terrorist teams in the world. Delta Force and the Navy Seals are great, but theirs is not a good fit with the way we work. I would like to have Nick Malone who has worked for both MI-6 and SAS on our team. Mr. President, he's not only as bad as they get, but also with him it's personal. He hates al-Qaeda more than you could ever imagine, sir."

"What is his story, Colonel?"

"Well, sir, he was on assignment for the Prime Minister in the Kabul region doing what he does best, seeking and killing al-Qaeda, when he was ordered by his superiors to come home immediately. No reason was given; just get home. When he landed, he was escorted to No. 10 Downing where the Prime Minister and Nick's commanding officer were waiting to inform him of his wife's death. She was visiting the holy city of Jerusalem with her church group when she and two other women were forced at gunpoint from their hotel to a waiting van. AQ demanded three of their senior members held in an Israeli prison be released in exchange for their release. They also demanded that Malone be recalled. We still can't figure out how they got his name, but they did. Of course you know what the answer to that was; Israel does not negotiate with terrorists under any circumstances. There were threats of rape and torture but the Israelis remained steadfast so the executions commenced. First was the rape, then the beheading. A video was made for Western eyes only. Nick's wife Becky was eight months pregnant with their first child. She was begging them to save her child when the order to kill was stopped. A man stepped out from the background and stood over her. Then he bent down and whispered to her that he was a medical doctor and he would save her baby. Doctor Ayman Al-Zawahiri, the number two man of AQ back then, began operating on her right then and there. One sharp slice below her abdomen, and the baby was delivered. No anesthesia, no nothing. She was sliced wide open."

"Al-Zawahiri took the baby and told her he would raise the boy as a Muslim and make a proper soldier out of him, so he could kill the infidels of his own blood. She was then beheaded. The whole process was being recorded for Al Jazeera so they could release it to the West. Even the screaming and gurgling sound was recorded. She used her last breath to tell her husband she loved him. Doctor Al-Zawahiri handed the baby to a woman who was cleaning up after the executions. 'Take care of the newborn,' he ordered, 'This child's future is with Allah.'"

"Nick Malone resigned his commission and moved to Canada. I have stayed in contact with him. He lives in Algonquin Provincial Park in Ontario. He has neither phone nor radio and picks up his mail at the Canoe Lake Store & Post Office. He has no contact with the outside world. I doubt if he even knows about Washington. I once asked him how he would get help in an emergency, and he said he would set the island on fire, so for sure his communication network is primitive."

The President knew he had the right man for the job. "Colonel, go to that island and bring him back. Tell him we need him. I'll contact the Prime Minister to let him know what we're doing. I'm sure I don't need to remind you to wear civilian clothes so we don't upset our Canadian friends. Bring him back, Colonel, and that's an order."

"I'll do my best sir."

"God speed, Colonel."

"Thank you, sir."

Chiswell stepped into the room to say that Sarah Walsh was on the phone. The President picked up the blinking line and said, "Sarah I am so sorry about your husband. He meant so much to me and always will. It was such an honor to serve him, let alone to be his friend."

"Thank you, Bill," the former First Lady answered. "David knows his life was not taken in vain. He seemed to have a sixth sense and he wanted America to be safe and sound once again, more like we were in the old days. He had high hopes for our country."

"I promise you, Sarah, I will see that his hopes and programs will be carried out. And I would like to ask you to think this over. There is no hurry with the funeral and all, but I would like to appoint you as Ambassador to the United Nations."

"Thank you, Mr. President. I am touched that you would think of me, especially with all that's on your plate right now. The answer is yes. This will be one step further in confirming my husband's legacy and I'm sure I can do some good as well."

The two said their goodbyes and hung up their phones.

Chapter 28

ALGONQUIN PROVINCIAL PARK
ONTARIO, CANADA

*T*he plane ride to Niagara Falls, New York, was uneventful. Meyers' unmarked Hawker was granted permission to land at Niagara Falls Air Force Base. He was supplied with a car, pointed it north, and went through customs at the Lewiston-Queenstown Bridge to Canada. From there he drove the few short miles to the Queen Elizabeth Way toward Toronto and to the 401. He drove to Huntsville, Ontario that evening and decided to spend the night. The next morning, Meyers checked in at the Park Ranger's gate by the entrance to Algonquin Provincial Park, got his pass, and drove directly to the Canoe Lake Store. The store is open just eight months a year and handles all the supplies, mail, phone service and rentals for the park. The small post office remains open all year. Steve parked his car and entered the store. After picking up a few items he asked directions to Nick Malone's island. They were easy, so a guide was not necessary. He rented a motorboat and bought a map of the lake. Soon he was on his way to "Becky's Haven" to see his old friend.

The island Nick called home was probably 20 acres in total, with a floating dock that could be removed and stored during the fierce winters of the north. The log house was small but adequate, about 900 square feet, featuring a kitchen with an old fashioned wood stove and electrical appliances powered by solar power, one bedroom, and a great room, which was glass from floor to ceiling. A giant fireplace made of local stone added to the already beautiful room and served as the house's main source of heat. Malone leased the island for 99 years from the Ontario Provincial Government and built the cabin himself out of cedar logs he cut on the spot. There was an old-fashioned well pump connected directly to the beautiful clean lake for running water, an adequate 'two holer' hidden well behind the cabin for privacy—not that he had any visitors to consider. Next to the dock was a 14-foot tripping canoe, handmade, of cedar strips and black cherry gunwales, and seats, by a craftsman from Northland Canoe Company in Huntsville. On the other side of the dock Nick had built a small shed of native cedar. He made sure the walls were extra thick and the cement floor was slanted and good for drainage. Each board was hand split, and the roof was made of cedar shingles. Every winter Nick would trek across the frozen lake to enlist the help of an old farmer friend who had draught horses. They would spend two or three days cutting and hauling ice from the lake to the icehouse shed and would cover it with a thick layer of sawdust. This prevented the ice from melting so it stayed fresh and clean all summer long. The only modern convenience was a flashlight.

Meyers pulled up to the dock, tied down his boat, and walked toward the cabin. Nick Malone was in his usual inhospitable mood and never moved from his rocking chair on the front porch as Steve approached. "Miserable bastard" chuckled Meyers to himself, climbing up the steps. There were many from SAS and SOE who believed Nick Malone was not only a perfect asshole but also a complete nut job. However, they all agreed, strange or not, he was the best there was at what he did.

"Nick, how the hell are you doing?" Meyers yelled to his friend. "I see you're still your same ornery self."

"Fuck you and I'm fine, I guess." Malone said as he got up to embrace his old friend. "What are you doing up here? You're the last person I would expect to see in this neck of the woods."

"Fishing," said Meyers with a sly grin.

"Must be pretty big fish you're after."

"They are," replied Meyers turning away to look out across the lake.

"Well tell your new President that if he needs some advice, I don't come cheap," said Malone, finally smiling at his old friend. "There were two things you could never do—lie and fish."

"And you never were one for the small talk," said Meyers with a loud laugh. "You're right, I'm here on business, Nick, and I don't have much time."

"I'm sorry about President Walsh," said Malone with more emotion than Meyers had expected. "He was a good man, but this is sure going to relieve America of some of its imperial hubris, isn't it?"

"You'd think, Nick, but as I said, I don't have much time. I'm here at the request of President Cassidy and your Prime Minister to ask if you will work with us."

"How?" Malone asked.

"The PM and the President want you to conduct a deeply covert assassination operation. They want al-Qaeda Central and all those who are associated with the bombings."

"So do I, but they're so insulated they'll probably die of old age," said Malone bitterly. "I could have had bin Laden himself nine years ago. You weren't assigned to SOE back then but, like now, the Yanks and the Brits were going to have a go at al-Qaeda Central in a joint operation that ended up in the usual FUBAR sort of way."

Malone took a deep breath, then continued, "I trained and re-trained with a group from your side, perhaps for nine or ten months. I lived and breathed bin Laden and AQ every second of every day. Several of my team spoke the language of the Pashtun mountain people so we could infiltrate very easily. No one on the team was blonde or blue eyed. We were all slight of stature and we fit like the proverbial glove—dark eyes, dark hair and lots of beard. Finally, the six of us shipped out. We landed in Kabul in the dead of night and changed into outfits like the ones worn by the Pashtun people. Our armor was the latest available which did not match our beat-to-shit clothes. If we were asked where we got the weapons, we would say off the dead Americans. We even made sure our hair was matted and, oh yes, we were even supplied lice. Don't forget the fucking lice. Do you know those CIA jerks actually breed those little fuckers just so you can look, feel and smell like one of those Taliban? What an experience! Those little bastards itch like crazy."

"Well, we hadn't bathed for three months, and we smelled as ripe as a goat farm. So you can imagine when we all get together with the Taliban assholes what it was like. What was good was that none of the enemy noticed any difference between them and us. At night we'd sit around a campfire and shoot anything that moved. When we shit we wiped our ass with anything we could find, leaves or rags and on a good day a few sheets of good old-fashioned toilet paper. The Taliban are so filthy I believe I caught one of them wiping the shit off the toilet paper and using the other side."

"Anyway, we were in Afghanistan and literally walked or rode donkeys to the Tora Bora. It took us months to get through the mountains and poppy fields. We lived mostly off the land, smoked game if we could find any, or purchased meat from a local village— usually goat. The price reflected their fear of the black turban of the Talib. Most of the villagers thought we were Talib and regarded us as heroes. This allowed us to move about with a certain amount of freedom to locate the target. We also had a laptop. Our orders were to make contact as soon as we had the target in sight and wait for permission to take him out.

"I'm here to tell you, Steve, I had the fucker in my crosshairs, bin Laden himself. We sent the request to fire as ordered by your people at NSA and the White House, and do you know what they did? They sent back a reprimand telling us about our incorrect English and asked for another request written correctly. Well, believe it or not, bin Laden was still in my sight when the second request went out, and it was strictly in the Queen's English, don't you know? The answer came back— Permission denied. The President chickened out, and that was that. 'Fuck it,' I said, 'I'm going home.' Typical government. The left hand doesn't know what the right hand is doing. Now, why do you think that I would be interested in going through all that shit again? I can cast a line and hook a three-pound bass, take my camera on a five-day canoe trip and snap pictures of all the wildlife I want or shoot the rapids of the Nippising River. Thanks but no thanks."

"Let's look at it in a practical way, Nick," replied Meyers. "Have you ever heard of the golden rule?"

"Of course, everyone has," Nick responded. "It's 'do onto others as you would have them do unto you.'"

"Well, that's one version, but the real one is "them that has the gold makes the rule."

"What's that supposed to mean?" Malone asked belligerently.

"It simply means you have retired and the Prime Minister controls your pension. I can't say for sure, but I would be willing to bet he'd be plenty pissed off if you turn him down. I'm authorized to tell you, you can pick anyone to accompany you or go it alone. No one will have control of the kill but you. Once you've completed your training you can be on your way. The President has also authorized me to tell you there is a five million dollar tax-free payment for signing on. That will be deposited in the bank of your choice. If you make the kill on Al Zawahiri or al Adel, he said you would be paid an additional 10 million dollars, again tax-free. Pretty nice pay check if you ask me."

"If I accept this assignment, who besides you and the President would know about it?" Nick asked.

Meyers answered definitively. "Only the President, his Chief of Staff, our Def-Sec and of course, the Prime Ministers of Great Britain and Israel. Those involved in the training operation would be on a need-to-know basis. Some of them are your people."

"You know, Steve, there's no one alive who wants those bastards more than I do. Ayman Al-Zawahiri, the #2 then and now the #1 who has my son, that's the kill I dream about."

"Does that mean you're in?" said Meyers.

"As you say, we must be practical, but between you and me I'd do it for free. Just to have my revenge," said Malone. "Just the other night I was thinking of Becky and thought how nice it would have been to catch bin Laden. I'm glad he's dead and Al-Zawahiri is alive so maybe I can have my sweet revenge after all. I would place them in separate cages stark ass naked. Then I would feed them rare bacon and pork sausage for breakfast, a pulled pork sandwich for lunch and chitterlings for dinner. I wouldn't even wash the chitterlings; just cook them the way they come, shit and all."

"What are chitterlings?" Meyers asked.

"They're the intestines of the pig and are considered a delicacy in some cultures, but sure as hell not by Muslims," Nick said with a grin. "Those sons of bitches would beg for me to kill them and I would, the same way my wife got hers, but slower and I may add only after I had them circumcised like the Jews."

"You're a sick bastard." Meyers smiled, "and that's exactly why you're the man for the job. I think your time has come. How about it? Now that bin Laden is dead, you can focus on the good doctor."

"Count me in," said Malone. "Just tell me where to report and when."

"Lock up your hutch," said Meyers, "you're coming with me."

Central Command, Tampa

The trip to Tampa was uneventful; neither man felt much like talking. As Meyers stared at the sleeping Irishman, he couldn't help but wonder what was going on in that mind of his. Every psychiatrist who had ever analyzed Nick Malone had given up. They had all come to the same conclusion: since Becky's death, Nick Malone was not fit for duty as an operative. However the SAS did not want to cut him loose so they offered him a desk job in operations with an equal amount of time as an instructor. Nick steadfastly refused; instead he took an early retirement and emigrated to Canada.

Meyers still believed Malone was the best possible choice for the job, no matter what the shrinks thought.

Chapter 29

UNLEASHED
MALONE, THE EARLY YEARS
HISTORY OF A KILLER

*B*orn in Ulster in 1974, young Nick Malone was running messages for Sinn Fein by the age of nine. Captured by an English army captain and five of his soldiers, he was taken to headquarters and detained until his parents were notified. The young Captain assumed correctly that he must have been enlisted by the terrorist organization with the knowledge of his parents. When they arrived at the detention facility, Nick's father was immediately recognized as an active member of Sinn Fein and arrested. He was told that he must inform on others in the organization or lose his wife and child to the Maize Prison. He caved in to their demands and Nick and his mother were released, but the Brits deemed the father too dangerous to be released. Nick never saw his Da again. This reinforced his dedication to Sinn Fein and, by the age of 14, was considered to be one of the best snipers in all of Ireland. With no formal training in the art of the kill, Nick, having already dropped out of school, would sit for days at a time eating dried beef and vegetables on a good day and whatever on a bad one while waiting for a target. He finally left home to protect his mother who was being constantly harassed by the authorities in an attempt to find out the whereabouts of her son. The constant stress of Nick's growing reputation was taking a toll on her health, for she knew that even at his tender age Nick would draw an automatic death sentence for treason and murder. She knew that she had lost her son to her husband's cause so she immigrated to Boston to live with her sister.

The English knew that Nick would be a valuable asset if he converted to their side. He was rapidly becoming a local folk hero and enlisting him would be a big win politically.

Nick learned to live on the lam and was constantly on the move, bouncing from house to house, moving at night, seeking shelter with fellow IRA soldiers or sympathizers, staying anywhere that was safe. He became a child of the streets and his cover was his youth.

Nick's years in the service of the Queen began after he was ambushed outside of Ulster. He had been ordered to a meeting of the Sinn Fein at a farmhouse on the outskirts of the city. His old neighbor and several key members of the IRA would be in attendance. When he arrived he noticed that the old farmer wasn't there. Suddenly the farmhouse was surrounded and all but Nick Malone were killed or badly wounded. The farmer showed up afterwards to collect his thirty pieces of silver, but instead he was shot in the back of the head and died as Nick watched. As he lay on the ground, Nick spat on him just before the soldiers handcuffed him and dragged him away.

The Brits have a way with terrorists. Whether they are AQ or IRA, one thing is for sure—they know how to get the information they're looking for and it was not long before young Malone came around to the English way of thinking. He decided to become an operative rather than hang. He knew that under British law a trial was not necessary and a summary execution would be ordered on the spot. Death at this stage of his young life was not an option. He began working for the Brits the following week and eventually, when he came of age, was assigned to SAS. He never returned to Northern Ireland.

After graduating from basic training he began his career as a field operative working on many difficult assignments. Eventually he was allowed to enter officer's candidate school where he graduated with honors. He became fluent in several languages, including Arabic and its many dialects. He had become one of the best and most trusted agents in the SAS when his world was shattered by the tragic death of his beloved Becky.

When Nick retired he traveled to Boston to see his mother who had gone there to live with her sister shortly after he'd left home. Their reunion, however, was bittersweet, for upon his arrival he learned that his mother was suffering from end-stage liver cancer. He remained by her side until her death. After the funeral Nick left for his beloved island where he lived in quiet solitude, trying to tame the demons that lurked within him.

Now he was on his way to meet the President of the United States. "Vengeance is mine," thought Nick. "This one's for you, my love."

Chapter 30

CENT-COM
TAMPA

*T*he plane landed and taxied to a far-off parking area where an army jeep was waiting to take them to the President. When they entered the makeshift office, they were immediately escorted in to see President Cassidy who was anxious to meet Major Malone. Prime Minister Lawton had cautioned his friend that the former operative had been classified as unstable after the death of his wife, but perhaps the years on the island had helped, and if the President wanted to take a chance on Malone, he would certainly consent to the loan. Personally, he thought the decision to hire the former SAS soldier was a hell of a start in bringing an end to this insidious Jihad.

"Major Malone, welcome to America or what's left of it" said President Cassidy as the two men entered his office. "I presume Colonel Meyers has filled you in?"

"Yes sir, he has," Nick replied.

"Good. Well then, I must tell you John Lawton is pleased that we have chosen you, and he sends his very best. He told me you're one hell of a soldier."

"Thank you, sir and please thank the PM as well."

"I asked you here because Colonel Meyers told me that you *are* the best, and for this operation that's what I need; it's that simple. Freedom has been attacked and freedom must retaliate, but I will not do it at the expense of the innocent. They bomb us, we bomb them, and pretty soon there's nothing left but more bombs. I want to use another option. I want to get the bastards who are responsible with as little collateral damage as possible. I have no intention of using my own security agencies because of their internal problems. I am aware of what happened to you during the Clinton years, and I can assure you that it won't happen again. As far as I'm concerned, when you've got them in your cross hairs, pull the fucking trigger. That's what I'm paying you for. Are we clear?"

"Crystal clear, Mr. President, When do I begin my training?"

"Right away, major. Colonel Meyers has been assembling a team to brief you on the latest Intel. He can bring you up to speed on where we are."

"I've kept in good shape," said Malone, "but I could be fitter. The Tora Bora is an unforgiving region."

"As I said, you are in control of this operation. You let Colonel Meyers know when and how you want to proceed."

"Yes sir, but I can tell you now that I prefer going alone. Not that I don't trust my fellow operatives, Mr. President, but I don't trust my fellow operatives. You know the old saying, "I can keep a secret but the person I tell it to can't.""

"Suits me fine, Major. Like I said, you're the boss." With that, the President stood and offered his hand. "I understand we both have our reasons."

"Yes Mr. President, we do."

"Thank you Mr. President" chorused Meyers, who had been silent throughout the meeting, and with that the two men took their leave.

Meyers and Malone decided to have dinner in Tampa. They both wanted big steaks and good wine, so they were driven to the famous Bern's Steak House on Howard Avenue. While their driver waited the two men toasted a lost love, a rediscovered friendship, and the future, whatever it might hold.

Training Camp

In the morning, Nick and Steve would start their briefing sessions. They arose early, dressed in civvies, and made their way to the commissary. The army took pride in serving really good food as part of its new image and putting on the feedbag reminded them both how much harder it was to 'take it off and keep it off' now than when they were younger. "Hey Steve," Nick chided, "why not have another order of biscuits and gravy?"

"I will if you order another one of those 14-ounce steaks plus two or three more over easy and, oh yes, have some more fried potatoes while you're at it."

They laughed, then Nick said, "How about you sign the voucher and I leave the tip?"

"It's a deal man, let's go." They walked the mile and a quarter to the meeting and found the rest of the team already assembled.

The three men and one woman represented a coalition between the SAS and SOE and the Mossad, the dreaded Israeli Secret Service. The SAS and Mossad members had been flown from Gloucestershire and Tel Aviv the night before and were expected to stay two or three days. The other man brought a rare smile to Nick Malone's face. Standing alone alongside the large square table was Master Sergeant Kevin McCarthy of SOE. The sight of McCarthy immediately brought back memories of the good times he had when he and Becky spent their off days with Kevin and his wife Denise. McCarthy had been on assignment to SAS, and he and Nick became fast friends.

"You old son of a gun," said McCarthy. "How the hell are you?"

"Better, much better now that I see you."

"It's been a long time. You know, Nick I never knew what to say when I heard the news about Becky. 'I'm sorry' sounded so innocuous in the face of what I knew you must have been going through. But you know that I am sorry, so damned sorry."

"It's okay. I received your card after the memorial and frankly, after Becky's death I shut out everything and everybody, I probably wouldn't have taken the call anyway. Mom passed too, liver cancer, you know? We'll catch up one evening but I'll just say knowing your part of this tells me this mission is serious and it will be a success. Those heathen bastards will get what's coming to them and hopefully it will be soon. Every last one of them is going to have an audience with the devil, and I'm going to be the one that gives them their ticket to hell."

"And that's exactly why we're here," said McCarthy. "Now let's get started."

The small group sat around a conference table where pots of coffee and tea had been placed. As soon as everyone was seated, the armed guard stepped out in the hall and locked the door behind him and Colonel Steve Meyers took the floor.

"I presume everyone here has already met, either in the past or this morning. We all know why we're here. I want to update Major Malone on where we stand with regard to Hamas, Hezbollah and al-Qaeda. It is the consensus of our respective agencies that even though al Fareed pulled the trigger it was really Quadafi who engineered the acquisition and the money for these bombs before he was deposed and it is bin Laden who pulled the rest of the strings before he was taken out. That is a vicious legacy and that's why we will focus primarily on al-Qaeda Central. We know they are located in the Tora Bora, but if not there, it's somewhere, and we will follow them to wherever. Our President will handle any diplomatic issues that may arise so we do not have to worry about anyone's feelings but our own.

Ladies first, so let's begin by hearing from our Mossad friend, Anna Kleberg."

Chapter 31

ANNA
THE EARLY YEARS

*A*nna had seen a lot for a young woman. She was born in Poland, and her parents immigrated to Israel when she was two. Anna grew up in one of the poorest sections of Tel Aviv but she was never hungry, as her father was a butcher and was allowed to bring meat home as part of his salary. Her mother worked as a housekeeper for a man named Yuri Asaluv, who was highly connected in the Israeli government. Throughout her childhood Yuri watched Anna grow into a beautiful, intelligent woman. Impressed by her remarkable grades in school, he offered to send her to college. He had no children and he looked upon Anna as his own. She wanted to study art history and languages, so when the time came Yuri arranged for her to attend the University of Florence.

In Florence, Anna excelled in her studies and graduated in the top one percentile of her class. After graduation, she decided to tour Europe with a group of her friends. It was there that she witnessed the growing tide of political unrest that was permeating the region. France, Germany, Algeria and many of the smaller countries had already spawned religious radicalism and seen it take root, especially in the Netherlands. The Islamic organizations, through false teachings at their mosques, had created a hotbed of hatred for the Western world and Israel. Anna, who through her love of languages had always appreciated cultural diversity, was about to experience first-hand the consequences of religious persecution. It was an experience that would forever change her life.

Anna had very innocently accepted an invitation to a political rally from some new friends she had met on her trip to Amsterdam. A lot of the people there were young Muslims whose radical behavior made her feel uneasy. She stayed for a short while, then decided to go home. When asked why she was leaving so early, she politely said she thought the group was staying later than she wanted and she needed some sleep.

Two young men involved with the rally insisted on escorting her home because of the late hour.

On the way, one of the young men made the excuse that he needed to stop off at his apartment to get something. Once there, the two males forced Anna into their room and began tearing at her clothes. One of them began asking questions and dumped the contents of her bag on a table. At first they had suspected Anna of spying on their mosque and reporting back to the Dutch authorities until they discovered her Israeli passport. "Jew bitch, fucking kike," they screamed at her. Then the larger of the two punched her hard in the face and ordered her to strip naked. When Anna refused, the other Muslim held her down while her clothes were torn from her body.

After the double rape, Anna was left alone in the room. She cleaned herself the best she could and dressed in what were now rags. She looked around the room, just to make sure she was alone, and noticed a chef's razor sharp boning knife in the kitchen. She quickly put it in her purse and left.

Anna was enraged but decided not to report her attack to the local police; a Jewish girl alone in the Netherlands would not find much support. She decided to take matters in her own hands and return to the rally. She hoped she would find her attackers.

The rally was still going strong with several hundred people still there and plenty of police to keep order. Anna stayed on the fringes, not mixing in at all. Finally, one of the rapists noticed her and attempted to follow her to the end of the street close to the park. "Hey, Jew bitch," he taunted. "Once wasn't enough? Now you want more?"

"I want to talk with you, that's all," she said, and the kid believed she wanted more sex.

"What would someone like me want with something like you?" he asked as he began to walk closer.

"I'll show you in the park," she said with a smile. "Let's walk down this way. It's quieter." It was only a few hundred feet before Anna found a bench and patted her hand on the wooden seat, gesturing for him to sit next to her. Before his rear touched the seat, Anna had the knife in her hand and slashed his face wide open. He screamed only once before the knife went straight into his heart. She flicked her wrist and withdrew the knife, leaving her attacker to bleed out. Anna threw the blade in the bushes after she wiped her prints off it and returned to her hotel only after she had dragged the body into the bushes.

When Anna got to her room she immediately called Yuri to tell him what had happened. He told her not to leave her room; help would be there soon. Within an hour, a woman arrived and identified herself as a friend of Yuri's and said she was sent there to help her. First the "Katsa" woman confirmed that Anna was raped and made sure she didn't need medical attention. Before Anna could say anything, the agent made a call to Yuri and confirmed her story. No, Anna did not need medical attention and yes, the young Muslim was dead. The agent told Yuri she had made contact with a "vacuum" (someone to clean the crime scene), which the Mossad had often used in the past. This time he was ordered to make the body disappear. If, for whatever reason, Anna could be identified as the killer, the fact that she is Jewish could create a messy situation for the Israeli government. She was given a diplomatic passport and flown out of the country that evening.

The plane landed several hours later at Ben Gurion Airport where another female representative of the Israeli Defense Forces or IDF met her. She was led to a waiting car and taken to a local hospital for a complete checkup. Unbeknownst to her, this was the first day of a long and dangerous career.

The Making of a Mossad

Yuri Asaluv was waiting in his office at what he preferred to call the Institute, when Anna arrived. She had never known what position Yuri held in the government but she quickly learned that he was head of foreign operations for the Mossad reporting only to the Prime Minister.

When Anna walked into Yuri's office, she was still in her tattered clothes. He gazed at her and thought, sadly, my daughter is not a little girl anymore. "Are you feeling a little better now that you're home, Anna?" Yuri asked.

"Yes Yuri, thanks to you, but I'll feel even better after I take a long hot bath and see my parents."

"Of course," he said. "In the morning, after you've had some rest, I want to see you back here. Call this number and a car will be waiting."

"Thank you, Yuri, thank you so much for everything."

"Anna," cautioned Yuri "please say nothing to your parents about your experience in the Netherlands. This must remain our secret. You're safe now; go home and relax. Your mother is still at my house working. Just tell her you decided to come home early."

"Yes, I will, Yuri and I'll see you tomorrow."

"Oh, by the way, Anna, you did Israel an immense favor."

"How's that?"

"The young man that attacked you was the leader of an Islamic youth group in Europe. He was in Amsterdam to recruit youths for ISIS. He was new to the organization but rapidly becoming one of their top operatives, and a very dangerous young man. Thus, as I said, you have done your country a great service."

"I don't feel very good having taken a life," Anna replied.

"You shouldn't, but there are times when it is necessary, for the greater good. Now go get some rest."

The next day promptly at 8am she entered the small and subdued headquarters of the Mossad on King Saul Boulevard. She walked into Yuri Asaluv's office and much to her surprise saw the Prime Minister of Israel waiting for her. "Good afternoon, Miss Kleberg, I am Eli Mordachi."

"Yes, Sir," said Anna "I know who you are. This is an honor for me."

"Thank you, my dear. My good friend Yuri has talked often of you and your family. He has much affection for you and is very proud of the woman you've become. We would like to offer you a post in the government. It is a very important job, and Yuri has assured me you are the best candidate for this position. Give it careful consideration, for your decision may prove critical to the future of your country." The Prime Minster got up to leave just as Yuri was coming in to join them. "Anyway, it's been a pleasure meeting you. Now I'll leave you two to talk."

"Good day to you, Anna," Yuri said as he sat behind his desk. "I see you have met the Prime Minister. He and I have a very busy schedule today, so I'm afraid that if we don't get started I won't have enough time to answer all of your questions. Is that all right with you, Anna?"

"Of course, Yuri" said Anna, "Can I begin by asking a question?"

"What do you want to know?"

"What is the Institute and what is your position here?"

"The Institute is the headquarters of the Mossad. Are you familiar with the Mossad?"

"Yes."

"I wear three hats here at the Institute. One is a Melluckha, or recruiter. I am head of that department. Second, I'm in charge of all Kidons. The two jobs intertwine because being familiar with the abilities of my recruits allows me to assign the right person to the right job. And last and most important, I am an advisor to our Prime Minister. So you see, my dear, my plate has been full for many years. By the way, do you know what a Kidon does?"

Anna shook her head no, not really believing what she was hearing.

"A Kidon, Anna, is one who specializes in assassination, and that's exactly what we want you to do, eventually."

Anna felt she must be dreaming as she listened to Yuri describe the roles of the various Mossad operatives. "That's how it is done today" she heard him say as she began to recover. "First, the selection of a target is a very complicated process. The Memune or Director General of the Mossad receives a recommendation to eliminate someone. If he agrees that there's enough evidence to warrant execution, then he and only he takes it to the Prime Minister. The Prime Minister must not only approve the execution, he must sign off on it. Signing off means that he and only he accepts sole responsibility. This is a heavy weight on his shoulders. We give it serious thought before asking the Prime Minister to sign off."

"What do I do first, Yuri?" Anna asked.

"Training is first. It is 12 weeks of long hours, lots of reading, and strenuous physical exercise. Your parents cannot know you work here.

Therefore, you will be set up with a no-show job in a department here at the Institute. Your type of work does not require you to punch in and out every day. I will enroll you at Hebrew University where you will study for your master's in art history. Your degree will prove invaluable to your job. It will allow you excellent freedom of movement overseas where your cover will be as a consultant to art museums and private collectors.

"I will assign you first to the department that trains our Bat Leveyha or female assistant agents. Then you'll go from there."

"I'm ready, Yuri."

"Good." Yuri knew he would have an excellent agent. A woman like Anna would be a tremendous asset, and one he could count on.

Yuri was right; over the next few years, Anna was responsible for retrieving vast amounts of important information. She was soon transferred to ASTU—Active Service Terrorist Unit. It was there that she excelled as a honey trap, luring unsuspecting enemies into compromising positions for the purposes of gathering information or executing a target.

Anna soon earned a reputation as one of the most brilliant and dangerous female operatives in the world.

The starting of well laid plans

Anna Kleberg was not only a beautiful woman but also one of the most efficient and feared of the Mossad operatives. Standing before the group dressed in simple black slacks, a white blouse and pearls, she had no difficulty holding their attention.

"Thank you, Colonel" she began. "As you know my name is Anna. I was sent here by Prime Minister Mordachi to commit the full resources of my organization to ensure the success of this joint operation. Let me start by saying that Israel believes death is the only suitable punishment for any act of terrorism. Our philosophy is quite simple: If you act against our nation in any way that causes the death of its citizens or members of its Armed Forces, you die. However, we too realize that all too often it is not the evil but the innocent who perish. Israel applauds President Cassidy's decision to preserve our planet and we are proud to partner with the United States and Great Britain in a mission that will eventually bring peace to a world buried in strife and fear.

"There have been some changes since you retired, Major," Anna said, eyeing Nick Malone. "We used to infiltrate a cell, eliminate all of its members, then move on to the next. However we began to realize that these cells were reorganizing and becoming even stronger. We realized that terrorists were being raised rather than recruited and the child was often more dangerous than the father."

Anna had an impressive record even by Mossad standards. So prolific was she at her trade that for a short time the Mossad had to keep her in hiding for killing an Arab prince. Reactivated in the past four months, she had been on assignments in Monaco, London and Vienna. These three cities were the newest playgrounds of the oil-rich Arabs who could enjoy the indulgencies forbidden at home. Alcohol, women, gambling, pornography, were all considered taboo in the Muslim world. These cities were getting unusually large numbers of Islamic students and many of the mosques were extolling Jihad and recruiting many of these youths to join al-Qaeda. The Imams were well compensated for their efforts by al-Qaeda.

Anna and her team were following the money trail when she received her orders to fly to the United States as part of an important joint operation with the United States and Great Britain.

"Since you retired, Major," Anna went on "the Mossad has focused on five basic points. Number one: in Western Europe and Spain the IRA and the Basque plus the Taliban have spawned the most lethal political alliance to date. Together they are responsible for most of the assassinations in the region, and are the largest producers of suitcase bombs, but not nuclear, in the world. They will sell to anyone with the right connections and lots of money, even a civilian. With the money they receive from al-Qaeda, they support their causes. They do a lot of al-Qaeda's dirty work as does ISIS. Their alliance began back when the three organizations were fighting the Russians, and, after the invasion they remained allies because of their echoing beliefs. Today, the Taliban receives tens of millions each year from al-Qaeda. Between that and the revenue from the poppy fields, their war lords have become very rich. In return al-Qaeda has been given asylum in Afghanistan, where they are flourishing, even after 9/11. This is especially true in the Tora

Bora because of the treacherous terrain. Most armies are not capable of conquering the mountains or the climate in that region. We hope that this alliance may give them a false sense of security that could lead to their downfall.

"Number two: Al-Qaeda has become very adept at laundering money. After 9/11, the United States froze all monies, assets and financial transactions in an attempt to limit their resources. Unfortunately, they farm out many of their overseas operations to private contractors, and the U.S. did this with a large company specializing in forensic accounting out of Dubai. There was a huge public outcry and, of course, the company was fired, but not before we learned a great deal about al-Qaeda's finances. Al-Qaeda had reverted back to a unique system that had been in place in that part of the world nearly forever. The antiquated but foolproof system employs the use of money changers.

"The system is brilliant in its simplicity. For instance, if a supporter of AQ wanted to donate ten thousand dollars to the cause, he could go through a storefront mosque, or one of those neighborhood delis often run by Muslims, or even an off-brand gas station that you see along the road. The mosque is probably the easiest because a church or mosque, once approved by the IRS, is tax exempt. The $10,000 is deposited in the church account so the donor has proof for a tax deduction. Once that money is merged with other monies, it is very difficult to find. Then the treasurer of this mosque draws out money for repairs on its building or for some other reason but instead gives the cash to a courier. The courier purchases an air ticket and flies to a prearranged destination. He then takes a cab or camel to his brother's tent where a different courier, but always a relative, delivers the money to another family member in, let's say, Algeria. Everyone along the way takes a small piece of the pie plus expenses, which never exceed 12%, and everyone is happy. All AQ does is make sure the money changers are sympathetic to their cause. This type of banking has been going on for a thousand years or more. When we catch one of the money changers, we are ordered to take them out immediately and turn the money over to the "office." Sometimes they may have several hundred thousand dollars or more in their possession.

"Number three: In many countries, communist dictatorships

have ignited simmering ethnic rivalries and hatreds. Bosnia is a prime example of this, as are the lesser-known conflicts in Nagorno-Karabakh and Georgia. Repeated attempts by the Russian army to suppress Chechen separatism is a dramatic reminder that the Russian federation is full of ethnic groups that bitterly reject Moscow's right to rule.

"Africa is the most tragic example of conflicts gone badly. Mass terror in such places as Rwanda has caused tens of thousands or more to flee or face certain death. Militias are sent in under the guise of establishing peace by the dictator in power, yet in truth, their mission is to pillage anything of worth for those in power. These attacks are marked by extreme savagery now known as "ethnic cleansing." It's common to see babies with their hands or arms cut off so when they mature, they are unable to pull a trigger. It's common to see babies taken from their mothers when they're still sucking. They are abandoned on the trail or fed live to the crocs as entertainment for the troops. The women are left to die after they're raped and disfigured or partly disemboweled so the birds and animals can eat them alive. More often than not these dictators use the country's natural resources as their own. Diamonds and gold are moved to Swiss bank accounts along with much of the foreign aid, especially from America. The balance is used for arms that are supplied to loyal troops as well as food. The people get nothing, and it is this overwhelming feeling of hopelessness and the abysmal conditions that are fodder for terrorist groups who promise food, shelter and respect in return for loyalty to the Jihad.

"Today, the area of conflict that generates the most hatred against the United States and its allies is, of course, the Middle East. After the war against England and Russia, the Taliban of Afghanistan emerged as the most ruthless and violent of the tribes. A warring people, they know no other way of life than one of conflict. Israel, Great Britain and the US have been forced to take drastic measures in our foreign relations policies to protect our countries from these zealots. We pray that peace will come to our region, but that's not going to happen, at least not in the foreseeable future. That's why we must do what we must do to stay alive.

"Finally, number four: The American economy is the most important in the world. Without the help of the United States many countries would not exist, and that includes some of the countries that so hate the west today. No doubt, over the years oil has created the monster. The Arab knows he can destroy the west by turning their thirst for oil against them. All enemies of radical Islam must be aware that its romance with black gold is its Achilles heel. If America and her allies are to succeed in the war on terror, they must implement strict controls to regulate fuel economy and aggressively develop the use of alternative fuels. The solution would be simple if it were not for the fact that the oil barons have control of your politicians, but that's a whole different topic that must be addressed at another time.

"What would happen in America if a suicide bomber strolled through a large mall and blew himself up in the midst of hundreds of people? The business at malls all across the country would decline. After three or four of these attacks, the retail business in the US, as we know it, would be on its knees. The malls would become parking lots to nowhere, and the Americans would have to find a different way to shop. But that's not the worst. Commercial real estate values would plummet, forcing office buildings and other venues to become worthless. Next would be train stations, and after that airports, and on and on it goes. It would have a trickle-down result that would soon affect the rest of the world. You say 'it would take years.' Well, you're right, and that may be the advantage that we have been waiting for. They know it will take years and years before their mission is complete and they are content to wait. That is the Arab psyche: they will wait a hundred years for something they want. That's why our time is now. We must cut the head off the serpent, or be conquered by their oppression. Israel looks forward to working with the Americans and the English so that we may end their reign of terror and watch as their assets tumble instead of ours.

"Gentlemen, Israel is at your disposal. We will work with you every step of the way, and thank you for this opportunity."

Dead silence followed Anna Kleberg to her chair. Nick Malone sat in deep thought while the two gentlemen from SAS rose to speak, followed by Kevin McCarthy.

Their meetings continued throughout the morning. After an hour for lunch in a private dining room, the group resumed their work. The day ended at 3:45 PM.

As Nick and Steve began their walk back to their quarters Meyers asked, "So, Nick, what did you think of Anna Kleberg? Pretty sharp, don't you think?"

"She knows what the hell she's talking about, but everything else was the same old bullshit. Kevin was good, but I had trouble staying awake when the two from the SAS were talking. Did you realize that some of the crap they were talking about came right out of *The New York Times*? It's the same old, same old, for an assignment like this, except for the Intel, you're pretty much on your own. I've said all along that's the way I wanted it, but Kleberg and McCarthy would be great backup. I would have no problem working with either one of them."

"Well, they're yours for the asking, Nick, so think about it."

"I'll do that," he said as they arrived at their quarters.

Once again, the two soldiers had two big steaks for dinner; though this time they stayed on base and ate at the Officers Club. The two old friends wanted to catch up with one another for a while without the distractions of the others.

Training Camp: Day Two

The next morning, Steve Meyers left his quarters early while Malone still slept. Meyers had an appointment with the President, and was immediately escorted into Bill Cassidy's office.

"Good morning, Colonel," said Cassidy. "How did it go yesterday?"

"Very well, sir," said Meyers. "I think Major Malone is amenable to the idea of having the Mossad agent and Master Sergeant McCarthy work with him. To tell you the truth, sir, I think it's a much better idea. That Israeli woman is not only brutal but also very savvy about the customs of many of the tribes in the Tora Bora and that's exactly what we need."

"What about McCarthy, Colonel? Don't you need him here to help you handle things?"

"I don't like sparing him, that's for sure," Meyers replied, "but if we have to, we have to. Besides, I think Malone will want him to stay back and handle all the logistics. After all, that's his real expertise."

"That's fine, Colonel. Set up a meeting with my Chief of Staff when you're ready."

"Very well sir, and thank you Mr. President." Meyers saluted and left the room.

Not far from the President's temporary office was the building where the meetings were being held. When Meyers entered, everyone was already seated, sipping coffee and waiting for him.

Meyers immediately walked to his side of the table and began by excusing himself for being tardy.

"Let's pick up where we left off yesterday," he said. "I believe that the three countries represented are all on the same track. After conferring with my President, and he with the two Prime Ministers, we have orders to start our mission ASAP.

"Major Malone, I suggest that you get on with the physical aspect of your call back to duty right away. When we're done here today, you will begin the intake interviews with our medical team so they can determine how long it will take you to be ready."

After everyone spoke for the second time, someone suggested calling it quits. They decided to retreat to the Officers Club to tip a few to a successful send off and the return of Nick Malone.

Malone and Meyers were walking over when Meyers said, "Well, what do you think?"

"Think about what?" Malone asked.

"How everything went today."

"The same as yesterday only more shit. Where did SAS ever get that guy? He spoke in such a monotone that I swear I had trouble staying awake. I'd rather watch paint dry than listen to him. McCarthy made a lot of sense, and Anna was smart enough to know that the success or failure of an operation like this rests with the person carrying it out on a daily basis. The other SAS guy could be a pain in the ass, a cross every 't' and dot every 'i' kind of guy. He must have been a bean counter in another life."

Steve asked Nick what he thought about Anna going with him. Nick replied, "I've never seen nor heard anyone quite like her, Steve. The Mossad is lucky to have her. She would definitely be an asset."

"Not only that, Nick, but she is speaking for the Prime Minister himself and their Knesset."

"You know," said Nick, "it might be easier traveling as a family than alone. I know I'll be stopped and searched several times along the way, As my wife Anna could easily conceal crucial weapons under her burka. It's taboo, you know, to touch a woman you're not married to. And forget about peeking with her husband standing there dressed as a Taliban. The only way we'll get busted is if there's another woman close by, but she may also be intimidated by a Talib."

"Nick, you're running off at the mouth."

"No, just thinking out loud. Is it all right if I talk to her?"

"It's your show, be my guest. Now I believe it's Miller time, let's go get one."

The group started to party at the Officers Club bar. By military standards, the bar room was nice and cozy with a few tables of four and lots of small booths along the walls with intimate corners and alcoves for quiet conversations.

Everyone was sitting around a large oak table for their first round when Steve and Nick walked in. "Have a seat," said McCarthy, acting as the self-appointed cruise director. "What'll it be?" The two ordered beer and a Jameson. Nick began sipping the Jameson and staring at Anna. After a short time, Anna caught on and discreetly moved closer to him.

"Is something bothering you, Major?" Anna whispered.

"Why do you ask?"

"You look like you're worried about something. I hope I haven't offended you in any way."

"No of course not. I just wish I had more time to think before I ask you some questions."

"What kind of questions, Major?"

"Oh, how about, do you like to travel, hike, and ride horses, carry guns and act like a cowgirl?"

"If you add killing terrorists to the equation the answer is yes."

"Anna, when this whole thing started, my deal was to go it alone. I have always preferred it that way. That is, until I met you. I can't help but feel because of the danger that you'd be in I have no right to ask you to accompany me. Does that make any sense?"

"Yes, Major, but that does not deter me from wanting to go."

"It's Nick, the name is Nick."

"Okay Nick," said Anna. "It makes sense because you lost your love at the hands of these monsters and as a gentleman you are reticent to place another woman in harm's way. But I must tell you, I lost my self-respect to them, so if you're asking me to accompany you, the answer is a definite yes."

"Good, I'll inform Meyers and the President."

"When do we start?"

"We will train for at least three weeks, and enter the region through the Air Station outside of Kabul. Then we'll travel up through the eastern part of Afghanistan, along the border of Pakistan to the north western frontier and into the Tora Bora."

"What if they're no longer in the Tora Bora?"

"Then it's been a long frigging walk for nothing."

"May I make a suggestion?" offered Anna. "Let's finish our training in Tel Aviv and rely on Mossad intelligence to confirm their location. Just an idea," she said, "and we should probably spend time getting to know one another, especially if we're partners in this. Besides, I can show you what our beautiful city is all about."

Nick didn't say a word, just listened intently to one of the smartest women he'd ever met.

"You know," Anna continued, "we have a special department that will dress the two of us in the clothes we require. You said earlier the robe and black hat of a Talib was your choice. I will dress in the burka with the appropriate head covers and travel as your wife."

"That's exactly what I was thinking. You must be some kind of prophet, living in the Holy Land and all," Nick said lightly.

They continued their conversation, and except for a few minor details, they were in complete accord. Nick felt much better knowing that Anna would be on the mission.

"We will be in Israel for just a short time, two weeks at the most," Anna continued, "a few days of briefing by my superiors, some physical training, and then a couple of days together so I can show you the sights before we take off. Let my superiors decide on the drop. They will probably use Kabul, as you suggested. They also have many connections in the region that can provide us with whatever provisions and ammunition we will need for the journey into the Tora Bora. Oh yes, I almost forgot, those clothes I mentioned, they're original; they've never been washed. You and I will stink to high heaven, but we'll smell normal to them."

Anna Kleberg was accustomed to getting her own way, but Nick's open-mindedness surprised her. She was well aware that she was making plans with one of the most efficient stone-cold killers ever associated with the SAS.

After a long evening at the Officers Club, Steve, Nick and Anna made their way to their quarters. After Anna had left the two men, Steve remarked to Nick, "You two looked like you were solving the problems of the world."

"Just half of it," replied Nick, "but I have changed my mind about going it alone. I'd love to have Kevin along, but I know you depend on him, and he has a family. I could never forgive myself if he got in trouble. Anna is single and so am I. Neither of us would be carrying any extra baggage. Besides, I want him as my point man back here as well as handling the logistics. Traveling as man and wife might just be the cover Anna and I need. Anna convinced me that Mossad headquarters would be the best place to complete our preliminary training."

"Nick, that's exactly what I told the President earlier this morning. He thought it was a good idea as well."

Steve looked at him squarely, "I'll bet she had a tough time trying to convince you of that," he said as he walked away, shaking his head and laughing.

"She made a good point, and I think it's safer all the way around," he hollered to his friend. Will you notify the President?"

"I already have, I told you."

"Within a week I'd like to be in Israel. I'll do some training with Anna and we'll receive our outfits. When we're ready we'll fly an unmarked Israeli jet right into Kabul."

"What about weaponry, Nick?"

"There's a special weapon I'll need to get shipped here."

The weapon Nick required was the Hackler & Koch PSG1 .308 counter-sniper rifle. It is the most accurate semi-automatic sniper rifle in the world, with a custom-made adjustable stock. The whole weapon is covered with Cam flex, a new technology that allows you to blend into any environment. If a soldier wears the Cam flex clothing and carries a Cam flex covered weapon, he's virtually invisible, just like a chameleon.

"Today's terror tactics often force the sniper to take out multiple terrorists at a time, and the traditional bolt-action rifle wouldn't be capable of handling the worst case scenario. The H & K PSG-1 also sports a built in Hensoldt Wetzlar telescopic sight which can be used during the day or during a pitch-black night."

"Nick, where in hell did you hear about such a weapon?" Steve asked.

Nick explained. "The SAS had experimented with it for years by using a prototype, but now it's pretty much standard in the field. The cost is hefty but worth it."

"Well, consider it done," said Steve. "I'll notify the company and have it shipped military airborne today. You should have it to play with by tomorrow night, and you'll be out of here within a week. Good enough?"

"Good enough."

The next week was made up of long days and longer nights. Nick had kept himself in good shape, and for the most part was able to keep up with the Drill Sergeants of Delta Force, making reinstatement little more than a formality. He repeatedly thanked Algonquin Park for this. Soon he and Anna would board a privately marked jet for Israel.

Chapter 32

A NEW HOME

"Mr. President," said Chiswell, "It's time to move you to another site. The Secret Service wants to fly you to Baltimore and then on to Site R, near Camp David via Marine One. Site R has been made ready for you and your staff. For security purposes, you will be transported late at night.

"When is all this going to happen, Jim?"

"Your bags will be packed and ready to go by 7 PM tomorrow night, sir."

"Very well," said the President, "but what about the First Lady? I would like to have her with me now that I'll be in a safer place. I miss her, Jim. She gives me strength when I need it most and she always tempers it with her own special brand of wisdom."

"I'll make the arrangements, Mr. President."

Camo David and Site R

Site R, officially known as the Alternate Joint Communications Center, serves as the backup Pentagon and has more than 700,000 square feet of floor space. It has a gym, a crematorium, a reservoir holding over 600,000 gallons of clear mountain water, sleeping quarters for 3,000 people, and a fully attended hospital capable of performing open heart surgery.

The underground city is located 2000 feet down in Raven Rock Mountain, about six miles north of Camp David on the Pennsylvania–Maryland border. Cut out of solid granite, it is a major center for the Continuation of Government. Established by President Dwight Eisenhower, it had often been the topic of heated congressional debates, with the naysayers complaining that it was just more wasteful spending. After all, Mt. Weather in Berryville, Virginia was already an established communication center.

However, after the bombing it was necessary to evacuate Mt. Weather due to nuclear fallout and the decision to construct Site

R was finally heralded as visionary. Now it served as the temporary home of the President of the United States, his Cabinet members and assistants, plus congressional leaders. The Joint Chiefs of Staff would be in attendance, and several other experts including representatives from FEMA. The Pentagon and the Supreme Court would operate from Site R. Approximately 600 military personnel were already working there, with more coming. Army and Marine Corps personnel with orders to shoot on sight guard the perimeter.

Help arrives

Most of the civilized countries in the world were ready to help and had offered to do so. Ironically, Japan was the first country to contact the President to offer real assistance.

The cleanup of the Capital had remained a puzzle to the corps of engineers but Japan's knowledge of nuclear destruction would prove to be invaluable. Federal health agencies had advised that no one would be allowed to enter ground zero and the surrounding area due to radiation fallout and disease. Only those who wore HAZMAT suits would be allowed in, and those were in limited supply. That problem would soon be remedied as Japan sent enough suits to allow full crews to begin the work of cleaning up the city.

The period after the initial blast was the most difficult. This is the third time in history, and the first time on our shores, that a nuclear bomb was exploded as an act of war. Adding to the confusion were the throngs of Americans who offered help and had to be turned away until the area was clear. They were told to return to their homes and listen to the airwaves for organizations that are in need of volunteers. COG worked as it did after 9/11, proving once and for all that it takes more than a nuclear attack to silence freedom's ring.

A new place; a new day

The trip to Camp David was uneventful. The Secret Service ordered Air Force One to fly up to North Carolina and over West Virginia to BWI (Baltimore Washington International) to avoid any fallout.

President Cassidy called for a Cabinet meeting as his first order of business at Site R and rose at 5:30 AM to finish prepping for it. He knew they were in uncharted waters, and he needed complete cooperation from his ministers. Not since the Civil War has a President asked for such extensive power.

The Secretaries had all assured him that they would remain in their posts throughout the crisis. He also knew the populace was terrified and needed assurance. He decided to hold daily briefings to bring the people up to speed. Cassidy was confident that he would get his requests through Congress, but the Cabinet would be more formidable. An important part of the team was missing, but he was doing well at forming his new government in spite of the crisis.

Lerrick McKenna, as the new press secretary, would certainly have her work cut out for her.

At precisely 7:03 AM the new President walked into the underground cabinet room to address his ministers in person for the first time since the catastrophe. Everyone rose from their seats and applauded as Cassidy entered the room.

"Gentlemen, today's meeting will be the first of many strategy sessions. We have a city to re-build, a government to re-organize, and a nation whose survival depends on us, so it is paramount that we work well with one another. Therefore, all of you will be privy to what each department is involved in. This government must be as cohesive and transparent as possible to its people. We must remain as tightly banded as steel wire around a bale of hay until all of this is over. I would ask that there be no interruptions until I have finished, then the floor will be opened for discussion."

The President then discussed the economy, retaliation, permission to put boots on the ground where needed, the DC cleanup and many other topics. It was a good meeting.

Chapter 33

ABOARD ISRAELI AIR FORCE JET
TRANSPORT # 194

*N*ick and Anna were relaxing and speculating about how long it would take to complete their mission. "It will take as long as it takes," Nick said, "perhaps three or four months, maybe more. Why, you getting tired of me already?"

"No, I'm not tired of you already," Anna said. "Just curious, I guess. I don't care how long it takes as long as we get the job done."

"Anna, don't expect to eliminate everyone in one trip. These people seldom group together in one place. We'll be lucky to take out one or two, and real lucky if we score three. They're as cunning as sewer rats. These animals will have guards around their leaders for miles. We'll call it a good day when we can get a mile away from them. That's why I chose the weapon I did. I could actually take them out at two miles under the right conditions."

"Unlike leaders from the West, al-Qaeda's inner circle is never seen together. They are almost always based in separate camps. They also have the most amazing message system in the world. They never, ever use cell phones for fear of being overheard; they learned that lesson the hard way. Some time ago bin Laden was on his phone and our people heard everything he said. By the time he realized his mistake it was too late; the American forces had heard everything. After his plan to blow up another building was thwarted, he implemented an age-old system of using messengers as they had in the past. The system is very slow but very safe. From then on, the chatter from al-Qaeda became almost non-existent."

"Will we be given a cell to use, Nick?"

"No, I refused," he replied. "In case we're caught, I don't want any giveaways. I'll have a tiny radio inside a toothbrush.

We'll start out on foot near Kabul unless we can get a couple of riding horses. We will hide out during the day and travel at night if possible. This is very difficult terrain; hopefully our animals will be more surefooted than we are. We have to make them believe we're the typical, happily married Taliban couple looking for a location with fertile ground to build our house and to raise poppies... to build our future. If we can pull off that charade we'll be accepted, and that will allow us to get closer and closer to our target. Prepare to sleep next to me for a long time and remember, *walk behind me, and speak only when spoken to.*" Nick flashed a rare smile and closed his eyes for the rest of the trip.

The plane's flight plan was so secret that the flight took off and flew south until they reached 30,000 feet, then banked and headed north toward Amman, Jordan and Iraq. Once they were over Iraq, Israeli fighter jets escorted the plane to Kuwait, where it turned South East over the Persian Gulf to the small city of Gwader, Pakistan. From there, they traveled due north, then west to Kabul. Even though they flew over four Islamic nations without permission, the flight was uneventful.

———————

The secret flight landed safely at the US military base fifty miles from Kabul. Nick and Anna were greeted by the base commander. He had no idea why they had arrived, but seeing the clothes they wore and the Talib black turban on Nick, he could only assume it was a covert operation. The commander offered the base's hospitality, inviting Nick and Anna to dinner as his guests and providing sleeping quarters for the night. Nick accepted the offer and headed to the dining hall with Anna. While they were walking Nick said, "This is a perfect time to practice our roles, Anna." She readily agreed.

They took a table away from the other patrons and ordered a simple meal of rice, mutton, and vegetables, standard offering to visiting Afghanis if they didn't care for the American fare. Of course, Anna and Nick smelled as if bathing was against their religion and a young soldier started showing off to his friends by making comments about it.

"Please leave us alone," Nick said to him in Pashtu.

"Too bad you don't speak English," the soldier said, grabbing Nick's beard with two fingers and shaking his head from side to side.

Nick pulled the private's fingers away from his face, which made matters worse. Then the soldier turned to Anna and cupped her breast. Nick grabbed his hand and twisted his wrist until he cried out in pain. Threats and language flowed profusely. The soldier called Anna everything from a whore to someone who should gang bang his whole battalion, if she hadn't already. His friends had the sense to shut him up and get him outside. The commotion had attracted undo attention from the rest of the diners, so Nick and Anna left.

As they walked back to the quarters where their belongings were kept, the four soldiers approached them. The troublesome one grabbed Anna by her burka and swung her around so she was facing him and said "Look at this, bitch." Holding his penis in his hand, he asked "Want some of this?" With a flash of her hand, Anna had her straight razor out, aiming it at the soldier's genitals. She was about to slice him when Nick intervened. "What the hell is wrong with you, private?" Nick asked in English.

"Hey mister, you speak English with an accent," said the soldier. "You should have said something. We would have left you alone."

"What does it matter?" Malone asked. "The accent, stupid, is Irish. And yes, I do speak English. Now get the hell out of here before you're all in trouble." The four men scattered quickly.

When they were gone, Nick asked, "Anna, what the hell came over you? You looked like a mad woman."

"I'm sorry, I just lost it," Anna replied. "A reminder of several years ago, I guess. Nick, I can put up with a lot, but that guy got too close for comfort."

"What are you going to do when we're out there?" Nick said, pointing toward a mountain range. "What if we come across a group of smugglers, what are you going to do, blow the mission because one of them exposes himself to you?"

"Of course not," she protested. "You know that."

"No, I don't know that. But I do know this: I don't care what some guy tries, let *me* handle it, OK? I'm supposed to be your husband, remember?"

"I'm sorry; it's something I've never gotten over."

"I understand and I'm not asking you to get over it; just get it under control."

"Understood," said Anna.

"Listen, when we're on the trail, we can talk more about it. When you get back, perhaps you should get some counseling, but until then don't let your feelings get in the way of the success of our mission. Our lives depend on you to be a subservient Arab wife. As your husband I will protect you. You must do as I say, and that's final. I hope you understand this, because if you slip it could cost us dearly."

Both opted for a good night's sleep and were glad they'd accepted the Colonel's offer to stay the night rather than push on. In the morning, Nick and Anna were refreshed and asked if breakfast could be brought to them. Neither wanted to risk a repeat performance of the previous night.

It also gave Nick the chance to cruise around with a Pashtun guide and shop for horses or mules. They came upon a farm that had one of each, only a few miles from the base. Nick bartered, and did well. The farmer recognized the black hat of the Taliban and gave Nick a very good price. He asked Nick if he fought the Russians and the Americans. Nick nodded in the affirmative, and the farmer gave him his blessing and a wide toothless grin. After the money exchanged hands, Nick took off, riding his horse and trailing the mule behind him. He still needed another mule to carry the equipment and reminded himself to speak to the Colonel, who was supposed to have one for him.

The next evening, supplied with three animals, Nick and Anna embarked on a trip that would change their lives forever.

Chapter 34

$\mathcal{N}$ick rode the horse and Anna trailed behind on the mule, leading the pack animal. The first five days proved to be a hardship for both. Anna wasn't used to sleeping on the hard rock and Nick wanted to move at a much faster pace than the terrain allowed. He was counting the days to when he could implement his plan and pull the trigger. He thought often of his son and wondered whom he favored, his mother or himself. Somehow he was going to get him back.

Nick and Anna were getting along well. They had a few rough moments, but chalked them up to the tensions of their journey. Anna wasn't used to this kind of life, and although she claimed to have been here before, Nick thought it must have been for only a short time. She probably took care of business and left immediately. He hoped she was ready for the treacherous winters of the Tora Bora.

Neither of them had taken into consideration how much the thin mountain air would affect them. Each suffered from altitude sickness, even though they had taken medication for it. Their journey would take them two extra days to travel around the Eastern tip of the Khyber Pass and into Peshawar. Once there, they would check in to a hotel in the old section of the town.

Anna said, "Thank God we'll get some rest in Peshawar. The thought of sleeping on a real mattress has become a favorite dream of mine."

"Don't get used to it," said Nick. "We're going to do our business and move on as quickly as possible. It's a dangerous place, loaded with smugglers, thieves, and al-Qaeda. We must be very, very careful."

———

Peshawar is a city of two million or more where people from all walks of life come to do business. All roads lead through the Khyber Pass to the Great Trunk Road that runs through the town of Parachinar and on to the big city fifty miles away. Nick and Anna had to avoid this pass in case there were border patrols and army troops—or worse, Taliban and al-Qaeda.

The bounties of cultures that made up the city were as old as the city itself, and dated back over a thousand years. Farmers and tribesmen came to do their bartering, whether for food and equipment or human flesh. The government, what little there was of it, turned a blind eye. Politically, the North West Frontier was a region that separated itself from the rest of the country; the people there lived by their own standards. The ruthlessness of the tribes that inhabited these lands caused even the Pakistani government to fear the violence.

Nick knew that if the two of them slipped up in any way, or didn't speak the native tongue perfectly, their cover would be blown. But if he were recognized as a Taliban warrior, he would be accepted immediately. These people considered anyone who fought the Russians and Americans to be a hero.

Because of its location, many ethnic groups came to trade in Peshawar. People walked back and forth from Afghanistan to Pakistan as if the borders were invisible; no one seemed to notice and papers were rarely checked. Because of this informality, the town was a safe haven for al-Qaeda. Most residents, especially those from the old city, were sympathizers to the Jihad and would gladly give shelter to the Taliban or al-Qaeda. Nick's black turban of a Talib warrior would not only gain acceptance for him and Anna, but would help get him information that was vital to the success of his mission.

An oasis in the city

The Qissa Khwani bazaar (Old Story Tellers Bazaar) is the most ancient bazaar in Peshawar and considered the heart of the city. Its history dates back to 1670 AD when the governor of Peshawar, Mohabbat Khan, decided he wanted a special place for the caravans and smugglers to congregate. Everything a traveler needed was available here. He built Caikhanas (tea shops) and Sarais (inns), where vegetarian and non-vegetarian foods were sold. The bazaar rapidly became an oasis in the middle of the city. It pulsated with the sound of men with hammers building booths to display their goods, smugglers working the streets with promises of great deals and the rhythmic, relaxing sound of horses' hooves. The smell of luscious fruit, roasting meats, and tobacco filled the nostrils of weary travelers who'd spent so many weeks living on the rocky ground. The local Pashtun, while friendly, kept their distance and a wary eye at the same time.

Anna and Nick found a room at a local inn to freshen themselves with a sponge bath, some nourishment, and much needed sleep. The inn provided stalls for their livestock.

Nick woke Anna early the next morning and said, "We've been here long enough. With all our guns and ammunition it's better that we leave as soon as possible. We can't afford a search of our room."

Suddenly there was a sound outside the door and Nick put his finger to his mouth as a sign of silence. He walked softly to the side of the door, wrapped his hand around the latch, and yanked hard. Like a shot, his left hand came forward and grabbed a young man perhaps in his twenties. He was dressed in the traditional way of the Pashtun and wore a Shalwar (trousers) and a Kameez (long shirt) that fell from his shoulders to his ankles in an unbroken line. In perfect Pashtun, Nick shouted "What are you doing, son of a dog, trying to rob me?"

"Please, Talib, don't hurt me!" the young man cried. "I am only here as a messenger from Mullah Izmat. He wishes you to join him as his honored guest for tea at his Mosque following the afternoon prayers."

"Where is this Mosque and what does he want?"

"It is in a town called Quetta, Warrior, a short drive from here." The Pakistani feared for his life; he was shaking profusely. Nick had the look of a killer and demanded to know how this Iman knew he was here.

"The bazaar 'talks,' Warrior, that's how. The Iman was told one of his own was taking rest with his wife after a long journey," the frightened man explained.

"Is this man Talib?"

"Yes, Warrior, one of a few."

Nick turned to Anna and told her to lock the door behind him, as he would be gone for a while. Being invited by an Iman to worship in his mosque and take tea with him and the elders was indeed an honor. Nick dutifully accepted as any Muslim would, thinking perhaps he could listen to tales of AQ bravado and other stories of bravery that tribesman liked to spin among themselves. He thought this might be useful. "Take me to your Iman," Nick commanded, "and be very careful. I would hate to send your head to your Mullah as a gift."

The journey was actually 60 miles from Peshawar to Quetta. The terrain in the Khyber Pass matched the quality of the roads that were built there—rough and rocky, and often impassable. The blustery weather reminded Nick of the bitter cold season that was facing him. When he arrived in Quetta, he was taken to a small but well-kept Mosque where the Iman stood waiting for him. He was wrapped in woolen blankets and winter shoes to ward off the cold blustery air coming down from the mountains. He extended his hand to his fellow Talib.

If Peshawar is regarded as extremist, the town of Quetta exceeds it by its own ferocity. Nick was in a town where local tribal law prevails. The Pashtun people and their devotion to ultra-traditional Wasabi Islam carry extremism to a whole new level. Nick was welcomed with open arms. The black turban showed that he was a man to respect.

By the time Nick arrived the prayer service was over, so he would pray at the next service. "May Allah find you well and prosperous," he said to the Iman.

"Allah has granted me the good life and the will to pass it on to others, Warrior," the Iman responded. "Please join me for sweet cakes and tea." He took Nick's hand in a welcoming gesture.

The two joined three others who shared the same political fanaticism as the Iman. After the cakes and sweet green tea were served, the Iman said, "Tell me, Warrior, why are you traveling only with your wife and no one else?"

"I want only to please Allah and fight for our cause as a Taliban soldier. My wife follows me so we may make a home together away from everyone. I have been married only since last summer, and Allah has not blessed us with children yet. I am by way of a trade, a farmer. I wish to grow vegetables and raise meat for market. I wish to have a small field to grow poppies, and I wish peace to all our brethren."

The Iman quickly responded with a question. "It does not disturb you to raise poppies when the use of drugs is banned by the Koran?"

Nick replied, "If the West wants to punish themselves with opium and other drugs, I do not see where I'm doing wrong. The infidels pay handsomely for this privilege, and it is just another way I can contribute to the Jihad."

The old man laughed, as did the others at the table. "You are correct, Warrior. The West has no use for the Koran—or Allah for that matter. We call this trade in poppies the holy trade." The rest of the talk was general, but Nick felt that not only the Iman was checking him out, but also the other three Holy Men. They said few words, but kept nodding and laughing in agreement. Nick felt there was a reason for all of this and told them of fighting for Mullah Omar against the Russians, as his father did against the English. The Iman asked, "What about the Americans? Did you kill Americans?"

"Some," Nick said, "until I was wounded and made a prisoner of war. Allah saw to it that I was healed. I, like many others, escaped and went back to our villages or what was left of them. It was then I decided I would take a wife and come east to settle. I like the idea of being so close to the Pakistani border, and I will do whatever is needed if Allah deems me worthy."

Finally the Iman stood, as did the others, and said, "I will pray to Allah you have your wish and also to see you again."

Nick was left in the hands of the young man who drove him there. He said, "Take me back to my hotel, and you should pray silently that my wife is unharmed."

"As you wish, Warrior," the driver said. The men left the Mosque together.

Back at the hotel, Nick reported his experience to Anna and told her he felt they should stay another two days. He explained that the men at his table were there for a reason other than to meet another Talib. He was sure he was right: They were somehow connected to AQ. Once they checked out Nick's story, they would find that he was telling the truth. Meyers had made sure Nick was on the roster of escaped Taliban POW's held in an American military prison. Nick had assumed the name of a dead Taliban, and the village he claimed to be from was destroyed by fire when the Americans came through. Mullah Omar was dead, so he couldn't talk and it would be difficult to find any details.

The two days passed slowly with little to do but shop. They would have to leave soon to find shelter, and there was no sign of any of the men Nick had met. In order to show they were serious in finding land and starting a farm together, Nick and Anna purchased more seed, tools, and dried food, plus another pack animal. They knew they were facing a bitter cold winter and had to find lodging before they were stranded. Some of the roads higher up the mountains were already snowed in.

They were making their way back to the hotel when Nick noticed that he was being followed. He quietly passed his hand around his 9mm, just in case. Anna, too, had her hand on her gun. The person doing the following came up to Nick and wisely said, "There's no need to draw a weapon, Warrior, for we're friends. We drank tea together only two days ago with my Iman. Besides, no man in his right mind would dare harm you or your wife."

It was getting toward dusk and visibility was not the best. Nick said, "Show yourself so I can see your hands."

The man stepped away from the crowd and did as he was asked. "May we talk, Warrior? I bring news from some of your friends."

"Walk with us to the hotel, and keep your hands where I can see them," Nick answered.

The two men and Anna entered the hotel and discovered their room had been searched. Not ransacked, just carefully searched, with everything put back into its place. Only a professional would know how to do this, and it disturbed Malone. He didn't want to give himself away, but he wanted his visitor to know that he knew someone had been in the room. "I don't feel like we're alone," said Nick to this man who called himself Faisal. "Tell me, Faisal, what is so important that you require the services of a poor farmer?"

"A poor farmer with a new wife is just what the sheikh needs. Armies must be fed, Warrior. We must talk quietly and alone."

"Where will my wife go?"

"She may stay, but in the toilet. I have come at the behest of my Iman. He offers you a chance to fulfill your dreams and do us a great service as well. He has land and a great amount of it in North

Waziristan, just on the Afghanistan border. You will grow food for our army, and you will take the profits from the poppies. We have training camps there that travel between the two countries whenever it suits them. It is a five-day walk from here, and it is safe from the infidels and the Pakistani ISI, security police."

"Why do I deserve such an honor?"

"You are a veteran of two wars on the same soil and a prisoner. Your home and village were burned to the ground, and your poppy fields were sprayed with a chemical to destroy them. You have lost everything and are a true hero. You proudly wear the turban of the Talib warrior and do not fear who recognizes it. We know what side you're on. The sheikh has asked for you because he needs men like you. He would be here himself, but you know that's impossible. So I humbly ask once more, will you come?"

Malone couldn't believe what he was hearing. Governments from all over the Western world have tried to get this close and failed. He, on the other hand, was actually being recruited. He silently thanked Becky for looking down on him.

Feisal added, "On the Imam's property is a house. The Holy man says it's yours."

Nick nodded and asked when he should be there.

"As soon as possible, Warrior. The snows will be here soon, and you must be ready for the winter planting. You will be supplied with livestock for breeding and butchering."

"Please take the message back to the sheikh that I will be there in four days and I am humbly honored."

"It usually takes five, Warrior," said Feisal.

"I said I will be there in four."

"I bid you good night, then." The AQ emissary left, and Nick and Anna were once again alone in the room.

Nick looked perturbed and Anna asked why. With fingers to his mouth he whispered, "While we were shopping our room was searched."

"I know that, but so what? We have nothing to hide except for this," Anna said as she opened her burka and smiled. Close to her skin and under garments was the special rifle that Nick had so much faith in. He pretended not to notice she was showing off her figure at the same time.

Nick was beside himself, silently laughing so as not to draw the attention of the soldier if he was still in the hall. In the same whisper he said, "Have you been carrying that long?"

"At least for the last two days, just in case. What pisses me off is you didn't notice how big my butt got with all that ammo taped to it."

Once again he couldn't help but notice how really beautiful Anna was. He couldn't believe she had carried that 18-1/2-pound weapon for that long.

The next morning, they were once again on their way. This time they would travel northwest instead of west, which took them further into the Tora Bora. They avoided all the small towns en route, figuring their appearance would cause more stir than it was worth.

The cold was the worst Anna had ever experienced. Her woolen clothes hardly made a difference and when the sun went down she shivered violently. Nick made camp every night while Anna gathered wood for the fire. It was so cold they took turns all night long stirring the coals to be sure their fire didn't go out. They had a tent that helped prevent the wind from torturing their bodies, but the best method was to wrap themselves into each other for warmth, and stay as close to the pack animals as possible, absorbing their heat.

Chapter 35

SITE R

$\mathscr{P}$resident Cassidy welcomed Lerrick McKenna to the makeshift White House. "These are unusual times, Lerrick. We haven't even completed your clearance, so I'm going to waive it for now until things settle down some. Fortunately, I have a friend who is an old hand with the press office and was assigned to the defense department when I was Secretary. He's been retired for years, but lives in Gettysburg and consented to help out. He's agreed to mentor you, and believe me, he's the best. You'll have complete access with the exception of a few cases, and Jim Chiswell will brief you on those. Your job description is simple. Hold daily briefings to let the American people know what their government is doing to get the country through this crisis. They have a right to know the truth, so no matter what, the word 'spin' is off the table."

The President was pleased that the Secret Service had been able to find Lerrick and Jeff. Thank God, he thought, they were on holiday when Washington was destroyed. President Walsh and his First Lady were very fond of her, and he'd felt she should be rewarded for not going against his order to not go public about the bombing of the bridge. He felt the same way.

Now there was a new problem. He had to face ISIS.

Lerrick felt relieved; President Cassidy had done his best to put her at ease. She had been worried that, with all the confusion in D.C. she would have to fly by the seat of her pants, and was glad to find out that she was going to have a mentor. After meeting the President for the first time, she sensed that he placed America above personal or professional gain. She looked forward to carrying his message to the people.

Lerrrick met wtih Jim Chiswell early the next day. She was overwhelmed, and Jim sensed it. "Don't worry Lerrick; everyone in this bunker will be there to support you. Just tell it like it is and you'll be OK."

"I'm ready," Lerrick replied, privately thinking how lucky she and Jeff were, being down south on vacation when the bomb went off. They'd arrived at Site "R" with not much more than the clothes on their back.

"Good. Tomorrow the Secret Service will take you into Gettysburg shopping. We know you both probably need everything. Later today I'm going to talk with Dr. Roberts about working for his country. Believe me, I think we can all use a good shrink right now." Chiswell laughed.

"The President said as much when I spoke with him yesterday," Lerrick said.

"That's good, then we can get started; now about your quarters. They are down the hall from the President's and next door to mine. You have a private facility with an office attached. You take the elevator to the third floor, walk down the hall about 100 feet to C-3. That's yours. Jeff's apartment is just down the hall. If you like, I can arrange for Jeff to share your quarters."

"No," said Lerrick, "I believe it's best to live alone under these circumstances, but thank you anyway."

Lerrick was sure she and Jeff would quickly settle in to bunker living and get on with their new lives. Each day would bring a new challenge, and she was determined to be up to the task.

Press Conference
28 September, 2015

The seat of the US government was now Site "R" at Camp David.

Lerrick held her first press conference at the auditorium and every seat was taken with standing room only in the rear of the hall.

Lerrick McKenna once a NNC staff reporter was now Press Secretary to the President of the United States.

Walking to the podium she enjoyed the standing ovation offered for her new posting.

Arranging her statement papers she began.

"Good afternoon and thank you for being here today. This will be the first of many bi-weekly press conferences that the President wishes, to keep the American people—and the world for that matter—appraised as to what your government is doing."

"To date the clean-up of our capital is progressing very well. President Cassidy wants the world to know how appreciative we Americans are with the outpour of support we have received.

"With that in mind, I want to talk about another threat that is not only to us here at home, but to the whole Western Hemisphere. There is an organization called ISIS, which stands for "Islamic State of Iraq and Syria," which is a deviant and pathological organization that wants to create their own Islamic State. They are the worst of the worst, beheading Americans and Englishman for no reason other than the passport they carry."

"The day to day leaders who order the tortures—including crucifixions and beheading of their own people—are the same men who were the lieutenants of none other than Saddam Hussein."

Quoting the President, she went on to say, "Remember they are the extended arm of al-Qaeda. They're the ones calling the shots. Remember it is folly to think they are too brutal and conservative for al-Qaeda. They are allies forged in the belief that they can destroy the United States and Israel. ISIS has proclaimed it an Islamic caliphate and will never be accepted by the world as we know it."

"We have a lot of work to do here and abroad and the President wants you to know it will be done. Thank you and good day."

Lerrick stepped off the podium into a large crowd of reporters wanting more information and also wishing her the best. She had defined her job and responsibility in a very short time.

Chapter 36

150 MILES SOUTH EAST OF FEYZABAD

*N*ick and Anna had been on the road for two and a half days and their patience was wearing thin; not with each other, but with the harshness of the landscape.

Nick was leading his lame horse down the mountain when he spotted a Toyota pickup truck with three men aboard approaching. He began to warn Anna, but she had seen the truck as well. "I'm ready," she said, "but we must switch; you ride the mule and I'll lead the horse." A bit later when the truck came upon the couple, they stopped and offered the traditional greeting. A large man weighing 200 pounds and standing over six feet tall opened the passenger door and confronted Nick.

Nick expected the worst. He had been warned that Roadmen were in the area and it was rumored that they would take your woman and sell her to the highest bidder, then help themselves to whatever you had that was valuable. If you were lucky, you got away with your life. Fortunately, this was not the case. These men had been sent from their village to escort Nick and Anna up the mountain. The weather was beginning to make passage difficult and the Mullah wanted to be sure they were alright. The largest of the men said he would drive the two of them to his village where they could spend the night. The next day, they were to finish the trip with his truck.

Nick accepted their kindness. All of their belongings were taken from the backs of the mules and loaded in the back of the pick-up truck. Nick was told that two of the men would walk the animals back to the village that was forty miles away.

Nick was shown a great deal of respect. As his wife, Anna was invited to ride in the front of the truck rather than in the open cold bed.

The winds were becoming fierce and most of the mountains were capped with snow. This gave Nick something to talk about while Anna held her hands clasped together across her stomach. Nick remarked,

"My wife is in the first stages of pregnancy, so I thank Allah for this ride. Allah has been good to me, and He has allowed me a child and a fresh start as a farmer."

"Yes, I know about the farming, Warrior, and it is good news about your wife."

"I pray that the all-merciful Allah gives you a son," responded the large man. "Please allow me to introduce myself. I am Khalid Gadahn, and I am the village elder. I was asked by the sheikh himself to guide you to your farm and make sure you are well."

Nick knew exactly who this man was–not because he had seen his picture, because there was no picture of him in existence–but because of his job. He was definitely either part of, or an aide to al-Qaeda Central, the leadership committee of the organization. He has been with al-Qaeda for years and more than likely fought the Ruskies with bin Laden himself. Nick looked at Anna as if to say "Just play our parts; you do your job, and I'll do mine."

The loving glance caught the eye of their host. It seemed that this man seldom missed a thing; perhaps that's why he has lived so long. "You care deeply for your wife, Warrior, which is good. Perhaps someday you will take another," he said, and smiled once more. "Allah has blessed you three times, once with a young wife, who is with child, and third, you have a farm. This is a good start. Your wife will be able to care for you when you reach an old age."

"I am truly blessed, Khalid. And the fourth blessing? Being part of such a worthy cause. I am very proud that Allah has chosen me to be here. Tell me, my friend, what is this farm like? Am I going to be able to sow seed this late in the season?"

Khalid responded with a not-to-worry look. "This climate is harsh, unlike the weather you enjoy in the south, but you should be there in time to plant your crops and your cash crop as well. Perhaps you would like some of my men to help you get started? That will guarantee the seed will be planted before winter."

"Thank you, my new friend, and I humbly accept your offer." Nick knew this man was no fool and that kindness was embedded in suspicion. The last leg of the trip should prove interesting. If he could convince Khalid, he could convince anyone.

The next day they arrived at their farm, a small house, good enough for two or three people. It was made of stone from the valley and instead of mortar, mud and goat manure was used to fill in the cracks. Once they'd unloaded, Anna built a fire in the cooking pit and everyone sat around warming themselves with hot tea, honey and the sweet cakes that she had made.

The farm was surrounded with old brick and stone fencing for protection against the elements. The small animals were kept close by, within the boundaries of the walls, while the larger ones grazed on the outside, near the barn. With all the outbuildings and the living quarters, there was enough room for six small families within the compound. This was more than just a farm. It would be considered a village; by Afghan standards.

Anna added more wood to the fire, creating hot coals with logs of walnut and mulberry which would heat the house during the night as well. This was done all year round because of the altitude.

The next morning, Anna and Nick rose along with their new friend and his soldiers who slept in one of the outbuildings. The group ate a traditional meal of tea, mutton, and vegetable soup. Anna packed food for each of the soldiers as a thank you. After saying their goodbyes, with promises of meeting again, they all went their different ways.

The Tora Bora
Beauty and Beast

The most renowned of all the mountain ranges is the Tora Bora, which is completely covered by snow most of the year. It dominates the Spin Gahr and lies totally within Afghanistan, while the Safed Range lies on the Pakistani side of the border. Both ranges are clothed in beautiful scenery. The weather is extremely severe, with long winters, short springs, and shorter summers. These adverse conditions, however, do not deter the many farmers who benefit from the rich soil and fast running streams that assure plenty of water. These farmers dominate the area with plant crops including orchards, vegetables and of course poppies, which are sold for the production of heroin, worldwide.

Centuries ago they also learned that the land was ideal for raising goats and sheep.

The Tora Bora is the most ideal redoubt in the world for al-Qaeda. Hundreds of caves zigzag up the mountain, making it a perfect area for someone to hide and still operate. The pattern not only shields its inhabitants from the frigid winds, but also protects them from enemy bullets and bombs. Some of the caves are hundreds of yards long and have been improved by their residents with heat, portable toilets, and propane cooking facilities. Osama and his soldiers occupied these caves when they fought the Russian soldiers, as did the Afghan Warriors of long ago when they fought the 'Angleez.'

Nick came to the conclusion that al Zawahiri and his war council had moved further west where they would still enjoy the protection that the range offered. Nick knew AQ Central would never start a training camp in this area if the doctor were still residing in the caves. Soon he would learn of his whereabouts, but in the meantime he and Anna would get the crops planted so he could deliver them in the spring.

The work at the farm proved more difficult than either of them had anticipated. They were both exhausted from their journey. The trek across the mountain region had been wicked because of the high altitude. It was especially difficult for Anna because she carried the majority of their weapons under her burka, and even though they had taken medication to prevent altitude sickness, she still suffered from shortness of breath and headaches during the trip to her new home.

As the weeks went by, Nick and Anna settled in. The planting was going well, thanks to the help of Khalid's soldiers, and Nick always showed his appreciation.

Nick was anxious to establish himself as a loyal member of al-Qaeda and was pleased that everything was going as planned. The two helpers on loan from Khalid ate their meals with Nick and Anna. Anna would cook and serve, then take her place in the kitchen where she ate alone. Green sugarless tea was served hot with honey and was a welcome treat with the rest of the dinner of cakes, fresh vegetables, and smoked meats of goat and horseflesh or sheep. Anna received many compliments on her cooking and sometimes Nick would invite her to share his table, since there were no women to share hers. The others didn't seem to mind.

After dinner Nick would tell some of his war stories, and then Anna would re-kindle the fire in the cooking pit to keep everyone warm. Exhausted from the long hard day, everyone would turn in early, so they would be ready for the morning.

Lying in bed with a night sheet over him, Malone wondered if the house was bugged. He felt that Khalid was testing him, so he assumed there were voice recorders and cameras hidden all over the place. Loyalty is what keeps al-Qaeda alive. Khalid would never confide in Nick until he was sure that he was trustworthy. Suddenly, Nick rose and walked to a large ornate screen similar to one in most homes of the Pashtu where women may have some privacy to change or bathe. He approached Anna and gently pulled her by the hair, back toward him, to quietly whisper his suspicion to her. She took the cue perfectly, and turned around and kissed him. She held on to him for a long minute, and then led him to their bed. After they had made love, Nick wondered if her spontaneity had been prompted by emotion – or was it an act for Israel. A complex woman, he mused, very complex indeed.

Nick made up his mind to go over the house again in the morning just in case he had missed something. He also decided to tell Anna to speak very little English, if any, and only when they were outside of the house. If they were caught speaking English it would not only be the end of their mission; it would be the end of their lives.

Nick's three mules and the horse, had been returned to him with another gift from Khalid – three pregnant ewes and a ram, plus three pregnant nannies and a Billy goat as a gift to the bride and groom. Nick commented, "Allah has truly blessed me once more. Tell Khalid I said thank you for everything he has done and thank you for delivering these fine gifts, so that I am able to start my herd."

When one of the men called him Ishmael, Nick showed his surprise. "Not to worry, my friend, I found out who you are through friends of Khalid. He says you are a hero of the Taliban effort against the Russians and the Americans. That in fact, you were with Mullah Omar for most of your career and were with him when he died. Mullah Omar's brother sends his greetings and good wishes for many sons in your new marriage."

The next morning Nick searched the house for any bugs al-Qaeda had planted. He found several. Images of Nick and Anna could be seen from every room in the house with only the tiny screen providing any privacy at all.

Anna was doing household chores when Nick took her by the arm and motioned her to go outside, pretending he wanted to show her something. Standing next to the stable, Nick told her what he had found.

Anna had been expecting it. "Are we going to clean them out?" she asked.

"Hell, no," said Nick "but I think it best if we minimize their suspicions. We must only speak in the local dialect for the time being. No English is to be spoken inside or outside."

"I agree, and I also think we should find a place to hide these guns. If I keep wearing them in the house we're going to get caught. Besides they hurt like hell. I'm going to look around these out-buildings; we should find a good place in one of them." In the second building they entered, Anna found a room that had been used as a workshop for the farm. In the wall behind an old Ford tractor, she discovered two loose wallboards where somebody probably once hid valuables. She carefully removed them and, with Nick's help, placed the sniper rifle and its tripod and scope, plus other equipment and ammunition, about four feet from the floor, then replaced the boards by nailing them shut. "That's done," she said, "Now I can clean up the chaff on my thigh."

Nick reached out to her and gently kissed her. It felt good to hold such a beautiful woman in his arms. He suggested she find another place to hide the rest of the arsenal, rather than having everything in one place. They began walking back to the house, hand-in-hand, smiling and talking like a couple of teenagers. Mahmoud was watching from behind the house and was concerned by their behavior. It worried him to see them openly display such affection, much like the people from the west. He thought of Nick as a friend and he wanted to trust him, but he had been tricked before and he wasn't going to let it happen again.

After dinner, Nick took Anna outside under the premise that they were going to check the livestock and get some fresh air. It was then that he told her he wanted to move the sniper weapon to the outhouse. "I want to hide it right inside the toilet seat, high up near the hole," he explained.

Anna's silence shouted her disapproval. "What if it falls into the hole? What the hell are we going to do then?"

"That's simple; go in after it. I'm positive it's a much safer place. An Arab would never look down the hole he shit in; that's as bad as eating pork. Besides, have you seen the condition of that thing? It's so unsanitary no one would even think of sticking their hand below the hole."

"Oh God" she said, "and I suppose it's a woman's job to retrieve it if it falls in?"

Nick laughed as he said "Right on."

"Suit yourself, it's your show," Anna said as she shivered in disgust. She had started walking back to the house when Nick called her back. Speaking in Pashtu he told her that he had noticed Mahmoud and Abu watching them. He reminded her again to speak Pashtu and walk behind him so as not to arouse any suspicion. He told her that he had something of importance to discuss with her.

Nick explained to Anna that Khalid had told him about a training camp still here in the mountains, a day's ride, which is where he will off load his farm yield. "The strategy we discussed was good but I will make my own plans as we go along," he said. "Our superiors expect a lot from us, Anna, and you know as well as I that to eradicate slime you must start at the top and work down. In other words, whenever possible, shoot the General and the troops will scatter. This will take a long time but the value of the end result is priceless." He continued to explain that as soon as the crops were ready, he would deliver them as ordered. During his first two or three visits, he would get the lay of the land and find an appropriate place to hide himself and his weapons.

"When will you strike?" she asked.

"In the wee hours of the morn when everyone should be asleep except the guards. To do this I must leave my weapons at a site chosen on previous trips to the camp. I am certain that the sniper rifle is accurate from two miles away, but I hope to find an adequate spot within a mile or so of the camp. After hiding the weapons and securing the site I'll travel to the camp as usual, loaded with vegetables and meat for the trainees." Nick was hoping that he could pick off some of the big guys, then call in the Air Force with their specially built C-130-A and create dust of the others.

As always when he arrived at the camp, he would be stopped and searched but they would find only a handgun and hunting knife, and to carry those was acceptable. He hoped he would be able to carry out his plan when al Zawahiri was holding a council meeting, but they were often held at night. Even though his weaponry was sophisticated enough to take out a target in the dark, the mountain terrain made escape in the darkness virtually impossible. Besides, he was probably not anywhere near the vicinity.

Anna was not happy. She had always followed the orders of her superiors and considered any deviation irresponsible and dangerous; although she trusted Nick's instincts and knew that his experience in the region far exceeded hers, she questioned his plans.

"Anna, you were told that at the beginning I had the final say and you agreed. Honestly, I don't like to fly by the seat of my pants either, but with the recent developments, I believe this is the better plan. I promise you; after I make my first trip in we'll rethink this together, because when it's time to make that final trip, everything about us has to convince them I'm legitimate or we've failed and we will pay for our failures with our lives. You must remember to be very careful when I'm gone. Frick and Frack will be watching your every move."

In bed, holding Anna tight, Nick whispered, "Smile, Anna, you're on candid camera." She rolled over on top of him, showing off to the cameras.

"I don't care," she said to herself as she made love to him.

The next day started out badly, but finally Abu and Mahmoud got the old tractor running and they were able to till the last six acres. Nick figured it would take him three days to plow the field fine enough for seeding and another two to plant it by hand. Potatoes, beans, carrots, cabbage, and squash would survive the harsh weather, and that was all he could do for this year's yield… aside from the poppies, of course.

Anna came out of the house and pulled the heavy cord that sounded the bell for lunch. Mahmoud and Abu were in the barn and came running. The cold mountain air, combined with the tilling and planting, worked up huge appetites for these men. Besides, Anna was a good cook and pretty to look at. She saw them smile and wondered how these mountain men could even eat with such rotten teeth. It's disgusting, she thought, and so unsanitary. She could not imagine having to kiss one of them.

Seated at the table, Nick commented on what a good job the men were doing. He told them he had thanked Allah for their help and couldn't have done this without them. The men were pleased. All the planting was done, and if everything went well, there would be a substantial yield. As for the animals, they were beginning to give birth.

Although some snow was on the ground, Nick was still assured an earlier crop than the farmers higher up the mountain could expect. Soon he would make contact with the commander of the training camp and let him know what he planned to bring in late spring.

Winter in the Tora Bora

The next day, Nick left Anna and his two workers with strict instructions for Anna to stay in the house and mind her own business. Nick wanted to visit the other villages in the area and introduce himself as their new neighbor. This was a step to firmly cement himself in the community. He rode his horse for what seemed like hours, stopping at each village and taking tea and warm food with his hosts. Twice on the trip he prayed with his fellow Taliban and was accorded the warmest welcome by everyone. Most of the villagers, the old men as well as the young boys, wanted to hear about his experiences in the wars against the Soviets and the Americans. He was a hero, and everyone was honored to have such a neighbor. Sitting around campfires, they begged him to stay the night, and in one village it was so late that he did. It was in this village that a young girl was offered to him by her father as a second wife. Malone knew very well this was a serious gesture on their part, and he had to handle it diplomatically. He finally told the girl's father he needed to think about it for a while because his new wife was pregnant and they were just settling in. This seemed to pacify the father, but Nick knew he would have to let him know soon.

Throughout the late winter and early spring, he and Anna got along well. Anna played her subservient role to perfection, acting as Nick's wife and taking care of household duties while he spent his time running the farm. Toward the end of April, they could see tiny shoots coming through the ground and knew that by the end of May they should have a healthy crop of vegetables to harvest. The poppies would take a while longer, but they would be worth a lot of money.

Abu and Mahmoud taught Nick how to harvest the poppies and to convert them to a thick paste-like substance ready for market. This would give him a good excuse to journey to the city and check on things. There he would sell his product, which could very well mean his survival in the community.

Late Spring

Their crops far exceeded all expectations, and Nick and Anna were overjoyed with the abundance. Mahmoud and Abu were pleased as well, and Nick told the men that they would share in the profits when he sold the poppies. Both refused payment because Khalid was paying them already, but Nick put his foot down. "Allah has truly blessed me with a profitable crop, and there will be more and more to come. Both of you deserve to be rewarded. I will talk personally with Khalid."

The next day he packed his mules with crops for the mouths of al-Qaeda trainees and made the journey farther north to the training camp. He took the two men with him after he arranged for a woman from the closest village to stay with Anna.

The trek was over the most difficult terrain Nick had ever known. The arduous journey made him long for his tiny island with the trout breaking water, hungry as hell and just waiting to jump into his skillet. It also made him think of his growing relationship with Anna. It was good that they were going to be apart for a short time; it would give him time to think about their relationship. Was it professional or personal, or was she as confused as he was? It happened so quickly and so easily that it had caught him completely off guard. It had been a long time since Becky passed. He had never permitted himself to enjoy the pleasure of another woman, but for some reason he felt that she would approve of Anna. They were both all about loyalty and dedication.

High up in the mountains, Nick stopped, gasping for air. Mahmoud and Abu laughed. Even though they were much older, they were accustomed to the altitude and could walk the range with ease. A lifetime of running up and down the mountainside had its advantages.

Nick's rest was far too short when he asked which way they should head. Both men pointed toward the Chinese border and the village of Mohan. Nick thought to himself, no wonder we can't find these bastards; the air up here is even too thin for airplanes. If a platoon ever found this redoubt they would pass out before they could make the kill. No wonder the English, Russians, and Americans lost.

Osama was never found hiding up here, nor was his successor. Nature had created the perfect hideout for the worst scourge on earth. Even though they were the enemy, Nick marveled at their resolve and steadfastness. Bin Laden had built a brilliant organization and it was going to take generations of dedication, patience, and the grace of God to overcome this enemy. Al Zahwari was probably his best choice to succeed him.

The journey had taken an exhausting three nights and four days before the village of Mohan became visible from the mountains of Waziristan. Thankfully they were only about three hours away, for all were tired and cold. A hot mug of tea and a good dinner would be a welcome reward for the weary travelers.

As they entered the village, two truckloads of Taliban and al-Qaeda soldiers stopped them on the road and demanded they be searched. In the chilly air of the mountain range, the three men were forced to strip naked and were subjected to a cavity search before they were allowed to go on. Nick said a silent prayer of thanks that his mother had refused to have him circumcised. If he had been, he would have been held as an American, or shot as a Jew. As the men were void of any unusual weapons, the searchers told them to continue and became very helpful once they learned where the food was going.

The men arrived at the village just in time to witness a woman stripped to the waist and tied to the back end of a pickup truck. It seemed the whole village was watching as a Talib soldier began beating her with a leather strap connected to a wooden handle. Nick was told she had been raped and warned several times never to leave her house alone, but she had chosen to ignore the warnings. The laws of the Wasabi are very clear regarding women. The court had determined that she was permissive and must be punished for her actions. It was ordered that she be struck 25 times by a Talib soldier in the public meeting place.

When it was over the girl was nearly unconscious. Nick's offer of first aid stirred the ire of several tribesmen, but before anything was said, he took the scarf from his head and they saw the black turban of the Talib. The men stepped back and offered apologies. The women, although silent, were pleased. It showed in their sad dark eyes.

An older man stepped forward and said, "Warrior, perhaps you would take her as your own. Maybe a new start, far away, would save her from Allah's displeasure; I'm sure you're aware that she cannot remain here. Her father has disowned her, and she has nowhere to go. If you do not take her with you she will surely die traveling through the mountains alone."

"What happened to her, old man?"

"Her name is Mara and she was raped by one of the warlords; now she is thought to be untouchable."

"I will take her, old man, and I will give her a good home. Cut her loose," he ordered, "and consider her mine. She will help me at my farm and be a companion for my wife, who is with child."

"May Allah bless you with a son, Warrior, and may your business in our humble village be profitable."

Nick couldn't let a 19-year-old girl die for such a ridiculous reason, but hoped he was doing the right thing. Several of the villagers walked by and spat at the girl until Nick threatened them. Some of the younger men, trying to show their fearlessness, moved forward like a pack of coyotes encircling their prey when Abu blocked their path and became the recipient of the first blow. Abu was a large man for a Pashtun, standing six feet tall and weighing at least 180 pounds, most of which was solid muscle. The blow landed solidly on Abu's cheekbone, and

Nick heard the crack of bone. In an instant, Abu grabbed the man by the throat, lifting his assailant off the ground when a beady-eyed, short man with thick glasses and a walking stick came into view. He was somewhat bent with age—age that had hit him early in life. Abu immediately released his grasp and stepped back in reverence to Iman al Zahwari who was standing amongst them, larger than life, with his hands together in the sign of peace.

"Abu, let the man go," said Nick.

"Forgive me, sheikh" said a terrified Abu "it was not an act of violence. I merely wanted to protect this warrior from a beating at the hands of so many."

"We must attack the infidel, not one another. I'm sure this warrior can handle himself. Now let me meet your master."

"Warrior, come meet the sheikh," said Abu, and Nick stepped forward and introduced himself to his sworn enemy, Iman al Zahwari.

"I have heard of you, Warrior," said Zahwari. "You are a known hero, and I have the highest respect for comrade-in-arms Mullah Omar. Those who killed him will pay with their blood, and sooner than you think. But enough of that talk until we have supper and pray. I am told Allah has brought you here on a mission. I am told you offer us your crops and you will bring poppies to Pakistan."

"That is true, sheikh, and the first of the bounty is with you now. I pray each day Allah will give me the strength to complete several trips here, with fresh food for those that are so worthy. There is much more to pick but I have no way of making just one trip. These are all the animals I have."

"Allah has blessed me, Warrior, by your presence," said al Zahwari, and he turned to the crowd. He told them they should honor him as a war hero who was here to help. He turned back to Nick and invited him to ride back to his quarters so they could talk. Malone bowed his head in humble gratitude and followed the sheik, praying silently that he could act sincere enough to avoid detection.

The Wasabis revered their leaders, especially Bin Laden and the new leader, who were both treated as holy men. Some of the younger tribesmen looked upon al Zahwari as a national hero, a thought that made Nick want to puke. That type of adoration was rooted in the western cultures that al Zahwari despised. Nick wondered if it were directed towards someone else would he denounce such public displays of affection. Perhaps his ego would prove to be his Achilles heel. Nick knew that he hadn't survived this long by being stupid.

Nick followed al Zahwari to a waiting truck. They sat together in the rear seat and the cunning new leader of al-Qaeda asked about the former war with the infidels and where Nick fought and with whom. He even went as far back as the Russians and was being very thorough. Nick knew he was being tested and silently thanked the Mossad for the rehearsals. Al Zahwari seemed pleased that Nick had fought with Mullah Omar and told him that the Mullah had been a great friend and, that he still mourned his death. Nick was glad he had taken the identity of a dead Talib fighter who was in fact attached to Omar. Zahwari wondered out loud why their paths hadn't crossed, especially since he and the Mullah were together many times during the conflicts. Nick answered that it was probably because he was allowed to go back to his village to save his father, but when he arrived he found that his father had been tortured and killed, and the entire village totally destroyed. That answer brought on a tirade about the Russians and how they got what they deserved and what he wanted to do to the Americans and the English. He ranted on and on about the sins of the Americans, extolling Las Vegas as an example of the way the Great Satan lives.

When he was finished Nick concluded everything that he had heard about him was true: Iman al Zahwari was a psychopath. He claimed to be a religious leader, yet trained young men to be Islamic martyrs, promising them honey and virgins; he led others as if he were a great general, yet he showed no compassion and was interested only in complete annihilation of any and all who opposed him.

Maybe, Nick thought, he should just take him out now. If ever there was a mission worth dying for, this was it. Then Nick thought of Anna and the girl; they would certainly be killed, and Anna's death would be slow and painful. No, he thought, he would play his part until the time was right. When it comes, he will rid the world of this lunatic and others like him.

After another security check, Nick entered a huge cave, which curved sharply to the left and then to the right before heading straight back—perhaps 200 feet—into a large room carved out of a natural cave. It had all the added comforts of home—icarpets, food, a generator, a small stove, bottled water, and more. Nick noticed the water was bottled in the USA; Zahwari must have thought the Great Satan was good for something. When he entered, Nick was invited to join in conversation with two other men. They were obviously proud to be in the presence of a fellow warrior and treated him as an honored guest. Nick was hungry after his long trip, and his appetite brought a smile to the sheik's face. He knew however, that he could not let down his guard, for even the slightest mistake would be fatal. Nick was careful to keep his answers simple and to the point. He accepted another mug of hot tea and was offered a plate of honey cakes to take back to the sleeping cell Zahwari's lieutenants had provided him.

Al Zahwari's beliefs were that of the Wasabi sect, the strictest of all of the Islamic sects known today. They are particularly rigid in their attitude towards women and have been known to execute a woman for showing her ankle or her face in public. Women's worth was measured only by their ability to produce children and serve their husbands. Beatings were routine for even the slightest infractions. Listening to music, going to school, seeing a movie, or just plain kite flying (which is a national pastime) are not allowed and come with severe penalties. Radio, television and newspapers were also against the law, which kept the people from being influenced by the world that existed beyond their towns and villages.

Nick listened intently as the three men denounced the United States and extolled the creation of Islamic states throughout the western world. He remained motionless while every nerve in his body screamed for him to seize his weapon and take the life of the man who had masterminded the murders of so many, including his beloved Becky. But Nick knew that killing just the leader alone, and not the other members of the inner counsel, would lead to a swift retaliation by a man who was as savage as they come. Nick wondered if his son was nearby. No, thought Nick, I have penetrated deeper into the organization than anyone else and the more information I can send back about the inner workings of al-Qaeda, the better chance we have of eliminating them. All of them.

"You seem distracted, Warrior, what is bothering you?"

"I become angered when I think of how the infidel disrespects our faith more and more every day. They want to strip us of our dignity and tell us how to run our lives and country; I'm not willing to accept that. I pray to Allah that I may take more of a role in seeing their end."

"And so you shall warrior, so you shall. I have no words to express how important our cause is. We will talk more at another time. Now I must take leave, but before I do I have a gift for you. Come, follow me."

Nick obliged him and walked out to the entrance of the cave. As he watched, a soldier drove up in a brand new green four-door Toyota Tundra truck with an extra 100-gallon fuel tank attached to the rear bed for long distance driving; the vehicle of choice for al-Qaeda. The new leader turned to Nick and said; "Now you can deliver your goods more efficiently, Warrior. I have arranged for my men to deliver your animals. They will be at your farm within a few days."

Nick was stunned and thanked him profusely for the gift, while thinking *I will use this to carry the nails for your coffin.* He took the keys and drove to the sleeping cell. He couldn't wait to leave. That would happen early in the morning with his helpers and the young woman.

The other men from the dinner offered their goodbyes, Allah's blessings, and their wrath on the Great Satan. Nick decided that one thing was for sure: that monster didn't live in that cave. He was hiding somewhere else.

The truck was packed with Mara's few belongings, and then the four of them set out on the journey home. Nick was anxious to get out of there and get back to Anna.

On the way home, Nick commented to his men about the gift and bragged to them how much he was honored. Abu and Mahmoud were pleased and appreciated Nick's comments. Even though everything had gone well, he resolved not to get too cocky: What's good today, could become tomorrow's nightmare.

The young woman sat in the back, looking sad and beaten, a tear running down her cheek. She would never see her parents again because she had disobeyed them. The rape would leave lasting scars, and she would forever be condemned as damaged goods. She was cast out in disgrace, with nothing but a few meager belongings. Abu had learned that apparently this particular warlord wanted Mara's father's property and when he was refused, he decided to show how powerful he was. Every time he came to the village he paid a visit to their home and had his way with Mara. The rapes had been repeated many times without consequence, so Mara, determined not to let him harm her again, fled her home at the first word of his arrival, even though it was against the laws of the village for a woman to go out unescorted. After several warnings, the elders ordered that she be lashed and banned. During the journey to her new home, Mara tried to put the horror out of her mind, felt she was safe, and hoped she was headed to a better life. Mahmoud said he thought the woman was beautiful, and he didn't mind if she wasn't a virgin. Nick stepped in and told him to be patient; that she needed time for healing.

Nick was beginning to worry that coming to Mara's defense might upset his plans. He knew Abu and Mahmoud were soldiers and only worked at the farm to inform Khalid of his movements, and he didn't want to create any unwanted suspicions. He also knew that as soldiers of al-Qaeda they were as zealous as their leaders and could cause immeasurable damage if they reported any suspicions to Khalid. The old saying, "sleep with both eyes open," was never more appropriate than it was now. Nick decided to set traps on his bedroom door just in case they tried to pull something while he was asleep. Maybe he should send them on their final trip sooner rather than later? No, he decided, the safest way was to kill them while they were working in the fields just before he and Anna left for good. He would definitely take Mara with them, give her some money, and take her to the States and offer her a chance at a better life. He was certain he could get her in, and when he did, he would make sure she got a good education. There was no way he was going to leave her in this wretched part of the world. He smiled thinking 'You bastard, you took my son, now I have one of yours. Yes, I now have a daughter.'

Late in the afternoon, just before it turned dark, the three men and the girl arrived at the farm tired and hungry. Anna was pleased to see them all and prepared a quick meal. Afterwards she asked Nick to take the woman who had been staying with her back to her parents in the next village.

Anna was staring at Mara, when Nick broke the silence by introducing her, and explained the circumstances surrounding her expulsion from the village. Anna took her by the hand and led her to a tiny room at the back of the house. She told Mara this would be her room, then left to find clean bedding and fresh water. Anna welcomed Mara, and explained that she would be expected to help with the household duties and assist with the farm work when needed. Her personal belongings, what little she had, were taken from the truck and dropped on the floor of her room. Anna then brought out the first aid kit and began cleaning Mara's lash wounds.

In bed that evening, Anna whispered in Nick's ear, "You must be crazy to bring that girl back with you. What were you thinking of AND what are we going to do with her?"

"I've thought about it and I want to take her with us to the states. Now go to sleep, and we'll talk more in the morning."

Anna was worried; compassion could get you killed in their line of work.

Several days of backbreaking work in the fields followed, and Mara proved absolutely invaluable. She worked as hard as the men and helped Anna in the house as well. All was going very well until Abu made advances and she wanted no part of it. Instead of getting angry, Nick took the high road and talked to Abu. He told him this was the wrong way to start a relationship, and he must let her heal first. Nick warned him that she was not to be touched. Abu had done nothing wrong; he just tried to kiss her; but she got scared, fearing that Abu wanted more. Nick and Anna calmed her down, and Abu, who regarded Nick as a friend, was embarrassed and left the house. There was another problem: Mahmoud also had his eyes set on her, and this could set the men apart. Perhaps it was time to consult Khalid.

Anna explained to Mara that she was safe at the farm. She also told Mara that both men found her very attractive and perhaps Mara should begin thinking about which one she would choose if the opportunity arose.

"Neither," Mara said emphatically. "They're Taliban and they belong to al-Qaeda. I want nothing to do with a marriage like that. They will die soon and what would I do in this world as a widow? I cannot go back to my village, so I would die alone out here and so would my children, if I had any."

Anna felt bad for the young girl who had no idea that her future was going to get brighter.

Chapter 37

FOUR MONTHS LATER AND THE FINAL TRIP

*N*ick decided to leave in two days for his 6th and final trip to the al-Qaeda training camp and instructed Abu and Mahmoud to load the truck high with fresh crops for the AQ soldiers. He told them what he wanted done at the farm during his absence and warned them both that Mara was off limits.

Later that night, Nick went to the outhouse to retrieve his sniper rifle. He extracted it from the waste pit, wiped it down, and stored it in his truck. He had created a storage area underneath the 100-gallon auxiliary tank that sat near the rear window of the Toyota. When disassembled, the compact rifle could be easily stored behind the tank. He then placed a wooden toolbox in front of the tank and bolted it in place on the truck bed. Now it was time for a good night sleep, but first he must talk to Anna.

She listened as Nick went over his plan. He refrained from telling her where he would hide his weapons, or where he would take his final shots, just in case she was forced to talk. She had cautioned him that there must be enough dirt and sand to brush the area clear of any tracks so that, upon his return, he would immediately be able to see if the site had been compromised. Nick confirmed that the area he picked out was perfectly suited to his needs. A narrow path that jutted off the main road about a mile from the training camp led to a sandy clearing that was encircled by trees and thick underbrush—well suited for hiding his gear. After he secured the site he would continue on to the training camp as usual and stay an extra day if invited by the sheikh. He told Anna to say a prayer that al Zahwari was there so he could kill him.

"It's ironic isn't it, that we ask God to help us kill," said Anna.

Nick didn't respond to Anna's remark; instead, he continued to discuss his strategy. "When I arrive at the camp they will search me as usual. However, it will be little more than a mere formality because of the number of times I have been there; most of the guards now call me by name. Once I'm done with the search I will deliver my goods and make small talk with the locals. They like that, and always want me to meet their kinfolk or their daughters. They could sit for hours listening to the stories about the deeds of the Taliban warriors. When the time comes to leave I will travel back to the hiding place, put on the Ghille suit, and prepare to strike at first light. If all goes accordingly, I will come home and kill Abu and Mahmoud. Then you, Mara, and I will make a run for the Peshawar border and wait to be picked up."

Anna asked, "How will you make contact?"

"I have a GPS tracker that tells Colonel Meyers where I am 24/7; it's buried in my arm pit somewhere. I was also given a radio by which I can contact a war plane that can come to my rescue in a matter of minutes."

"Why didn't you tell me that?" she asked.

"I didn't think it was necessary. But while we're on the subject I have something else for you, too." He pulled a small capsule out of his pocket and gave it to her. "If they find out you're a Jew they will torture you until you beg for the mercy of death."

"I have one, remember. I'm Mossad."

"I almost forgot," Nick said with a slight smile. "I've been playing the protective husband, remember. Seriously, I don't want to think that what happened to Becky could happen to you."

"Nick, while you're out there, if you think of anything except the mission it could be fatal for all of us. I will do my part here but if something happens to you, how will I know? Will someone contact me?"

"Take this," said Nick and he handed her a small transmitter similar to the one he carried. "If for some reason they lose contact with me, this unit will become activated and Colonel Meyers will contact you. Be careful to limit your words in case the Taliban can pick up the transmission; however, if these mountains protect them, they should also protect us. Meyers will dispatch the warplane to come and get you and Mara, unless the shit really hits the fan. Then it's time to take the pills."

"I just hope you come back, because the thought of riding that friggin mule back to Pakistan doesn't do much for my disposition."

"Let's walk back, Anna. It's time to get some sleep."

The house was quiet, and the two made passionate love and gave the cameras one final show. "I would like to do this with some meaning behind it," he told her.

"Someday soon," she whispered, "when we're back home."

The next morning came too soon. Nick got up from a sound sleep and had to shake Anna to wake her. She made him a large breakfast and packed extra food in case he had to make a run for it. Mara bade him goodbye and wished Allah to provide a safe journey. Abu and Mahmoud sent him off with all the usual blessings one bestows on a fellow soldier, and Nick assured them he would be back in a few days.

Chapter 38

CAMP DAVID
SITE R

*P*resident Bill Cassidy had a few moments to reflect on what had happened in these past months before his busy day began. He was thankful that everyone he appointed was doing his job and doing it well. He was close to accomplishing the goals he set for his first year in office. He had three years to go, and it was way too early to think about running for his own term, but the idea had occurred to him. He knew that filling the term of David Walsh didn't give him enough time to accomplish everything he wanted to do – things like believing in a smaller national government and thinking he would be much happier when he could drop Martial Law and give Americans back their rights. It was important for them to get on with their lives. He also knew that in order to get the job done, he would have to remain as steadfast as possible.

Cassidy changed his thoughts to Warren Dunn and the terrible disservice he caused his country. Several months had passed and the weather was changing rapidly, but that didn't affect the morale of the thousands of workers who were working to create a new capital on the same foundations as the old one. The capital was beginning to show great progress and his promise to re-build was becoming a reality.

He reached for his phone and asked his secretary to find Colonel Meyers and Master Sergeant McCarthy and ask them to be available by tomorrow morning at 9AM.

McCarthy and Meyers had been waiting just a few minutes before they were escorted to the President's office.

"Gentlemen," said the President, "after you found Nick Malone for me, I should have sent you right back to Houston to finish the job David Walsh had originally ordered. The country doesn't need any more grief, and that's why I am going to order you and Master Sergeant McCarthy back to Houston to visit Mr. Dunn for the last time. While you're at it, find out who this mysterious Arab woman is that's hanging around and bring her to your safe house. Her knowledge of who is guilty in our house and senate is invaluable. It will be up to your discretion as to how, but do whatever is necessary to end this problem. You have complete carte blanche from this office."

The two men were dismissed.

––––––––––

The President then turned his attention to Sarah Walsh, the new Ambassador to the United Nations.

When she entered his office he stood and hugged her. This was the first time he had seen her since her husband died.

Sarah was proving to be as effective as Eleanor Roosevelt, and commanded the utmost respect from her peers as she committed herself to her President's bidding.

"Sarah," said Cassidy, "I want you to address the UN Assembly and explain to them the new ways our government is working. We are going to take care of ourselves first and foremost; then we will work on world peace. Tell them I am not one for world order, but for freedom to choose whatever order they wish. Tell them I will put an end to this crazy war against religion and cultures. We want everyone to have what we have in America—peace amongst ourselves, and the ability to rule through natural order.

"That will be a start before I address them in a month, telling them what I'm about to tell you now."

The President then told the former First Lady what his total plan was to rid the world of terrorism, and where he expects to steer his government for a better tomorrow. Her job, specifically, was to tell her fellow ambassadors exactly where her president, and the United States, stands.

Chapter 39

REGION OF TORA BORA

Nick Malone was on the last leg of his trip, with just a few miles to go. Soon he would be able to settle down and complete the second part of his plan. He arrived at his kill site and hid his truck in the brush. He reached in the hidden compartment and slid his hand down, hoping his package hadn't dislodged due to rough roads. Thankfully, it was there, and Nick grasped the oil cloth bag and pulled it out. The TISS—Tactical Integrated Soldier System—was a very important part of his weaponry. This particular unit was made small and compact, just for a sniper. The transmitter had no vocal radio receiver so the user couldn't give up his position. If Nick decided he needed to contact the circling C 130-A—in range every day at a prearranged time—he could do so without giving himself away. He would receive an affirmative answer from the tiny blue light that flashed three times on the screen. He needed to hide his radio, gun, and his specially made Cam flex Ghille suit at the hideout he had chosen a mile or so from the training camp. He knew this operation would be best late at night, or in the wee hours of the morning.

It didn't take long to walk the mile to his hideout, and he figured this was still the best place he could find. He poured over every piece of ground, wearing his Ghille suit to protect his location from predators. Better to take the prudent road than to be sorry. On a previous visit, Nick had placed traps around the encampment, so that if there were footprints he could tell immediately that he needed to find another location.

As he looked out over the rugged terrain he couldn't help but notice the raw beauty before him. These mountains had an effect on you like no others in the world. But as beautiful as the Tora Bora was, it was as wild and unforgiving as one could imagine. It was a landscape of fear where invading armies soon disappeared. It had been that way for thousands of years. He privately bet himself that if he dug deep enough he would find evidence of the hordes of warriors who came over the Chinese border to wreak havoc, loot, and plunder. History probably wouldn't have any evidence of these conflicts. It was sad, very sad, and he was about to make it worse. Plundering was never an option, however he hoped that there would be several al-Qaeda absent from their breakfast tables in the morning, as Becky was absent from his. Serves the heathens right, he thought. The more he could kill, the happier he would become.

Nick completed his task, then made contact with the C130-A. He gave the quadrants and the time he wanted the plane to attack – early in the morning while everyone but the guards were asleep. He settled on 4 A.M. The tiny blue light blinked three times, acknowledging the message, and Nick hid the radio with the rest of the gear.

Al-Qaeda Training Camp

After the usual search of his truck, Nick was allowed to drive farther in, toward the center of the camp. He saw row after row of tiny pup tents with small fires in front of each, reminiscent of an old Civil War encampment 150 years ago. Their parade grounds, which were also used for shooting practice and hand-to-hand combat, were off to one side. Nick noticed the extra security; he had to follow strict regulations and be escorted by a guard every foot of the way. He was sure that the extra security was for the benefit of al Zahwari. A dead giveaway for sure, and all the better.

He stopped his truck at the warehouse and was offered help in unloading. When finished, he was invited to share a meal with some of the soldiers and was given his own tent for the night. This was so much better than having to sit for hours listening to a lot of old men with hair growing from their ears and nose talking about the past with their bullshit war stories. During dinner, one young AQ happened to mention a very important meeting going on at the top of the mount. As soon as dinner was over, the young man boasted, he was to report for guard duty. Nick said to himself, "Adios, mother fucker."

After dinner, the soldier left to guard the big wheels and left Nick hoping Dr. al-Zahwari was there. There must be a way of finding out, Nick thought, so he took a walk through the camp with his escort, engaged him in conversation, asked and answered questions of past wars, and talked of the sacrifices everyone must make to accomplish the mutual goals of the future. Finally, the man began to open up and sure enough, there were six of the leaders of AQ Central along with the doctor having a meeting in the very room where Nick shared stories, tea and dinner. He hoped they would not take their leave until the early hours of the morning, as was their custom.

Nick decided to tell his hosts that because the camp looked especially busy, and his wish to see the sheikh might be impossible, he would lie down to rest before leaving early in the morning. He also mentioned that his wife was with child and he wanted to get back to her and the farm. He left at midnight and raced to his hideout but not before several of the soldiers wished him good luck. They all said they would pray to Allah for his wife to deliver a boy baby.

Nick drove the mile to the sniper lair, hid his truck, and wearing night goggles climbed the side of the mountain to the rocky ledge, leaving plenty of time to prepare.

He reached back into the hole where his gear was stowed, pulled out his Ghille suit, and began dressing himself. Wearing the Ghille allowed Nick to blend into the environment like a chameleon. Next out of the hole came his special rifle. The rifle stock and silencer, along with the telescopic lens, were all wrapped tightly in the same material as the Ghille to ward off reflection. Nick braced his tripod amongst the rocks and attached the rifle to it. He adjusted the telephoto lens one last time, as he had done several times in the past months. To be ready was to remain alive. When he was completely set up, he laid Campro netting over everything, just to be on the safe side. There was a wait of about three hours, so Nick laid his head down, staying completely disguised under his Ghille, and closed his eyes.

When he awoke, he had about an hour before all hell would break loose, so he started to select his targets. Fortunately for him, every guard in the camp was sitting by a small campfire under a blanket to keep warm. The guards up on the hill, however, weren't as lucky; they had to pull duty in the freezing wind. He would pick off the guards on the ground first, then train his rifle on the mountaintop. That way members of the council would be the last to know what was going on.

Malone started to think about what his instructors taught him at SAS School and what he already knew from his IRA days. He was taught to be aware of sound, so he brought a specially-made hearing aid like the ones that hunters use. He also brought a special pair of night glasses which enabled him to see every quick or jerky motion that would normally escape the human eye. Nick wanted the wildlife settled down before the operation began; he knew they would scatter when startled. He had to be aware of odors from the body, like scented soap or after-shave lotion. Forget about insect repellants, camp cooking, and last but not least, no smoking.

It was getting close to the 4 AM mark, so he began his final scoping. The quicker he could train his rifle on the target, the better it would be. He needed to silence the guards quickly before the plane arrived to kill the rest in their sleep and prevent escape. He took his first aim on a kid no more than sixteen years old who was sitting in the very center of the camp, dozing. The bullet made mush of his brain. Next was a man in his 60's. He was maybe 75 feet away from the kid, and didn't notice anything unusual. *Good*, thought Malone, *this one should be easy*, and it was; the bullet tore through the man's throat, ripping his head two-thirds of the way off. This went on for 10 minutes—approximately one guard every thirty seconds. As far as he knew, all the guards were dead, so Nick decided not to take out the special guards on patrol at the mountain top. Shooting them could be a dead giveaway and why upset the applecart? Besides, Becky's revenge would soon be taken.

It was 4:02 AM when Nick detected the faint sound of an aircraft. Arriving almost exactly when expected, the C 130-A was over the camp at about 5000 feet. The plane banked and circled, getting closer and closer with its lights off and the engines now rigged for silent running. Malone was about to see, for the first time in his career, one of the most accurate, most powerful, and most vicious war machines ever produced. Outside of the production personnel, only a handful of people have seen this warship in action. It was so top secret that no one has had time to build a defense against it.

After a few minutes, the plane began circling the camp and came right on target from 600 feet up. With its two newly designed 50 caliber machine guns roaring all four barrels at full capacity of 4400 rounds per minute per gun—or 8800 rounds total—the target area was quickly beginning to disappear. The barrage of bullets came so fast that even the guards on the mountain sounded the alarm too late. Nick watched through his scope and couldn't believe what he was seeing. The plane actually banked first around the camp—about the size of a football field — where over 500 men and boys lived and trained. Then it began firing. Most everyone caught in the camp said hello to his Allah. Then the bullets hit large rocks and exploded them into pebbles. The sleeping camp, or what was left of it, finally came to life, but only for a minute to see who was sending them honey, fruit, and virgins. Clearly, this would be a big dent carved out of al-Qaeda's flesh, and something for Dr. Iman al Zawahiri to think about.

Once the floor of the valley was cleaned out, the C 130-A trained itself on the side of the mountain. The infrared detectors indicated that there was life, and the plane showered the area, practically grinding the mountain to rubble, even crumbling the entrance to the cave where Zawahiri and Nick had their many conversations. Nick never saw an escape hatch when he was there, but couldn't believe there wasn't one. One could always wish.

Nick stuck around till daybreak, hoping he could pick off some of the higher ups. He was successful in taking out Abu Laith A-Libi, the AQ field commander and Midhat Al-Sayid Umar, the man responsible for AQ's weapons of mass destruction program and, most likely, the son of a bitch who masterminded the attack on Washington.

It was a good day, but still less than Malone had hoped for. Nick Malone had killed close to 500 trainees and two majordomos from the inner circle, but that didn't matter. He promised himself he wouldn't rest until all the top leaders, especially, Al-Zawahiri, were dead. He would kill them someday soon, but not today. Today he needed to get back to the farm and get Anna and Mara the hell out of this godforsaken country. They would travel in the truck as his wives, in case there were inquiries on the road.

The farm actually looked inviting compared to what he had just been through. He pulled up to the front of the compound and found Mara in his bedroom, cowering in fear, and Anna trying to console her. She was a mess. Anna explained that less than two hours ago, Mahmoud and Abu decided it was party time. Since Mara had rejected them, both the men were pissed and their egos bruised. They decided to have some fun anyway and Anna said she heard screaming and sobbing and Mara begging to be left alone when she was feeding the goats. She ran out of the house and heard the commotion from the other end of the barn.

Anna drew the slide back on her 9-mm Glock and inserted a bullet. She ran first to the barn and then to Mara's room. It was there that she found them, one holding her down while the other, in full splendor, was beginning to have his way. Remembering what happened several years ago in the Netherlands, Anna didn't hesitate for a second. She shot the man in the back of the head, not once but twice, as she was trained—"when you use a pistol for a kill, pull the trigger twice just in case the victim is still alive." Abu was dead, and Mahmoud rose from his kneeling position with the fear of God etched on his face, begging Anna not to shoot. He slowly worked his way around to where Anna was standing, explaining to her that none of this was his idea. Suddenly, he lunged for the gun and Anna shot him in the face. Twice.

"Nick, I have never seen a more evil look on a person's face. I knew he was going to kill us both. Unfortunately for Mara, she had never seen someone die before, especially the way he did. Needless to say, she was hysterical but I got her calmed down long enough to help me take the bodies to the shed. I figured if you weren't home I would set it afire."

"You did well," said Nick, nodding to Anna. He then reached for the girl and said in Pashto, "We are leaving this place in the morning, and you will be with us. You will travel with Anna and me as my number two wife. I am bringing you to America."

The girl smiled and said, "Somehow I thought you were Western, but in case I was wrong I kept my mouth shut."

"Well, you are wrong. I'm not American, I'm Irish, but I work for the Americans, and Anna is a Jew. Does that bother you?"

"No, not at all. You both risked your lives for me. I may be uneducated because of Taliban law, but I'm not stupid. I appreciate everything you've done for me."

"Don't worry, Mara," Anna told her. "Your world will be opening up very soon. We will see that you are educated and show you a life that's second to none. That's why your culture hates us, you know.

Frankly, they're jealous, and Americans are easy to pick on, but difficult to beat. None of us will accept defeat and risk losing our freedom. But you will see all that for yourself. You will be taught our language and our ways, and you will learn to cope with your new freedom. You'll be able to choose a man for your husband instead of having one chosen for you. You'll be able to go to a movie and wear less inhibiting clothes and you'll be able to listen to music of your choice. That, Mara, is just a small sample of why we're hard to beat. It's because we're free. We can discuss all this and more when we get underway."

Mara was smiling as she started to pack, thinking of her future. Then Malone asked her why she suspected he was American. Mara told him she heard him and Anna giggling and whispering in English one night during their lovemaking. Nick was sure there was no danger to that because you'd have to be in the house to hear them, and thank God the recorders didn't pick it up! Nick left it alone and made his way to the shed while the women finished packing.

The two bodies were stacked on a large wooden workbench—the perfect bier for cremating. He could do it the way the Hindus did —build a fire under the table and stack more wood, teepee style, on top of the bodies. The Hindus just ignited the bier with slow burning kindling but Nick preferred a quicker way. He doused the bodies with gasoline and soaked the shed as well. He figured he would have to check the fire several times during the night to make sure their bodies were consumed properly. Discovery of two murdered al-Qaeda soldiers was not an option.

———————

The next morning, Nick packed their belongings on the back of the truck and the three took off for Peshawar. The shed was still burning so he left it alone without bothering to check it. The roads were disastrous… only one lane. Coming down the mountain on patches of ice was worse than heading north towards the Tora Bora. At the speed he was traveling, it would take at least three days. Nick wanted to do it in two if possible.

Mara was doing much better and felt safe with her two benefactors. Nick was concentrating on the difficult driving while the two women sat in the back seat, talking about Mara's future. It was impossible to sleep outdoors because of the miserable winds and ice, so when nightfall came they just pulled over to the side of the road and slept in the truck for a few hours.

On the second day of traveling, on a boring road that seemed never to end, Nick ran into trouble. An armed man of eighteen or twenty attempted to pull them over. Soon, more bandits with guns appeared from the gullies that lined each side of the road.

Nick shouted "Danger!" and alerted both women. Unfortunately, Mara was not armed but Anna and Nick were armed well enough for six men.

Malone said, "These bandits will probably want children to sell in Peshawar. Be very aware and do what they say. They are extremely dangerous and will kill at the drop of a hat, especially if you have nothing they want. That makes them angry. I will do the talking and remember, Mara, to act as my second wife. Without children to steal maybe they will settle for money."

Nick pulled the truck over and was ordered out on the road. One of the bandits forced the women out and told them to face the truck with their hands on the hood. Anna and Mara complied. Anna kept her cool but she noticed that Mara was very scared.

Malone was asked where he was headed and responded, "To Peshawar to purchase much needed goods for my farm." Fortunately, he was wearing the black turban of the Taliban soldier when they began searching him. "This must mean you have much money with you?" asked the smuggler.

"Without money, how do you expect me to purchase any goods?" Nick said.

One of the men discovered the weapons Nick was carrying and wanted to know why he was so well armed. Nick said, "I raise sheep, goats, and crops for the sheikh to feed his camps and must be prepared to fight the Great Satan at a moment's notice. There's no telling when these weapons would be useful, so it is acceptable to carry them."

These bandits were of the Asian/Arab mix and had no use for Allah or al-Qaeda, just their pockets. The human trade was their specialty, and they would do exactly what they were doing now—pull over every car on this desolate road and take people's money and valuables and, of course, their children. This has been a lucrative practice for these nomads for a thousand years. When they reach their destination, they bring the children to auction, selling to the highest bidder, making a small fortune, and not caring a bit how anyone feels. Of course, they have competition in the form of Afghani couples who can't afford to feed their babies or young children who also bring them across the border to Pakistan and sell them to the highest bidder. The young girls are usually sold to brothels while the little boys are bought by the rich Arabs to play with as "boy toys."

"How much money do you have, Talib, and don't lie. If you do, I will cut off the finger of one of your wives."

Nick showed the man his money and invited him to search the truck and luggage. He asked if they would leave a little so he could cover expenses, but all he got was laughter. Nick was stripped of his weaponry and money, with the exception of a 9-MM Glock in an ankle holster. The bandits were now paying all their attention to Mara and began searching her. She tried to fight them off when Nick gave the nod to Anna, who had not taken her eyes off of him, waiting for this moment. Anna opened the front of her burka and revealed an AK-47. At the same time, Nick reached down for his Glock. They began shooting simultaneously, and within two minutes the bandits were dead. Nick retrieved his money, made sure Mara was OK, and repacked the vehicle. Soon they were on their way, leaving the bodies by the side of the road.

The atmosphere inside the truck was tense but Anna calmed Mara down.

Nick turned to the two women to reassure them and said, "Time is closing in on us." Anna wanted to know what he meant, and Nick told her that his superiors land a plane twice a week in Peshawar especially for the purpose of extracting them to Germany and then the U.S. He felt they couldn't afford to dally any longer in case the bandits or al Zawahiri and his people were looking for them.

Their only option was to get out of Afghanistan… and quickly.

Chapter 40

HOUSTON, TEXAS

The Hawker-10 jet landed at a private airfield with two pilots under Steve Meyer's command. They were ordered to stand by while Meyers and McCarthy took care of business.

There is an area of the city of Houston that is similar to the old Garden District of New Orleans. Large graceful mansions on huge lots are adorned with perfectly trimmed bushes and trees and long brick driveways with electronic gates and guardhouses. Usually these gatehouses are occupied with armed guards.

The two of them knew exactly where to go and drove directly to the home of Warren Dunn. McCarthy drove past the house on Culpeper Court that was set back from the road by at least 500 feet. Permanent employees of Dunn's, rather than the unprofessional rent-a-cops, occupied the two gatehouses. Meyers took a good look at the inside of the shacks to determine if they were occupied. They were.

These two handpicked commandos, who only served the President of the United States, were ready. Their assignment was to eliminate whomever stood between them and Warren Dunn. What they didn't know was that Dunn was having a dinner party for several high rollers in the oil industry. Meyers and McCarthy had changed into black coveralls on the plane to save time, and with no moon they were difficult to see.

The SUV was parked half a block down the street. Kevin made sure he was parked legally and left the doors unlocked. Meyers opened the rear hatch and they strapped on their Glock 45's and attached their suppressors. The pistols they were carrying held fifteen rounds in the clip and one in the chamber. Each man had two more clips attached to his belt. Also attached to their belts were handcuffs and a Taser C2, a small personal-protection device about the size of a cell phone that delivers 50,000 volts when the trigger is depressed. The range of this little beauty is only 15 feet, but it is a great asset when facing more than one perp. Steve and Kevin were ready. Walking down the road, Kevin remarked that he hoped no patrol cars were in the area.

"They're not around," said Steve.

"How do you know?"

"Because everything has been taken care of."

The men approached the front gates from opposite sides of the driveway, crouching low in the bushes, and opened the guard doors at the same time.

McCarthy dispatched the guards within seconds: One bullet per second, with one dead center to the face and one to the heart. The second guard received two shots to the head, blowing the back of his skull clean off. McCarthy closed the door behind him and left everything as it was. He turned toward Meyers and saw that one guard was already dead with a hole in the right temple and brain matter splattered on the window. There was no need for the second shot.

Through the glass doors of the guardhouse McCarthy saw that Meyers had the chief of security, George Purvis, on his knees. "Tell me who's there in the house."

"Go fuck yourself. If you think I'm telling you anything, you've got another think coming," Purvis said.

"Bad attitude, Georgie" Meyers said as he squeezed the trigger and blew out Purvis's knee. "Now tell me, who's in the manor house?"

In less than a minute the guard, writhing in pain, blurted out the names of the five men inside. He also said there was a woman he had seen before, but didn't know her name. They were there for a business meeting and that's why there was extra security on the grounds tonight. "Usually there are only two guards, and tonight there are eight," he said.

"There were eight. Now there are four." With that, Meyers took aim and blew the man's head right off his shoulders. *Love these Glocks,* he thought to himself.

It was a long walk down the path to Dunn's house, so the men were wary. They weren't positive the information they got from Purvis was accurate.

"Where do you think the rest of the guards are stationed?" McCarthy asked.

"Don't know. We'll just have to wait until we're closer. If I were

Dunn, I would have dogs, cameras, and sound monitoring equipment all over the place, but so far, so good, right?"

McCarthy spotted him first. A shadow from one of the spotlights on the lawn showed exactly where the guard was running. Instinctively both men drew and shot at the same time, depositing a total of four bullets in his head and torso. He was dead before he hit the ground. McCarthy knelt and fired once again with his silenced weapon after unloading a direct hit on another security guard. Not a headshot, but nevertheless fatal. Steve said, "Keep your eyes open. We've killed only six guards."

Searching the grounds for the best way in, the two men removed two more guards. One of them got the drop on Meyers as he was looking around the front of the house and radioed his partner to come immediately. McCarthy, meanwhile, was still in the bushes, waiting. When the two guards were together, McCarthy sneaked up from behind them and shot both in the back of their heads. "Thanks, I owe you one," said Meyers.

"What's next?" asked McCarthy.

"A nice window in the back of the house would suit me. Let's hide these bodies first."

The back of the huge mansion boasted three decks, all of different heights and shapes, built specifically for entertaining business clients and personal friends. All three had individual Jacuzzis, each capable of seating twelve people. Around the side of the mansion was another Jacuzzi built for four, located in a romantic spot for intimate rendezvous. Directly below the decks were two pools. One was Olympic size with fresh water; the other was a large free-form salt-water edition for those who wanted to be near the ocean.

"Someone is coming," whispered McCarthy.

The door opened to reveal a former member of the Cabinet during the Reagan years and one of their targets, the woman who was thought to be an agent for al-Qaeda. She was as beautiful as she was reputed to be, and it was easy to see how men could be manipulated by her charms. Her dress and mannerisms were those of an aristocrat, and her English was impeccable. When she spoke, you got the feeling there was no one else in the room but you. She was always totally focused on her subject, staring at him with beautiful almond black eyes. Men were mesmerized and it was easy for her to persuade wealthy targets to invest in dummy corporations owned by al-Qaeda. It was a simple plan where everyone profited except the target, which most always lost sizeable amounts of money, yet none of her victims ever turned on her. Instead she hid behind a veil of security, provided by her many suitors, that allowed her to avoid arrest and deportation.

This evening she sat at the corner of a table and crossed her legs just enough so the former Minister could see straight to her thigh. Tonight's target was just one of many that she had enlisted to help Warren Dunn secretly fund al-Qaeda. In return, al Zawahiri would see to it that Dunn was rewarded with more exclusive oil contracts from the Arab region. These contracts were worth billions, even after al-Qaeda took its hefty share. Dunn would end up controlling the majority of the world's oil supply, which put the Western world—and especially the United States—in a compromising position, with him being arguably the most powerful man in the western world.

Dunn needed the cooperation of the congressmen and senators, whom he entertained lavishly at his home. His Amigo parties were the best ever, and if the politicians didn't go home with a happy ending, it was no fault of the host. His payback was their support, and if it didn't come around, then the photographs were presented. He would go to any length to get what he wanted, even ruining a promising career or a marriage. He didn't give a damn as long as he reaped the harvest.

This mystery woman openly hated Dunn for what he was and would have nothing to do with him. No matter what he did or offered, Dunn was turned down. This had caused a rift between them, but she was there to take care of their business and not him, plain and simple. It drove him crazy seeing her touch other men and allowing him to watch while she played with his friends night after night. If she had her way, she would drive a knife into his lungs and let him slowly bleed out. What made her smile, however, was knowing that Dunn would be toast once al-Qaeda got everything they wanted.

She sat, flirting with her partner for the evening, as Meyers and McCarthy lay flat on their bellies listening. They sipped the rest of their wine, and then she let the man kiss her before they walked back inside the house.

Steve selected a medium-size window and took out a glasscutter, crazy glue, and a wooden handle with a rubber backing. He applied the glue to the rubber backing and then stuck it on the window. When it dried, he scratched the glass with the glasscutter and pulled. The action broke the glass along the scratch and enabled Kevin to remove the section of glass that remained; he then reached inside to unlock the window without any noise. He pushed it up and climbed into the laundry room, which was right off the kitchen, "Perfect," said Meyers. "No one does the laundry while entertaining guests. Sneak around the rooms back here and tell me what you find. I'll do this end and then meet you back in the wash room in five."

"Understood."

All the rooms were clear, as were the servants quarters. The chef and his assistant were busy in the kitchen. Meyers hoped for a late dinner and early cocktail hour so that by the time everyone sat down they would be nice and toasty. That made the job much easier. The collateral damage could be huge, with a lot of innocents as victims, unless he could do something to save them. There were eight outside security guards dead by necessity. The two cooks, one kitchen boy, three servants and five house guests need not die, if possible. Warren Dunn and the woman were really all he was interested in. "Do whatever is necessary to get the job done," said Cassidy.

Meeting back in the laundry room, both men agreed they should start now. "What's your plan, boss?" asked McCarthy

Meyers quickly answered, "Let everyone be seated and allow the staff to serve the first course. Right in the middle of it, when the servants disappear to get ready for the second course, you make your entrance. I'll take care of the house staff. You hold the guests at bay, but be careful; everyone in Texas carries a gun. I'll be in to help you out as soon as the service people are secure. Remember, if they make the slightest move, whatever it is or who it is, take them out."

"No problem." McCarthy walked toward the huge dining room while the staff were readying themselves for the first course —a crabmeat bisque au sherry. He counted seven seats, but six men including Dunn, which concerned him because there were seven at the cocktail hour.

The girl was missing. With the Taser in one hand and his 45mm in the other, he allowed them to taste the soup before all hell broke loose.

He barged into the dining room, gun drawn, ordered everyone to place their hands above their heads. One congressmen/guest reached for his ankle weapon, and Kevin zapped him with his Taser.

Meyers, meanwhile, assembled the staff at gun point and made them tie each other up with butcher's twine. Some of the maids screamed so he stuffed kitchen towels in their mouths. All were then tied to the heavy kitchen equipment that was bolted to the floor. "Don't get any ideas," he screamed, "or you're dead." He hated taking good lives when it was unnecessary.

Meyers had just started to search the rest of the guests for weapons when he noticed that the woman was missing. He turned to McCarthy and asked "where is the female?" Kevin answered, "I don't know."

"The fucking bitch left," said Meyers.

Turning to Dunn, he demanded to know where she was and was told "Go to hell." Then Dunn started laughing, and said he really didn't know. "Well, maybe this will stir your memory," Meyers said, as he shot Dunn through the foot. The smile vanished quickly as he fell back on the table screaming. He then said she had left for a private club called Amigos.

"What are you saying, Mr. Dunn?"

"I'm saying she left early to prepare for a special event she is having for a few of my clients."

He was so cocky, even with his wound, and so sure of himself that Meyers decided to let Dunn watch as he tasered his friends into la-la land. Saving the best for last. But Dunn wasn't going to be allowed to just stand there with no pain, so Meyers shot him in the knee. Dunn fell to the floor screaming at Meyers and cursing him. When asked again, Dunn couldn't speak. Meyers made him stand up which made the pain worse, and gave him a roundhouse below the belt. After two of Meyer's specialties, he began to talk freely.

"I don't know for sure," Dunn said, in terrible pain, "but I believe she is staying at the Ritz Carlton."

"What room, Dunn? Hurry up," said Meyers, but Dunn said he wasn't sure. "Is the reservation in your name?" Meyers asked.

"No, I don't think so. I don't know whose name it's under," Dunn said.

Meyers asked, "What's her name?"

"I only know her as Naomi."

"You lying piece of shit! I know you do business with her, and a lot of it, so tell me her name or I won't ask again." Meyers brought his fist up and Dunn pleaded, "No, no please don't hit me again. Her real name is Riana Abbasid."

"Where's she from and who does she work for, besides you?"

"She works just for me, you fool, and that's all I'm telling you. I don't know anything beyond what she does at this house. She's just an expensive escort, that's all."

Steve's fist came around and caught Dunn in the same spot as before, and he passed out. Meyers quickly revived him and said, "Oh, no you don't. That would be too easy for you and that's not allowed. Besides, you need to see what's going to happen. Now watch this, Mr. Big Shot." Meyers gave the go-ahead to McCarthy, who began systematically shooting each person at the table.

The killings took no time at all. One bullet to the back of the head, followed by another through the heart, and it was all over. Then they both turned to a terrified Walter Dunn who was standing at the dining room table completely losing control of himself and begging for his life. A vile stench filled the room and Meyers began to laugh. "Jesus, Mary and Joseph, Dunn, did you soil your breeches?" Dunn, terrified, quickly agreed to tell Meyers anything he wanted to know if he would only spare his life.

"As long as we get the information we want. All of the information, not bits and pieces, understand?"

"Yes, yes I do," said Dunn.

For the next two hours, Meyers grilled Dunn for the information that the President needed while McCarthy made sure nothing of value was touched. Money, jewelry, and other valuables, including ID, stayed with the bodies. Meyers wanted it to look like a hit rather than a robbery.

At last Meyers was sure they had all the information they needed, but Dunn was still scared out of his mind. "Walter, what the hell are you worried about? I told you I wasn't going to hurt you, so calm down. I must tell you though, the President of the United States ordered your hit, but since I can't go back on my promise, Master Sergeant McCarthy will handle it. Thanks for everything, you fuck."

It actually gave both men pleasure to watch Walter Dunn squirm, then cry, and then break into a sweat. As he started to beg, McCarthy took a face shot.

"Let's get the hell out of here."

Both men put their black, bloodstained coveralls into the fireplace and headed for their car. "That SOB did commit treason, Kevin. He admitted it."

"I know, Steve, I heard it. But look at the money and embarrassment we saved the country and the President."

"He aligned himself with al-Qaeda and several other terrorist organizations."

"And the treason goes way beyond Walter Dunn. There must be dozens more."

"Yeah, well, let the POTUS worry about that," said Meyers. "If he wants us to do something about it, he'll tell us. Until then, let's look for that Arab broad."

McCarthy got behind the wheel and pulled into traffic, driving toward the Ritz Carlton.

"If we do catch her, be careful she doesn't try to swallow something, like a cyanide pill." McCarthy understood.

———

Riana Abbasid had left Dunn's house early because she had another appointment. She knew she'd see everyone later at the "AMIGOS" party that Walter Dunn was hosting. Riana had arranged for the best escorts and food Houston had to offer, so she was damn sure the party would be a success. She needed sleep; Dunn had kept her going ever since she flew in from London, and this was the best time to catch a catnap. Riana always rented two rooms, one in her name and one in another, just to be on the safe side. She kept the keys on her person at all times, and always had an exit plan. She headed for her secondary room and entered. Everything was fine, so far.

When Meyers and McCarthy arrived at the Ritz, they walked to the front desk and asked for the room number. Steve knocked on her door while Kevin held his silenced Glock at the ready, just in case. There was no answer, so Meyers took locksmith picks from his ditty bag and opened the door. The room showed no signs of life but there were several suitcases, some contained personal papers, things put to paper that should have been confined to memory, memos that could send her to Gitmo for life – plus, and a lot of very expensive clothing and jewelry. "Let's get out of here, Steve. I think the best bet is to wait for her at the Amigo's Club."

As they were leaving, the men spotted her leaving her secondary room. McCarthy literally ran to her and body-slammed her to the wall, pushing his hand into her mouth to prevent her from biting down on a cyanide pill. "You are under arrest," he said.

Riana just seemed relieved of all the tensions that were brought upon her by her superiors and showed no struggle. Meyers then went back to her room and grabbed a washcloth from the bathroom to stuff in her mouth. When he got back he also handcuffed her so McCarthy could free himself.

They pushed her into the elevator and then to their rented car.

Meyers then ordered McCarthy to go back to her room and pack up her valuables and any other information he could find.

Sitting in the car, Meyers proceeded to explain to Riana the reason for her arrest and to inform her that she had no rights as an enemy combatant. He also informed her of the fate of the guests at Warren Dunn's house including Dunn himself. She was not surprised, nor was she showing any emotion. "Cold bitch," Meyers thought.

Within a half an hour McCarthy was back in the car, heading for the airport.

When the plane was at 30,000 feet, Meyers called the President to tell him the news: Mission accomplished. He also told the President, that Riana was alive and he was taking her to the SOE safe house in Gordonsville, Virginia for questioning. Cassidy was pleased and said her information could be a fountain of intelligence. The President hung up but not before asking Meyers to keep him in the loop on a daily basis. He did not seem worried about the several congressmen and business associates that were exterminated during the raid. He would deal with that later.

Chapter 41

CAMP DAVID
SITE R

*T*he President picked up his phone and began talking to Ian McPherson. "Ian, I have decided to order our fleet to stand down. I will not have a nuclear attack on my watch unless absolutely necessary, but I still want to teach those Libyan bastards a lesson. I have decided that although the E-Bomb was a success, I want more. I am ordering you to commence with a conventional bombing of every single port, village, town or city within the borders of Libya. Make that country look like Nagasaki after the drop. In other words, flatten it... *the whole damn country*. I do not want a building left standing. As you know, we have just taken out at least 500 AQ in the Tora Bora. Leveling Libya will be the icing on the cake."

"Yes, sir, Mr. President. As ordered, sir." And Pearson hung up.

Cassidy then called for Lerrick McKenna, his new Press Secretary, and ordered her to explain at her daily briefing that several congressmen, while dinner guests of Warren Dunn, were murdered, and that the Houston Police and the FBI were investigating. She was to give more information to the press as the investigation progressed.

"Spinned properly," he told Lerrick, "would give them more time to find the rest of the culprits. The American people have suffered enough. No reason to drop everything in their lap at once. Let's do our magic first. We're gonna make sure this country is clean again."

Lerrick asked about the "woman." The President told her she would be the source of very valuable information, but at this point she was not to be mentioned. All he wanted was the announcement of the deaths at Dunn's mansion.

Chapter 42

FORMER AMERICAN UNIVERSITY
DUMP SITE #1
WASHINGTON, D. C.

The workers had started the cleanup a long time ago, and had barely made a dent in the rubble. This site was near the NW University Park area that embraces much of embassy row, plus the 100 blocks encircling American University. Nothing in this area was standing, and trucks were hauling waste 24/7. The trucks would be filled, then driven to the site and dumped. Huge bulldozers would pile the junk ever higher until the area was full. Then they would spread the junk to make room for more.

There was no fear of radiation now that the government had declared the city safe. Some areas weren't hit as hard as others, but workers had to take exception to this because of rotting body parts from humans and animals. This required special handling and cremation as soon as possible to prevent disease. Assistance came from virtually every city and hamlet in the country, plus an outpouring from many foreign countries. The volunteer list kept growing and growing. It seemed that everyone wanted to do his or her share in re-building the nation's capital. In order to keep up the momentum and do the job as quickly as possible, the government chose to use the golf course at Chevy Chase Country Club to house volunteers. The course could hold at least a thousand camp sites. The Army supplied food, transportation, and medical aid to and from the job site. The work was backbreaking, so workers were on two days, then off two days.

Even with a hundred dumpsites throughout the district, it was estimated that it would take at least eighteen months, working three shifts a day, just to clear the debris.

The President and Congress were told that every federal building, including the Capital and the White House, would be re-built exactly the way they were. The Capitol Building and White House would mirror what they were originally, using the same drawings from 200 years ago. Architectural firms banded together so they could give the American people the best talent possible. One firm specialized in marble construction while another specialized in stone, and it went on and on.

The cooperation was breathtaking and, more important; the government was working especially well under these incredible circumstances. As well perhaps, when the Pentagon was rebuilt after 9/11.

Chapter 43

THE ROAD TO PESHAWAR

The journey to safety was a long one. After the struggle with the road bandits, Malone was stopped two more times. Each time, he was forced to give money he didn't have or that they were convinced he didn't have. After the first go-around with bandits, he removed the cash they stole after he shot them. Now the money was stowed in the same compartment where he had carried his sniper rifle. Nick was very convincing, but he traded personal belongings for their safety. After the smugglers got what they wanted, they got rough, demanding more. He was about to kill them all when they discovered he was a Taliban hero. It wasn't the black turban this time but a survivor of the al-Qaeda training camp. He had left the camp after the raid and rejoined his 'family', who were these bandits. Recognizing Nick was all that was necessary, and the bandits returned the booty stolen from them with apologies. There were many questions regarding the raid, and he gained valuable information that the U.S. and Israel could use. The time he spent with these thieves was not wasted, but now he would have to wait longer for the plane to pick them up.

Malone estimated their arrival into the city to be about seven hours. It would be necessary to stay at a hotel for a couple of days.

Those remaining hours were grueling, with most of the driving done at night. The roads were so bad that several times the women made him stop because of carsickness.

Finally they arrived at the outskirts of the city. The area they were driving through was squalid beyond belief. The people were mostly Afghanis who came across the border in the hope of escaping the oppression of the Talib. Many were educated; some were even doctors or teachers who couldn't practice their profession in their adopted country because of the political influence of the Taliban on the current government. They were told 'practice your profession and you will die,' so there was no money and nowhere to go. Nick was in a dangerous situation because he was a Taliban warrior and needed to get out of the area immediately. They'd just as soon kill him as look at him.

Fortunately, there were no incidents and the three found cheap lodging just on the outskirts of the city, not too far from the central market. Nick made sure the women were safe in their room, then stayed in the truck to protect their belongings, and to make contact with the base that was to carry them out.

Contact was clear. The three of them must be at the base by 10 A.M. the day after tomorrow. First they would go to Germany for a stopover, then to Tampa, Florida, for a debriefing, then back to Israel for another debriefing. Kind of crazy, he thought, with computers and all, but the old saying "there's the right way and the army way" was never more true than now.

Sitting in the truck was difficult for Nick. Keeping his eyes open after such an arduous trip was not how he would have liked to spend the evening. He began thinking of the damage he had done and how many people had to die. For the first time in his career, Nick was having reservations. Perhaps he would see somebody when he got back to the States; professional help is not all bad. There were several things left undone, but one thing for sure: he was homesick and needed to get out. Pakistan was just like Afghanistan, no difference at all, just a shit hole. He would love to ask the Pakistani president what percentage of the three billion dollars a year in aid from the U.S. goes into his Swiss account. And why can't he control the NW corner of his country? Cancer spreads quickly, and it will soon take effect on both countries where the landscape is one of fear and evil. He was only one man, and the U.S., Israel, and Great Britain needed to create a force of the very best men and women dedicated to the elimination of terror. It must be small and stealth, and especially focused on ending it all. Maybe he'd make that suggestion to Meyers.

The other thing was Anna. He felt very alive when she was close to him. He hoped her lovemaking was real, that she didn't just feel duty bound. Together they had taken on a responsibility, and they had promised Mara a better life. He would see to that, even if Anna backed out. There was something good and special about Mara. He wanted her to be a part of his life, and he hoped this wasn't just wishful thinking. He would legally adopt her, and he could afford the very best schools and a good life for her. He would make that happen.

This was the first time Nick Malone had a chance to clear his mind and he felt good about it.

There was a noise in the back of the truck. Malone turned to the left quickly to see two men stealing his belongings. As he turned, a pistol was aimed at the back of his head from the right. He was told to get out of the truck and place his hands on the hood. Malone complied and was told they were looking for money and jewelry and they were taking his truck. Shit, he thought, how the hell am I going to get out of this one? His gun was at his hip and the noise from his 9mm would surely draw an unwanted crowd, but he had no choice. Unfortunately, the suppressor was packed with the rest of his stuff. He could draw and shoot but there were three of them.

He chose to use the knife that was holstered behind his neck.

He was ordered to turn around, keeping his hands in the air, which he did. The man came closer and as soon as he began searching Nick's body for money, Nick slowly moved his hand to the hilt of his knife. He quickly brought it across the man's face, leaving a six-inch long gash on the side of his cheek. The man screamed in agony but it gave Nick the advantage. He was able to have his Glock ready when the other two ran to the front of the truck. Malone kicked the attacker's gun out of the way while moving swiftly and using the front of the truck as a shield. He took aim and realized these guys had no other weapons except knives. One of the men pleaded for him not to shoot, and Nick demanded they drop their knives. They did, and he ordered each one to strip naked for further proof of no weapons. Malone thought this should prove interesting, and it was.

Once they were undressed and standing exposed, he searched each one. He ordered them to put their clothes back on and began asking questions. It turned out there was no useful information, and Nick was about to let them go when the wounded one drew a gun he had failed to see. The small-bore 22-caliber pistol fired one shot that hit Nick in the arm. It was superficial but a hit nonetheless. Within two seconds the man was dead, with a large part of his skull three feet away from his head. The other two men were crying and begging for mercy. They were told to leave and carry their friend's body with them. Nick decided that as tired as he was, he would leave immediately for the Air Force base. He went inside the hotel to tell the women.

The pain was intense and he was bleeding badly. He didn't realize the bullet had lodged in his arm and was not just a surface wound. The only bandages came from his Crescent Aid kit that was kept in his truck and that helped very little.

Because of the wound, driving was almost impossible. As soon as he was outside the city, Anna took over. The final journey took several hours, but the thought of being back where they belonged within the next two days was almost more than they could stand.

———————

Arriving finally at the Air Base, Malone and the women had to go through security. Once he was inside, the tension disappeared. He was escorted immediately to the medics and was told the bullet must be removed before infection could set in. The operation left Nick's arm in a sling but he was informed that the wound would heal quickly.

They were given a two-bedroom private house and a pass to the PX for anything necessary. This was the first time Mara had seen running water and Anna actually had to show her how to shower. Too tired to cook, they ate at the officers club as the guests of the base Commander. Sitting at a private table, they realized that the stench from their clothing was almost unbearable. It was so noticeable that people moved away from their table! Nick and the Commander were aware of what was going on. Nick offered that they would leave, but was told in no uncertain terms to order dinner as his guests. Besides, he wanted to talk with him. During dinner, Commander Gerald Wesson, speaking in English, told Nick and Anna there had been a lot of chatter from al-Qaeda and their Taliban allies from the Tora Bora to Peshawar and surrounding areas. "They have put a price on your head for destroying their camp."

"How did they find out it was me?" Nick asked.

"I believe there was a name that was used prominently in several conversations. On one occasion, this story was told to Ayman al Zawahiri himself, Nick. There is a man called Khalid who loaned you two of his men to help with the farming and gifted you with livestock.

Well, he paid a visit to the farm and found the bodies of his two operatives, or what was left of them. Apparently the fire you set went out, leaving the corpses only half cremated. He identified them as his men and couldn't find you, so he added two and two."

"How safe is it on the base?" asked Nick.

"We have a lot of local workers here and frankly some are questionable. Last year, as you know, we caught a man who was very high up in the Taliban. He was working as a cashier at the PX and spent most of his time recruiting. He wanted the young people to martyr themselves. Of course, now he's living at Chateau Gitmo. But to answer your question, with a price on your head, and with the new leadership getting serious for the first time by offering the money, the sooner you're up in the air and out of here the better. When you get back to your barracks there will be some clothes waiting for you. And that's for all three of you. Wash, change, store your shit clothing in the bags that are provided, and put them in the closet. My people will take care of removing them when you're gone. As for your stuff on the truck, take what you want and we will remove the rest, including the truck."

"Commander, the only thing I need to get is the money I have hidden, and I must tell you it is quite a bit. Plus, there are weapons."

"We will store the weapons in our armory and take your money to the exchange and trade it for US dollars. Fair enough?"

"Fair enough."

Nick was first in the door, then Mara and Anna. Mara was more excited than she had been on the whole trip, trying on the new clothes while Nick once again jumped in the shower. He slipped on a pair of jeans and a Tommy Hilfiger shirt. The best part, though, was brushing his teeth for the first time in months and shaving off the scraggy looking beard. He did keep his Glock 9mm and a razor sharp knife. Anna did the same, just in case. Mara looked great in her western clothes and the fear of leaving her homeland and village was rapidly escaping her.

———————

Early the next morning, Nick decided to take a walk. He was alone, striding toward the tennis courts and gym. A man was walking on the other side of the street and crossed to Nick's side. He was in western dress and looked unassuming as he approached Malone. In perfect English, he said, "Major Malone, we know who you are and we know what happened was your fault. I am here alone as a humble messenger who brings a message. It is not safe for you anywhere on earth. Death will happen when you least expect it. We will have your head to add to your wife's. As for your reward, you will never see your son. Our leaders happened to leave the mountain early so you see they're all alive. Your mission failed Major Malone. Dr. al Zawahiri is visibly upset over what you did and he holds himself personally responsible. He took you in, gave you gifts, and extended a continuation of a pride and trust that he rarely offers to others. As a matter of fact, Major Malone, he has never offered what you received to anyone else. Yes, we know your name and rank and someday you will pay dearly, you and that Jew bitch you work with. The Mossad will sorely miss her." Nick moved forward, wanting to take him out, but noticed some of his compatriots watching over him from across the road. "Perhaps not today, but someday you will get what you deserve. Here are the last gifts my leader sends to you with his compliments." The man handed Nick two photos. One was of his son playing as a normal little boy and the other was a photo of Becky's head. Then, as fast as the man had arrived, he tried to disappear. Malone blocked his way, staring at him and at the pictures and reconfirming his vow to kill every one of these bastards that were responsible for murdering his beloved Becky and taking his boy. "I believe that yes, you will get to me, but not before I take out hundreds more of you. My solemn vow is to rid this world of pond scum like you, your wives, children and grandchildren. I promise you I will show no mercy." Then Nick walked quickly away to report the incident to the Base Commander, but not before turning back and saying, "La-ilaha-illa-Allah, (there is no god but the God) and He will have his vengeance."

Malone and the two women quickly boarded their plane without incident. He decided not to tell Anna about the morning's confrontation until they returned to the States. They all needed some rest and a major clean up before meeting with the President.

Nick placed a call to Meyers from aboard the jet and found him in his new office at Site R. The two talked briefly and Meyers told him to contact him as soon as he landed. He would arrange for them to be choppered there and stay as guests at one of the cottages at Camp David. Meyers asked about Anna, and Nick told him they were all tired but fine. Nick said he had someone special he wanted to introduce to America, and Meyers wanted to know how he wound up with Mara. Nick said he would relate all the gory details over a beer. Steve promised he'd have whatever she needed, such as an American passport upon arrival. Meyers congratulated Nick on a job well done, and told him the President would like to see him and Anna as soon as they had gotten some rest. The call ended with both men promising to catch up over drinks and dinner.

Nick Malone took out the two pictures that were given to him that morning. He needed to put the horror behind him and concentrate on his future with Anna. He tore the picture of Becky into shreds, then sat back and stared one last time at his son before shredding his picture as he had his mother's. He then sat back and ordered a stiff drink. He tried to relax, but tears came instead.

He knew one thing though, and that was he wanted Anna with him, and he wanted to adopt Mara. He wanted a family... and the sooner the better.

As for his son, he could always hope for a miracle. Perhaps one day he would have the chance to meet the boy he would have called Kevin.

www.ingramcontent.com/pod-product-compliance
Lightning Source LLC
Chambersburg PA
CBHW020605260626
47157CB00003B/879